The CHAMPAGNE QUEEN

The CHAMPAGNE QUEEN

The Century Trilogy

Petra Durst-Benning

Translated by Edwin Miles

amazoncrossing

Previously published as *Die Champagnerkönigin* by Ullstein Buchverlage GmbH in Germany in 2013. Translated from German by Edwin Miles. First published in English by AmazonCrossing in 2016.

Published by AmazonCrossing, Seattle

www.apub.com

Amazon, the Amazon logo, and AmazonCrossing are trademarks of Amazon.com, Inc., or its affiliates.

ISBN-13: 9781503937581
ISBN-10: 1503937585

Cover design by Shasti O'Leary-Soudant

Printed in the United States of America

Chapter One

The Palatinate, Germany, January 1898

"You were raised to marry, not to peel potatoes!"

Isabelle nearly jumped out of her skin when she suddenly heard her mother's voice and then her chirping laugh, the same laugh with which Jeanette Herrenhus had always dismissed Isabelle's protests.

Isabelle put down the knife she had been holding. Was she going insane? If she were, it would really come as no surprise. She looked around the kitchen, noting its low, soot-blackened ceiling and small windows. Like the rest of the house, the kitchen was cramped, and more and more, Isabelle felt like a bird trapped in a too-small cage, with too little air to breathe.

A strand of her curly red hair had worked loose from her braid, and she tucked it behind her ear. Then she went back to peeling potatoes. It would be a terrible thing if her mother were to appear there. The woman would have a nervous breakdown on the spot. And Isabelle wouldn't really be able to blame her.

There was a small Palatinate village close to the French border, deep in a basin-shaped valley. Little light made it through the tiny windows of the half-timbered house. To the west were dark, towering forests that were actually across the border in France, while to the east were a few vineyards that grew Sylvaner and Pinot Gris grapes. In between lay the village of Grimmzeit. Just thinking of the name of the village made Isabelle shudder. Grim times: no name could be more apt. The village consisted of a few dozen stout, traditional houses, a church, and a village school. There were no shops, so to buy anything at all, one had to travel to the next town. And even there, it felt as if everything had been buried alive. Which is just how she felt in that house—not that she had anyone but herself to blame!

Around Grimmzeit, a handful of gloomy castles lurked on the mountainsides. They were built by long-forgotten nobles in earlier times. Leon had announced his desire to visit them with her in the coming spring. He had gone on at length about the history of the region, as if he had worked on the formidable structures himself, and he had talked about the Celts, the Romans, and the Germanic tribes. Although Isabelle had said nothing in response, the prospect of outings to old piles of stones sounded about as appealing as sitting around in Grimmzeit itself.

Even if Isabelle had maintained contact with her family in Berlin, she would never have had the heart to write to her father, the successful businessman Moritz Herrenhus, or her mother, the erstwhile prima ballerina of the Berlin State Ballet: *I live in Grimmzeit. Come and visit!*

Isabelle laughed drily. Her parents had not sent her to finishing school for *this*. Isabelle Herrenhus, the beautiful debutante, was supposed to make a good match. Money marries money, as they say, and power sleeps in the same bed as both of you—that had been her father's plan. He had unearthed one potential marriage candidate after another—factory owners' sons, young counts, overseas diplomats with the best contacts, and even an aging baron. He had put so much hope in her and had invested a great deal of money. The most beautiful dresses, extravagant jewelry, elaborate hairdos—only the best was ever good enough for his princess. She was the center of attention at every party she attended and was always surrounded by budding suitors. Her charm, straightforward manner, and infectious laugh had earned her at least as much admiration as her good looks. In addition to milk-and-honey skin, she had waist-length locks that tumbled over her shoulders and down her back like molten copper. Dark-brown lashes crowned and accentuated her emerald-green eyes, and her finely curved eyebrows made them look daring and challenging, as if to say, *What price the world? I don't care. I can afford anything!*

She had received proposals. Several, in fact. But whenever a suitor had come to her, bouquet in hand, stammering out his request for her hand in marriage, Isabelle had always shaken her head and said, "No, thank you." She was holding out for the great love of her life.

Leon Feininger. Isabelle would never forget the way he had walked into the Berlin cycling club, his head held high, chest out, as confidently as if he owned the place. His curly brown hair hung devil-may-care around his face. His striking, masculine face spoke of adventure and audacity. With his powerful calves and fit, muscular torso, he was so different from the feeble, pallid drones who populated the salons of Berlin. At that first sight of him, her heart began to pound as if about to burst, and she knew that she wanted to—no, that she *must*—get to know him better. And the attraction had been mutual.

On their cycling tours through Berlin's hinterland, Leon had talked. About his family, who lived on a winegrowing estate. About their centuries-old roots and about the traditions to which the Feininger family felt bound. He had told Isabelle they lived like the landed gentry of England but in the Palatinate region instead. He had enthusiastically described the grape harvest and the traditional celebrations and wine tastings in enormous cellars, the wine invariably served with hearty food. In her mind's eye, the images grew more and more vibrant—romantic, rural scenes like those the great painters had immortalized in oil on canvas. And she was in the middle of it all as the *grande dame* of the estate . . .

receptions in the rose garden, wine festivals where she was always the most beautiful woman present, cozy evenings spent around the fireplace with close friends and good red wine. At Leon's winery, she would have a free hand, and finally—finally—not have to dance to her father's tune. She could scarcely wait to put her skills to some useful purpose.

Why Leon had left the Palatinate when everything there had been so wonderful—well, *that* was a question Isabelle had never asked. Had he really only wanted to pit himself against the best cyclists in Germany? Or had he been unable to put up with the confinements of his homeland? And why had she never questioned his depictions or dug a little deeper? That would have been the smart thing to do. Instead, she had eloped with him blindly, like a heroine in a cheap novel. She was no longer surprised that those stories always ended when the prince and his princess rode off in a coach or on horseback. Because what came next wasn't really suited to the romantic dispositions of the women who read those stories. Who wanted to watch the princess turn into a housemaid?

Oh, Leon, if I didn't love you so much . . . , Isabelle thought, not for the first time.

Leon's family had taken his sudden reappearance after his many months away—and with a new bride in tow—with astonishing indifference. His mother, a careworn woman aged beyond her years, had bashfully stroked her son's arm just once. Only later did Isabelle understand that, for Anni Feininger, the simple gesture was a demonstration of great love. Leon's father, Oskar, a burly, taciturn man, had nodded at Leon—nothing more—and Isabelle could have sworn that his expression had darkened a little when he did so. Father and son had practically nothing in common.

Of course, there had been questions, along with a few reproaches and congratulations on their marriage. But that was all. They were given one of the bedrooms on the second floor—directly beside the room where Leon's parents slept. That had been the first shock for Isabelle, who had thought that she and Leon would be given a side wing of the estate. But the "side wing" of the farmhouse was home to the cows. At the time, Isabelle had determined not to stay there a single day longer than necessary, and she refused to unpack her bags. The next day, when she saw how her elegant dresses were being crushed in their cases, she realized that she had no choice but to hang them in the far-too-small wardrobe. She would put up with the situation, but as a stopgap, no more. After that, Leon would have to find a new place for them.

But the very next day, Leon had needed to help with the grape harvest, and he had no time to search for a better house or even a comfortable apartment. He had not even been able to show her the entire estate, which was really no more than a simple farm. Isabelle had discovered the little there was to see by herself: the large barn filled with wine barrels, the stall for the two cows whose rear ends were always smeared with dung, the pigsty in which she still hadn't set foot, and a mesh chicken pen that had been patched with wire countless times. There wasn't a trace of the "landed gentry" romance she'd imagined. While Isabelle tiptoed between the pigsty and the barn in her fine suede shoes, Leon's effusive descriptions of his home dissolved like smoke in the wind. But the sun shone, casting a golden veil over the rugged landscape, and the fruity odor of freshly pressed grape juice added a certain sweetness to the country air. In September, not yet two months after their arrival, there had been a festival to mark the end of the harvest, and it had come close to the celebration that Isabelle had pictured in her mind. She and Leon danced through half the night, and when they got hungry, they fortified themselves with chunks of hearty onion pie.

The morning after the harvest festival, Isabelle had gone to hang a jacket in her wardrobe, and her elegant salon dresses caught her eye. They were leading a lonely existence in there. *So what!* she thought. Everything was different than she had expected it to be, but maybe she could get used to life on the land—at least once they had found a suitable home for themselves.

Then the golden autumn came to an abrupt end, and the sun was replaced by fog. With the fog came the boredom, something to which Isabelle was entirely unaccustomed. In Berlin, she never had enough time for her activities: seeing her friends; training on her bicycle with her best friend, Josephine; and all her work in the cycling club, in addition to all the social engagements her parents took her to. The idleness of her new life was now nearly driving her crazy. No one wanted or needed anything from her. Anni had her household firmly in her grasp, and Isabelle was only occasionally allowed to help in the kitchen. There were no jobs to be had in the area. Her dreams of an independent life burst like soap bubbles.

"Come out for a ride with me! You'll feel so much better afterward," said Leon when she complained about the leaden wasteland that was weighing so heavily on her. But Isabelle waved him off. Ever since taking a bad fall during a long-distance race the previous spring, cycling had become the last thing she wanted to do.

"Why don't we try to find a house of our own?" she asked.

"Now, in winter? When everything's so bleak? I don't think that would be a good idea," said Leon, and he promised they would look for something in the spring. Isabelle was left only with the nights. In Leon's arms, at least, she found the fulfillment that she was denied during the day.

Though Isabelle knew she should be grateful to have been given a task, she couldn't help but feel overwhelmed by the mountain of potatoes in front of her. If anyone had told her in her previous life how much work had to be done to fill the bellies of five adults, she would not have believed it. The red earth of the Palatinate that clung so obstinately to the potatoes crept deeper and deeper into the little creases of her knuckles every day and clung so persistently under her fingernails that none of her talents as a manicurist could get them clean again.

Isabelle sighed deeply again. Hands like a farmer's wife and potatoes, morning, noon, and night.

"Think you'll get through all that today?"

Isabelle did not have to turn around to know her mother-in-law was standing in the doorway. Fog-dampened air and the stink of the pigsty had entered the kitchen with her.

"The knife is dull. I can't do it any faster," Isabelle said.

"It's a poor workman who blames his tools!" Anni Feininger pulled up a chair and joined Isabelle at the kitchen table. "Imagine, a letter arrived for Leon. A letter from—" She broke off abruptly when she saw the potatoes Isabelle had already peeled. "And you've once again cut off half the potato with the peel! Won't you ever learn?" Anni snatched the knife out of Isabelle's hand, then picked up one of the dirty potatoes. The letter—at the mention of which Isabelle had detected, for the very first time, a trace of excitement in Anni's voice—was tossed carelessly onto the table, the red-brown dust from the potatoes immediately soiling the cream-colored envelope.

How many times does she plan to show me how to peel a potato? Isabelle wondered, glancing curiously at the letter. "Herr Leonard Feininger" was written on it in stiff handwriting, but Isabelle could not make out the name of the sender. She did not like to think about who might want something from him.

"Like this!" Leon's mother held a paper-thin curl of potato skin triumphantly in the air.

"Then do the work yourself," said Isabelle. "I was not brought up to peel potatoes!" She stood up and swept out of the room.

Where was Leon? Isabelle peered out through the door of the house. The blanket of fog that had draped itself over the village was so thick that she could barely make out the neighbors' houses. He wouldn't ride far in this murky soup, would he? Then again, Leon went cycling whenever the mood took him—never mind the weather or anything else. Her beautiful, wild cyclist. Perhaps a little fresh air would do her good as well. A walk up the hill behind the house and down again, just to make sure she didn't lose her figure. Isabelle grabbed her jacket and a scarf from the wardrobe.

The air was moist and heavy, and just breathing hurt her lungs. *What am I doing?* she thought angrily when she nearly lost her footing at a slippery spot on the hillside. She looked out in disgust at the foggy wasteland all around her. How did I wind up here?

"*We raised you to marry well.*" Again, Isabelle heard her mother's voice. Suddenly, it felt as if the conversation had taken place just the day before, though it was long ago.

That day, more than two years earlier, Isabelle had gone to visit her friend Josephine in her new home. Clara had also been there. Josephine, Clara, and Isabelle had been inseparable, and Clara and Isabelle had been curious to see how Josephine had set up the little house she'd inherited from old Frieda. To Isabelle's astonishment, everything looked just as it had before: the same threadbare furniture with the patchwork rugs on the floor. The place even smelled like it always had—of the potatoes stored away in the cellar and of the musty woolen blankets old Frieda draped over every sofa and armchair. Mousie the cat, who lazed around wherever it felt like it and left its fur behind, had added its own distinctive bouquet to the mix. Josephine had changed nothing after moving in, nothing at all. To Isabelle, the whole place looked shabby, but she had been moved by the fact that Josephine had chosen to preserve the memory of her deceased benefactor in that way.

Josephine had suggested they cook soup with the vegetables and meat she had on hand. Aghast, Isabelle had stared at her friend. She'd been expecting a chilled bottle of sparkling wine, a few tasty snacks, or at least an inaugural cake!

Clara, however, had found nothing wrong with Josephine's suggestion and had calmly started peeling carrots and potatoes with Josephine while Isabelle looked on enviously from a chair. She had felt rather lost back then, as if some kind of invisible wall separated her from her friends. But even if she had wanted to help with the food, she had no idea how to even hold a paring knife.

That evening, when she had told her mother about her helplessness at Josephine's "housewarming party," her mother had replied with those pregnant words: "Don't worry your pretty head about it. You were raised to marry, not to peel potatoes!"

At the time, Isabelle had thought no more about it. People like her hired staff for such work. That's just the way it was.

Perhaps her parents would have done better to raise her to survive, she thought now, when she paused, panting, atop the rise behind the farm. Then perhaps her adjustment to the life she now had to lead would not be so difficult.

She narrowed her eyes to see better. The fog had thinned somewhat, but from up there, she couldn't see any sign of Leon. She sighed. To a point, she could understand Leon's passion for cycling—after all, she had been part of the sport herself until just recently. But things couldn't go on like this, she concluded, as she slipped and stumbled back down the hillside. Something had to happen, or she'd go out of her mind before spring arrived.

The next few hours passed very slowly. Isabelle paced around their bedroom, the floorboards creaking tauntingly with every step. Like all the upstairs rooms, the bedroom was not heated. Isabelle pulled a woolen shawl around her shoulders, but it didn't help much. Going down to the heated parlor was not a good alternative, because it meant having to put up with the pipe smoke from Oskar Feininger and his even more taciturn brother Albert, who also lived on the farm.

Feeling depressed, she looked around the dimly lit room. She'd run out of reading material weeks before, and there was nothing in the Feininger house to read apart from a Christian periodical. Finally she sat down and began to write a letter to her friend Clara. But she stopped as soon as she'd written *Dear Clara*. Apart from her moaning and misery, she had nothing to write about. As a doctor's wife, Clara managed a large practice. And, of course, she had her own household to look after, as well as little Matthias—a full schedule, really, and then some. When Clara found out that Isabelle was sitting around twiddling her thumbs—even though she had no choice in the matter—her reaction would certainly be one of incomprehension.

The same would be true of her friend Josephine, who was running a successful bicycle business with her husband. And when she thought about Lilo in the Black Forest! Lilo and her husband managed no fewer than three luxury sanatoriums. Isabelle had imagined something similar for her own life in the Palatinate. In her naïveté, she had dreamed of taking control of the winery, together with Leon.

Dreams . . . as a young woman, she'd had more than enough of those. *Maybe that's why our friendship held?* she thought, still staring at the unwritten page in front of her. Apart from the fact that all three of them had lived on the same street, Clara, Josephine, and Isabelle could hardly have been more different. Clara, the good pharmacist's daughter; Josephine, the rebel of the trio; and then Isabelle herself, the rich daughter of a factory owner. But whenever they were together, they laughed and told each other their secrets, and what they had in common had been stronger by far than all the social differences that separated them. Each of them had her dreams, and to all appearances, her friends had made theirs come true. But here she was, stuck in the wilderness, all out of dreams.

Disgusted, Isabelle threw her pen and stationery into a corner before a thought occurred to her: The letter that her mother-in-law had been so excited about—why hadn't Isabelle taken it with her? Then she would at least have something to read. And the letter would probably affect her, too, wouldn't it?

When she abandoned Berlin so precipitately, she did not tell anyone except Clara what her new address would be. Even so, it had obviously been easy for her father to find out where she had gone, because a letter from him arrived just a few days after her wedding. The letter had been addressed to *Mrs. I. Feininger.* He had not even written her first name. In curt, clear words, he had told her that she was dead to him. And until today, she had not heard a word from her mother. Only from Clara, now and then, came a few sparse lines. All her bridges were charred ruins.

Isabelle occasionally looked out the window, but there was no sign whatsoever of Leon. It was almost dark. When was he finally going to return?

To divert herself, she went to the mirror on the wall. In the pale light of the gas lamp, she did her best to pluck her eyebrows. Her face had become so round! And her eyes had lost all their shine—all the boredom she felt was reflected in them. To think that she had once beguiled every man she met with her provocative eyes. Nervously, Isabelle tossed the golden tweezers onto the vanity. Then she picked up her sewing box and began to let out the waistband on one of her skirts—something she had to do for all her dresses. In Berlin, she had danced through the nights and trained long hours on her bicycle, and her figure had been slender. But with the inactivity and the rich, plain food in that house, her slim waistline had disappeared. As much as she might hold in her breath, she could no longer lace up her bodice all the way.

Leon's mother had already remarked that it looked as if a new family member might be on the way. *Pregnant, my foot! I'll start looking like a potato myself soon*, thought Isabelle, adding a good inch of material to the waistband of her skirt. Perhaps she should get some of that horrible brown woolen yarn from her mother-in-law and knit herself a jacket. With something like that, she could perhaps conceal her curves. And she'd have something to do. Oh, good Lord, she couldn't even imagine doing needlework.

With clammy fingers, Isabelle sewed away at her skirt for a while. But her thoughts kept returning to the letter. Why hadn't she taken it with her? With every stitch, her conviction that it had something to do with her grew—Anni wouldn't have mentioned it to her otherwise! Had something happened to her parents? An accident in her father's factory? The thought frightened her, but what frightened her even more was the unexpressed pleasure she felt at the idea that in an emergency, she would *have* to return to Berlin. Everyone would understand that. Leon and his family, her family, her friends in Berlin. She wouldn't owe anyone an explanation. And then they would see where things went.

With her heart beating hard, Isabelle went back to the kitchen. She had to read the letter, immediately! But where had her mother-in-law put it? It wasn't on the sideboard with the doily, nor was it in the basket with the shriveled apples. Disappointed, she was about to head back upstairs when she saw it after all, tucked in behind the yellowing mirror. Isabelle sighed with relief. She had the letter in her hand when she heard Anni's sharp voice behind her. "Put that down! It's for Leon!"

Chapter Two

Leon came home from his extended ride feeling on top of the world.

"Isabelle's upstairs," his mother had announced bitterly when he arrived.

His darling wife probably had ducked some housewifely duty again! Leon had sensed that his mother expected some sort of response from him or that he would take her side, but he would not be drawn in. It made no difference to him which of the two women made sure the food was on the table at the right time. He liked his mother's cooking, and when it came to Isabelle, in bed she was everything a man could wish for. Leon grinned. As he climbed the stairs to the bedroom, he glanced at the clock on the wall. It was just after five, and dinner was at six—enough time for a little activity under the covers. Far from wearing him out, his training ride had only fired him up.

"I'm back, *chérie*! Did you miss me?" he called, turning the door handle expectantly. Isabelle was sitting on the edge of the bed, and her expression was not relaxed. She was in another one of her moods. He went over to her and leaned down to kiss her, but she fended him off.

"How can you do this to me?" she railed. "I sit around here bored out of my mind, while you go off and have the time of your life!"

Oh, for God's sake. One would think he'd been gone for months! Leon had trouble stifling a grin at the dramas she managed to conjure up. His beloved wife really could make a mountain out of any molehill.

"Why aren't you downstairs? Mother has chestnuts on the stove, and the whole house smells wonderful," he said as he pulled off his mud-splattered trousers and threw them on the floor. In the last few months, he'd discovered that the best approach to Isabelle's moods was to ignore them. "Now I'm back again." In his underwear, he sat beside her on the bed and kissed her neck. How wonderful she smelled, of peaches and vanilla. Leon felt his excitement quicken, as it always did when he was close to Isabelle. The scent of her perfect skin, her long red hair tumbling wildly down her back—thank God she hadn't wrapped her magnificent mane into one of those braids he hated. He traced his middle finger slowly down her back.

"*Chérie*, I'm sorry, and I would be only too happy to atone for my sins . . ."

But instead of giving in to his cooing, Isabelle abruptly turned away. "Leon, really, it's not all right, you going out every day and riding for hours while I sit here with the walls closing in. You could certainly take care of me a little more." Her voice was unusually doleful.

"Are we both supposed to sit around and be bored?" Leon replied. "Everybody knows that life on the land is bleak in winter. But in two or three months, spring will be here, and it will be a completely different world."

"Waiting for spring is the last thing I want to do. I'm thirsty for a change of scene and a breath of city air . . . or I'll die like a primrose you forgot to water," she said angrily. "And then there's this stupid letter that came for you that I've been going crazy about all day." She told him all her horrible suspicions about what was in the letter.

Leon's brow creased. "That can only be the invitations for the races in Kaiserslautern and Worms. Or a newspaper report about the New Year's race in Mainz, which I won, after all!" he said proudly.

Isabelle snorted. "Don't you have anything in your head anymore except your races? Why don't you go downstairs and get the letter, and then we'll both know."

"It's from a notary in Pirmasens. Strange . . . ," Leon murmured when he was sitting beside Isabelle on the bed again a few minutes later. He opened the envelope, careful not to tear the papers inside. "I'm supposed to go there in two days!" He looked up with a grin. "See? Your wish for a little city air is my command."

"An appointment with a notary? What in the world could it mean?" Isabelle was looking excitedly over his shoulder.

Leon looked up at her with a frown. "I don't have the slightest idea."

One of their neighbors offered to drive Leon and Isabelle into the city in his carriage. Wearing her best dress and wrapped in her warmest coat, Isabelle eyed the decrepit vehicle suspiciously. Sun, rain, and other weather-related phenomena had left their marks on it, making the wood molder and causing deep cracks that ran from the front axle all the way back. And it was supposed to get them to Pirmasens?

As fragile as the coach was, the horses that the farmer harnessed in front of it were a pair of young and frisky three-year-olds that leaped ahead in fright at every shake of a branch. The carriage groaned ominously, and Isabelle feared a broken axle or worse. Although he cursed aloud, the driver did his best to keep the horses calm. Isabelle's fear grew. What if they had an accident between two villages and drove into the ditch beside the road? In this thinly populated region, it could take forever for anyone to come to their aid—if anyone could find them at all in the soupy fog!

To Isabelle's great relief, they made it into Pirmasens unscathed. She peered excitedly out the window as they passed several factories on the way into town. The air smelled sour, a mix of tanned leather and the smoke rising from the factory chimneys all around. Almost every company sign depicted shoes or a cobbler: "Neuff Shoe Factory," "Rheinberg Shoe Factory," "Peter Kaiser Shoe Factory." Under normal circumstances, as the daughter of a factory owner herself, she would have had a keen interest in finding out why so many shoes were manufactured in Pirmasens. And, naturally, she would also have risked a glance into this or that showroom window, but just then the only thing that interested her was what was waiting for them at the notary's office.

When they pulled up in front of a stately building close to the town hall at the end of the Palace Square, Isabelle let out a sigh of relief. Finally!

The notary wore a brown suit that made him all but disappear against the brown-veneered furniture in his dusty offices, and he read the final will and testament of Monsieur Jacques Feininger in an uncomfortably high-pitched voice. A second man, dressed in dark-green wool, sat beside him. He was a translator officially certified by the district court. At some point in his life, the deceased had taken French citizenship, and because the testament had been written in French and the beneficiaries were German, by law every sentence had to be translated. Isabelle, who had spent years studying French, spoke the language well, and understood it even better, could have happily done without all the wearisome translations.

"I, Jacques Feininger, do hereby leave to my nephew, Leonard Feininger, as sole heir . . ."

Leon was inheriting something! In her excitement, Isabelle dug her fingers into Leon's arm.

". . . my vineyard and winery located in Hautvillers . . ."

A vineyard in Hautvillers? She hadn't heard anything about that before. Was Hautvillers also in the Palatinate? And who was this uncle, Jacques Feininger? Isabelle, feeling rather confused, looked from the notary to Leon. But he, too, seemed completely at a loss. A deep crease appeared across his forehead, and he seemed to be unable to stop shaking his head, as if he were having trouble assimilating what the notary was reading.

After an hour, the notary slapped the leather file in front of him closed. The wooden legs of his chair scraped painfully across the graying parquetry as he stood up. Isabelle and Leon rose as well. The translator, his forehead dotted with beads of sweat from his exertions, remained seated as he filled out a form.

The notary cleared his throat, then reached out to shake Leon's hand.

"Congratulations, sir! A wine estate in the province of Champagne—I have seen many a poorer legacy."

"An estate in Champagne! Oh my goodness." They were not even out of the door of the notary's office when Isabelle laughed out loud and fell into her husband's arms. Good-bye, Grimmzeit! This was the chance she'd been waiting for. A vineyard and winery of their own . . .

Leon still looked somewhat lost and sheepish. Isabelle tugged insistently at his arm.

"Why didn't you ever tell me about Jacques? And why, of all people, did he leave it to *you*? A vineyard in Champagne! What does it mean?"

A grin slowly spread across Leon's face. "Simply this, *chérie*: it means that from now on, we're rich! We can do whatever we want!" With a gesture of exaggerated gallantry, he held out his arm for her to take. "Time to celebrate!"

"Uncle Jakob is—I mean, was—father's brother, younger by two years. I have no idea when he started calling himself Jacques." Leon shrugged.

"He left Grimmzeit when I was three or four years old. There was some sort of quarrel between him and my father. As a child, you only pick up on these things indirectly, and you never know what it's about, exactly. My mother cried a lot at that time, I remember that. She must have been about your age, and she often sat me on her lap, as if she might find consolation in me. Strange. I remember it like it was yesterday, how her face was often wet from her tears. Still, I loved being so close to her. Later on, moments like that were rare." Leon looked off into the distance, lost in thought.

In the weak light inside the small café, Isabelle listened to her husband intently. It was rare for Leon to speak openly about his feelings, and his words moved her very much. Anni Feininger as a young woman and fragile mother . . . she found that hard to imagine.

"What then?"

"After that, we didn't hear anything from Uncle Jakob for many years. His name hardly ever came up, but I thought about him quite a bit. In my childhood imagination, I assumed he'd gone off to sea and become a pirate. Or that he'd emigrated to America to fight the Indians. There was something adventurous about him, something daring and fearless. He had an opinion about everything and never shied away from announcing it! Nothing like Uncle Albert, who never says a peep about anything for the sake of peace and quiet." Leon twisted his mouth to one side. "Jakob was really a daredevil, apparently. I mean, just up and leaving like that . . . that takes some courage, doesn't it?"

Isabelle nodded. She'd done just the same when she followed Leon to the Palatinate. But in the enthusiasm of telling his story, the parallel to hers seemed lost on him.

"Jakob broke free of what was tying him down. For me, he was always a hero. And perhaps a bit of a role model, too." Leon laughed softly. Isabelle could not stop herself from reaching out and stroking the dimples that appeared in his cheeks when he laughed like that.

Leon took her hand and kissed her tenderly. Then he said, "I only discovered two years ago that Jakob—Jacques—lived just a couple of hundred miles away. He sent me a letter, inviting me to visit him."

"So you know the place?" Isabelle set down her glass of tea so abruptly that the brown liquid splashed onto the tablecloth. "I thought that was all a mystery to you, too!"

Up to that moment, it had all sounded like a dream, an illusion that she did not want to trust. But if Leon had really been there and seen it all . . .

"Yes, I know it. I was there for three weeks back then, although I spent most of it out on the bicycle. The roads of Champagne are outstanding. I was already racing successfully back then, and of course I had to keep training. At the Munich Race in the autumn of '96, for example, I came in second—"

"Leon!" Isabelle interrupted. "The winery. What's it like? And how did you get along with your uncle?"

Leon screwed up his face as if he'd bitten into something sour. "To be honest, there was nothing left of the hero of my childhood. Instead, I found a cranky old coot who'd argue about anything with anybody, including me. I don't think he was very popular among his neighbors. But his vineyard is beautiful. And"—he paused, as if to build the suspense—"the estate includes not only its own vines, but also its own cellars! Jakob was what they call a vigneron, a grower who produces his own champagne." The pride in Leon's voice was unmistakable. "I can honestly say that, for me, my uncle's champagne tasted wonderful."

Their own champagne . . . an elegant sales room. And equally elegant customers who would buy the champagne by the crate. And there she would be, in the middle of all of it, organizing everything. Isabelle's thoughts were whirling through her mind. *Keep those kinds of thoughts in check, young woman!* an inner voice whispered in her ear at the same time. *Not everything that glitters is gold. You've seen that for yourself in Grimmzeit.*

"Hautvillers, by the way, is only about fifteen miles from Reims, which is the heart of the province of Champagne. At least, that's where the biggest and best champagne producers are based, and champagne is sold there in huge quantities."

"On my eighteenth birthday, Father had champagne served. I think it was Moët, and the cork popped and hit the ceiling. I remember very clearly how surprised I was when I first felt the little bubbles bursting on my tongue." Isabelle laughed rapturously at the memory. Champagne—the word alone carried so much promise! Her eye fell instinctively on the glass of thin black tea in front of her. A film had formed on its surface. She smiled seductively at her husband. "You know, to celebrate this day, we really ought to order a glass! Your treat?"

"Champagne in the middle of the day? Why not order yourself a piece of cake instead?" Leon replied. "What would you say if I told you that Moët champagne actually comes from Hautvillers?"

"But not at your uncle's vineyard, surely?" Isabelle's mouth was dry with excitement. Perhaps she could allow herself a dream after all?

Leon shook his head. "No, but the Moët cellars are just a block away. There are a lot of resident champagne makers in Hautvillers. And the village itself happens to be very pretty. As a racing cyclist, I don't pay much attention to lovely landscapes or towns; I keep my eyes on the road. Still, the Montagne de Reims, the area around Reims, made a great impression on me. It felt as if I was riding through a green-and-gold sea of grapevines—"

"Leon, please, stop! You're a wonderful storyteller, and I could listen to you for hours," Isabelle interrupted him, laughing. "But frankly, I'd prefer to go to our new home without any visions of it in my head." Doing *that*, after all, had already gone awry once.

She grabbed her handbag and gave a sign to the waiter that she wanted to pay. "If it were up to me, we could leave today. I—" She frowned at her husband as an anxious thought occurred to her. "I sincerely hope you're planning to run the winery yourself?"

Chapter Three

"*Jacques* Feininger—my God, that makes me angry! He couldn't live with the good old name of Jakob that our parents gave him?" Holding a knife and fork high, like two weapons, Oskar Feininger leaned across the dinner table. "And French citizenship—that takes the cake! Did he have to chum up to the frogs? Is that it? Oh, of course, he was a *maker of fine champagne.* Our good Palatinate wine wasn't good enough for him anymore, no sir!"

Isabelle grimaced. If her father-in-law got any more worked up, he'd start foaming at the mouth. The way he derided his brother was terrible.

Albert sat as placidly as ever, as if none of it had anything to do with him. Anni didn't say anything, but instead of eating with her usual appetite, she only picked at a slice of bread. When they had returned from Pirmasens and Leon told his mother about his uncle's death, she had clasped her hands to her chest in shock and run from the room. When she had returned, Isabelle could have sworn she'd been crying. She had prepared supper in silence and inadvertently set out honey instead of butter on the table.

"Aren't you happy for Leon at all? Accepting an inheritance like that is a wonderful thing. And a great honor, too," said Isabelle, as her father-in-law gulped down a mouthful of wine.

"A great honor! You don't know what you're talking about," Oskar spat. "That man added nothing to our family but trouble and unrest. Even now, he's sowing strife and discord in this family from the grave."

"That's enough! If anyone in this family is causing strife, it's you," said Anni, so loudly and unexpectedly that everyone at the table jumped. "How can anyone be so vindictive? Sometimes I truly wonder—"

"What? What do you wonder?" Oskar snarled at her.

Isabelle followed this brief exchange between her in-laws uneasily, but she could make no sense of it. Instead of answering her husband, Anni turned to Leon. "I take it you'll be wanting to pay a visit to the place as soon as you can?"

Leon nodded. Then he took her right hand in his, as if he wanted to ask for forgiveness in advance for what he was about to say. "Mother, when we leave, we're leaving forever. I know what's waiting for me there, and it would be smart to make the move sooner rather than later."

Isabelle rejoiced inwardly. No more dithering, thank God! But when she saw the pain in Anni's eyes, it put at least a small damper on her excitement.

A week later, Isabelle and Leon were packed and ready to leave. Isabelle could hardly have imagined a cooler farewell from her father-in-law. A quick handshake, a scowl, and that was it. That he had agreed to take them, with all their baggage, to the train station in Pirmasens, felt to Isabelle like a miracle. Anni must have put enormous pressure on her husband; Oskar would never have done it otherwise. Choosing Champagne over the Palatinate had made Leon, in his father's eyes, another renegade. Instead of giving his son some useful tips to get him on his way, he had taken every opportunity to put him down.

"*You're* going to try to run a winery? You can't even do a decent day's work here. If you still think riding your bicycle comes first, you'll run your estate into the ground before you know it."

Leon acted as if his father's words couldn't hurt him, but Isabelle knew that he was churning inside. She could have cheerfully killed her father-in-law! But it annoyed her just as much to realize that Oskar Feininger's words had planted a seed of skepticism in her about Leon's abilities as the future owner of the estate. Oskar was at least a little bit right: to that point, Leon had not exactly distinguished himself on the farm. His cycling always had been more important. *What a miserable, disloyal wife you have turned out to be!* she chided herself inwardly, more than once. Leon would certainly do things differently once they were settled on their own estate.

Isabelle reached out stiffly to take her mother-in-law's hand. "All the best. And thank you," she said halfheartedly.

Anni, always so down-to-earth as a farmer, shook Isabelle's hand feebly. Then she nodded slightly and turned to Leon.

"Leon . . . my boy . . . ," she whispered, choking up, then she threw both arms around her son. "Farewell."

Isabelle felt a chill go through her, and not only because of the merciless east wind whipping across the train platform. The weather would have been more suited to Siberia than the Palatinate, where now, at the end of February, the first crocuses were already beginning to appear in Pirmasens.

"We'll write every week, I promise! And when you come to visit, we'll throw a huge party, and the champagne will flow!" Leon said encouragingly to his mother. In that moment, he looked as if he even believed what he was saying.

But Anni raised her hand in a gesture that spoke another language: about animals that had to be tended, about their own vineyard, about Leon's father's rejection of everything that had to do with Jacques and the Champagne region. She knew that she was unlikely to see her son again soon.

Awkwardly, Isabelle turned away from Anni, who still clung to her son like she was drowning. The poor woman. For the first time, Isabelle had some idea of what she had done to her own mother by eloping. Once they had settled in on the estate in Hautvillers, she thought she might pick up her paper and pen and write a few lines home to Berlin. Her father didn't need to find out about it. She could send the letter to Clara, who would hand it to Jeanette Herrenhus personally.

The shriek of the incoming train jolted Isabelle from her thoughts, for which she was glad.

"Well, that's that," said Leon, his voice husky as he watched his parents walking back toward the station entrance.

"Do you want to hire a porter or two?" said Isabelle. "We'll never get all of this luggage on the train alone."

"I'm not going to throw money away on someone to carry my bags for me. Let me do it." His voice was suddenly cheerful, and he seemed happy for the distraction from the pain of parting. Leon pressed a kiss to Isabelle's lips. "Watch the rest of our things while I load the bicycles, okay?"

Along with the bicycles, they had two large suitcases, a travel bag containing her personal things, plus several bags that belonged to Leon. *Well, no one can accuse us of traveling light,* Isabelle thought as she watched Leon heave their two bicycles into the baggage car section. At least they didn't have to change trains; the train would take them directly to Metz via Neunkirchen and Saarbrücken. From there, however, they would travel toward Verdun and then on to Reims by coach—no trains rolled through the vast French forests. Leon estimated that they would arrive in Reims the following afternoon, but they still had little idea of where they would sleep that night.

For maybe the twentieth time, Isabelle reached down, assuring herself that she had her handbag. She was carrying not only her own and

Leon's papers, but also her jewelry, which she had taken with her when she left Berlin: several valuable pearl necklaces and diamond rings, a pair of ruby earrings and a pair of sapphire earrings, some garnet brooches, and bracelets in gold and silver. In Isabelle's view, she had earned her father's generous gifts by acceding to his wishes and presenting herself on the marriage market like some sort of prize cow. She had not for a moment considered leaving the jewelry behind in her parents' house. But in Grimmzeit, Isabelle had had no opportunity to wear it; instead, she had tucked it away under the bed as a kind of rainy-day nest egg, hoping all along that she would never have to make use of it for anything so dire.

Grimmzeit . . . she wasted no tears on the place or the grim times. She hoped something better would come. Feeling better than she had in a long time, Isabelle took one of the longer jewelry boxes out of the bag. She placed the rose-colored pearls around her neck and fastened the clasp. Why not get dressed up to travel? She no longer needed anything for a rainy day, after all.

The journey was uneventful. The train was only half full, which meant that, for most of the time, they had a compartment to themselves and could talk without being disturbed.

"It all still seems so unreal! You and me on our own estate. I can't imagine what to expect," said Isabelle as the train chugged through the last foothills of the Palatinate forest. "What do you think our life will be like in the future?" It was not the first time she had asked Leon that question, but so far she had not received a satisfactory answer; instead Leon had remained extremely vague. Now, however, she was determined not to let him off the hook.

"What will our life be like in the future?" Leon repeated. "Well, it's easy, isn't it? We'll sell champagne and get disgustingly rich!" He beamed at her as if he were deeply satisfied with his reply. "And we'll have some help doing it, too. There's an old man named Claude Bertrand who lives in a little house at the end of the property. He is, or rather *was*, Jacques's overseer, and he made sure everything was as it ought to be. I still remember how surprised I was when he spoke to me in very good German. His ancestors came from the Alsace region; his mother was German, his father French. And he explained that in Alsace many people grew up speaking both languages. I'm sure Claude will be happy to have us keep him on. I wrote to him last week and told him we were coming."

"*You* thought to do that?" asked Isabelle in disbelief.

"I'm not going off to Champagne as naïvely as my father might think," said Leon coolly. "There's a *chef de cave*, too—he's the man in charge of the cellars—but I don't remember his name. A bit of an odd bird. He's only got one eye, and he's hunchbacked."

Isabelle listened with interest. The prospect of already having staff on hand awaiting their arrival—and who also spoke German—was a huge relief.

"And is there a maid? Or some other help in the house?" she asked, trying to sound as casual as possible. Isabelle had not yet been able to make Leon understand that a young woman of her background should not waste her time on housework.

He nodded. "When I visited my uncle, Claude Bertrand's wife cooked for us. She's an excellent cook. I presume she runs my uncle's household, too. No doubt that she'll also be happy to stay on as our employee."

Isabelle, reassured, smiled.

"And there are hands for the vineyard work, too. At least, when my uncle showed me around his vines, there were a lot of men and women busy tying things up. Whether they're permanently employed or just there at certain times of the year, I really couldn't say. I didn't have much of a head for the details back then, but my impression was that the estate was managed well—if not by my uncle, then by his people.

If one simply keeps an eye on everything and makes sure that things get done . . ." He shrugged, as he always did when he considered something to be easy and obvious.

Isabelle felt as if she'd just been rescued from a sinking ship. Everything sounded so wonderful! Her mind wandering, she toyed with her pearl necklace. She could already see herself, elegantly dressed, standing in a luxurious salon with a champagne glass in her hand, welcoming wealthy customers to the cellars. A life as exhilarating as champagne itself.

The hotel they checked into in Reims stood beside the Place Royale and was simple but clean. While Leon made sure that their luggage was safely stowed away, Isabelle freshened up in their room. The hostess had set out a bowl of lukewarm water for her on the vanity, and to Isabelle's surprise, two slices of lemon were floating in it. Lemons in the middle of winter? Smiling, she had squeezed the juice into the water and luxuriated in the refreshing tingle the acid left on her cheeks.

They had been on the road for two days. The previous night had been spent in a dismal guesthouse, and the last stretch of the trip had been slow and tiring, but neither Leon nor Isabelle had any desire to rest. Both of them wanted to get out and look at Reims, the city that would be so much a part of their future life.

The sun that had accompanied them throughout the day was weakening in the late afternoon. Feeling a chill, Isabelle wrapped her scarf a little closer around her throat.

"Look around—this is just how I remember Reims from my last stopover here. So rich and inviting," said Leon euphorically. "And it's clean. No dog waste or garbage lying around. Isn't this a splendid town?"

Isabelle, her eyes shining, looked up at the artfully wrought streetlamps that were already illuminating even the farthest corners she could see. The city had not skimped on anything. And then there were all the lovely stores—fashion shops, men's outfitters, perfumeries, and a beautiful pharmacy, and beside that, a shop that sold nothing but chocolate and fine confections—the street was no less fine than Berlin's Kurfürstendamm. Isabelle would feel at home here; she could already sense that. It would have been so unimaginably dreadful if Reims had turned out to be another Grimmzeit! Her relief at not having another soap bubble burst before her eyes was so immense that it sent a shudder through her body.

"All these beautiful shops! You know what I feel like? Doing a little shopping. We probably won't have any time to come back here in the next few weeks. And we absolutely must look at the cathedral! They say it's a Gothic construction, one of a kind, really, the place where all the French kings have been crowned." She had read that in the travel guide that she had snapped up in a bookshop at the train station in Saarbrücken. She tilted her head back and gazed all around. On the journey, they had seen the high towers of the cathedral, with their missing spires, from far away, but now that they were in the heart of the city, where multistory buildings were lined up side by side, she could no longer see them.

Leon nodded disinterestedly, then he pointed to a brightly lit restaurant on the other side of the street. "Look. On the board, it says they have roast venison. Now that I think about it, I'm starving."

"But . . . ," Isabelle protested. The guide had listed so many sights! Museums, elegant squares, even a third-century triumphal arch. And just here, this hat shop! She looked in longingly at a purple composition of feathers, lace, and beads.

"Tomorrow is another day," said Leon resolutely. "Let's enjoy some good French cuisine."

In her former life in Berlin, Isabelle would have had no reservations about eating in a fine restaurant like the Café le Théâtre. On the contrary, in fact. Fashionably dressed, on the arm of her father, who was always shown to one of the best tables, she would have felt as comfortable as a fish in water. But now, with Leon, she looked around self-consciously. Every table was covered twice in white linen. Candles in opulent, multiple-armed candlesticks stood on every table, and the cutlery was highly polished sterling silver. Even more highly polished were the other diners. The women wore their hair in elaborate hairdos held in place with pins and decorative combs, and they were dressed in the latest French fashions. Their cheeks were rouged, their lips were red, and many of them had ringed their eyes or traced their eyebrows dramatically with a dark pencil. The men looked casually elegant in their dark-green jackets with stand-up collars and horn buttons. Diamond jewelry glittered on every woman's neckline, while their escorts consulted gold pocket watches.

The balls Isabelle had frequented in Berlin had always been glamorous affairs, but there had always been a trace of Prussian modesty about them. Here, by contrast, a wasteful opulence held sway. In her traveling dress, beneath which she was not even wearing a corset, she felt poorly dressed—or, even worse, practically indecent! If only she had at least gone to the trouble of putting up her hair properly!

But the waiter who served them gave not the slightest hint of condescension, as she might well have expected in a fine Berlin restaurant. He cheerfully explained the dishes on the menu, and Leon acted so interested that one might actually have believed that he could understand what the man was saying. Isabelle smirked.

"We'd like the poached salmon as an appetizer, followed by the roast venison," said Leon when the waiter had finished. *"Et une carafe d'eau."*

"I thought you couldn't speak any French," said Isabelle in astonishment the moment the waiter was out of earshot.

"Well, I can get by. I told you that I'd raced successfully in France, didn't I? You pick up a phrase here and there. I can speak a little English, too. When I was racing over in London, I had the feeling that I was learning the language very easily." Musing, he added, "You know, I never had the chance to go to secondary school. All there is in Grimmzeit is the village school. And it never occurred to my parents to send me off to school in Pirmasens or somewhere else. I would have liked to learn more. But my parents believed that secondary school was only for the rich, not for boys who grew up on vineyards. So I began to look around for something I could prove myself with, and I came across cycling. My parents had no objections, because it fit in well enough with the work on the farm. I finally had a few far-reaching goals of my own. But sometimes I think I could have been a bit more than just a good cyclist."

"Oh, Leon," said Isabelle, moved. "I know what you mean! My father never put much stock in me, either. For him, I was nothing but some kind of merchandise. The best future he could think of for me was to marry me off to a good match. But what really counts is what we have here and now! You'll be a wonderful landowner, secondary school or not. And I plan to show everyone that I can be more than just a bauble on the arm of a rich businessman. Together, we're strong."

Leon nodded. "You're right. From now, we'll show everyone what we can do!"

While they waited for their food to arrive, Isabelle gazed around the obviously popular restaurant. All the tables were occupied, and a virtual armada of waiters was hard at work bringing food and drink to the tables. Now and then, a whiff of something delicious wafted over to them. Beautifully decorated pastries, caviar piled in the finest crystal bowls, whole fish baked in a salt crust and filleted at the table—only the best was served here! Champagne bottles cooled in ice buckets, and the guests raised their splendid glasses in toasts to one another. At the next table, at which sat a particularly well-dressed group, a new magnum of champagne was just being served. No wonder the spirits at that table seemed particularly high. With a sigh, Isabelle sipped at her glass of water.

"That's the regular table of the champagne makers," the waiter whispered to Isabelle. "They meet here once a month, and right now they are in a wonderful mood." He smiled generously, then set two plates in front of Isabelle and Leon. With a flourish, he lifted the silver cloches that covered the individual dishes. "Poached salmon *à la maison*—bon appetit!"

While Leon went to work on the appetizer as if he hadn't eaten for days, Isabelle felt her own feelings of insecurity dissolve. She took a little of the delicate fish, and it was simply delicious. The festive mood inside the restaurant was heightened by the lively tunes of a string duet.

Isabelle winked at Leon.

"If everyone here is drinking champagne, it can't be so horribly expensive, can it? Don't you think we could . . . I mean, if not now, then when?"

"Monsieur, the champagne list!" Leon called to the waiter. But when the man handed him the open leather-bound menu, Leon's smile faded. "There must be over a hundred kinds of champagne here!" he said, loud enough that a few heads at neighboring tables turned in their direction. A few women giggled.

Isabelle leaned over to see the menu, too. Veuve Clicquot Ponsardin, Piper-Heidsieck, Moët, Louis Roederer—the list went on and on. And then there were the prices! A single bottle would dent their resources.

While Isabelle tried to think of a way to extricate themselves from the situation gracefully, one of the women from the champagne makers' table leaned over to her. Her hair was piled high on her head and held in place with pearl-studded needles, and her face was made-up dramatically. She wore an off-the-shoulder dress, and although she was no longer particularly young, her décolleté was as impressive as any twenty-year-old's and was adorned with a gold collier and a teardrop-shaped diamond pendant as big as a hazelnut.

"May I make a suggestion?" she said in an unusually deep voice. As she spoke, she raised her champagne glass as if she wanted to toast them.

"If it comes from such a beauty . . . ," said Leon.

Isabelle heard a certain undertone in his voice. His pupils widened a little, as they always did when he saw a woman he liked the look of. Isabelle twisted her mouth to one side.

"Not everything that is expensive is good," said the woman, and she swept her hand as if to discard the champagne menu. A gust of perfume swirled around her words. "Order yourselves a bottle of Trubert Millésime, and you will have the best that Champagne has to offer!"

Her words were confirmed by a laugh from the others at her table, and the woman laughed, too. They all started speaking at once, and they called out the name of one champagne after another.

Leon joined in their laughter, but Isabelle grimaced. Though she didn't understand what they were saying at the next table, she had the unpleasant feeling that a joke had been made at their expense. Abruptly, she turned to the waiter, who was still waiting patiently.

"A bottle of Feininger, please," she said loudly and prayed that the champagne made by Leon's uncle was on the list.

Chapter Four

Isabelle turned her head to the side so that Leon could kiss her throat more easily.

"You smell so good," he murmured, nuzzling her neck. Then he bit the lobe of her left ear tenderly. "So sweet, like a candied cherry." His fingers traced her nipples, his body pressed against hers. Sighing with desire, Isabelle pulled him even closer. She wanted to take him inside her, to feel him . . .

"I have an idea," said Leon, as they lay side by side, fulfilled by their lovemaking.

Golden sunlight filtered through the wooden shutters, falling onto the bedcovers and Isabelle's naked body. She stretched luxuriously and said, "We stay here the whole day and do what we just did again?"

Leon laughed his usual throaty laugh. "Half-right, sweetheart. We'll certainly stay here, but not in this room." Playfully, he picked up a lock of her long red hair and draped it across her breasts. "We'll be at the estate soon enough, and the work isn't going to go anywhere. One day of idleness now is just what we need. Besides, after last night, we definitely have to find a restaurant that serves Feininger champagne."

Isabelle laughed, too, but inside she was torn. On the one hand, she was already so curious about Hautvillers! And hadn't Leon told the overseer that they would be coming that day? But on the other hand, this would probably be her last chance for a long time to enjoy some big-city life.

She rolled over and plucked her travel guide from the nightstand. "What shall we see first? This old triumphal arch, or—"

"*Chérie*, darling," Leon interrupted her. He took her hand and planted a kiss playfully on her palm. "*My* plan is a little different."

Dressed in an elegant—if no longer completely modern—ensemble of strawberry-red velvet and a cream-colored woolen jacket, Isabelle set off a short time later in the direction of the world-famous cathedral. She had put on several pearl necklaces and had tied her hair into a sizable bun on the back of her head. A few loose strands curled behind her ears, accentuating her slender neck. All in all, she thought, catching sight of her reflection in a showroom window, she looked more like she'd just come from Berlin than from Grimmzeit.

The sun was shining, but there wasn't any warmth in it. Shivering, Isabelle regretted—not for the first time—that she hadn't taken any of her furs with her when she abandoned Berlin. But it had been late summer when she left, she had packed her bags in a hurry, and the furs had been stored away so she had no idea where to find them. Who thinks of sable and silver fox when they are blissfully in love?

As soon as they were settled in and champagne sales were going well—she assumed they would after seeing, in the restaurant the previous evening, just how freely the bubbly liquid could flow—she would get herself a new fur coat. Already she had her eyes open for a shop that would be able to sell her one. Her very first fur coat that her father had not paid for!

Her ire at Leon's preference for seeing Reims from the saddle of his bicycle rather than on foot with her soon melted away. As usual, she could not stay angry with her cycling husband. There were advantages to her being out alone, too, because it meant that she could admire the window displays of all the lovely shops in peace.

In a perfumery, the window display of which advertised French scents, Isabelle bought soap and a hand cream. She was already paying when she caught a glimpse of a collection of tiny jars, their lids decorated with colored stones. Her mother had possessed just such a tiny jar.

"May I see that?" she asked in French. The language felt strangely out of place in her mouth as she asked, although she had spoken French regularly at the aristocratic balls she'd attended in Berlin.

"Our finest color for cheeks and lips, my lady," the young saleswoman explained. She obligingly screwed the lids off several of the jars, and Isabelle saw that they were filled with creams in different colors. She found one particular copper tone particularly appealing.

"S'il vous plaît?" The saleswoman held out the jar to Isabelle invitingly.

Isabelle did not need a second invitation. Like a starving woman, she dipped her right index finger into the jar, then dabbed the color on her lips. It had been so long since she had worn perfume, so long since she had put on any kind of makeup. *Grimmzeit is far away*, she thought, and a smile crossed her face.

The cream felt delicate and soft, like a kiss from Leon. When she looked at the mirror the saleswoman held for her, she had to smile—she suddenly looked just as French as the elegant women she had seen in the restaurant.

Isabelle left the shop a few minutes later, satisfied with her purchases but with far fewer francs in her purse. Again and again, she stopped in front of shop windows to delight in her reflection and her copper-red lips. She felt better than she had in a very long time. Smiling to herself, she stopped at a street dealer carrying a vendor's tray of postcards of the city. The cathedral, the town hall, and there— that regal-looking pharmacy she had admired in real life the evening before. She bought the card for Clara; she knew her friend in Berlin would like it, and she would be surprised to receive a postcard, out of the blue, from France.

As Isabelle walked down a long street with a tramline running down the center, she suddenly understood what it was, apart from the shops and the overwhelmingly hospitable people, that made Reims so special: it was the white sandstone that was part of practically every building she saw. It reflected the sunlight in a transcendentally beautiful way. The thought that this splendid city was just fifteen miles from her future home and that she would come here often filled her with joy.

Notre Dame de Reims was already in sight when Isabelle passed a shop that had nothing in its window but an empty champagne bottle and two glasses arranged on material that looked like molten gold. The tableau looked not only exceptionally elegant but almost arrogant, as if the person who had conceived it wanted to say, *This is all one needs, isn't it?* The small scene radiated an intimacy as well. It was just an empty champagne bottle and two glasses, and one of the glasses was lying on its side as if someone, in the heat of emotion, had knocked it over. A guest at an elegant table. A lover in his beloved's embrace . . .

Isabelle abruptly turned her gaze up and away from the window, as if she had been caught in the act of peering secretly through a keyhole. "Champagne & Champagne" was written in black letters on an imposing cream-colored sign above the window. Not "Champagne and Wine" or "Champagne and Spirits." What was the owner trying to say with a name like that? As if magically drawn, Isabelle pressed her nose to the window; the next moment, a man's face appeared from inside. Shocked, Isabelle jumped back. Then she hurried on down the street.

Life-size figures, small figures, angels, fabulous creatures, the Virgin Mary . . . Isabelle couldn't take her eyes off the world-renowned Notre Dame de Reims cathedral. In her travel guide, it said that the centuries-old building was almost five hundred feet long and that more than 2,300 figures had been counted on the facades. Isabelle found the "smiling angel" that she discovered just to the left of the west entrance especially enchanting. Faced with so much beauty, she was a little afraid to step inside.

But when she finally did so, she felt a lump form in her throat from sheer emotion. It was even more beautiful inside. It was comforting that this church smelled just like any other on the inside—of dust and candle wax, old stones and incense, sins and forgiveness.

The soft strains of organ music mixed with the dull knocking of the stonemasons working on the restoration of the external facade. The sunlight streaming through the stained-glass windows refracted into thousands of prisms, like a kaleidoscope. With every step, Isabelle felt more like Alice in Wonderland. She flinched slightly when, close beside her, she heard a light scraping sound that she could not classify. It was a middle-aged man with a small knife in his hand, scratching something into one of the steps that led up to the choir stalls. A name, perhaps? Then Isabelle saw that on every stone windowsill, every step and wall, there were thousands of scribbles—letters, names, whorls, strange symbols. Did the visitors want to be one with this place, becoming part of the structure and leaving behind something of themselves? For a moment, she thought about whether she, too . . . she had a nail file with her . . . But then she decided against it and instead lit a candle at one of the many candle altars. She knelt and closed her eyes and prayed.

Dear God, thank you for this fairytale that has already begun, here in Reims.

When Isabelle left the cathedral an hour later, she felt nothing but serenity and confidence. The estate would be a unique opportunity for Leon and her to grow into a good team. He might not yet have fully grasped the enormity of their undertaking, but with their arrival at the farm, he would understand that the time was ripe for something other than cycling.

The champagne shop she had seen earlier reappeared ahead of her, and she slowed her step. Left and right of the door, there were two large, hip-high vases that had not been there before. They were filled with white lilies and looked exceptionally graceful. Inside the shop itself, several chandeliers had been lit, and they only heightened the stylish radiance of the place.

Isabelle stopped short a few yards from the entrance. As an aspiring champagne maker, whatever the shop offered was bound to be of interest to her, but she still was wary about going inside. What nonsense! She turned the handle with determination and opened the door.

The owner, a strikingly attractive gentleman, was, to Isabelle's relief, busy with another customer. He smiled and nodded to her, and with a gesture, he invited her to browse.

Isabelle returned his smile cautiously. Inside, the shop was just as lovely and unusual as it looked from outside: on the polished granite floor lay a magnificent Aubusson carpet, and instead of pictures, several mirrors in different sizes with ornate golden frames graced the cream-colored walls. Isabelle cast a skeptical look at her reflection, as if to ask, *What do you think* you're *doing here?* When she walked toward the wine racks that took up the entire left-hand wall of the shop, the carpet swallowed the sound of her footsteps. Isabelle found the sight of the hundreds of bottles impressive, perhaps even a little intimidating.

"For a father, it is always painful to let his daughter go," the owner said. "Even when he knows she's in the best of hands and that the future son-in-law is as respectable as . . ." As he spoke, the man took a champagne bottle out of a cooler and opened it expertly. Two long-stemmed glasses were on the counter, and he poured both half full. He had beautiful hands, Isabelle saw from beneath lowered eyelids. At once strong and sensitive, like the hands of a pianist. Every movement he made radiated self-confidence and dignity, as if he were carrying out a sacred deed. Mesmerized, Isabelle could hardly look away.

"Isn't it a consolation to know that champagne offers us support at times like these? Joy and suffering—siblings, they are! Who could know that better than we *Champenois,* with our eventful history? So many wars, so much unrest, and in between the most marvelous *savoir vivre.*" The man behind the counter gestured in the air, a casually elegant motion. "Let's leave big politics out of it. I'd much rather tell you a small personal story. When my dear friend Louise Pommery saw her daughter married off to Comte Guy de Polignac, she naturally served the best champagne that her house could offer at that time: the 1874 Pommery. And what can I tell you?"

The customer looked at him expectantly. And Isabelle, standing by the wine racks, was transfixed.

"To this day, whenever anyone who was at that wedding comes into this shop, they talk about that dry, powerful champagne they found so breathtaking."

The customer nodded, obviously impressed. "The guests at Marie-Claire's wedding should also have something to talk about! Money is no issue. What I want is a truly spectacular champagne. One wants to show what one is capable of, after all. Am I right?" He laughed, then stretched his arms out, as if doing that might underscore his words.

The owner smiled back with reserve. "Then may I invite you, my esteemed Comte de Chauvinaux, to sample this outstanding *millésime*? It comes from the house of Mumm and is characterized by . . ."

Isabelle, who pretended to inspect the champagne bottles in the racks, listened breathlessly to the shopkeeper's words. What a civilized way to do business! While the owner took an order for thirty crates of champagne, she surreptitiously looked at him more closely.

Isabelle estimated that he was in his early fifties. His dense dark-brown hair was cut with military precision; his hazel eyes, crowned by strong brows, were intense. His skin was lightly tanned, the lines of his face even and soft, but not weak. On the contrary, with every movement he made and every sentence he spoke, the man radiated vitality. The dark-gray suit he wore was the epitome of the clothier's art, and Isabelle had never seen such perfectly tailored men's clothes on even the most dashing officers of the imperial bodyguard in Berlin. His black leather shoes had been polished so highly that he could probably use them for a mirror. In her mind, Isabelle whistled appreciatively. What a good-looking man!

**

Although, to all appearances, he had no more than glanced sidelong at her, from the moment his young customer stepped into his shop, Raymond Dupont observed her closely. At the age of fifty-five, he was a connoisseur of not only fine champagnes, but also beautiful women, although he knew that he probably defined beauty a little differently than most men, who might not have liked the young woman's tousled locks. Raymond, however, could almost sense the resilient bounce of her hair beneath his hands. *Like warm autumn leaves*, he thought. Another man might assert that the freckles that dappled her cheeks looked common or even rustic. But in Raymond's eyes, they brought her milk-white complexion to the fore. Her cheeks, chin, and nose might be considered by some to be a little too accentuated, as on the face of a porcelain doll. But Raymond knew that her face would transform in time and that nobler features would appear. She would go from being pretty to being classically beautiful—a transformation that very few women were capable of. But this young woman was a rose in the process of emerging. *Like a champagne that needs time to mature*, he thought, as the Comte de Chauvinaux departed.

He inhaled deeply, as if he might breathe in the young woman's aura. She was a head shorter than he, but her proud, upright bearing made her appear taller and even more charming. Bearing—in his eyes—was an important element of beauty.

"My name is Raymond Dupont. I'm the owner of this establishment. How may I be of service, madame?"

"I . . . well . . . I'll be living in . . . Hautvillers and . . ." She took a small, uncertain step back.

The stammering did not fit his image of her, and Raymond sensed that the young woman herself was annoyed about it. Was it because French was not her native tongue? Or was something else to blame for her agitation?

Nervously, she stroked her skirt smooth with both hands, then she raised her eyes and firmly said, "I have to learn as much as possible about champagne as quickly as possible!"

And that was all. No more explanation was forthcoming.

"You'll be living in Hautvillers? Congratulations! It's a very lovely location. The famous monk Dom Pérignon lived there, once upon a time. He did a great deal to advance the making of champagne. If you have the time, you should go for a stroll and visit his grave."

The young woman nodded but did not respond to his banter. So she was not especially talkative or coquettish or affected, as he had so often experienced.

What an enchanting vision—ravishing, even! Raymond smiled. He should really have been preparing for the visit of his next extremely wealthy customer, Madame Depeche, but he surprised himself when he said, "Would you like to taste the champagne? One learns best by doing, don't you think?" With a sweep of his hand, he invited his visitor to follow him to where several armchairs were grouped around a heavy table. For Raymond, champagne was something to be taken seriously, and pretty chairs artfully set around a delicate table would have been out of place. The last thing he wanted his customers wondering about was where to put their elbows and legs. He wanted their senses to be stimulated—or even better, aroused. As if making passionate love, a devotee of champagne ought to be able to forget the world around her and simply feel, smell, taste, and see . . .

"May I ask what . . . that would cost?" the woman said, lowering her eyes slightly.

"Why, nothing, of course," replied Raymond airily. "Or did you see me charge my customer for tasting the champagne just now? Now, please." He took three bottles of champagne that had been sitting in ice in a large silver bucket behind the counter. They had been intended for the arrogant Madame Depeche, who was coming in search of new champagnes for her picturesque restaurant on the banks of the Marne. But because she had no sense of taste of her own and relied entirely on his, he could present her with others.

"You're German?"

"Forgive me. I haven't introduced myself at all. My name is Isabelle Feininger. And yes, I'm from Germany. From Berlin, actually." She reached out her hand to him, and a smile appeared on her face for the first time. Raymond felt her relax a little.

Feininger? He became more alert. Wasn't there a German winemaker in Hautvillers by that name? A strange fellow. Raymond had never crossed paths with him, but he'd heard about him occasionally. Was she his wife? Or was the name just a coincidence?

"Then you must certainly know that there have been many Germans here in the Champagne region, and they profited greatly from their products. Think of Mumm, Heidsieck, and Krug. Even today, there are many wine specialists who find their way here from Germany."

"For me, it's rather that the opposite is true—I know nothing about champagne. In Berlin, they normally serve sparkling wine at parties and celebrations. They say that Kaiser Wilhelm gets downright angry if anyone dares open a bottle of champagne. Though, my father *did* serve champagne on special occasions, so I have had the opportunity to enjoy it from time to time," said Isabelle.

There was no vain boasting in her words. No inordinate high-society conceit. She spoke so casually of Kaiser Wilhelm that he might have been a close friend. And she was not wearing perfume; all Raymond could smell was a trace of lemon. When it came to tasting wine, perfume only got in the way.

"You know, you've just put your finger on the greatest difference between you Germans and we French?" he said, smiling. "A German wine lover opens a bottle of French champagne only on grand occasions. We French, on the other hand, open a bottle of champagne to make a grand occasion out of every moment." He skillfully removed first the foil, then the wire *muselet* from the first bottle. Instead of then twisting out the cork, he first removed the metal cap from it.

"This is what they call the plaque. For you, madame. A lucky charm—maybe it will work?"

While she happily inspected the silver-colored plaque, he opened the bottle so that no more than a soft hiss could be heard. Then he repeated the process with the next two bottles. Three would be enough to start with. He poured two glasses half full and handed her one of them.

"Champagne is a very special drink. A single swallow is enough to put one in the best of moods, but how great is the pleasure one takes from an entire bottle? It seduces people, enlivens any conversation, banishes sorrow and pain, and"—he paused for effect—"champagne is *the* drink for flirting." Instead of looking her in the eye, as he would have liked, he regarded the white-gold liquid in his glass. "See all the millions of bubbles? I could look into a glass of champagne for hours without getting bored. And it seems I'm not the only one, because more champagne is produced, sold, and drunk today than ever before. People are simply addicted to it!"

"And what do you think is the reason for that?" Isabelle asked seriously, apparently not seduced in the slightest.

Raymond shrugged. "Companies in practically every sector of our economy are doing very well. New factories and firms are springing up everywhere, like mushrooms. There's a lot of money around and, for now, no hint of war or other conflicts on the horizon. We live in very good times indeed. But please don't get the impression that champagne is just a passing fashion! Even under King Louis the Fourteenth, it was an exceptionally popular drink." Raymond was relieved to see that she knew whom he was talking about. A lack of education would have ill-suited his guest. Education and charm—two more crucial elements of beauty. And the ability to move gracefully. Isabelle Feininger moved with the grace of a young deer.

"They say that the Sun King wanted no other drink. The things he said, the things he did—these were observed in minute detail not only by the members of his court, but also high society in every country in the world. Louis the Fourteenth singlehandedly made the drinking of champagne a fashion. But enough history. Try it!" He raised his own glass encouragingly. "What we have here is a Dom Pérignon *millésime* produced in Hautvillers, the place you—"

"I heard that same expression last night!" she interrupted him, and a faint blush colored her cheeks. "A *millésime*." She let the word pearl off her lips. "What does that mean exactly?"

He would have liked to know in which company she had heard the word. "With champagne, as a rule, wines from different years are mixed together. This allows a cellar master to use wines from a good year to balance out wines from weaker years, which in turn allows him to produce a consistent quality product year after year. One could call these kinds of champagnes '*non-millésime*,' but most of the time that designation is simply ignored. With a *millésime*, on the other hand, only the grapes from *one* particularly good year are used, and this is noted with pride on the label. It has been some years since the last *millésime* . . ." Raymond could not prevent a soft sigh from escaping him. It had been "some years" for so many things . . .

"But that's not how it is with normal wine, is it? Only the grapes from one year go into a bottle." A small crease appeared on her forehead.

So she knows a little after all, Raymond thought. And she's not afraid of asking questions. With an avidity that he had not felt for a long time, Raymond went on with his exposition.

"This kind of complicated assemblage of wines from different years is, in fact, unique to champagne. And only three kinds of grapes are used. Pinot Noir, which gives the wine its long life; Pinot Meunier, which gives it its fruitiness and lightness in the glass; and the Chardonnay grape, without which a champagne would be coarse and boring. The proportion in which these three grapes are mixed is a closely guarded secret and varies among cellar masters. There is also an exception, and that is the champagnes that are made only from Chardonnay grapes, and—" He broke off when he saw that Isabelle was looking confused. "Madame?"

"It's just as I was afraid it might be—terribly complicated." Isabelle sighed, raised her glass to her mouth, and drank a small mouthful. As she did so, her full top lip curled slightly. "A good drop," she said, though she did not sound particularly euphoric.

Raymond, who knew this reaction from many champagne tasting sessions, smiled in amusement, although he normally rolled his eyes on the inside.

"Champagne is not there to be sipped, my dear. If that were the case, you could have gone straight to a cheap liqueur. One should enjoy champagne in large mouthfuls, because that is what brings out its aromas the best." To confirm his words, he took a large mouthful from his glass and was happy to see that she did the same. Then she looked at him in amazement.

"It actually tastes completely different now. Much . . . fuller!" She took another mouthful, closing her eyes in pleasure. "Am I mistaken, or does this champagne taste a little like cognac? And there's something else, a woody note . . . and something smoky."

Raymond felt a shiver run through him. The abandon with which she dedicated herself to the champagne—there was something almost erotic in it. He cleared his throat and said, "What we have before us is a completely mature champagne, not some flighty, fickle thing. I also find the slight hint of orange and cinnamon very stimulating."

Isabelle looked at him wide-eyed. "That is exactly what I was just about to say, but monsieur"—she drank another mouthful—"there is something else again . . . marzipan?"

Raymond held his breath. It was rare for an unpracticed palate to recognize these fine nuances. Isabelle Feininger seemed to have a true gift.

"My compliments, madame! Marzipan. Or more accurately, a trace of bitter almond. The flavor is so distinctive that one can discern a Dom Pérignon *millésime* among hundreds of champagnes simply by tasting," he said. "The second champagne we'll try is made in a completely different way."

After trying two more champagnes, Isabelle's eyes were gleaming like the most brilliant Brazilian tourmalines. Her lips seemed fuller than before, as if the tingling of the champagne had made them swell like the buds of flowers. She reached out her hand to the dealer, smiling.

"Thank you very, very much for this wonderful tasting! You have opened a door for me into a world that I never even knew existed. Oh, forgive me, I don't normally babble on so." Embarrassed, she withdrew her hand. He could have held it for hours.

Raymond smiled, but his chest ached. "I would really have been very disappointed if my champagnes had not worked their magic on you. If you would like, madame, we can continue this lesson at any time."

Chapter Five

With practiced ease, but under Leon's watchful gaze, the coachman tied the two bicycles onto the huge flat back of his wagon. Then he did the same with the rest of their baggage. He drove the stretch to Hautvillers several times a week, and when Leon and Isabelle had booked the journey, he assured them that he knew the road well.

"Your luggage weighs at least as much as a load of champagne bottles, so I won't be pushing the horses very hard," he said. "But if everything goes smoothly, we'll be there in three hours."

Three hours, Isabelle thought as Leon helped her up onto the seat. Maybe she should take up cycling again after all; then she would be able to get back to Reims easily. The thought cheered her up and made it at least a little easier to say good-bye to the city that had already touched her heart.

They were finally on their way to their new home. The sun shone brightly, as it ought to at the beginning of March. Birds were chirping for all they were worth, and the scent of the first forsythia blooms filled the air. Isabelle snuggled close to Leon, who had also climbed up onto the seat of the coach to sit between her and the driver.

"'*Bonne chance*,' the man in the champagne shop said. Isn't that nice? Good luck. We could really use some of that."

Leon put his arm around her. "One thing I have to give the *Champenois*—they really are very friendly," he said, and told her again about the professional cyclists he had met the day before. They had given him many tips about the best cycling routes.

"So much forest? I really did not expect that in Champagne," Isabelle said to the coachman after they had seen nothing but trees for half an hour. Fallen leaves from the previous winter carpeted the ground between the still-bare trees, creating a morbid atmosphere. The sun, which had been shining as brightly as the daffodils in the front gardens of Reims, shed its light here through the trees in a pallid glow.

"The world-famous vineyards are coming," said the coachman, and grinned.

And, indeed, at a certain point, the forest thinned out, the land opened up, and the sun shone down again from a cloudless sky.

The driver turned around a curve and reined in the horses.

"*Et voilà!*" He swept his hands wide, his gesture taking in the gently rolling landscape of the Montagne de Reims.

Isabelle exhaled audibly. "This . . . is unbelievable!" Her gaze turned across thousands—no, millions—of grapevines, growing in rows as far as she could see. The vineyards here were not steep as they had been in the Palatinate; in places, the vines even grew on flat land. *Like an ocean crossed by a low swell*, thought Isabelle, overwhelmed by the sense of distance and endlessness. But even more impressive was the knowledge that this landscape was the result of human work. *Work and the blessing of God*, she thought, and the notion felt utterly strange to her, something that had not come to her either in Berlin, with its enormous factory buildings, or in the Palatinate. She felt overcome by a strange emotion.

"Somewhere in the middle of all that are our vineyards, too. Isn't that amazing?" said Leon.

Isabelle gripped his hand. Speaking quietly, she said, "I never imagined it would be so beautiful." She nodded in the direction of the nearest grapevines. "What are those bushes standing at the end of every fourth or fifth row of vines?"

"Roses, of course," Leon replied casually.

"Roses are almost as typical of the Champagne region as the grapevines," the coachman said. "There's a reason for them, too. In certain weather, the roses succumb to a mildew infection very fast, so if a winemaker sees a rose bush that's been hit, he knows he has to treat his vines against the mildew."

"I'm sure it must be wonderful when the roses are in bloom." She could not remember ever being so impressed by a landscape—she, a child of the city. *This is where you belong*, said a soft voice deep inside her.

"See there?" The coachman was pointing to a village in the distance. It was situated atop a hill that was higher than most of the others around, which made it look somehow majestic and very close to the clouds. "Hautvillers."

Isabelle blinked several times. She had arrived. Hautvillers. Her new home.

A steep main street wound up the hillside. Well-tended houses lined both sides of the street, with little space in between. None of the houses was more than two stories high, and it seemed to Isabelle that the residents were doing their best not to outshine the grapevines that, in places, grew down to the walls of the houses. Maybe that was the reason that everything here seemed to exist in such harmony. Almost every house was decorated with a wrought iron sign depicting the profession of the person who lived inside. As the horses stretched their necks forward and leaned into the steep climb up the main street of Hautvillers, their coach passed a basket maker, a general store, a laundry, and a cobbler's workshop. Isabelle beamed at everyone she saw—after all, these people would be her new neighbors.

After a few minutes, they came to a marketplace, around which Isabelle noted the town hall, a bakery, and a small restaurant called Le Grand Cerf—"The Great Stag." A very pretty young woman with her hair loosely tied up was energetically sweeping out the entrance to the restaurant, and as the coach drove past, she looked up. Her eyes shone like dark-brown sealing wax, but she returned neither Isabelle's smile nor her greeting. *If that's how you want to be*, thought Isabelle.

"Look there!" Leon cried, and he pointed to a sign attached to the garden fence of a house on a corner. It pointed the way to the Moët champagne estate, but Isabelle did not see a similar sign pointing to *their* estate anywhere. The horses had almost reached the top of the hill—and therefore the end of the village—when Isabelle spied, beyond the houses on her right, a magnificent estate built atop a small rise. It lay some distance outside the village, a tree-lined lane leading toward it. Finally! Isabelle squeezed Leon's hand excitedly.

The coach turned to the right, into one of the last streets of the village. The houses and gardens were larger there, and everything seemed more open and less crowded than in the village below. *It is lovely here*, thought Isabelle, as the coach pulled up in front of the last building on the right. It was not possible to drive any farther, however, because the street ended just a few yards ahead in a cobblestoned cul-de-sac, beyond which were gardens and fields. Isabelle frowned. There was no way to drive to the estate on the hill from there.

"I thought the driver knew the way! What now?" she said reproachfully to Leon. Instead of answering, he jumped down from the wagon.

"We're here, my dear!"

Isabelle's disappointment at finding that her new home was not the large estate in the distance did not last long. Jacques's elongated two-story house was not grandly situated among the vineyards. It was on the very edge of the village, and there was no tree-lined lane leading to it. But there was a large forecourt with space for many horses and carriages, and the house itself was the largest on the entire street. "Champagne Feininger"—the name stood out on the plain but elegant sign mounted above the large double-winged wooden gate in the middle of the building. Champagne Feininger. Isabelle felt a warm tremor run through her at the sight, but she could not bask in her anticipation for long; too many other impressions were pouring over her.

The dark-brown gate was so huge that their coach could have driven through it with ease. The roof, made of rust-red tiles, made a pleasing contrast to the white plaster and the dark-brown wood framing the window. And the windows! On the ground floor alone, Isabelle counted five windows on the left of the gate and as many on the right, while the upper floor was the same, everything perfectly symmetrical and exceptionally pleasing to the eye as a result. Every window reflected the late-afternoon sun.

"Well? Did I promise too much?"

"The house is beautiful," said Isabelle. She thought she should pinch herself to make sure she was not dreaming. For once, Leon had not exaggerated. This was just what she'd imagined an elegant country house would look like!

She pointed to the vines climbing the white walls. "When those flower, the house must look like a fairytale palace."

Leon scowled. "That needs to be cut back urgently. See how it's already gotten up onto the roof? I have no desire to wait for the vines to get in under the tiles and damage the roof."

Isabelle glanced admiringly at her husband. Leon really seemed to know what he was talking about. But her thoughts were interrupted by the appearance of an elderly man coming around the corner of the house. Isabelle guessed he was sixty years old, and he wore work pants and a jacket that were not particularly clean. His face was marked by years of weather, and his eyes were friendly. He wore a cap, beneath which sprouted tufts of gray hair. A scruffy knee-high dog trotted beside him, carrying a stick in its mouth.

He smiled and shook hands first with Isabelle and then Leon. "Claude Bertrand's my name. Bonjour, Monsieur Feininger. Bonjour, madame. How lovely that you've made it!"

Once the men had carried the luggage into the house, they immediately set off on an inspection tour. Isabelle stayed behind—what she wanted to do most of all was explore the house!

With her heart beating hard, she stood in the dark entryway, from which, left and right, two halls led off. Opposite the large double gate that formed the main entrance to the house was another, almost as wide as the main entrance itself. Isabelle went over to the door and had to use both hands to turn the handle to open it. The room on the other side was dark and cold, and a sour smell rose to meet her. With a frown, she looked at the strange machine that took up almost the entire space inside: a kind of wooden vat fitted with various metal bars. No doubt the entire apparatus had something to do with the production of the champagne, she decided, and closed the door again.

Behind the first door in the right-hand corridor was a pantry. Sacks of flour, salt, sugar, and other foodstuffs were stored on wooden shelves. Heads of cabbage shared a shelf with squash of different colors; there were jars of preserved fruit and marmalade and more jars containing bell peppers and other vegetables. From the ceiling, sides of ham and smoked sausages hung on various hooks. Isabelle raised her eyebrows and nodded—someone had certainly been looking ahead the previous autumn. On the floor, there were several baskets with onions and potatoes.

In the next room on the right, sturdy work boots were lined up next to light summer shoes, all of them more or less caked in dirt. Several heavy coats hung from iron hooks alongside a few old gray-brown cardigans. The room had no windows and smelled like sheep's wool and dubbin, soil and sweat. Isabelle crinkled her nose. A bad habit, that the farm workers would store their work clothes in there! Well, that would change from now on, she decided on the spot.

Next came a laundry room with two huge washtubs and a stove for boiling water, and an adjoining room in which clotheslines stretched from one wall to the other. But there were no clothes, unwashed or fresh, to be seen. *All that's missing is the kitchen*, thought Isabelle.

And, indeed, hardly had she opened the next door when the smell of freshly baked bread wafted over her. Two long loaves of white bread stood invitingly on a heavy wooden table. The crusts were lightly browned and looked so delicious that Isabelle was tempted to break off a piece. On a stoneware plate beside the loaves lay a piece of ham, a small round cheese, and a bunch of yellow beets. Isabelle smiled. It looked as if somebody had prepared a meal for her.

The kitchen was the largest room she had seen so far. The pantry and laundry had each had only one window, but here there were two. On either side of the windows hung floral drapes that lent gaiety to the room, but there were no curtains over the windows themselves, so the sunlight streamed through the windows. In the glow of the late-afternoon sun, the brown tiled floor looked to be made of copper. The centerpiece of the room was a large stove in which someone had already lit a fire. Feeling slightly chilled from their journey, Isabelle held her hands in front of the stove and enjoyed the heat it radiated.

A pot of water bubbled away on the stove. Isabelle considered calling for one of the staff. After the long drive, a cup of coffee or tea would have been wonderful. But it could wait; she had something much more urgent to take care of. She had needed to use a toilet for some time but was too embarrassed to ask the coachman to stop.

When she opened the final door on the right and discovered exactly what she wanted, she sighed with relief. Luckily for her, Leon's uncle had been a rather progressive man, so she wouldn't have to use an out-house as she had in Grimmzeit. That had been terrible. Here, however, Isabelle was positively enchanted to find a small bathroom with a real bathtub in a room that adjoined the toilet.

A little later, greatly relieved, she stood in the corridor again, ready to tackle the rest of the house. If the right side was the domestic domain, then the manorial rooms had to be on the left side. There, however, instead of reaching the individual rooms from a long corridor, one passed from one room into the next. The advantage of that arrangement was that it allowed windows on both sides of the room.

She was instantly delighted by what she found in the first room. It was a large living room with dark furniture and many lamps. There were two separate sitting areas in front of the windows; the armchairs were upholstered in velvet the shade of honey and looked comfortable, if a little worn. Large paintings of flowers decorated the walls, and trays of colorful wine glasses added even more color to the room.

Isabelle sat in one of the armchairs, just to try it out. The view over the valley beyond the top of the hill was beautiful. There were grapevines planted over on that side, too, as far as the horizon, and they came so close to the house that Isabelle felt as if she could reach out through the open window and touch them. *They must be Feininger vines*, she thought, rejoicing in the feeling that, in every sense of the word, she had arrived. She imagined sitting here with Leon in the evening, the day's work done, a glass of champagne in her hand.

The next room was a library, with bookshelves running along all the walls. Among the books, Isabelle noticed immediately, were a large number of specialist volumes about viticulture and champagne manu-facture. There were books about chemistry and other technical topics, but also a lot of novels, biographies, and ancient tomes clad in leather, with text on the covers that Isabelle could not decipher—she assumed that they were valuable antique treasures. Most of the books were in

French but a number were in German. Isabelle could not help thinking of how much she had been starved for books in Grimmzeit. Her own library—she would certainly never get bored here.

The third room was a study, in the center of which stood a very large escritoire. As in the previous room, a lovely tiled stove stood along one wall. With so many stoves, they would never have to be cold. As soon as Leon came in, she would ask him to light a fire; she wanted their first evening in their new home to be cozy.

Every room radiated so much airiness and joy that Isabelle's own heart grew lighter, too. Clearly the man who had lived there had enjoyed having beautiful things around him. Was this the French *savoir vivre* that so much had been written about? Enjoying life with all one's senses—was that how Leon's uncle Jacques had lived? With every room she entered, she had the feeling that she was discovering more facets of the man's personality—such a pity that she had never met him herself.

She hurried up the stairs to find the bedrooms. To the right were several smaller rooms, no doubt the accommodations of the domestic staff. To the left were three bedrooms that could be used either as guest rooms or for children. The last room at the end of the corridor was the biggest and grandest of all. It was furnished with white-lacquered furniture, which did not fit in very well with the rest of the house but was beautiful in itself and seemed very stylish. That evening, she would sink into Leon's arms in there, and they would inaugurate the bedroom in their own way. Isabelle sighed with longing.

Then a gold-framed picture hanging over the bed caught her eye. A portrait in oil. It was . . . Leon . . . body and soul! The artist had even captured the small furrows on each side of his mouth. And his brown hair—so much detail that Isabelle could only stand and wonder. But why would Leon's uncle hang a painting of his nephew in his bedroom? The next moment, it was as if the scales fell from her eyes. The man in the picture was not Leon. It was Jacques himself! And the remarkable resemblance could only mean . . .

Isabelle stared in bewilderment at the picture, then a smile spread across her face. Was this the reason that Anni's eyes lit up whenever Jacques's name was mentioned? Was this why Oskar Feininger always reacted with such hostility if someone so much as mentioned his brother? If Leon really was Jacques's son and not Oskar's, it would certainly explain the generous inheritance.

Chapter Six

"There's no help in the house? What do you mean?" Isabelle laughed in confusion. "Who do all those heavy boots and clothes in the workroom belong to if not the farmhand and the maid?" Aghast, Isabelle looked across the table at her husband.

Because no maid had appeared, she had carried the bread and other victuals into the living room herself. From one of the many silver trays, she had taken two colorful wine glasses and a carafe, which she filled with ice-cold water from the well. She had not yet ventured into the cellar, so there was neither wine nor champagne on the table.

When he had come in, Leon had sat down at the table and, without a word of praise for her industriousness, immediately began to tell her all about what he had found out on his rounds with the overseer. Now he bit hungrily into his second chunk of bread—which she'd discovered Claude had left for them—and, with his mouth full, he said, "Claude's wife, Louise, passed away last year. Jacques didn't take on anyone else after she died. He got the laundry done somewhere else, but Jacques and Claude divided up the rest of the work between themselves. The system seemed to work, too; from what I've seen, the place is in great shape."

"You don't seriously think I'm going to stand over a stove or sling a rag around like some maid! And who's supposed to look after the animals you told me about? And there's that huge vegetable garden!" Isabelle was almost shouting.

There were two horses and a coach, and two wagons, Leon had reported enthusiastically. Add in a few chickens, a herd of sheep, and even two peacocks. *It's a farm*, Isabelle thought with horror when she heard Leon's description. Had she ended up in a French Grimmzeit after all?

"Calm down, my dear!" Laughing, he took Isabelle's hand in his and gave it a kiss. "You're acting like you've just been threatened with ten years in a dungeon! We'll find a solution for everything, I'm sure. Claude can look after the animals. If I understood him right, that was already one of the things he took care of. I'll ensure that the work in the vineyards is done properly, and making the champagne is the cellar master's job. His name is Gustave Grosse, by the way, and he'll be here tomorrow around midday to show us how everything works. I can hardly wait! There's nothing to do in the vegetable garden yet, so all you've got is the bit of work around the house. And I'm sure you'll cope with that."

Isabelle looked speechlessly at her husband. The two champagne glasses that she had set at the end of the table caught her eye. She'd actually been thinking that on their first night in their new home, Leon would open a bottle of champagne for them. But here he was, telling her unpleasant stories instead.

"Just think about how good you've got things now," Leon went on in his most persuasive tone. "At my parents' home, it always annoyed you that my mother had the final word. But here, you're the mistress of the house. *You* make the rules!"

"The rules . . . I will most definitely do that," Isabelle replied vehemently. "First thing tomorrow, I'm going to ask around among our neighbors to see if they can recommend a young woman who can clean and do the washing for us. And I'll be keeping a lookout for a good cook, too. I'm sure it won't be too hard to find the people we need. If you think I'm going to waste my time with that kind of thing, think again! I'll have enough to do just being the face of the estate and keeping the house organized." Satisfied with her own resolution, she sliced off a sliver of ham and put it on her bread.

"It isn't that easy, Isabelle."

"Oh, really?" she said archly. "I see no difficulty at all."

"I don't know how to say this . . . I mean, we've never talked about money. While my uncle left me this estate, he did *not* leave me any money with it."

Isabelle found the sight of him helplessly scratching his head, messing up his hair, so moving that she softened right away. There they were, sitting together on the first evening in Hautvillers, and they were fighting over nothing at all.

"Don't worry. I'm not planning to buy anything big. The house can stay as it is for now," she said gently. "I'll make sure that the staff is as frugal as can be. Of course, we will have to have some kind of here-we-are party for our neighbors, but we don't have to break the bank with it. A small dinner, three courses, four at the most—"

"Isabelle, my darling, there you go getting carried away again! You'll just have to be patient for a little while with the invitations. And we simply don't have any money to pay a maid or laundress. The little bit that my mother gave me we spent in Reims. And so far we haven't had any support from your father, either. For now, things are tight."

Thunderstruck, Isabelle could only sit there while she tried to understand what he was saying. Her husband was penniless? He thought that money would come from *her* side?

Until that moment, she had always assumed that Leon had a certain income at his disposal. After all, he was one of Europe's best racing cyclists! And in the big races, the prize money was certainly considerable. Besides, what kind of man proposed to a young woman knowing full well that he would not be able to support her? It was unimaginable. For that reason, Isabelle had never thought about money, not once! And when they had lived in Grimmzeit, she hadn't needed any, because she had simply lived in Leon's parents' household. Mentally, she quickly calculated how much she had left in her purse. After what she had bought in Reims, it wasn't much.

"Now don't go looking so horrified," said Leon. "It's really just a temporary hole in the wallet. I'll win another big race, and things will look different again."

"Cycle racing! I don't want to hear about that anymore," Isabelle replied harshly. "We are champagne makers now, in case you forgot. Somewhere down there"—she pointed in the direction of the cellar— "there must be many, many bottles of champagne. What we need to do is sell them off as quickly as possible. *Then* we won't have to worry about money. I really cannot comprehend how you can even *think* about a race now. We should go straight into Jacques's office and look for the addresses of his customers. Then you can visit them tomorrow and sell them as many cases of champagne as possible," she said, feeling both impassioned and relieved at the same time. Everything was just a matter of a few days. With her mind made up, she stood and began to move toward the office to look for the papers.

But Leon took her firmly by the arm. "Don't you dare think about work now. This is our first night in our new home!" He pulled her to him and kissed her passionately.

Isabelle felt the old, familiar tingling deep in her body. Maybe the champagne business could wait until tomorrow after all.

The next morning, the sun was already beaming from the sky at eight o'clock, enticing Isabelle to open a kitchen window. She was wearing one of her best dresses: deep-red velvet with a black border. She wanted to look as pretty as possible to take on her new home. In the sunlight, the color of the dress reminded Isabelle of the Dutch tulips that bloomed in the same deep red in the garden at her parents' house.

The twittering of birds came in from the bare vines outside, increasing the feeling of springtime, but the kitchen grew noticeably chilly in just a few minutes. Isabelle shivered and closed the window again. She pulled her wool shawl a little closer around her shoulders, then turned around and looked at the remains of her breakfast. To make things easier, she had eaten in the kitchen instead of carrying everything to the living room. The coffee had been a little bitter and the bread hard, and she had to chew it for ages to choke it down. The evening before, she had forgotten to put it in the large clay pot intended for just that—a mistake, as it turned out. But these were just trifles, weren't they? In their night of lovemaking, her hunger had been satisfied in other ways.

She was in the process of heating some water to wash the dishes when Leon appeared with two thick files under his arm.

"You have to see this." He pushed the plates and cutlery aside to make room for the files.

Isabelle was about to protest, but when she saw the furrows on his forehead, she stopped herself.

Leon tapped on a page he had opened to, and said, "It looks as if Jacques only had customers in America. Look here, a Carlisle Restaurant in Springfield, Missouri, the Hotel Bristol in Knoxville, a Grand Hotel in a place called Dayton—"

"Those cities are certainly not on the East Coast, or we'd have heard the names before," said Isabelle, as she tried to comprehend what it all meant.

"The Park Hotel and the Sweet Joey in Springfield. Lots of overseas customers, but in places we've never heard of, and no sign of Boston or New York." He swallowed, and his Adam's apple jumped. "Now what? Does this mean I have to go to America, like Adrian Neumann?"

For a moment, they stood in silence.

Adrian Neumann was the husband of Isabelle's friend Josephine, in Berlin. He imported bicycles from America, and he and Josephine sold them in Germany. Josephine had always had a good head for business, and Isabelle had silently envied her for that.

Forget Jo! Your *time has come,* her inner voice whispered. *Now you can prove yourself!*

"You uncle must have customers around here, too. Or . . . somewhere else in Europe. In Germany, for example. That would at least be close. Have you looked through everything?" she asked doubtfully. She knew how slapdash Leon could be, after all.

"If you don't believe me, go through it all yourself," he said, and stomped out of the kitchen.

Shaking her head, Isabelle sat down at the kitchen table and began to leaf through the files. Orders, bills, a little general correspondence, all neatly organized by year. When Leon returned to the kitchen, she said, "Everything points to your uncle traveling to America once a year to sell champagne. Here's his invoice for the passage last year."

"It's like I said," Leon replied. He pulled on his jacket. "Let's talk about this topic another time. I have to go."

"Go where?" asked Isabelle, irritated. "You can't seriously go off cycling now!"

Leon grinned. "Can't I? I have to check the lay of the land when it comes to selling champagne around here, don't I? Before we talk about sailing off to America, I want to see if I can pull in a few local customers."

Isabelle watched as Leon rode off. Her mind was swirling with thoughts. Did he really want to see the situation for himself? Or was he really just going for a training ride? And if that was the case, wouldn't she be better off handling matters herself?

A short time later, Isabelle marched off with a notepad and pencil. She had to get an overview of the estate and what it took to run the place before she could even begin to make any plans.

The house was built on an embankment in such a way that beneath the ground floor there were several lower floors, cellars, and exits. The garden, too, was laid out over several levels connected by stone steps. For a long moment, Isabelle stood and gazed out over it all. The view of the gently curving hill was so beautiful that it almost brought her to tears. How magnificent the vineyards would look when the first new leaves sprouted! But when did that actually happen? She decided to read some of Jacques's books that very evening to learn about the rhythm of the vines over the course of a year.

She walked on and came first to a narrow vegetable garden, then to an extended fruit orchard, where two peacocks strutted as if they owned not only the field but the entire world. The sight of them brought a smile back to Isabelle's face. But then one of the large birds began to stalk toward her, and she hurriedly moved away.

Farther down, at the same level as the lowest cellar, there was a small field where some bushes were growing. Currants, perhaps? Or raspberries? Isabelle thought of the many jars of preserved fruit in the pantry. She hoped they would be able to employ a cook before harvest time.

She crouched down and placed her hand on the cold earth. The vegetable garden and berry bushes were still hibernating, but the fertile earth would soon wake to new life. The grass would come up and the bushes would bloom. It already smelled so good! She breathed in the earthy air as deeply as she could, filling her lungs.

All of this was theirs, now and into the future, and it was not a dream? The extensive garden, the animals, and the vineyards? She headed toward the chicken pen, walking over narrow planks laid on the ground beside the field. At least she could walk here without getting her shoes wet. In Grimmzeit, the mud had often been ankle deep! Isabelle counted twenty chickens and two roosters, all scratching for food. She opened the door of the coop and a sour smell escaped from inside, but she ignored it. Carefully, she felt around in the straw nests. An egg! And another! And there, a third. She gathered twelve eggs in all and placed them carefully in a bowl that she discovered beside the door. At least she knew what they would be eating for lunch.

Motivated by her success, Isabelle moved on. The next shack she inspected was a stall that, she assumed, was meant for the sheep. But it was empty, and the floor was covered with trampled, filthy straw. Several planks were missing from the wall and others were dangling loosely. *Overseer to repair*, Isabelle noted on her list. But then she thought again, crossed out the first two words, and wrote *hammer and nails* instead. She could do this sort of thing herself! She would get Claude Bertrand to show her how to use such tools as soon as possible. If her friend Josephine could fix bicycles in Berlin, then Isabelle could certainly hammer a few nails into wood, couldn't she? She didn't want to bother Leon with it; he had to put all his energy into selling the champagne. *If this place is ever going to amount to anything, and as long as we have no staff, I'll have to do as much of the day-to-day work as I can,* she thought as she moved on toward the next shack. That, it turned out, was the stable for the horses. The top half of the Dutch door was open, and two pretty horses, both brown, were looking out curiously. When Isabelle reached out toward one of them, it kicked the door hard with its forefoot. Isabelle jumped. The horse kicked the wooden door again.

"What is it? Do you want to come out? Or are you hungry?" She looked around, but the grass around the stable was still too short for her to be able to tear out a handful. In the barn beside the stall, she discovered a few bales of hay. She plucked an armful of hay from one of them and took it back to the horses. They whinnied gratefully, but then Isabelle watched them bicker over the feed, their ears lying flat. Hadn't the overseer fed them yet? It was already after nine.

Claude Bertrand lived in a house at the end of the property, Leon had reminded her the evening before. Isabelle could see the house from where she stood. It was small and looked solid, though a little run-down—just like the rest of the estate. There wasn't much she could really put her finger on, but when she looked closely, she spotted a small hole in the fence around the chicken run here, a loose plank there, and over there was a broken step . . . It seemed clear to her that, since Jacques's death, no one had really maintained the place as they should have. But that would change.

Isabelle was pulled out of her thoughts abruptly when a shadow appeared beside her.

"Our stock feed is running low, I'm afraid, like so many other things." Claude Bertrand opened the door to the stable and threw a few carrots into their food trough. "I drove the sheep out to the meadows last week, though it's really much too early in the year. But if I move them every couple of days, they'll get enough to survive. I need the hay for the horses. But I'm afraid we're going to have to buy more, even if hay is expensive at this time of year." He leaned down and stroked his dog's head; like the day before, the faithful mutt was at his side.

"A herd of sheep, horses, peacocks—why haven't the animals been sold yet?" She watched sympathetically as the horses crunched hungrily at the carrots.

Claude Bertrand shrugged. "I'd been advising Monsieur Jacques for years to do that! In the past, most of the producers in the region kept sheep; they'd sell the wool to balance out a bad grape year. These days, almost every vigneron has given up on sheep. All of them are concentrating on their main business. But Monsieur Jacques wanted to stick to the old tradition. And Monsieur Leon also told me yesterday that he wanted to hold on to the sheep, like his uncle."

Well, we haven't had our last discussion on that topic, she thought. She kept the thought to herself and said instead, "Monsieur Bertrand, could you show me the wine cellar? I'd like to get a first impression of our stock."

He looked at her in bewilderment. "But, madame, that is not my area. I don't even have a key to the wine cellar. Gustave Grosse would knock my head off if I set foot in his shrine!"

Gustave Grosse. Isabelle pressed her lips together. Where was the cellar master? Shouldn't he have been there the day before to greet them?

"But you can at least tell me which vineyards belong to us, can't you?" There was a lot more she would have liked to say, but she didn't want to get into an argument with the overseer, who struck her as a very friendly man.

"What you can see. The one ahead, that joins the orchard—see it? And the two blocks beside that?" The overseer pointed forward with one hand, and his dog instantly leaped in that direction as if its master had thrown a stick for it to fetch. "All three parcels belong to the Feininger cellars. A very good situation, though one of them is lying fallow right now. There are many other vineyards all around the village, too. Gustave Grosse can show you all of them. Why don't you stroll around for a bit? It's good to see the sun again after the long winter."

Isabelle walked off feeling like a schoolgirl who had asked her teacher too many tiresome questions and had been sent away as a result. She would put up with it for that day, she decided. But in the future, Claude Bertrand would have to get used to her questions.

Chapter Seven

As he did every Wednesday morning, Daniel Lambert set off to inspect the Trubert vineyards. After the long winter months, the plants in the Champagne region were slowly starting to return to life. For him—a cellar master with more than thirty vineyards to look after and the one to decide when and where the work had to start—it was an important time. Daniel had an unerring eye for the changes nature brought with it as the year turned. And what he couldn't see, he could feel. In most areas, the winter dormancy of the vines was over. But, as usual, the northern slopes of the Trubert estate were a few weeks behind. The vines had not been cut back, so they were growing wild and unkempt beyond the trellises.

Merde! Daniel felt a cold fury rising inside him. Why had he failed the previous fall, yet again, to convince Henriette Trubert of the importance of pruning her vines even more rigorously? Fewer grapes per vine meant higher quality—that was the argument he had tried to convince her with.

But she was unmoved and had simply replied, "Trubert champagne *is* good. After all, we have the best cellar master for miles around, and that is always one of the best buying arguments for our customers."

"But, madame, please understand. With better grapes, I would be able to achieve an even better result!" he had pleaded with her.

"If it makes you happy, then for God's sake cut the vines. But I don't want to hear a word about cutting them back to just *one* cordon! I insist on a good harvest," she had said. And that had been the end of the discussion.

Daniel had decided not to raise the subject with Alphonse. Henriette's husband had a thousand things to think of—but his business, unfortunately, was not one of them. He left that entirely in the hands of madame.

While he sat on one of the boundary stones, Daniel thought again about looking for a new position. He was always getting offers, but so far none of them had really attracted him.

Although he had more than enough work waiting for him back in the wine cellar, Daniel sat for a while on the stone, eating a little bread and cheese and enjoying a moment in the sun, which was strong enough to give a little warmth. Early bees were already exploring, and their soft buzzing was the only sound in that landscape of vines.

Would a new boss really mean more freedom? he wondered. Delivering pretty speeches—all the vignerons could do that! But in the end, how much of a free hand they gave their cellar master . . . well, that was a different matter. He'd assumed that his previous employer trusted him and his judgment. But when it came down to it, Jacques Feininger stuck his nose in everywhere, making Daniel's disappointment all the more bitter. At the start, Daniel had smiled and swallowed his pride and tried to change things by making good points. In vain. By the second year, they had fought so fiercely with one another that he'd finally packed up and gone to the Truberts. *From bad to worse*, he thought.

He swung his gaze to the right, and a bare slope of the Feininger vineyards caught his eye. The pang that he felt in his heart was short-lived, but it hurt. It had once been Lambert land. One of the best locations in Champagne. He sniffed contemptuously. Pearls before swine: Jacques Feininger was simply no good as a vigneron. He had not even come close to getting the best out of that fertile land.

As if he needed any more proof to back up his conviction, Daniel looked farther out, to a more distant vineyard. At the edge of the property lay a pile of old uprooted vines that had been replaced by newer, younger plants. Practically babies, the new plants, and they had barely survived their first winter. Lunacy, no less! It was one of the best-situated blocks, far and wide. And the vines they'd pulled out were not even twenty-five years old and still had a good ten or twenty years ahead of them. Mature plants that produced mature grapes with a lot of color, not just immature, young fruit!

"Everyone is always going on about the importance of the terroir *for the wine. But the* terroir *is God-given, and a vintner has no power over that. But what a vintner can do, my dear son, is to know every vine like he knows his best friend."* Daniel suddenly heard his father words in his ear, as he so often did when he was working out in the vineyards by himself. *"Vintners are good at overlooking the fact that every plant has its own characteristics and preferences and weaknesses, and all of it is tied up with where it's growing in the vineyard and many other factors. Every single plant has to be pampered like a child, because all of them together give a wine its own peculiar identity."*

What would his father say if he knew that many of today's producers didn't care at all about the "identity" of a champagne and were far more interested in making as much as they possibly could? Champagne was the drink of the rich, and all over the world, people paid a lot of money for the pleasure it brought. The *Champenois* rushed to meet the increasing demand, and quantity often mattered more than quality. Frederick Lambert would turn in his grave if he knew that his own son, Daniel, had become part of that game. Though his father was the last one who had any right to go casting aspersions.

"Damn it," he murmured, and tried in vain to replace his gloomy thoughts with something more pleasant. Perhaps he should forget about work for the day and spend the time drinking Ghislaine's house wine instead. Nothing special about it, nothing to tantalize one's palate, but simply a wine with which he could drink himself into oblivion. But then, in his sister's tavern, he'd be sure to run into Alphonse Trubert, and he had no desire to do that. He would never understand what Ghislaine saw in the man.

His thoughts were interrupted by the sight of a person climbing to the top of the hill—at this time of year, that was not something he would have expected. It was an unfamiliar woman, one dressed so elegantly that she looked more prepared for a ballroom than for a vineyard. Her hair glowed amber red in the sun. *What must it feel like to wrap a strand of red hair around your finger?* he thought. The thought came unheralded. She paused every few steps, and while it seemed as if she was enjoying the view, at the same time her chest rose and fell like that of someone who has been running for her life. Daniel grinned mockingly. Typical city woman. Madame was out of breath, and on a slope as gentle as that one.

But the next moment, his grin froze as he realized who it had to be: *l'Allemande* and none other! She and her husband had arrived in Hautvillers the day before; he'd heard as much from Ghislaine, because they had driven right past her tavern. Her husband was probably creeping around here somewhere, too. That was all he needed! Quickly, he packed up the rest of his food.

He was about to leave when the stranger caught his eye again. She was darting frantically from one vine to the next, looking around in a panic. Daniel watched her drop to her knees and scratch at the ground, or maybe she was pulling something out. The next moment, she seemed to be sobbing and rocked back and forth like a woman in mourning. Daniel felt like he was witnessing something he shouldn't. What had shaken the woman like that? He was a little scared, but was

he misreading the situation? Had she lost something and was just looking for it?

Although he had already made up his mind that he wanted nothing to do with Jacques Feininger's heirs, he walked toward the woman.
When he was a few steps away, he cleared his throat.

"Can I help you, madame?"

She jumped back and pressed both hands to her breast, but quickly
pulled herself together. She had, truly, been crying, and she wiped her
teary face with the sleeve of her dress. A beautiful woman, he realized.
And much younger than he had thought she was from a distance.

"What are you doing here? Are you one of the workers?" she asked
in surprisingly good French.

"Not really," he said, smiling a little feebly. "But perhaps I can still
help you?"

There was doubt in her eyes as she looked at the rows of vines. "I
don't know much about these things, but . . . there!" She pointed at the
ground between them. "Those must be weeds from last year, right? And
plants like that have no place in a vineyard, do they?" She bent down
and pulled out a handful of dried-up chickweed, then held it up in
front of him reproachfully, as if he'd personally planted it there. He was
about to point out that he was not responsible for the unkempt condition of this particular vineyard, when she went on. "And if that isn't bad
enough"—she pointed at the young vines, from which sap was weeping
copiously—"there, those vines! They're dying, aren't they? All of them.
Can't you see that? I thought this would be our great opportunity, and
now this." Her last words transformed into sobbing, and she turned
away in embarrassment. "Forgive me, but seeing all of this destroyed, I
would never have believed it."

Confused, Daniel looked first at the distraught stranger, then at the
tiny pools of sap that had formed along the vines. *Les pleurs . . .*

Then he laughed. "Madame—" He wanted to explain to her that
what she saw was completely harmless, but she cut him off.

"What do you have there?" She pointed at the secateur that always dangled from his belt. The pruning shears were one of the few things that he had inherited from his father.

"Did you . . . *cut* these vines with those?" The red-haired woman looked at him so angrily that Daniel was afraid she might attack him. "You saboteur!"

Daniel could not believe what he was hearing. "You don't think that I . . ." He twisted his mouth in disgust, and without another word, he turned and walked away.

He had not yet reached the bottom of the vineyard when he saw another woman coming toward him. But instead of wearing a fiery-red dress, this woman was attired in businesslike dark blue. *Merde, not her, too,* he thought.

"Madame," he said politely when they were face to face. He would have preferred to simply go his own way, but because Henriette Trubert stopped, he had to stop as well.

The vintner shielded her eyes with her right hand against the bright sun. Her gaze was following the red-haired woman, who was running and stumbling in the direction of the Feininger winery.

"So what they say is true—the Germans are here. Now I've seen it with my own eyes. So the Lambert estate really has fallen into the wrong hands."

Daniel clenched his teeth together so hard that it hurt. "The *Lambert* estate hasn't existed for a very long time," he said, making an effort to keep his voice calm. "The Feiningers are the rightful heirs of Jacques, and they can do whatever they want, even if they don't know the first thing about this kind of work."

"My dear Daniel, as indifferent as you might act, you can't put anything over on me!" Henriette laughed derisively, and countless wrinkles appeared around her mouth. Her lip rouge filled the tiny furrows.

At one time, Henriette Trubert had been the most beautiful woman in the entire Champagne region. But her exposure to the frosts of winter

and the summer winds during her constant inspections of the extensive land belonging to her estate had aged her prematurely. Fine lines
also had formed around her eyes, and the skin of her cheeks and chin
sagged. As attractive as she still looked in the muted candlelight of her
living room, under the cold sun of March, each of her fifty-five years
was visible.

"It must hurt, mustn't it? Knowing that it isn't *you* working these
vineyards but strangers from God-knows-where who probably don't
know a grape from an olive."

Daniel swallowed. He could not have described his mood any better, especially given that ridiculous scene with the German woman. But
he'd be damned if he was going to give his employer the satisfaction of
agreeing with her.

"Things can't always be the way you'd like them to be," he said airily.

"That humble tone isn't like you at all. You're normally much more
pugnacious," said Henriette wryly. She laid one hand on his right arm,
and it took some self-control on Daniel's part not to pull away. Her
eyes were imploring, and every scrap of sarcasm disappeared from her
voice when she said, "If you think I'm going to stand by and watch the
Feininger estate get ahead, you're mistaken. I'm going to do everything
in my power to get my hands on that land. Picture yourself as cellar
master there; you could decide what happens to all of this." She swept
her free hand across the vista in front of them, including the vineyards
around them. "Who knows? Maybe I'll even manage it before this year's
harvest. If we play our cards right . . ."

"*We?*" Daniel's throat was dry; the word sounded more like he was
clearing his throat. But whether he wanted it or not, his spirit had
opened itself to Henriette Trubert's vision of the future. Like a donkey
trotting behind a carrot, he was both angry with himself and unable to
shut out the visions in his mind's eye. If he were in charge . . .

"Of course, *we*!" Henriette chided him. "Your reputation is impec-
cable, and your word counts for a great deal around here. People tell you

things they would never reveal to me. I expect you to tell me anything that has to do with the Feiningers. With the right information, the rest should be child's play for me."

"And why would I do that, madame?" he asked stiffly. As much as he hated the idea that the Germans were here, every part of him resisted betraying the trust of others just to help Henriette.

The woman smiled. "How would you like to see a champagne edition with Trubert-Lambert on the label?"

***

What gall! The way that man had stood before her and grinned brazenly at her after what he'd done to the vines. There would be consequences. Isabelle was still shaking with anger when she reached the overseer's house.

Claude Bertrand was sitting with his back against the wall of his house, eating his lunch. His dog watched every movement of its master's hand, hoping that something might fall from the plate.

"Did you have a pleasant walk?" he asked when he saw her approach. "I'm sure you must be hungry, madame. Please, sit. It's a simple repast, but I'd be happy to share it with you." He pushed his cardigan, which was lying on the bench beside him, out of the way to make room for her.

"I wish it had been a pleasant walk, but I made an extremely *unpleasant* discovery in the vineyards," said Isabelle ardently. With her hands planted on her hips, and in a most accusatory tone, as if the overseer could do anything about it, she added, "The grapevines are losing all their sap from countless wounds! It looked so horrible ."

"Is it already that time?" Claude said, more to himself, his voice calm as he sliced a piece off a thick sausage. "There's no need to worry about the vines weeping. That's just what happens at this time of year. When the earth warms to more than forty-five degrees, the plants wake up from their winter dormancy. They begin to draw up water from very deep in the earth, and at the places where the vines were pruned the previous fall, they bleed part of the sap out again. It goes on for about two weeks, and it's perfectly harmless. *Les pleurs*, the vintners call it. The weeping of the vines."

Isabelle swallowed. *Les pleurs*—didn't that man out there mumble something like that?

"So that's . . . normal? Not sabotage?"

"What made you think that?" With a smile, he held out his knife to her, a piece of sausage impaled on the end.

Isabelle turned down the offer nervously. Her knees felt weak as she lowered herself onto the bench beside the overseer. He poured red wine into a heavy glass and pressed it into her hand.

Dazed, Isabelle took a large gulp. The wine tasted slightly acidic and herbal, and she found it invigorating.

"Just a regular house wine, good enough for me." Claude Bertrand shrugged. "As improbable as it might sound, there are actually wine-makers in Champagne who make something besides champagne."

"But don't they earn far more money with champagne?" asked Isabelle, happy to change the subject. Her stomach was growling and, rather timidly, she took a slice of bread from the basket on the table. Bertrand immediately held out a small butter dish for her.

"They do. But making champagne is a complicated and very drawn-out process. Some of the makers cellar their bottles for a year—others for six years or longer—but that means their money is tied up for that long, too. And"—he paused, as if to be sure of her fullest attention—"the competition is tremendous! You have to keep in mind that there are more than three hundred champagne producers these days. We have a good dozen here in Hautvillers; the two biggest are Moët and Trubert. And all of them want to sell, sell, sell! And come hell or high water, they make sure everyone knows about their champagne. They hire the slickest agents, men with fast mouths and fancy suits; these men have the best contacts and they don't come cheap. And the modern machines—it's all extremely expensive. If you want to be successful in this business, then you have to be rich before you start."

Expensive advertising, big-talking salesmen, and modern machines? Isabelle thought about her empty purse and her cycling husband, and her heart trembled.

"But Feininger champagne has a very good reputation in the industry, doesn't it?" she asked, and held her breath.

The overseer shrugged again. "You should save those questions for Gustave Grosse. I take care of the land and buildings; the champagne isn't my side of things."

Isabelle sighed inwardly. Claude Bertrand clearly did not want to intrude on the cellar master's territory. She cleared her throat.

"I ran into a very strange man just now, out in the vineyards. I'm wondering what he was doing out there."

"What did he look like, this man?"

"In his late twenties, I'd say. Not especially tall, wiry. He was blond, with wavy hair down to his shoulders. His eyes were the color of pennies."

The man had been shamelessly good-looking. When he was standing in front of her, she felt a shock run through her, partly of fright . . . but there had been something thrilling in it, too. It was something she had felt only once before, and that was when Leon had swaggered into the cycling club and announced, "My name is Leonard Feininger. You might have heard of me."

"And he had a pair of pruners hanging from his belt," she added.

"Well, *that* is nothing special, madame. Everyone carries a pair of those; they call them secateur, by the way. It's practically a growth on a man's hand around here, but you'll see that for yourself soon enough," Claude said, and he raised his eyebrows in light mockery. "But from the rest of your description, it could only have been Daniel Lambert.

He prowls through the vineyards like a lonely fox patrolling his ancestral territory." The old man laughed. "You should be happy, Madame Feininger. On your first day here, you've met the best cellar master in the entire Champagne region, maybe even the best of all time!"

Isabelle pulled her head down between her shoulders like a beaten dog.

"So he wasn't . . . just a worker?" A butterfly had settled on the tulip-red sleeve of her dress. She pretended that she was admiring the creature closely.

"Far from it! Daniel is known throughout the region. He's a very popular fellow indeed."

A slightly strangled sound escaped Isabelle. No doubt the whole village would soon know about her impressive "debut."

"He worked here once, too, actually. About six years ago. Jacques could have counted himself lucky when the youngster started here. Daniel inherited his father's keen eye and sense of taste—Frederick Lambert was a gifted cellar master! Unfortunately, Jacques did not recognize young Daniel's brilliance, and he kept putting his nose in where it wasn't needed instead of just letting the lad get on with it. There was a lot of strife back then." The regret in Claude's voice was unmistakable. "These days, Daniel works for the Truberts." The overseer waved his hand in the direction of the large estate across the valley, the same place that Isabelle had wrongly thought was to be her new home.

"He can't be too brilliant," she said primly. "Or he would have set me straight about *les pleurs* immediately." She preferred not to remember that she hadn't even given the man a chance to speak. And even less did she want to think about the first impression she must have given—scratching around in the dirt with her nose running. "And apart from that, he had no business wandering around our vineyards. I don't go invading stranger's gardens, after all," she said indignantly.

Claude smiled mildly. "In this special garden, madame, he is not what I'd call a stranger. The Feininger estate originally belonged to his family. His father, Frederick, lost it in a game of cards when the boy was about eight and his sister ten. The winner was Jacques."

"Leon's uncle won the estate in a game of cards?" Isabelle, thunderstruck, leaned across the table. "I don't believe it!"

"Oh, you can ask whoever you like—the story might be more than twenty years old now, but everyone around here remembers it. Frederick took his own life a little while later, probably when he realized what a great mistake he'd made. After that, young Daniel and his sister grew up with an aunt on this very street, just a few doors down. Madeleine was her name, but she's dead now, too. If things had followed their normal course, Daniel Lambert would have been the rightful heir to all of this. All things considered, he's probably to be forgiven for being attracted to the vineyards of his forefathers. He's bound to this soil like no other."

Isabelle set down her wine glass and sighed.

"You're right to say that there are many things that I can't yet know. But one thing is certainly clear to me: this place is suffering from neglect and sloppiness!" She tore a page out of her notebook and laid it on the table in front of Claude. Trying hard to sound objective, she said, "I put together a list of the most urgent repairs. I'm more than happy to lend a hand; the main thing is that these tasks need to be completed as quickly as possible."

Claude looked from the list to Isabelle. "Madame, with all due respect for your efforts, it isn't as simple as that."

"*What* isn't as simple?" Isabelle shot back, bracing against the uncomfortable feeling of déjà vu, having heard essentially the same words from Leon less than twenty-four hours earlier.

"Madame, it's best if I say this right out: there is no money for repairs, or I would have done them long ago. Do you think I enjoy seeing everything in this run-down state? There is no money for wood or nails or new wire—we don't even have enough for hay or other feed for the stock! The carrots I gave the horses earlier came from my own supplies. I haven't been paid for three months and have been living on my savings, but they are dwindling." The overseer lifted both hands in a gesture of resignation and let them fall in his lap.

"I'm truly sorry, madame, but I want to survive. And for that reason, for better or worse, I'm going to have to look for another situation."

Chapter Eight

"Well? What do you think?" Gustave Grosse looked expectantly at Isabelle and Leon with his right eye. Where his left eye should have been, he wore a patch. "An accident," he'd remarked casually when he saw Isabelle's curious look.

When the *chef de cave* had suggested starting their tour of the cellar with a wine tasting, Isabelle had agreed that it would be a good idea. Now, however, she was no longer so sure, because while she and Leon were still on their first glass, their cellar master was already on his third. The man would soon be completely soused! And the more he drank, the more his good eye twitched, a characteristic that Isabelle found extremely jarring.

She was trying to concentrate on the champagne in her glass, but in contrast to her tasting at Raymond Dupont's shop in Reims, she could distinguish nothing special: no citrus, no scent of vanilla or other aromas. Was it because she was so excited? This was their own champagne, after all.

"It tastes quite sweet," Leon said vaguely.

Gustave Grosse nodded proudly. "This is champagne from the old school! I learned to make champagne like this in the south of the region, before the phylloxera came and destroyed all our vines. I don't think much of the new fashion for making champagne drier than old toast. Wine has to be sweet; then you'll happily drink another glass, wouldn't you say, monsieur?"

Leon nodded.

"Is Feininger champagne actually very popular?" Isabelle asked. "I mean, there are so many different kinds, and the competition is very great. When we went to dinner in Reims, it wasn't on the menu."

"Reims!" Gustave waved his hand dismissively. "You can sell champagne anywhere in the world, not just in Reims. When people hear the word *champagne*, their eyes get that gleam in them, and it doesn't matter what brand you're talking about. Of course there are bigger names than Feininger, but if it's a grand name you're after, I can take care of that. I know an old man who used to be a butcher by the name of Yves Pommery. If you take him on, you can relabel your drop as Champagne Pommery! It'll bring in a pretty penny then, believe me." The man laughed heartily.

Isabelle could not believe she'd heard right. "That would be fraud!"

"I wouldn't say that, madame. It's all a matter of how you look at it. In America, the customers go mad for a special name."

"But—"

"That's something we can think about later," Leon interrupted, trying to head off a confrontation. "Perhaps we should get started with the inspection?"

With a sweep of his arm, the *chef de cave* presented the large apparatus that Isabelle had discovered the first time she looked around the house. "Not too many of the vignerons have a wine press like this. Most of them have to have them done in a municipal press or one run by a cooperative. I used to work in an operation where the cellar was a good three miles from the village press; first, we had to haul all the grapes down there, then haul the juice back again. We've got things much better here on the Feininger estate."

"Excellent!" said Leon. "Then I can put all my energy into sales." He turned to Isabelle. "When I went riding earlier, I noted several beautiful guesthouses that looked rather expensive. In the next few days, I'll pay them a visit with bottles of Feininger champagne. I really don't know why Jacques went to all the trouble of shipping his champagne off to America when we've got more than enough restaurants and bistros around here."

Gustave nodded his agreement vigorously.

"I'm telling you, our money worries will soon be behind us," Leon whispered in Isabelle's ear.

"I very much hope so, or we can start looking for a new overseer," she whispered back. When she saw Leon's confused look, she added, with significance, "There's quite a bit I have to tell you. Later." Then she pointed to the large double gate and said, "And the grapes are delivered by horse and cart through the big gate?"

"Right you are, madame. This pipe here? The juice and skins and seeds from the pressed grapes—what we call *must*—flows through this into a large round tank one floor down. Come with me. I'll show you!" Gustave wedged the open champagne bottle beneath his left arm, opened a narrow door in the wall behind the press, and made his way downstairs. Isabelle and Leon followed him down to an intermediate floor, where the ceiling was so low that they could barely stand upright. It was dim and chilly, and Isabelle shivered. She needed to remember to throw on a warm shawl the next time she came down here.

"This tank is where we filter out the last of the contaminants. All the big stuff—binding wire, grape seeds, and leaves—stays behind in the press. You can only make good champagne when the juice is perfectly clean."

So far, all quite comprehensible, thought Isabelle, while they followed the low gleam of the cellar master's lantern down another set of stairs. It was even chillier and very poorly lit. Isabelle found herself in a cave-like vault. She looked around. Enormous barrels stood on heavy wooden racks on the left and right, along brick-lined walls.

"The clean juice is pumped into these barrels. Hungarian oak. Monsieur Jacques always put great store in that."

Isabelle felt as if she were in a very special world. The idea that she could be part of that world in the future filled her with joy and pride.

"And who are those men there?" In the back of the cellar, several young men were busy with something that Isabelle could not make out.

"Day laborers, but very experienced, all of them. Today, we're cleaning out all the barrels that are not in use just now. It's a job I couldn't do alone," said the cellar master. He placed his hand on one of the barrels behind him. "The juice goes through the first fermentation in the barrels. The yeast feeds on the natural sugar in the juice and turns it into alcohol. At the same time, you get a huge buildup of pressure, and to stop them from the exploding, the barrels are only two-thirds full. You get a similar pressure later in the bottles, and I know very well what can happen when one of those explodes." He tapped at the patch where his other eye should have been.

Isabelle blinked sympathetically. "And what are these?" she asked, pointing to words written in chalk on small wooden blackboards, one of which was attached to the wall beside each barrel. Her eyes had still not fully adjusted to the darkness, and she had to strain to be able to read the inscriptions. Apart from the cellar master's dim lamp, the only illumination came from the little bit of daylight that filtered in past a large wooden gate in one wall.

"This is where we note which vineyard the grapes came from, what kind of grapes are in the barrel right now, and when it was filled. Only one kind of grape juice goes in each barrel, of course. In this one, for instance, we're fermenting Pinot Meunier from a southern exposure, and the grapes were pressed on September ninth."

"So early?" Leon said in amazement. "In the Palatinate, we started the harvest in the middle of October."

Gustave said, "We had a hot summer and picked earlier than usual. But we've had years when we've harvested as early as the end of August."

As he spoke, he pushed open the top half of the gate. "From now to November, when the fermenting takes place, the temperature in here has to be kept between sixty and seventy degrees constantly. And once the fermentation's complete, we have to open up the doors and windows to let the cellars get cold. But before that, we've got to avoid drafts at all costs; a chill can kill off the yeast."

Isabelle, impressed, nodded.

"This way!" With a sweep of his arm worthy of a castle lord, Gustave Grosse beckoned them to follow him.

Arriving at the bottom of a ramshackle spiral staircase, the *chef de cave* said: "*Voilà—les celliers!*"

Isabelle looked around in amazement. They were many feet below ground. Several passages led off to the left and right of the bottom of the staircase. It was very cold, and the air was filled with a peculiar mix of odors: limestone and wine, cork and vinegar. Along the seemingly endless passages, the champagne bottles were stacked as high as a man could reach.

"The caves were left behind when the monks of Hautvillers were excavating stone for the construction of their monastery. They took the materials they needed and created these empty passages. You find them all over the region. No wonder, with all the churches and monasteries around here," said Gustave. His voice sounded hushed.

"There have to be . . . thousands and thousands of bottles down here! It's a treasure trove!" Leon exclaimed, rushing from one side of the corridor to the other.

"There's another cellar one level down," said Gustave, waving the champagne bottle toward the spiral staircase. "But the only champagne down there is from before my time. It's probably undrinkable by now." He waved dismissively. "But who cares, with all the riches up here?"

Leon nodded vigorously in agreement. The next moment, he went to Isabelle and took her hand. Grinning broadly, he swung her around in a jaunty dance.

"We're rich, darling! Didn't I tell you?" he whispered in her ear.

Isabelle willingly let herself be infected by Leon's joy. For the first time that day, she laughed aloud. Oh, if only she'd seen these cellars the day before! All her fears had been unfounded.

Two hours later, exhausted, Isabelle sank onto one of the kitchen chairs while Leon rekindled the fire in the stove, which had gone out in their absence. After the tour of the cellars, they had gone to visit a number of the vineyards. They had crossed hill and dale, uphill and down, as the sun slowly set. Gustave Grosse had referred to the white boundary stones repeatedly to make sure they were actually on Feininger property. At one point, he claimed to be on their land, but then Isabelle had discovered the name "Moët" on a soiled stone.

"Grosse doesn't seem to know which vines belong to the Feininger estate. But I guess it's no surprise, considering how spread out they are," said Isabelle as the room gradually began to warm. For the first time in hours, her shivering subsided, and she stretched her arms to ease the tension the chill had caused in her neck. She took off her shoes and massaged her aching feet. She could not remember ever having walked so far in a single day! At the end of their tour of inspection, it had begun to rain, and they had returned not only tired, but also wet. With no maid that she could hand her wet clothes to, Isabelle had hung their clothes in the laundry. She had to get out dry clothes for herself, so she went ahead and unpacked her suitcase completely. This time, however, she had felt much better about it than she had in Grimmzeit!

"It's a little impractical, don't you think, that you have to go so far just to get from one vineyard to the next?" Isabelle yawned.

"They have the same kind of land divisions in the Palatinate. Inheritance, disputes, debts—you'd be amazed how fast a parcel can get broken up. Two neighbors start to quarrel, and one of them sells off a small strip of land along the border to his neighbor's property—boom, suddenly you've got three fields instead of two. Then the new owner leaves his narrow strip of land to his two sons equally, and it just gets messier and messier," Leon replied. He'd brought back a fresh loaf of bread from his ride, and he cut it into finger-thick slices. He put the breadbasket on the table, along with a bottle of champagne. "But this fragmentation of the properties has its good side, too. If one vineyard gets hit by a hailstorm, you can always hope that the others have been spared." He poured the champagne generously into two cut-glass goblets.

Isabelle smiled. In the future, they could drink champagne like other people drank water—what a life!

"There's something about Grosse that I don't like," she said between bites of the airy white bread. The crust was baked crisp and tasted simply delicious. "He's an unpleasant type, and he's got an answer for everything. And at the same time, I still feel like I'm a long way from understanding all that I need to. It can't be that we've got vineyards lying fallow! From all I've heard today, there's hardly any land more valuable than the land here in Champagne." Isabelle took a swig of the champagne, which she still found far too sweet for her taste. "And then there were all the weeds from last year." She shook her head. "If you ask me, Grosse is a shiftless old fox who'd much rather guzzle champagne than see to the care of the vineyards."

Leon looked at his wife half in astonishment, half in annoyance. "You're acting like you're already an expert in this field! Don't be so quick to judge. Give the man a chance to prove himself. If he's his own best customer, he'd have to know something about champagne, wouldn't he?" He laughed.

"You're right. When it comes down to it, I can't judge him," Isabelle admitted. "Perhaps it's really for the best to let things run along as they have been for a while." Still, the uneasy feeling in her gut, precipitated by their encounter with the cellar master, remained.

Chapter Nine

Isabelle was woken the next morning by the crowing of the rooster. As she pulled on her heavy woolen socks and cardigan, Leon's reclining figure caught her eye. She wasn't surprised to see that he was still deep in sleep. Once again, it had been very late before they fell asleep.

Downstairs, the first thing Isabelle did was light the fire in the kitchen stove. A short time later, in the pale gleam of dawn, she sat by the window in Jacques's library and browsed through a book entitled *Three Steps for Soil Preparation in Vineyards*. The writer talked about topsoil, midsoil, and subsoil. About homogenization and interchange. About vegetation layers and buffering capabilities. *This is something for Leon*, she decided after a few pages, and pulled another book off the bookshelf. It was in French and bore the title *Études sur la Bière*. The writer, a man named Louis Pasteur, described yeast as consisting of what he called microorganisms, which were crucially important for any fermentation process. While he wrote about beer, it would be the same for champagne. Without yeast, no fermentation would take place, Pasteur claimed, and he had apparently proved it in tests in his laboratory. When Isabelle came to the part where he described the different kinds of wild yeasts, she clapped the book closed. All she wanted was to find out a little bit more about the process of making champagne! But she had no intention of getting a degree in chemistry to do it.

Suddenly, she thought of Clara. Wouldn't it be lovely to have her friend there now! Clara would have tips for Isabelle about running the house. And she'd certainly have a better grasp of what Pasteur was writing about than Isabelle herself did. Even as a young girl, Clara had longed to study pharmacology so that she could later take over her father's pharmacy. She always had her nose in this or that medical textbook. After her wedding, there was no more talk of studying, but Isabelle assumed that Clara was continuing her studies in private.

Lost in thought, she took a sip of the herbal tea she'd made herself. She took it as a personal triumph that she had actually managed to light the fire in the stove. If she was honest with herself, she'd always laughed at Clara a little. In secret, she called Clara, whose parents had sent her off to a home economics school for prospective wives, "the little wifey." Isabelle shook her head. How arrogant she'd been toward Clara, who was certainly far less helpless than Isabelle felt herself to be, at least when it came to cooking, cleaning, and everything else it took to keep a house running.

"I'm sure I could learn from Clara," she murmured to herself. She missed her friends in Berlin so much! The closeness they'd shared, the trust that allowed them to reveal their weaknesses to one another, and the way they had always encouraged each other, too. In her mind, she heard Clara's voice: *You can do it!*

Isabelle nodded silently. Then she went to Jacques's desk and began opening the drawers. In the second one, she found what she was looking for: writing paper and an envelope. She took them to the small table by the window.

Dear Clara, she wrote.

I hope you and your family are well. A lot has happened since my postcard from Reims. Leon and I are now living in the Champagne region of France, on a vineyard estate. Everything is so new and exciting, but I'll tell you all the details another time. Right now, I urgently need your help . . .

Half an hour later, satisfied with her letter, Isabelle put the pen and paper aside. At the same time, she heard Leon stirring upstairs. He'd soon come thundering down the stairs calling for a decent breakfast, just as he'd been used to at his mother's house.

"Cooking an egg can't be that hard," Isabelle muttered, going into the kitchen. Until the cookbooks and household advice she'd asked Clara for arrived, she would have to make do somehow. Anyway, she did not have time to prepare elaborate meals or to give the house a thorough cleaning; far more pressing was the need to go through Jacques's office files to try to get an overview of the state of the place. Apart from that, she wanted to spend some more time studying in Jacques's library; though she'd stay away from the complicated science, she couldn't remain as ignorant as she was about winegrowing forever. And how were they supposed to handle chickens and peacocks and horses? Well, there had to be a book about that in the library, too.

When her husband appeared in the kitchen in full cycling gear and carrying a few bottles of Feininger champagne, she impulsively threw herself into his arms. "Oh, Leon, I can't tell you how happy I am," she whispered in his ear. "You taking care of the champagne sales, me looking after everything else . . . the two of us, pitching in together. I've been dreaming of this!"

***

Leon pedaled off energetically. From Hautvillers toward the Marne, it was downhill between vineyards almost all the way. Then came the good, flat roads that followed the river; he estimated that he was averaging almost twenty miles an hour. There was little traffic, and to his regret, he saw no other cyclists at all. Occasionally, he had to overtake a wagon stacked high with wine crates. In summer and fall, when there was so much to do in the vineyards and wine presses, he guessed the traffic would be much heavier. He felt incredibly fortunate that selling champagne combined so well with cycling! As dearly as he would have loved to register for the races in Munich and Paris—with the excellent training conditions there in Champagne, he knew he'd be among the leaders in the spring races—his new life would leave him no time for that.

Content with himself and the world, Leon slowed his tempo, then turned into the courtyard of an idyllic restaurant beside the Marne. The owner of the restaurant, whom he had met the previous day, greeted him warmly. Then Leon produced one of the bottles from his backpack and set it grandly on the counter. "*Voilà*—Feininger champagne!"

The host opened the bottle skillfully, then he poured two glasses half full. After a couple of mouthfuls, he nodded in a way that made Leon rejoice. It was easy to do business with the people here. He grinned at the man. "Very drinkable, our champagne, wouldn't you say?"

Instead of answering, the restaurant owner took out a pack of cigarettes, lit a cigarette, and inhaled with satisfaction.

"Something that I was really interested in when we met yesterday: your bicycle out there looks so sleek! Do you really race with it? Tell me about it. Until the first guests arrive, I've got time." As he spoke, he generously poured champagne for both of them.

Feeling on top of the world, Leon left the restaurant two hours later. He was off to a good start—the man had promised to buy half a dozen bottles.

The next stop on his sales round was just three miles downstream, a restaurant called Chez Annika. Annika, the owner's wife, was a pretty thing with large breasts, long legs, and a rear that she flaunted with every step. He could well imagine that the proprietress's charms, for some of her guests, were reason enough to pay a return visit.

He had hardly stepped inside the restaurant when Annika hurried over to meet him. "Monsieur Leon, how lovely to see you again!" She led him to a small table by the window where two glasses and a plate of pastries were already set up. Leon grinned. The view over the shimmering green river was gorgeous, but the view of his hostess's revealing cleavage was far more interesting.

"A champagne as thrilling as love, don't you think?" he said when they raised their glasses, and he looked into Annika's eyes as he said it.

She returned his gaze with a flutter of her eyelids and murmured, "After two or three glasses, one would probably be up for anything. Perhaps I should think about buying a few extra cases." Beneath the table, her knees brushed against his.

The next moment, he felt a heavy hand on his left shoulder.

"If I might kindly ask you to leave, monsieur."

Leon's smile froze. The gruff baritone voice belonged to Annika's husband.

"To the kitchen with you! You've got work to do," the man growled at his wife. A sharp exchange of words in French followed. Annika turned and swept away, pouting.

Leon cleared his throat. "Monsieur, I came here to present my Feininger champagne. Perhaps you would like to sample it in your wife's place? I—"

"I choose the champagne I serve here. Always have and always will." He picked up Leon's backpack and pushed it into his chest. "Scram, fast!"

Outside, Leon mounted his bicycle angrily. Everything had been going so well. He would certainly have been able to sell a lot of champagne to Annika if her husband hadn't shown up.

"Feininger champagne? Never heard of it. As long as I can remember, we've served Veuve Clicquot Ponsardin. But you can leave one or two bottles."

"Feininger? I lost to that old man at dice, once. I wouldn't drink his champagne."

One more restaurant, thought Leon as he opened the door to Chez Antoine, then he'd go for a longer ride. Making a sales call to a restaurant during the busy lunch period would not be a very good idea.

"Feininger? I didn't think that sweet stuff was still around," said the proprietor, busily setting a table.

Leon spread his arms wide. "Of course it's still around! You're looking at Leon Feininger, in the flesh. And this . . . is our superb Feininger champagne!" he said as he pulled out one of the now lukewarm bottles still in his backpack.

"You can put that away," said the proprietor. "I can't serve a sugary brew like that to my guests. Around here, all they want is dry champagne, like the kind that Trubert makes."

"Well, each to his own," said Leon, putting the bottle in his backpack. He was about to leave when something else occurred to him.

"We sell eggs, too. Excellent eggs. Could you perhaps use a few for your cakes?"

***

Resolutely, Isabelle carved one slice after another from the dried sausage she had found in the pantry. She laid the slices in a semicircle on a plate along with a piece of hard cheese and some dried fruit.

It was true they had no money for a party, but she could go and visit her new neighbors, even if it meant having to invent a German tradition. With a smile, she set the platter in a basket in which she had already arranged two bottles of champagne and several glasses. She glanced at herself in the gold-framed mirror, adjusted the pearl necklace around her neck, and stepped into the daylight.

An older woman with gray-blond hair, gray eyes, and a severe expression on her face opened the door at the first house Isabelle came to. She wore an apron and her hands were wet.

"*Oui?*" she said curtly.

Isabelle instinctively curtsied, as she always had for the teachers at school.

"My name is Isabelle Feininger. I'm your new neighbor, and I've come to introduce myself." She held out the plate of cheese and sausage to the woman. "Please, help yourself!"

The woman stared at the platter. "You're bringing something to eat?"

"It's a German tradition. It's something we do to get to know our neighbors," Isabelle lied. "Of course, we will also be throwing a party, but we have to find our feet first and then . . ." Her smile began to fail; suddenly she felt ridiculous, standing there with her offerings.

The older woman wiped her right hand on her apron, then held it out to Isabelle. "I'm Marie Guenin. It's not exactly a good time, but I suppose you'd better come inside."

There was another woman in the kitchen. She was sitting on a chair in the center of the room and had a comb in her hand. On the table next to her, there was a plate of hairpins. Her dark-brown hair was streaked with gray and hung over the back of the chair like a tattered curtain.

"This is my sister-in-law, Micheline. She's the sister of my husband, Albert, God rest his soul," said Marie. "Now we keep the Guenin estate running together." Turning to Micheline, she said, "Our new neighbor's come to introduce herself."

Micheline smiled and helped herself to the proffered food. "What a lovely custom, don't you agree, Marie?"

Isabelle guessed that both women were in their early sixties. But in contrast to willowy Marie's weatherworn face, Micheline's face was plump and unlined, almost like that of a young girl. And while Marie came across as the no-nonsense type, Micheline seemed a little dreamy. The two sisters-in-law lived under one roof, to be sure, but they could not have been more different.

"I can see you're busy," said Isabelle. "I don't want to disturb you. I'm sure we can chat another time."

"You're not disturbing us, young lady. On the contrary," said Micheline. "Perhaps you can even help us resolve a little dispute we're having." She glanced belligerently at Marie, then turned back to Isabelle. "If a woman is faced with an important undertaking—and I mean a *very* important undertaking—does she wear her hair in a stiff braid or pinned up neatly? Or does she just leave it loose?" She sounded very earnest.

"First, your undertaking is not *important*. It's *impossible*," said Marie, and Isabelle could tell from her tone that this was not the first time that she had argued her point. "And second, Madame Feininger, don't you think that a woman of Micheline's age should *never* wear her hair loose?"

"Well, I guess it would depend on what kind of important undertaking this is," said Isabelle, trying hard to be diplomatic. "If it's an important business matter, or something difficult to take care of, then I believe a tight braid that doesn't get in the way would be in order." She touched one hand to her own hair. "Unfortunately, I'm no expert in this area. My own braids always work loose far too fast."

Marie looked triumphantly at her sister-in-law. "A tight braid! What did I tell you? Madame Feininger, please, sit down."

"The young lady hasn't finished speaking yet," said Micheline petulantly. "So . . ." She nodded to Isabelle as if to prompt her.

Isabelle sighed inside. She thought she'd managed to extricate herself, but no.

"If a woman—of whatever age—were to have a rendezvous with a nice gentleman—of whatever age—then she would go to a great deal of trouble to pin her hair up as artfully as possible." She indicated the hairpins. "I know a few very nice tricks, and I'd be happy to show you."

"You'd help me pin my hair up nicely?" Micheline popped another piece of cheese into her mouth excitedly.

Isabelle, sensing the other Madame Guenin's baleful look, smiled and nodded.

"But only on one condition! Or rather two. First of all, I'd like to open the bottle of champagne I brought along, because offering a drink is also part of our German custom. And second, after that, I'd like you, dear Marie, to show me how I can put together a decent braid."

When Isabelle left the house an hour later, she still did not know what Micheline's "important undertaking" was, but she did have the feeling that she had made her first friends there.

At the next house, there was an iron sign displaying a sewing machine and the name "Blanche Thevenin." Isabelle knocked on the door, but no one answered. She shifted her weight impatiently from one foot to the other, then knocked again. She was about to leave when the door opened, and a pale middle-aged woman looked out. Her thin hair was pinned up into a bun, which drew attention to her pointy nose. She had a tape measure slung around her neck and at least a dozen pins were stuck into her jacket.

Isabelle introduced herself and repeated her speech about the German custom.

The woman looked at Isabelle from red-rimmed eyes. "*Merci*. But I'm afraid I don't have time to chat. No one's given me a winery yet, and I have to work for my living." She held up the ends of the tape measure as if that would explain everything.

Taken aback, Isabelle put her platter of cheese and sausage away. "Could I maybe help you with something? I have time."

The woman laughed bitterly. "I wish I could say the same! But there are never enough hours in my day. And right now . . ." She sighed. "Three weeks ago, I was commissioned to tailor an evening dress for *madame*. And it's supposed to be *extraordinary*." The ironic undertone she used to talk about her customer suggested that she didn't like "madame" very much. "I'm not usually at a loss for ideas, but this time, I can't come up with anything!"

Isabelle thought of the many hours she'd spent in different fashion studios at her father's behest. After that, *this* ought to be a breeze! "Perhaps something might occur to me if I see what material you have. I've got a little experience when it comes to fashionable clothes." She held up her champagne bottle temptingly. "What would you say to a glass of champagne first? That's sure to inspire some ideas."

"Champagne?" The seamstress raised her eyebrows. She looked Isabelle up and down, then shrugged. "If we really must."

While Isabelle and Blanche Thevenin sipped their champagne, the seamstress told Isabelle that a big festival was to take place at the Trubert estate at the end of March. Madame Trubert and her husband wanted to celebrate the eightieth anniversary of their champagne cellars and invite all the important families in Champagne.

As they talked, Isabelle inspected the rolls of fabric on a large cutting table. Fine Brussels lace in a rose shade, with matching borders in claret red. Mulberry-colored velvet. Lining material in a medium brown—all of it very dignified and expensive but also very boring.

"What's that?" Isabelle asked, pointing to a large basket beneath the window.

Blanche Thevenin waved dismissively. "Oh, just old scraps."

Isabelle was already rummaging through the brightly colored left-over cloth. "I think I have an idea." She took out a section of red fabric and laid it beside a bottle-green remnant, then joined a piece of gold-colored cloth along the edge.

"What do you think?" she asked triumphantly, once she had laid out several lengths of material in the same way.

"Lots of strips of colorful cloth to make a skirt?" Blanche sniffed. "That might be some kind of national costume in Germany, but it's nothing for an elegant festival here in Champagne. It would be best if you left, madame. I really have more important things to do than waste my time with you."

Feeling disappointed and angry, Isabelle left the house. Her inspiration might well have missed the mark, but did the dressmaker have to act so ungraciously? Blanche Thevenin would probably never be a friend of hers. Isabelle again thought about the familiarity and intimacy of her friendships. Back in Berlin, she had taken Clara and Josephine for granted, only recognizing how much her friends meant to her after they were hundreds of miles away.

She took a deep breath and knocked at the third door. The image of a wine barrel on the iron sign told her that it was the home of a cooper.

"So you're from Germany? Berlin . . ." Carla Chapron, the cooper's wife, sighed rapturously, as if she were picturing Berlin at its loveliest.

Isabelle sipped just as rapturously at the café mocha that the woman had immediately offered her. They were sitting in a sunny living room, and on the round table in front of them was a plate of confections finer than anything Isabelle had ever tasted. *Macarons parisien*, they were called; apparently, they were a favorite of the French king and one of her, Carla's, specialties, the cooper's wife explained.

"Isn't it true that emperors and kings are always meeting in Berlin?" Carla asked, leaning inquisitively toward Isabelle.

Isabelle wiped a crumb from her lips. "That's true. Once, my parents and I were even invited to a ball at the emperor's palace."

Carla listened intently as Isabelle put her heart and soul into one story after another.

In the past, the Berlin party round had often been a horror for her. Having to take care with every word, every gesture, and always having to look perfect, not giving her father anything to reproach her for . . . it had all been so exhausting. But now she positively raved about it, and an hour passed before she stood and said with regret, "I'd love to tell you more, but it will have to be another time. I really must go. I want to visit at least one more of our neighbors before my husband gets home." She pointed out the window to a small and rather untidy looking house on the other side of the street.

"You want to visit *la maîtresse*? Then you should check first that Ghislaine doesn't have a man in the house," Carla said through pursed lips.

"A *maîtresse*? Somebody's mistress? On our street? I don't understand," said Isabelle with a frown. Instead of leaving, she sat down again on the wine-red sofa. "Maybe there's time for *you* to tell *me* about some things."

Chapter Ten

The sun was already beneath the rolling hills of Montagne de Reims when Leon got home. Isabelle, hair flying, ran out to meet him and flung her arms around his neck.

"How many crates of champagne did you sell? Do we have a little money again?"

With a laugh, Leon extricated himself from her embrace and propped his bicycle beneath the eaves. His stomach growled as he headed for the kitchen, hand in hand with Isabelle.

"Couldn't have gone better."

Isabelle grinned. "I knew you'd be a good salesman! I'm sure they must have been fighting each other for the champagne. Tell me!"

"Later, sweetheart. I'd much rather hear about all the good food we've got for dinner."

"Dinner?" Isabelle squeaked. "Honestly, I didn't manage to get anything cooked at all. But you'd be amazed at all the things I learned today—we've got an actual *maîtresse* living in our own street!"

Leon kissed her on the tip of her nose. "You can tell me all your gossip another time. Let's go out for dinner. Le Grand Cerf. Claude told me yesterday that they do good, plain food in there." He was already pulling on his jacket. "According to him, the whole village meets there in the evenings. We can get to know a few people."

Isabelle hesitated as he held her coat for her. "I thought we had to save. Can we afford it?"

He waved off her misgivings. "Surely I can take my wife to dinner to celebrate our first sales. Really, darling, you do ask some questions!"

Leon had been inside many village taverns. Most of them were dingy, joyless places where a few permanent sots drank away the hours and where the air was sour with the smell of spilled beer and tobacco smoke. Most of the time, he'd only stopped in briefly to take a break from cycling and eat a cheap meal, if there was even something edible being served. So he was all the more amazed when he pulled open the door of the village inn of Hautvillers and stepped into a welcoming atmosphere. Instead of long tables and benches, there were small round cloth-covered tables with green-lacquered chairs around them. The walls were decorated with pastel artwork; the bar was white, with brass-colored taps for the beer.

At the bar, there was a group of elegantly dressed men, all drinking champagne and in high spirits and enveloped in a cloud of aftershave and cigar smoke. Among them was a tall gentleman with impressive muttonchop sideburns, who—with an equally impressive gesture—seemed to be in the middle of proposing a toast.

Leon said a general greeting to the group, which one or two of the men answered with a nod. From their appearance, he thought they had to be champagne barons. Should he join them or sit with Isabelle at one of the small tables? He had not yet made his decision when the man with the muttonchops spoke to him.

"Are you Monsieur Feininger, by any chance?"

Leon nodded, happy to see that, even here, they would recognize him as a cyclist!

The man said something to the others in the group, who laughed quietly in response.

"Why not come and have a drink with us?" said one of the men, handing Leon a champagne glass.

Leon turned to Isabelle. "Darling, Claude Bertrand is just back there. You can sit with him, and I'll come join you in a minute."

Isabelle, somewhat put out, walked off in Claude's direction.

"I'm Simon Souret," said the man with the muttonchops as he shook Leon's hand vigorously. "Sales agent for Champagne Trubert. This is my fellow agent at Trubert, Stephane Manot. Then we have Silvain Grenoble from Pommery & Greno, and beside him our man at Piper-Heidsieck."

Leon happily shook hands with one agent after another. Champagne barons! He couldn't have been more wrong! These were the famed sales representatives he'd heard so much about in the last two days—experienced, globetrotting men with a talent for selling and an even greater knowledge of champagne. *And at least as big a thirst for the stuff*, he thought with a grin, while the hostess opened another bottle for the group.

"So how's business on the Feininger estate?" Simon Souret asked, clinking his glass with Leon's.

"Very good for the start," Leon replied. "I'm hard at work finding new customers." He was suddenly unsure what he should say. While he was flattered that these men had accepted him into their ranks so quickly, they were the competition.

"New customers. That's wonderful! We have enough on our plates with the old ones, right, gentlemen?" the Trubert agent said, and he laughed so hard that his whiskers shook. "I'm just back from a trip to America. And a very successful trip, if I say so myself. Which is also the reason for our little . . . celebration." The men laughed.

"America?" Leon was suddenly all ears; he might be able to learn something from the man. "Where did your travels take you, exactly?" His question was met with loud guffaws from the others.

Simon Souret grinned broadly—first at his colleagues and then at Leon. "All over the place. In Springfield, Missouri, in Knoxville, Dayton, Cincinnati . . ."

"I don't believe it!" Leon's mind was racing. "We've got customers ourselves in just those cities," he said, which touched off a new round of laughter. *What was so funny about that?* he wondered.

"You *have* customers there? Or was it perhaps your deceased uncle, Jacques Feininger, peddling that sweet swill of his?" The salesman was still smiling, but his voice now had an edge to it. The men around them, one or two of whom had been throwing in the odd remark earlier, fell silent.

"What are you trying to say?" Leon asked quietly, glaring now at Simon Souret.

"I'm not *trying* to say anything. Wherever I went in the backlands of America, everyone assumed that the Feininger estate didn't exist anymore." He shrugged in mock sympathy.

The Pommery agent took up the thread immediately and said, "And because you were so full of compassion for the poor abandoned customers, you offered them your Trubert champagne in consolation, right?" Then he turned to the others. "The son of a bitch beat us to it again!"

"You . . . you stole Jacques's customers?" Leon was suddenly so upset that he had difficulty getting the words out. The hostess and a few other guests turned to him.

The man beside Leon clapped him comfortingly on the shoulder. "Don't take it so hard. Next time, you'll be the one luring away a maker's clients."

"That's how the game is played these days," the Pommery salesman added. "On the plus side, you've saved yourself a trip to America."

Again, the men laughed raucously.

"Let's drink to that. The next round's on me, again!" Simon Souret said pompously.

Leon's glass rang as he set it down hard on the bar. "I've lost my thirst!"

***

Isabelle was already at Claude's table before she realized who was sitting beside him. Micheline Guenin winked at her conspiratorially. But Isabelle's smile froze when, at the next table, she saw Daniel Lambert. That man, with his loose tongue . . . that was all she needed! Luckily, he had not noticed her. He was deeply involved in a tasting session; there were several glasses and bottles in front of him. The way he swirled his glass, sniffed its contents, and examined the rosé-colored liquid was strangely intimate, and Isabelle looked away quickly. She went to one of the few free tables in front of the floor-to-ceiling transom windows.

She wondered how long Leon planned to stand around with the men at the bar, when loud laughter from the group rang out. The last thing she wanted was to sit around alone, and she was eager to find out how much money he had taken in from champagne sales that day and what he was planning next. The fact that he was taking her out for dinner, at least, was a good sign.

A rushed waitress came to her table, and Isabelle ordered a glass of water. Isabelle took a closer look around the restaurant. Almost all the tables were occupied, the visitors deep in animated conversations. Beer, wine, and champagne flowed freely, and the hostess behind the bar had her hands full keeping up with the orders. Isabelle immediately recognized her: it was the young woman with her hair casually tied up, the one Isabelle had seen in front of Le Grand Cerf the first time they went through Hautvillers.

So that was *la maîtresse. Close up, she's even more attractive*, Isabelle thought. Not so much as a blemish marred her skin, and the same was true for her figure: she had a slender waist and was as petite as a ballerina. Her legs, which showed beneath the flowing fabric of her skirt whenever she moved, were as long as a racehorse's. As beautiful and bursting with vitality as the woman was, she could have stood up to anyone on a Berlin stage, and nothing about *la maîtresse* looked in any way disreputable or degenerate. *Then again, she doesn't seem particularly friendly*, thought Isabelle, as she watched the woman hand Leon a glass of water.

"The morals don't show on the outside, do they?" Isabelle jumped as someone suddenly whispered in her ear.

It was Carla Chapron, the cooper's wife.

"Can you read minds?" Isabelle whispered back with a smile.

"Ignaz, may I introduce our new neighbor? This is the woman who drank sparkling wine with the emperor of Germany," said Carla to her husband with pride in her voice. "May we join you?"

Isabelle nodded quickly, relieved that she didn't have to sit alone any longer.

"See the man standing at the bar? Over on the left, away from the others?" Carla pointed covertly to a man in his early sixties. He was not as elegantly dressed as the group with whom Leon was standing; his pants and jacket looked more utilitarian, like the clothes Claude wore. His bushy moustache was a mottled gray-black; he had a double chin, a red nose and jowls, and his belly was so big that it touched the side of the bar. Just then, he seemed thoroughly amused at some joke that *la maîtresse* had just made, and his whole body quaked with laughter.

"*That* is Alphonse Trubert," the cooper's wife murmured meaningfully. "Ghislaine's lover. Or rather, *one* of her lovers."

Isabelle stared at the rather unattractive man in disbelief. He had to be twenty-five years older than his mistress. "What does Madame Trubert have to say about the way her husband dallies with his lover like this, in public?" she asked.

Carla Chapron was about to answer when Leon came to the table.

"My turn for an introduction," said Isabelle. "My husband, Leon Feininger. These are our neighbors, Ignaz and Carla Chapron." When

Leon had greeted both, Isabelle asked archly, "Did you have a nice chat with the men at the bar?"

"Depends," Leon growled. "But you didn't miss anything."

The next moment, instead of the waitress who had come to the table earlier, *la maîtresse* herself slammed a carafe of water and a few glasses on the table. "Do you want something to eat, too?" Rarely had a question sounded so hostile.

Isabelle gave Leon a puzzled look, but when he did not react, she said, "Yes, we would."

A smile played across the lips of *la maîtresse* then. "But of course, madame. I recommend the baked *andouillette.*"

Isabelle raised her eyebrows. It was not something she knew.

"A specialty of Champagne, but really quite distinctive," said Carla in a tone that Isabelle could not place.

"Baked sausage? We love that in Germany. Two, please," said Leon, without asking Isabelle. Ignaz Chapron ordered the same.

The sausage looked like a pale German bratwurst. It had been crisply baked and was smothered in browned onion rings. Two slices of bread lay on the edge of the plate—Isabelle found the sight so inviting that her stomach let out a low growl.

She had just sliced off the first piece of sausage when she noticed a smell. Something vaguely fermented. It smelled like . . . horse urine. She looked around, perplexed. Where was it coming from? And why didn't someone close the window? A reek like that during dinner was anything but appetizing. But no one else seemed to have noticed it, and Leon and the cooper were digging into their food enthusiastically. Isabelle pulled herself together and put the first piece of sausage into her mouth.

The feeling that she was about to retch was almost overwhelming. It was only with the greatest effort that she managed to choke down the sausage, and then she had to hold her hand over her mouth to smother her coughing and gagging. What . . . was . . . this?

Ignoring the inquiring looks of the others at the table, Isabelle began to examine the sausage more closely. Sticky, gelatinous chunks in different shades of white and pink had been pressed together into a kind of aspic—the sausage was absolutely nothing like a German bratwurst. Isabelle turned to Carla and asked her hesitantly, "So what is this . . . *andouillette* made of?"

"Oh, you need countless ingredients to make it, and every butcher has his own recipe." Carla's eyes lit up, and she was obviously enjoying the opportunity to describe the special sausage. "One will use the stomachs of calves, cows, and ducks, but our butcher here in Hautvillers swears by adding lamb's stomach to the mix. Then you add the intestines of the same animals and their kidneys, spleens, and udders. Everything is cut up very fine, which helps bring out the distinctive flavor. And so as not to damage that, practically no spices are used at all. And it's a real treat cold." Carla Chapron sounded so proud that one might have thought that she'd come up with the recipe herself. "Do you like it?"

Isabelle, whose nausea had only worsened with Carla's enumeration of the ingredients, said miserably, "It's really a very . . . special sausage, isn't it?" She could not stand the smell of the innards anymore.

A short time later, the hostess returned to clear the table. With her eyebrows raised, she looked at Isabelle's all-but-untouched plate.

"You didn't like it? You're probably just used to boring old potatoes." The disdain in her voice was unmistakable. "You'd better get used to it. There'll be a lot more that you'll have trouble swallowing."

Chapter Eleven

"We had a wonderful evening. We drank wine and chatted away and laughed." Micheline Guenin sighed wistfully. "Claude tells such good stories. I could listen to him for hours."

A smile flickered on Isabelle's face as she looked from the washbasin to her neighbor, who was leaning against the window. Micheline sounded like a young girl in love!

She had gone to visit the Guenin sisters briefly to borrow a piece of soap. The basket of dirty wash was overflowing, and she could not put off the chore any longer, as much as she would have liked to. When Micheline had offered to help her, she accepted gladly. Since entering Isabelle's house, the old woman had been going on about her evening at Le Grand Cerf. The picture she painted of Claude Bertrand was completely different from the one that Isabelle already had of him. Claude recited poetry? His cryptic humor had Micheline in tears? Well, it was always said that beauty lies in the eye of the beholder.

As wonderful as the evening had been for Micheline Guenin, Isabelle herself had found it terribly frustrating. And then, on the way home, Leon had told her that the agent from Trubert had apparently stolen away all their American customers. Isabelle had been stunned, scarcely able to believe what she heard. What an outrage!

She and Leon had sat up together in Jacques's office until late in the night, debating what this meant for them. Leon, for the time being, was ready to write off the American customers and look for others closer to home, but Isabelle was not so willing to admit defeat. She wanted to write a letter to all the customers explaining the situation and asking them to reestablish the business relationships Jacques had started. In the meantime, Leon could court a new clientele in France. With this plan, Isabelle had fallen asleep at around two in the morning, exhausted but at least a little calmer.

The air in the laundry was so stiflingly hot that sweat was rolling down Isabelle's forehead. With wet hands, she tugged at the window, but apart from breaking a nail, nothing happened. She sighed and made a mental note to repair the window as best she could when she was done with the laundry.

"Should I add more soap, or is it too foamy already?" she asked, looking at the opaque broth in the vat in which her delicate knickers and camisoles were drifting around like belly-up fish. Micheline was too busy staring dreamily out the window to answer, so Isabelle reached for the scrubbing brush as she had always seen Irmi, her mother's maid in Berlin, do.

"For goodness' sake, don't!" Micheline cried. "Fine things like those need a gentle hand. Look, like this." She reached into the lukewarm water with both hands and began to knead the thin fabric carefully.

Isabelle watched attentively. Running a household was a lot of work but also a lot of fun, she had been surprised to discover. Just the previous afternoon, she had hauled all of the Persian rugs out of the house, slung them over a rail, and beat them until the color came through properly again. Now, whenever she went through the rooms, the first thing that caught her eye were the carpets, and she was happy with what she'd achieved. She would have been ten times happier to take the first orders from Leon and process them, but as long as there was nothing for her to do on the business side, she could certainly make herself useful around the house.

"Done!" said Micheline, pulling Isabelle out of her thoughts. Leon's underwear and Isabelle's lace knickers and camisoles were already hanging wet and white in neat rows on the clothesline.

Almost tenderly, Micheline smoothed a pair of Isabelle's underwear flat. "What I wouldn't have given to be able to wear something like this when I was young. But for whom?"

Isabelle, who was emptying the washtub, looked at the older woman. "May I ask why you . . . I mean—"

"Why I never married?" Micheline finished Isabelle's question. "It was how it is so often: the man I wanted married someone else. And I had no interest in the men who were interested in me. When it became clear that Marie and my brother would be childless, I thought it would be best if I stayed on the estate. An extra pair of hands couldn't hurt, right? Not with all the work that needs to be done."

Isabelle smiled and nodded. But a moment later, she grew serious again. "Your brother and Marie must have been very sad when they realized that God was not going to give them any children."

"Oh, they had a child," Micheline replied, which took Isabelle by surprise. "But the little one was not well. Not . . . normal." Micheline was visibly sad as she relived the misfortunes of the past in her mind. "A boy. He was three weeks old when he died—it was a terrible thing. The doctor told them that there was a danger that the next child would be just as unwell, and Marie decided not to even try. After that, the three of us grew even closer."

Micheline's story had begun to give Isabelle the chills. But a great love in her old age . . . she would wish that for Micheline with all her heart.

"Not everything in our lives goes the way we once dreamed it might. But sometimes you get a second chance. And I don't care what

Marie says about it, I'm going to take that chance!" Micheline's eyes shone as she turned back to the window, as if she hoped to see Claude outside just at that moment.

"Did Monsieur Bertrand mention to you that he might like to find a new job?" Isabelle held her breath.

Micheline looked back at her in surprise. "No! Should he?"

Isabelle hurriedly assured her that he did not.

"Well, you really put a fright into me," said Micheline, laughing. "I can't begin to imagine Claude moving away. Enough of that! You said earlier that you had a lot of work ahead of you today; if you like, I'd be happy to help you with some of it. Over there, all I'm going to hear are Marie's admonitions and how improper a romantic liaison is at my age. Honestly, I'm not in the mood for that at all."

A short time later, the two women were hard at work on the furniture in the living rooms, rubbing in a special liquid with old rags. It was a polish made of a few spoonfuls of oil, red wine, and a pinch of salt—a secret recipe of Micheline's that quickly took care of all the scratches in the lackluster wood. That afternoon, when Isabelle stood back and admired their handiwork in the golden sunshine falling through the high windows, she felt pride and satisfaction.

"It might sound strange, but I'm in love with this house," she murmured. "Whenever I go through the rooms, all I want to do is touch the furniture or stroke the velvet curtains. Whenever I walk past one of the windows, I have to stop and enjoy the magnificent views." A little embarrassed, Isabelle smiled at Micheline. "Even today, I can't imagine ever living anywhere else again. I feel so . . . like I'm where I belong!"

When they were done with the furniture, Micheline showed Isabelle how to cook potatoes and brew coffee properly.

"There's so much to learn. In the house, the yard, the vineyards. In Jacques's study, too. And all of it is important one way or another. I don't know if I'll ever get it all in," Isabelle cried despairingly.

"Give yourself a little time, my dear. Reims wasn't built in a day, either," said Micheline with a wink. Then she untied her apron and said good-bye for the day.

Isabelle watched the old woman leave. She should give herself time? She and Leon had no time to spare! The last bit of money they had was disappearing like morning frost in the March sun. The competition had snatched Jacques's American customers away, and they'd exploit every other weakness she or Leon showed, any way they could. They could only protect themselves if they kept their eyes and ears open and came to grips with the estate as quickly as they could.

Turning her thoughts back to the house, Isabelle wished Clara would send her a few cookbooks with simple recipes. Then she could at least check off the kitchen and cooking and spend her time on more important things.

When, a few days later, the postman really did bring a package for her, Isabelle let out a shriek so loud that it made the man jump. "Mail from Berlin!" As she signed for the package, she glanced past the postman and caught sight of Daniel Lambert on the opposite side of the street. He knocked on the door of the house of *la maîtresse* and went in without waiting.

Isabelle's face darkened. It came as no surprise to see him at *that* house. Visiting a prostitute in the middle of the day seemed just like him.

The postman followed her gaze, and said, "Ah, Daniel is visiting his sister, Ghislaine."

Isabelle looked at the man for a few seconds before she could speak. "What did you say? Daniel Lambert is the brother of *la maîtresse*—" She slapped her hand over her mouth, shocked at her own words.

But the postman merely grinned. "Didn't you know? He owns half of Le Grand Cerf, and he advises Ghislaine on what wines to buy. And should I tell you something else?" The postman leaned a little closer conspiratorially, and Isabelle automatically stepped back. "A long time ago, both of them lived here, in your house! That was when the estate belonged to the Lambert family, but it's been many years now."

"I knew that Daniel Lambert had lived here. But that Ghislaine was his sister and that she also called this home . . . some things are clearer now," Isabelle murmured to herself. No wonder Ghislaine was so hostile toward them. In her eyes, Leon and Isabelle were, as Jacques had been, interlopers who'd snatched away their family home.

She wished the postman good day, then carried Clara's package into the kitchen and set it on the table. She cut through the wrapping and lifted out three books: a cookbook, a general homemaker's guide, and a smaller guide with tips for spring cleaning. Isabelle was amazed such a specific book existed. She opened it at random and read, "The best way to get rid of scale is with vinegar." *Good to know*, Isabelle thought, remembering the buildup of lime that was half blocking the faucets in her bathroom. But far more valuable than any household tip was the letter from Clara. Isabelle felt a pang in her chest when she saw Clara's crisp handwriting.

Berlin, March 1898

Dear Isabelle,
What a wonderful joy to hear from you! You hadn't written a proper letter for so long and I was getting so worried.

Oh, Clara, what was I supposed to write about? Isabelle thought, feeling a tinge of bad conscience.

But now my fears have been put to rest. An estate in Champagne—that sounds like just the kind of place where you could find happiness. Dear Isabelle, I see you in my mind right now, keeping the whole place organized, keeping the staff on their toes, and pitching in yourself wherever there's a need.

Staff? *If you only knew,* Isabelle thought and smiled.

I still remember how you so wanted to find something to do with your life, how you couldn't stand the idea of being stuck with the boring duties of a good wife to some businessman. And now, beside your attractive cyclist, it seems your wish is coming true. Now you can show everyone just what you have inside!

Isabelle was reminded of what a good listener Clara had always been, and she bit her lip to keep from tearing up.

I miss you terribly, you and our own dear Josephine, who also almost never has time to meet up, by the way. Don't be angry with me if I admit this, but I had actually been thinking that you would turn your back on the Palatinate and come back to Berlin. I went to the library and read that the Palatinate is a very rural—some would say "backward"—corner of the German empire. Which I'm sure is not something anyone would say about the Champagne region, would they? After all, the most famous drink in the world comes from there! I'm sure you won't ever want to leave, which means that Josephine and I will have to come and pay you a visit sometime. Well, I'm sure there are worse things than that.

A visit from her two friends? Isabelle's heart began to beat faster. That would be wonderful!

As she looked up from the letter, a coach driving quickly up the street caught her eye. The team cut the curves so sharply that the postman, who was standing in front of Ghislaine's house, had to jump aside to avoid ending up under the wheels.

What kind of inconsiderate oaf would drive a coach up here like that? Isabelle thought angrily. But then the coach pulled up in front of her house, which was puzzling since she hadn't been expecting anyone.

She recognized the elegantly dressed woman immediately. It was the same woman who had been sitting at the next table at the restaurant in Reims and who had given them unsought advice about which champagne to order. What was she doing here? And did she also recognize Isabelle? If she did, she gave no sign of it.

"I'm Henriette Trubert. I've brought you some bread and salt, which is how we wish someone the best of luck in their new home—it's an old tradition among the *Champenois.*"

Henriette Trubert, from the estate of the same name? The woman who had stolen their American customers? What did she want from Isabelle? Isabelle brusquely accepted the bread, which had a clay saltcellar baked into the middle.

"Would you like to come in?" Isabelle asked, just to be polite, hoping that the other woman would turn the invitation down.

"I'd love to," said Henriette Trubert. She smiled, baring her teeth.

"So have you settled in? Living in Champagne must be completely different from living in Berlin."

Isabelle looked at the woman over the rim of her coffee cup. How did her neighbor know that she came from Berlin? "My husband and I feel very much at home here in Hautvillers. Apart from one or two . . . uncertainties, the way of life here is very romantic," she replied primly.

"Romantic?" Henriette Trubert raised her eyebrows mockingly. "How nice for you, madame. For my part, I only know about the romanticism of the vines from a few idealistic oil paintings, and I'm quite sure the artists never so much as took part in a grape harvest. You'll find out for yourself soon enough that making champagne is a year-round ordeal. In spring, you fear late frosts will destroy the young buds. In summer, you're afraid of hailstorms, and later in the year, you pray to God that your cellar master can come up with the perfect cuvée. And if you're lucky enough to come up with a good champagne one year, then you pray that no one starts a war, which will also ruin your business." She shrugged in resignation. "We're more like slaves than masters! And as if that weren't enough, you've constantly got the competition breathing down your neck."

She could talk! Isabelle snorted. "While we're on that subject, could you explain to me what your agent had in mind when he poached our American customers? If you ask me, that was simply not fair!" It was not normally her custom to be so blunt, but it didn't seem as if subtlety would work with Madame Trubert.

Henriette let out a deep sigh. "You're absolutely right, child, but that's how things work around here."

Child? Isabelle's jaw tightened, but before she could respond, Henriette continued. "Jacques Feininger would have jumped at the chance, if he'd had it, believe me. Let me explain something to you. Here in Champagne, all our resources are limited: the ground on which our grapes grow, the sunshine our vines need, and the customers who buy champagne. A limited number of wholesalers, restaurants, and hotels buy champagne for their own clientele. Champagne makers are constantly being forced out of the market or bought by others. One company grows, another shrinks—but the sum total doesn't change. When I sent my best agent to America, we were of the opinion that there was no heir for Jacques's estate. He never said a word about a nephew." Henriette set down her coffee and reached out to Isabelle with her right hand. "I hope you're not angry with me about something so trifling. It will never happen again. You have my word."

Oh, I believe that! thought Isabelle. They had no more customers for anyone to poach. In her view, the matter was far from trifling, but she held her tongue and shook Henriette's hand briefly.

Henriette's eyes glittered triumphantly. "Let's talk about something more pleasant," she said. "Your husband is a cyclist, I've heard. Such an exciting pastime. Tell me, does that fit in with all the work in the vineyards and cellar?"

"Leon only rides his bicycle for pleasure. The estate is most important to him, of course."

"And business is . . . good?"

"Couldn't be better," Isabelle replied with a voice of conviction. "My husband has a very engaging manner, which is always an advantage and especially so in this profession. In any case, he doesn't need to use unfair means to do his job."

Henriette's eyebrows shot up. "Oh, and there was one other thing," she said, already pulling on her gloves.

Chapter Twelve

"Henriette Trubert called what she's invited you to her 'little gala'? From what I've heard, the Trubert party is *the* event of spring, if not the entire year. They say the Truberts have invited all their important customers. Guests from around the world will be there. How exciting—meeting all those sophisticated people. You lucky thing! I'd give anything to be invited." Carla Chapron sighed wistfully.

The sky was dark that morning, as if it did not really want to lighten. She and Carla had run into each other at the village bakery, and Isabelle took the opportunity to find out more about the party and its hostess.

"The event of the year? Guests from all over the world? Now I don't know what to think." Isabelle hesitated. "The way Madame Trubert talked to me about it, it sounded as if she were inviting a few of the neighbors," she said as they climbed a steep hill. Only a few days earlier, she had stopped to catch her breath a couple of times walking up this same hill, but now she kept up with Carla easily. A light rain began to fall. Isabelle took a scarf out of her bag and tied it around her head.

"The neighbors—that's a laugh!" Carla said bitterly. "For Henriette, the only thing that counts is who owns a vineyard or sells a ton of champagne. Everyone else is a second-class citizen, but what would her cellars be without the barrels that my Ignaz makes for her? Does she think that we'd embarrass her? We might not be as rich as the fine winemakers and their wives, but I would be sure to dress the part for an event like that."

Isabelle heard the anger, envy, and years of frustration in every word. *I should have kept my mouth shut,* thought Isabelle. "Madame Trubert probably just wants to be nice to us, because we're new. We'll only be invited this once and never again, I'm sure," she said weakly.

Isabelle reached home and was about to go inside when she changed her mind and went to see her neighbors. Nobody answered her knock, so she went around the outside of the building and looked out across the Guenin's garden to the next vineyard. When she saw Marie and Micheline among the vines there, she set off toward them.

"A little courtyard party?" Micheline Guenin repeated as she used hammer, nails, and new slats to repair the wooden trellis that the vines grew along. "If the Truberts throw a party, then they do it in style, and don't let anyone tell you otherwise."

"Are you going, too?" Isabelle asked hopefully, admiring the skill with which the two women handled the tools.

"Why would you think that? We are about as insignificant as vintners can be."

"And we're not much use to Henriette, either," Marie added.

"But what are we?" said Isabelle, throwing her hands in the air in a very French gesture. *We're poor wretches,* she thought, grimacing, *if Leon doesn't manage to land a few customers soon.*

"I reckon that Henriette has certain hopes in mind when it comes to your estate," Marie Guenin replied, with a meaningful edge to her voice. She and Micheline exchanged a look. With tacit approval from her sister-in-law, Marie went on. "When Albert was still alive, we were also invited to all the Truberts' parties. She fawned all over him! It was disgusting."

"Henriette tries to worm her way in with every man who can be useful to her. That's all it was," said Micheline, as if belatedly trying to defend her brother.

Marie nodded. "A few days after Albert's death, Henriette appeared on our doorstep and told us that she wanted to buy our estate. That was nothing new—when she smells a chance to increase her holdings, she's there before you can say boo, isn't she, Micheline?"

"She talked her head off, trying to persuade us. Do you remember? We were supposed to think how lovely it would be not to have to run the whole business, etcetera, etcetera. Pfff!" Micheline sniffed indignantly.

Isabelle looked from one woman to the other. "I assume you didn't want to sell, right?"

The Guenin women nodded.

"And now you think that Madame Trubert wants to get her hands on our estate?"

"She tried to get it from old Jacques, but without any luck, so, yes, that's what she wants to do," said Micheline.

Isabelle shook her head. "Not for anything in the world! We're not exactly in the best position right now—Madame Trubert and her unscrupulous agent stole our American customers, so she's at least partly to blame for that—but the tide will soon turn, I'm sure of it. Believe me, Leon and I will show Henriette and the rest of the world what we're capable of!" Isabelle looked out across the valley, toward the Trubert estate.

Micheline followed her gaze. "Maybe it would be best not to go to the party at all, but to find some sort of excuse—"

"Nonsense!" Her sister-in-law interrupted her. "Henriette hasn't done anything to either of them, and whether she has any plans about the Feininger estate is pure speculation." Marie turned to Isabelle. "That party will be a splendid affair, and there will be guests from all over, interesting people with a lot to tell. And Henriette, I'm sure, has invited all her best customers from near and far. It's an opportunity for you to get to know some important people. If you want my advice . . ."

"Yes?" Isabelle said hesitantly. She didn't want to get caught up in another difference of opinion between the two women.

"Look as lovely as you can, and wear your most beautiful ball gown from Berlin."

"And do your hair elegantly," Micheline added, to Isabelle's astonishment. "Henriette, I'm sure, is hoping that you'll show up looking like a kitchen maid and embarrass yourself."

Isabelle laughed. "Then she can get ready to be disappointed!"

As Isabelle walked back to her house, one thing Marie said kept going through her head: *"Henriette, I'm sure, has invited all her best customers."*

From nowhere, Isabelle suddenly thought of one of her father's favorite sayings: revenge is a dish best served *warm*! A daring plan was forming in her mind. Poaching customers? She and Leon could do that, too. And what better an opportunity than at Henriette's gala? She was already counting down the days.

***

By the middle of March, spring had truly established itself: everything was green and blooming, and the vines were sprouting profusely. The last thing they needed now was another frost! Men were cutting back the vines throughout the region, but things were falling behind on the Feininger estate.

"Back in the Palatinate, pruning the vines early is extremely important. Every grower knows that he'll only get decent quality if he limits the volume of grapes. On top of that, the vines get worn out if you let the grapes grow uncontrolled," Leon said. He stood with his hands on his hips, glaring at Gustave Grosse. "Grab a few guys and start pruning—like all the other *Champenois* have been doing for weeks—and do it fast!"

"What do you care about the others? An unpruned vine gives you enough grapes for four bottles of wine, a pruned vine enough for just two bottles. Think how much money you'd be throwing away! Champagne grapes are robust; the vines don't tire so easily. And when they get old and the yields drop, you replace them! In the south of Champagne, where I hail from, they see it the same," Gustave said, slurring his reply. He swayed from one leg to the other. Dark shadows rimmed his eyes, and his cheeks and nose were red.

Repulsed by the cellar master's appearance, Isabelle stood off to one side as she listened to them quarrel. Gustave was completely hungover and in no condition to work. She held her breath, waiting for Leon to reprimand him.

"I don't care what they do in southern Champagne or anywhere else," Leon replied. "Without pruning, the vines will be so overgrown by harvest time that we won't be able to move around. Is that what you want? I don't, so we cut them back!" When the cellar master looked like he was about to reply, Leon cut him off. "I will not tolerate any more discussion. Enough, no more!" He fumbled in the pockets of his cycling pants, pulled out a few coins, and handed them to the one-eyed man. "Here. You can pay a few helpers with that."

Gustave snatched the coins furiously from Leon's outstretched hand. "If that's how it is, then in God's name, so be it! But I have a few things to take care of in the cellar first." Without another word, he staggered off.

"I'll bet you he's going to sleep off his hangover somewhere. If I catch him doing that . . . ," Isabelle said.

Leon laughed. "It wouldn't be the first time. If it's any consolation, he's usually in one piece again after an hour or two."

"He's shown up drunk for work too often in the short time we've been here." Isabelle furrowed her brow. "Why do you put up with it?"

Leon crouched and tied his shoelace. "What am I supposed to do? He's a sot, and hard work is not one of his virtues—your first impression of the man was right. But as long as he does his work reasonably well . . ."

"He shows up here whenever it suits him and leaves again when he feels like it. God alone knows what he does in the wine cellar! And he's constantly complaining that he doesn't want to do this or that. If it were up to me, I'd fire the lazy lout today."

"You wouldn't dare," said Leon, pulling on a cap. "I can't divide myself up and take care of the wine cellar, the vines, and the sales at the same time. I don't have the time *or* the knowledge. We need him; remember that."

Isabelle nodded in concern. "The money you just gave him was the last of what we had, wasn't it?" She tried not to sound too reproachful. Pruning the vines was certainly important, but so was a full stomach.

"It doesn't matter." Leon waved it off. "One or two good orders, and we'll be flush again. Probably today; just let me at 'em!"

They kissed long and deeply in parting, then Leon swung himself onto his bicycle.

Isabelle waved after his diminishing figure. He was planning to ride through the area north of Reims to search for new customers, but would he be any more successful there than he had been elsewhere? A few bottles here and there—so far, that was all Leon had managed to sell. The money he brought home wasn't even close to enough. And now he'd given their last pennies to the cellar master.

Panic rose inside her as her eyes swept across the extensive lands around the house. The peacocks, the horses, the chickens—they all needed to be fed! In two weeks, it would be the end of the month, and she would have to pay Grosse and Claude their wages. She had promised them that she would have their money by then. She had to buy groceries, too. How was she supposed to do all that?

Leon could not explain why they hadn't had any success yet. It certainly was not for lack of hard work on his part; every day for two weeks he had paid visits to prospective customers. Restaurants, bistros, hotels. But the establishments already had suppliers and were not willing to change, or they had too much champagne in stock to even consider buying more. Or they had no money. Or the customers preferred wine or beer. Or . . . or . . . or . . .

The night before, they had argued about it. Leon had claimed that the champagne the establishments bought was a matter of preference, but when Isabelle had responded that the other vintners were selling their products, he had shouted angrily at her.

"Do you think I'm too stupid to sell? I've talked myself blue in the face, believe me!"

"You're probably just talking to the wrong people. You have to visit the top-notch places, you know?"

"Oh, of course, and you're the only one who knows the meaning of first class. All I know is stinking hovels, is that it?"

One harsh word had led to another, and only later, in bed, had they made up again.

In the distance, she saw Leon riding along the main road toward Épernay. She looked beseechingly toward the sky, which was the color of violets and shot through with high, streaky clouds.

Dear God, give him some success today. Send him home with a little money!

Although Isabelle had had little to do with the cellar master, she had had a good deal of contact with her overseer. It was clear that Claude had realized that Isabelle's interest in the estate was neither superficial nor fake and that she really was truly willing to pitch in wherever she could. As a result, he had begun to familiarize her with the day-to-day workings of the place. Gradually, Isabelle began to understand how the various cogs of livestock, vineyards, and gardens meshed; how much time and money would be tied up in different tasks; and what could be accomplished with minimal outlay. She had surprised Claude a few times now with an idea that cost little or no money but that nonetheless proved useful.

After finishing the breakfast dishes, Isabelle stopped by Claude's house, as she did every morning. Under her arm she carried a thick waxed tarpaulin that was so heavy it threatened to fall out of her grasp at any moment. She had found it in one of the attic rooms, and when she had unfolded it, dust had flown around and a stale smell began to emanate from it, but she had found no tears or holes. In the past, in Berlin, she would have pushed something like that away in disgust with her foot or chided the domestic staff for leaving such trash lying around. Today, however, the tarp was a treasure.

She presented the thick bundle to the overseer and asked, "What do you think? Would this material do as a new roof for the chicken coop?" The old roof had been leaking in several places for ages, and the chickens did not like being rained on inside their only refuge.

"It most certainly would!" Claude said, impressed. "Where did you come up with this?" When Isabelle explained where she had stumbled across the tarp, he replied, "You can find things like this as often as you like!"

Now, if only I could find a pile of money up in the attic, Isabelle thought as she walked back to her house. When she got home, she avoided looking into the pantry, which was slowly getting emptier. The bare shelves depressed her and made her anxious—what would they live on when there were no more pumpkins, no more potatoes?

She sat in Jacques's office with a cup of tea and continued going through Jacques's papers. She wanted to get a clear picture of which vineyards belonged to the Feininger estate. Until she unfolded the huge map that showed the various parcels of land around Hautvillers, Isabelle thought it would be easy to figure out. But after studying it for no more than a few moments, she realized that the markings on the map did not follow a clear pattern: here and there, she saw the names of individual champagne estates, but many of the properties were only marked with numbers or sometimes with additional letters. She found documents on which similar numbers and letters appeared, and some of the documents carried official seals and several illegible signatures, while others were so faded that they were almost impossible to decipher. Were they legal deeds of ownership? And if they were, what did they say?

Sunshine poured through the window, dousing the table in golden light and blinding Isabelle so that she had to close the curtains. In the half dark, she started to run her finger over the map again. This vineyard here belonged to Moët, and this plot, too. The one next to it only carried a number, and the one beside that seemed to be Feininger land. Or perhaps not? Blast it, how were they supposed to work with their land when they did not even know exactly what belonged to them and what didn't? They could end up ignoring one of their vineyards entirely. Or—what almost seemed worse—they might start working on a stranger's property.

After spending a long time pondering over the map in vain, she carefully folded it up, laid it on top of the file with the deeds, and wedged both of them under her arm. A little fresh air and some help— she needed both.

She hurried out in the direction of the vineyards. From what she knew of her cellar master, he would start with pruning the nearest vines. God forbid he should take one step more than necessary! But the numbers, letters, and names on the map would certainly mean more to him than to her. Arriving at the foot of the hill, she glanced around, shielding her eyes against the sunlight. But whichever way she looked, she saw no trace of Grosse or any laborers among the vines.

This cannot be, she thought, fury rising inside her. *Just you wait, Mr. Grosse!*

She found him in between two huge wine barrels on the middle level of the cellars. His mouth was open, and he snored loudly. He still reeked of alcohol, lying on a bed of blankets and pillows that looked as if they had seen regular use.

Isabelle felt a terrible rage swelling inside her, and only with a huge effort did she manage to control herself. She, Leon, and Claude were out breaking their backs from early morning until late in the day just to get by, and here was her cellar master, sleeping off his hangover! And she was supposed to pay him for this?

She jabbed him in the side with the point of her shoe. "Wake up! Right now!"

All the man did was fart and grumble.

Isabelle repeated her jab, harder this time and with more success: Gustave Grosse jumped like he'd been bitten by a tarantula.

"What do you think you're doing, lazing around here like that? Didn't my husband give you a clear job to do?" said Isabelle sharply.

"I only lay down for a moment. Just feeling a little faint, but it's passed now, madame," said Grosse, pulling himself together. He hurriedly pulled on his eye patch, which he had removed to sleep. "Just after your husband left, I went in search of a few field workers. But there were none to be had; they're all busy pruning for others. Tomorrow, madame, I'm sure to be able to find somebody."

"You should have hired laborers earlier!" Isabelle snapped at him. "What do you do down here the whole day long?" She swept her arm wide, taking in the entire cellar.

Grosse sighed. "Madame, my days are not long enough for the tasks of a cellar master, and here you want me to explain this exceptionally difficult craft in a few words? Is that what you really expect?"

"I expect you to *do* something and not lie around like a loaf of bread," Isabelle shot back. She was furious, but also helpless.

"May I be of any further assistance?" Grosse asked, sounding bored and folding up his blankets as if it were the most natural thing in the world. He did not seem particularly embarrassed to have been caught napping.

Isabelle hesitated. She had no desire to spend any longer than necessary in the man's company, but surely he could provide information she needed. "I'm trying to get a clear picture of all the Feininger vineyards." As she spoke, she unfolded the map. "But I'm still not sure which parcels belong to us and which don't. It would be best if we could go through everything together, and you could show me—"

"Pardon, madame, but *my* job is to make the champagne and keep the wine cellar in order. Monsieur Jacques always took care of the vineyards. He was the one who organized and supervised the harvest, and he was the only one with an overview of his properties. Having your husband order me to take care of the pruning in the future is one thing. You can't ask any more of me!"

"And then I said . . . I said he should, yes, he should at least try it! But the . . . bastard, he—" Leon broke off abruptly and took another gulp from the bottle. His eyes wandered around as if he were looking for something. A solution. A way to escape.

"The bastard didn't even want to try it! He said his 'honored guests' would only drink Lanson champagne. Lanson, pah! Why should Lanson be any better?" He took another swig from the bottle, and champagne trickled from the corner of his mouth; he wiped it away with the sleeve of his cycling jacket. He had not even changed clothes since returning in the early evening. Instead, he had gone straight to the cellar and come back with a few bottles. Since then, he'd been sitting at the kitchen table, drinking and complaining.

With a sinking heart, Isabelle watched her husband empty the second bottle. In all the time they had been together, she had never seen Leon like this. Oh, he'd had a drink or two with his club mates after a race in Berlin. Back then, he would get funny and a little loud. Sometimes, on evenings like that, they had started kissing madly, right in front of everybody, until the proprietor of the clubhouse had to tell them off. But he had never really gotten drunk, and certainly never gloomy.

He looked at her with wavering eyes. "No one wants our champagne! Why not? Tell me, why not?" he wailed. "And the Americans . . . our customers there . . . they're gone, too. They don't want anything to do with us anymore. Don't you get it?"

Oh God, he wasn't going to cry, was he?

"Leon, please pull yourself together," said Isabelle firmly. "It isn't over yet. We're still at the beginning, and we're not about to let ourselves be discouraged so quickly." She tried to inject as much confidence as possible into her voice. But at the same time, she felt like crying herself. Her conflict with the impertinent cellar master, the unanswered questions about which lands were theirs—these were things that she wanted to talk to Leon about. He had to do something, and soon! But when he came home like that, beaten like a dog, she couldn't bring herself to burden him more.

He held out the bottle to her. "At least you can drink with me! Or isn't the Feininger champagne good enough for you, either?"

For his sake, she sipped at her glass but put it down again immediately. "That's enough for today. We'll have to solve our problems another way, but we can tackle them again tomorrow." She stroked his arm. "Come on, let's go to bed."

Leon growled and balked. "Problems, problems! I can't stand it anymore. Ever since we came to this miserable farm, we've had nothing but problems. I'd rather ride my bicycle; I don't have any problems with that. And I'm the one that decides when I've had enough!" With a shaking hand, he tore the wire cage off the cork of the third bottle. Then he pulled the cork out of the bottle so violently that the champagne overflowed everywhere, splashing the table and Isabelle's dress. Leon laughed loudly and wildly. "If no one likes this stuff, then I'll just drink it myself," he said, and raised the bottle to his lips.

Isabelle stood up abruptly. "You're intolerable! Don't come to my bed drunk. I'll bring you a blanket and pillow; you can sleep in the living room," she said, and with heavy steps and a heavier heart, she climbed the stairs.

Isabelle lay awake long into the night, thoughts racing through her mind. "*No one wants our champagne,*" Leon had said earlier. What if he was right? All the champagnes that Raymond Dupont had offered her had far more aroma; they were finer, more elegant.

She wanted nothing more than to pull the blanket over her head and cry her eyes out. But what good would it do?

Finally, Isabelle got out of bed and sat in an armchair by the open window. The cold night air felt good. She breathed in deeply.

The sparkling starry sky looked so close. Isabelle could not remember ever having seen so many stars at one time. There were no big-city lights here to distract from the firmament, and the evening star shimmered auspiciously. At some point, she began to feel chilled and closed the window again. But even looking out through the glass, she could not take her eyes off bright, consoling Venus. The star seemed to want to show her the way and to say, *Don't lose your courage.* The longer she sat in the dark looking out, the more confidence returned to her. Admittedly, the position they were in was far from rosy. But she had never been a shrinking violet, so why was she letting a "few" problems make her anxious? She had to defy them, and sooner or later the brighter days would return!

Enough lamenting. Enough conflict. The time had come to find solutions, and she was sure Leon would feel the same way in the morning.

***

The next day, when Leon awoke with a throbbing skull and stumbled from the living room into the kitchen in search of a cup of strong coffee, all he found was a hastily scribbled note on the table.

Chapter Thirteen

Eyes closed, Raymond Dupont took a mouthful of the champagne that Daniel Lambert had poured for him. Countless tiny beads shattered on his tongue, and he reveled in the feeling, as if it were the first time. Then he went to work. With small motions of his jaw, as if chewing, he rolled the liquid through his mouth. Almond. Roasted almond! Cloves, marzipan . . . He opened his eyes. There was appreciation in his expression as he said, "The perfect champagne to beguile a mature woman."

The young cellar master smiled. "Very true! Certainly not the first choice for a party, but for an intimate evening for two . . ."

Raymond raised his glass to Daniel.

They were alone in Raymond's shop; he had locked the door, wanting to ensure the tasting wouldn't be disturbed. Many years earlier, he had made it his habit to invite the cellar masters—not the agents—of the champagne houses to his shop, to the chagrin of the *Champenois*. "*We pay our salesmen outrageously high salaries, and you don't even invite them in?*" they complained to him every year. But Raymond didn't want to hear the carefully rehearsed sales pitches of a Simon Souret from Trubert or a Silvain Grenoble from Pommery. What he wanted was to hear what the cellar master himself had in mind with a certain *assemblage*, with a particular mix of Pinot Noir, Pinot Meunier, and Chardonnay.

Daniel, who knew well what mattered to the champagne dealer in Reims, said, "There are plenty of young, fizzy champagnes around, at Trubert, too. But I wanted to create a champagne that you could put on the table late in the evening instead of cognac. A champagne with depth and fullness, one that would warm two lovers and make a short night longer."

"A champagne to warm two lovers—I hear the maestro speaking," said Raymond with a smile.

"In my dreams, perhaps. And in this case, a dream is the *only* thing behind the concept," Daniel replied with a sigh. "Apart from my love for making champagne, little else is going on."

Raymond regarded his guest in silence. It was well known that, when it came to women, Daniel Lambert was not averse to an occasional affair, and many, in fact, had been ascribed to the attractive man with the long blond hair. Even if not all the stories were true, there was still no doubt that Daniel had been welcome in many beds. It was also well known, however, that no woman could put up with him for long. In time, competing with the seductions of a good bunch of Pinot Meunier or Chardonnay grapes always proved to be too much. Or was it the other way around? Was it Daniel for whom no woman was exciting enough in the long run?

"How is Henriette?" Raymond asked in the most harmless tone he could. Henriette Trubert would have been very happy to turn her business relationship with her cellar master into a personal one, a fact that was evident to anyone who saw her in Daniel's company in the wine cellar, at tastings, or anywhere else. The way Henriette—one of Raymond's own former lovers—practically devoured the young man with her eyes was embarrassing, Raymond thought. Even with her best years behind her, Henriette was still a reasonably attractive woman, but more than that, she was powerful.

Raymond's own liaison with Henriette a few years earlier had not lasted long. She had been too demanding for his taste, and without wasting many words, they ended the affair. They had not remained friends; two people could only remain friends if they had been friends to start with. But they realized each other's value in business, and when their paths crossed, there was no animosity between them.

Daniel gave him a look that said, *I know what's behind your harmless question, but it's got nothing to do with me.* "Madame Trubert is very busy right now. She has big plans."

Raymond laughed. "Why so secretive, my young friend? Do you think I can't guess that she has her eye on your old estate? I'd be surprised if she didn't, considering her hunger for more land. How many acres did she buy last year? There was the Serlot estate, then the Eglotát place—was it eighteen acres? Twenty?"

"Twenty-three," Daniel said flatly.

"And now she's eyeing the Lambert lands." Although the estate proper and its outlying vineyards had carried the name "Feininger" for years, Raymond had never got used to it. For him, Frederick Lambert had been more than the best cellar master of all time. He had also been a good friend of Raymond's. And Raymond preferred to overlook the fact that other people now worked Frederick's land. Still, since her visit to his shop, he could not get the lovely Madame Feininger out of his head. A hybrid tea rose about to bloom . . .

Raymond refilled both their glasses with champagne. "From all I've heard, Henriette stands a good chance," he said. "It seems the Feiningers are struggling, to say the least."

Daniel snorted. "If someone took away all your customers, you'd be struggling just as much. If you think I condone behavior like that just because the land used to belong to my family, you're wrong. If the Feiningers are responsible for their own ruin, that's one thing. But I'm not part of Madame Trubert's dirty tricks, as much as she might like to make it look like I am."

Raymond raised his eyebrows a fraction. In all the years he had known Daniel, the young man had never said a critical word about his employer, although there had been plenty of opportunities to do so. "The way Simon Souret poached the Feininger's American clientele wasn't exactly sportsmanlike," he said.

Since Isabelle Feininger's visit, Raymond had found out quite a bit about the estate and its new owners: Although Jacques's nephew came from the Palatinate and was a vintner, he had no experience with champagne. With their overseas customers gone, the estate was in a bad position—bad enough that Leon Feininger was peddling his champagne door to door!

Daniel sighed. "The idea of working Lambert land again is tempting, to be sure. I still know every single vine, every aspect of the place. When I see what Grosse is doing with it all . . . let's just say it makes me very angry. Adding apple juice or some other ingredient that doesn't belong there certainly doesn't make for an honest wine."

"He *cuts* it?" Raymond was suddenly alert. For him, as a lover of the great champagnes, there was no greater sin.

Daniel nodded, then he smirked.

"Speak of the devil." Daniel gestured with his chin to the stores across the street. "If Madame Feininger can afford to visit the most expensive jeweler in Reims, things can't be all that bad."

"She rides a bicycle?" Raymond exclaimed. *The German is certainly an astounding woman*, he thought, as Isabelle pushed open the door to the jeweler's shop and stepped briskly inside.

Daniel cleared his throat. "So, tell me: What do you think of my champagne? I've only made a small quantity. Madame Trubert doesn't really appreciate such adventures, so I'm only allowed to do so if I'm successful with them. And it isn't cheap; I've put the best grapes into it. Luckily, there are some who have the nose for that certain something."

"And you're looking at one of them," said Raymond with a smile. Enough daydreaming about the beautiful redhead! He had a business to run. He straightened his shoulders and said, "I'll take all you've got." Selling such an extraordinary champagne would be child's play.

They were winding up their business when Isabelle Feininger knocked on the door. She looked pale and exhausted, and Raymond hurried over to open the door for her. Daniel followed him.

"I'll see you at Henriette's party," Daniel said to Raymond before turning to Isabelle. "Madame, I trust you have not found any more saboteurs among your vines?" With a slight smile, he tipped his cap in greeting.

Instead of returning his mockery in kind, Isabelle looked at him seriously and said, "I fear that the worst saboteur is inside my own cellars, and nowhere else."

The two men exchanged a glance, then Daniel said his good-byes.

"Please come inside, madame. The doorstep is no place to stand," said Raymond.

***

Isabelle's heart was beating hard, and her knees felt weak as she set her heavy bag on the table in Raymond's shop. She wasn't sure exactly why she was so agitated. Was it her visit to the jeweler? Or the unaccustomed trek on the bicycle? After all, she'd had to ride the bicycle just so she could go to Reims without Leon or Claude knowing of it. Certainly not Daniel Lambert's dark eyes . . . or the pleasant warmth she felt in her belly when they were standing so close together in the doorway. Was she going to react like that whenever she was near the man?

"What a pleasure to see you again, Madame Feininger. Let's sit down for a moment; then tell me how I can help you."

As Raymond sat in the chair opposite hers, Isabelle was suddenly reminded of her father. The graying hair, the perfectly fitted suit made of the finest wool, the self-confident air, so worldly, so experienced. All at once, she was sure that coming here had been the right decision.

"I would like to have another champagne tasting session with you. But this time, *I* would like to provide the champagne."

Raymond Dupont laughed in astonishment. "Madame, please don't feel you need to reciprocate! It is a pleasure for me to taste champagne with you. Let me quickly fetch a few bottles, and we can begin."

"No, Monsieur Dupont, please!" Isabelle cried. "It's not what you think." She hurriedly pulled out the five bottles of Feininger champagne she had taken from the cellar that morning. The wine had been shaken up vigorously from the ride, but the bottles were still reasonably cool. "I know that this is not ideal, but . . ." She bit her lip before going on. "I would like to know what you think of this champagne. Would you be so kind as to try it?" She held her breath, waiting for him to reply.

Moments later, Raymond Dupont held a glass of her champagne at eye level. "Pale yellow. I'd almost call it mustard-colored. And slightly cloudy. There are some impurities—at first glance, it is not a particularly alluring champagne, madame. But wait. Testing a champagne involves all the senses: the eyes, the nose, and the palate, of course." He brought the glass just under his nose and inhaled deeply. Then he raised the glass to his lips. It was barely perceptible—but Isabelle still saw it: a grimace.

"The sweetness is so overpowering that everything mineral, everything that the champagne grapes naturally give to it, is buried. I would not be surprised to find out that apple or pear juice was added to it."

"Apple juice?" Isabelle lifted one hand to her mouth in shock. "Do you mean to tell me the champagne has been adulterated?"

Raymond nodded and took a second mouthful. "And very little of *l'effervescence* develops in the mouth."

"You mean it isn't bubbly enough?" Isabelle frowned. This didn't sound good.

"Exactly!" Raymond sighed and pushed the glass away. "This is the champagne from your estate, isn't it?"

Isabelle nodded dejectedly. She felt like picking up her bag and running away. Her heart was racing. She crossed her arms over her chest as if doing so might protect her from the pain she felt.

"What do *you* think of this . . . sparkling wine, madame? If I remember correctly, you have an outstanding sense of taste."

This startled Isabelle. It was a question she was not prepared for. "Honestly, I feel quite helpless in this, and I would like to hear your unvarnished opinion."

Raymond sighed again.

"Please."

The champagne dealer lifted the glass and held it directly in front of Isabelle's eyes.

"This champagne, in terms of the craftsmanship that has gone into it, is woefully lacking, as shown by the impurities and the limited effervescence. The taste is far down toward the bottom of the scale. It possesses absolutely no fruit aromas and no complexity." When he saw the question on Isabelle's face, he said, "No character, no charm, you see? The cellar master who committed the crime of making this champagne has even managed to conceal its origin, for I can detect no trace of chalk or limestone. We *live* on an enormous mountain of chalk covered by a thin layer of soil. This is something one should taste, smell, feel!" Raymond suddenly sounded angry, as if he considered the wine a personal affront.

Isabelle looked at him with deep concern. "And the sales potential of this champagne? How would you gauge that?"

"The sales potential," Raymond repeated, as if he wanted to stall for time. He seemed to struggle inwardly for a moment, then he looked into Isabelle's eyes and said, "I'm sorry to have to tell you this, but a sweet brew like this is practically impossible to sell these days, at least here in Europe. Twenty years ago, things were different. People had different tastes back then, and a champagne had to be as sweet as possible. But the days of adding sugar or syrup to compensate for the lack of sweetness of the grapes here in Champagne are over. Today, the skills of our cellar masters are so advanced that they can take what was once the great disadvantage of being situated so far north—namely, the lack of sweetness in our grapes—and deliver a virtuoso performance. They bring acidity and sweetness together in such harmony that the champagne drinker is enthralled—and prepared to pay a small fortune for the privilege." He set the glass down again and drank some water.

It took everything Isabelle had to prevent herself from bursting into tears. A cheerful sentence, something to lighten that leaden moment . . . She was utterly unable to come up with anything.

"Keep your chin up, Madame Feininger. Perhaps there is still a chance to sell the wine in some less pampered part of the world."

Isabelle sat there, stunned. Dear God, let this be a bad dream.

And she had suspected Leon of not doing his best.

"Would Russia be a possibility?" she asked, trying to sound as businesslike as she could.

The champagne dealer shook his head. "The Russians are certainly known for having a sweet tooth, but also for their appetite for the best of the best."

"I see. Would it be all right if you also tested the other bottles?" Isabelle croaked. Her mouth felt as dry as sand.

Chapter Fourteen

"So much for a few necklaces!" Leon gaped at the pile of banknotes that Isabelle had tossed onto the table.

She smiled. "I certainly imagined I'd get quite a lot, but I was surprised that the jeweler in Reims gave me quite this much for my jewelry. In Germany, it would be more than four hundred marks."

The tantalizing smell of a meat ragout wafted from the kitchen. Isabelle had paid a visit to the charcuterie in Reims, and she rode home with two pounds of beef, plus a whole pie and some ham. She'd found a suitable recipe in Clara's cookbook and put the ragout on right away. That was good, for she had things to address with Leon, things for which he could certainly use a solid meal.

"Darling!" Leon jumped up and kissed Isabelle passionately. "This is absolutely fantastic! We're saved. There's enough here to pay Claude and Grosse and a few laborers besides. Feed for the horses, and we'll need to take them to a smithy soon, too, Claude told me. It's all easy, now! What a wonderful idea to sell off that old junk."

Isabelle freed herself from his embrace. "To be honest, parting with that *old junk* was hard. The pearl necklace was a gift from my mother for my eighteenth birthday, and the chain was something she'd inherited from her own mother. My father gave me the ruby collier when I graduated from secondary school." She sighed. "But now is not the time for sentimentality." Her jewelry box was still well filled, and she would have to be happy with what she had. If they got down to it, she could always trade in more of her jewelry, though she hoped that it would not be necessary.

Leon's pride and self-confidence were blazing in his eyes again. His depressed mood of the previous night had evaporated. "This is just the spur I needed! Tomorrow morning, I'll head off toward Troyes. I haven't tried to sell anything down that way yet. I'll talk for what my life's worth, and from now on, it will work. I can feel it! Then I'll be bringing home money, too, even more than this."

Isabelle nodded slightly, then she served the ragout. But while her husband went at the dish hungrily, Isabelle merely prodded at the food in front of her. How was she supposed to tell Leon that the Feininger champagne was no good? That *that* was the reason all his efforts had been in vain?

She waited until he had finished eating. Then, as calmly and objectively as she could, she described Raymond Dupont's tasting and the crushing verdict.

Leon listened, his Adam's apple bobbing as he swallowed nervously. "Sediment? Mustard-colored brew? Poor craftsmanship, and doesn't even taste good?" He angrily interrupted Isabelle. "What does this guy know? He could tell you anything. It's an outrage!"

Isabelle shook her head. She had been waiting for this reaction. "I trust Monsieur Dupont's judgment. I would not have gone to him otherwise. As a dealer, he has a lot to do with champagne—all kinds, all qualities. He knows what he's talking about. If Dupont says that our chances of selling the champagne at a reasonable price are practically nil, then that's how it is."

"But we've got thousands and thousands of bottles down there. How do you know they're all the same . . . bad quality?"

"Leon, please! I took Monsieur Dupont five bottles of champagne, and I selected them from five different parts of the cellar. All were equally bad."

"So what are you saying? Should I pour it all out?"

Isabelle laughed helplessly. "Monsieur Dupont's opinion is that we should look for a new cellar master. A young talent, someone fresh, someone who knows how to make champagne. A *chef de cave* who knows what today's champagne customers want."

"Oh, lovely!" Leon huffed. "And can you please tell me where we're supposed to find such a sorcerer's apprentice? All the cellar masters I've met so far earn their bread and butter elsewhere. And even if we found one looking for a job—what could we possibly offer?"

"There's still some time until the next harvest. We'll come up with something by then," Isabelle said.

For a long time, neither said a word. Leon riffled through the banknotes, straightened the pile, riffled again, straightened again. He was making Isabelle so nervous that she wanted to snatch the bills out of his hands, but she knew that he needed at least a few moments to digest what he'd just heard. She herself had needed the entire journey back from Reims to come to terms with it.

After a time, Leon reached for one of the champagne bottles left over from his binge the night before and looked at it thoughtfully. "This stuff really is very sweet, isn't it?"

Isabelle nodded. "Oh, yes."

As they looked into one another's eyes, they each recognized their own naïveté, stubbornness, and ignorance mirrored in the other. They began to laugh, and it grew louder and more hysterical.

Tears ran down Isabelle's cheeks, and she realized that it was possible to laugh yourself dry in the same way that you could cry yourself dry, although she had little experience with either. But all the negative feelings that had been dammed up inside washed away. The tension and fear were gone. In their place, she felt a seed of confidence burst open.

She inhaled deeply, but this time without the oppressive weight pressing down on her chest. She was about to speak when Leon said, "And I was thinking that I was too stupid to sell it." With a sigh, he wiped the tears of laughter from his own face.

"You're not," Isabelle replied firmly, meaning it sincerely. "I'm beginning to think that Jacques made this sweet brew especially for his American customers. He certainly found some success over there."

"Do you know what that would mean?" Leon sounded doubtful. "A sales tour to America would take quite a few weeks, certainly. And it wouldn't be cheap."

"You don't have to go to America. I've got another idea. The Americans come here, like the mountain to Muhammad," she said enigmatically.

"I'm sorry?"

Isabelle smiled. "I told you about the party at the Trubert place, the one we're invited to. They have customers coming from all over the world."

"So that means . . . we'll be meeting Jacques's old customers?" Leon looked at her through narrowed eyes. "Now I get it! Ha! If the Truberts can do it, then turnabout is fair play. They stole our customers, and now we steal them back."

Isabelle's grin widened. "You with your charm and me in my prettiest dress. We make a good team, don't we?"

Chapter Fifteen

Isabelle looked at herself in the mirror and was pleased with what she saw. She had skillfully piled her hair high, pinning it in place with ruby-studded combs; the color of the jewelry perfectly matched her evening dress. She carried a beaded handbag and had picked out a colorful fan. The ruby necklace that she had sold in Reims would have been the perfect accompaniment, but . . .

She turned and, as well as she could, she admired herself from behind. She smiled. Who needed gold and gems when there was something much better? She had her slim waistline back, and she was in better shape—much closer to what she had been in her best days as a long-distance cyclist. All the hard work had done some good for her, too.

Her genteel, citified pallor had also vanished, and her skin had taken on a golden sheen. She even had a few freckles sprinkled across her small snub nose. In the past, she would have complained about them and tried to hide them with powder. Today, she liked the way she looked. Standing straight, her chin lifted boldly, Isabelle nodded to her reflection. Her green eyes sparkled provocatively as she said, "You can measure up to any Henriette Trubert around. Don't let them tell you that you've lost!"

From a distance, the Trubert estate was impressive, and it was far more imposing close up. It consisted of a large two-story main building and several outbuildings, all massive, well-maintained structures. Freshly planted flower boxes hung beneath every window. The open courtyard between the whitewashed buildings was paved with cobblestones in a complicated pattern, and there were a number of halved wine barrels generously planted with spring flowers. Flaming torches stood between the barrels, illuminating the courtyard. The champagne cellars themselves were in the building to the right of the main house; a huge sign painted with "Champagne Trubert" in ornate silver lettering indicated as much. From the style, though, the building reminded Isabelle more of her father's workshops than cellarage for champagne.

Leon whistled softly between his teeth. "Not bad, eh? Seems they've got a real champagne factory going here. Nothing like our little cellars."

Isabelle furrowed her brow in doubt. "A champagne factory? I must say, that doesn't seem very exclusive to me." She pointed to the many guests waiting ahead of them to be greeted by their host and hostess. "Oh. It looks like we're among the last to arrive."

"This party seems to be a very big show," Leon murmured, pulling his jacket smooth.

While they waited their turn, Isabelle looked at Leon and thought he looked very nice. Her husband could match any of the gentlemen present for elegance. He was wearing his black pants and his white shirt, which Isabelle laboriously scrubbed on the washboard and then even more laboriously ironed. Over the shirt, he wore a linen jacket that he'd bought himself in Berlin from his winnings—Leon had always had a good sense of fashion.

Their eyes met, and they grinned happily at each other.

Isabelle grew more tense with every minute they had to wait. There were only four or five other couples ahead of them. She tugged at Leon's sleeve and whispered, "Let's run through our plan one last time. First, we just look around. Then, once we've found the Americans—" She broke off when the woman in front of them turned around.

Leon smiled charmingly at the woman. "Don't make me nervous," he hissed. "We've gone through it all enough."

Isabelle looked away from Leon. Only three couples ahead of them, now. To see more, she stood on tiptoes. The women in line were all dressed in the latest fashions and wore expensive jewelry. And the men, too, in their sportily elegant ensembles, were impressive. But the next moment, she almost fainted on the spot.

"That dress! Look at Henriette Trubert's dress!" A few heads immediately turned in her direction.

Leon gave her a reproving look. "Your dress is lovely, too," he whispered. "You'll be the belle of the ball this evening."

Ignoring the compliment, Isabelle settled down again. It was too complicated to explain what it was about the dress, but she would get to the bottom of it. She would make sure of that! She breathed in sharply. Only a few more steps.

"Madame and Monsieur Feininger!" Beaming broadly, Henriette welcomed them to her estate. "This is the famous cyclist I told you about," she said, turning to her husband.

Alphonse Trubert shook Leon's hand happily. "You'll have to tell me all about such an exciting preoccupation." His salt-and-pepper moustache flicked with every word he said. When he shook Isabelle's hand, his prominent stomach almost touched her body.

"May I introduce my son, Jean? He's come in just for today's party. He's usually away at boarding school at a Jesuit monastery. Isn't that right, Jean?"

The young man nodded unhappily. Isabelle reached out her hand to him.

"And our daughter, Yvette. She's at a secondary school in Reims."

Henriette must have been that pretty once, too, Isabelle thought as she greeted Yvette. Then she turned to her hostess.

"You have a lovely dress there, madame. It reminds me of a colorful rainbow," she said. She was still dumbfounded at the sight of it. When she had suggested to Blanche Thevenin that she sew together strips of different kinds and colors of fabric, the seamstress had dismissed the idea as pure nonsense even though she hadn't been able to think of a design to impress her client: *"That might be some kind of national costume in Germany, but it's nothing for an elegant festival here in Champagne!"* Isabelle could still hear the mockery in the dressmaker's voice.

"A bespoke work by my seamstress. She discovered the model at the most modern couturier in Paris and copied it for me especially," said Henriette, pursing her gaudy red lips proudly.

"In Paris? How interesting." Isabelle tried not to let her wrath show. Blanche Thevenin, you miserable fraud!

"A dress can only be as lovely as the woman wearing it. You, dear lady, would look enchanting in a linen shirt," said Leon flatteringly, and he kissed Henriette Trubert's hand.

Henriette raised her eyebrows appreciatively. "You were right, Madame Feininger. Your husband is quite the charmer."

Isabelle smiled tartly. She hated it when Leon flirted with other women. And as far as their plan was concerned, it didn't help in the slightest.

"Something for you," said Isabelle somewhat abruptly as she handed over the elegant box of pralines that Leon had bought using the money from the jewelry. The *chocolats* had been terribly expensive, and every franc they had cost caused Isabelle pain, but they agreed that skimping on a present would be a mistake. "One has to look rich and successful to become rich and successful," Isabelle had said, quoting a nugget of her father's business wisdom, and Leon had nodded.

"Well, then . . . let's get on with it," said Alphonse Trubert in a doleful voice, and he sighed deeply, as if the last thing he wanted was to spend the evening there. He gazed down into the valley longingly, which earned him a poisonous glance from Henriette.

Isabelle grinned with cruel pleasure. It looked as if the man would rather be with his lover at Le Grand Cerf than at his own party.

Henriette clinked at her champagne glass with a silver spoon. The crowd of guests fell silent and to Isabelle's surprise, Henriette herself, and not her husband, stood up to address them. *"Mesdames et messieurs . . ."*

After a few words of greeting, Henriette went through a seemingly endless list of names of those who had played a role in the eighty-year history of the company. The guests occasionally chuckled or murmured with appreciation.

A "little soiree"—ha! There had to be a hundred people gathered there! It all reminded Isabelle of the parties she had often attended in Berlin, although here in Champagne there was a lighter, more festive mood. At one end of the hall, a group of musicians had set up their instruments; there would probably be dancing later in the evening, which made Isabelle happy. She could not remember the last time that she'd been dancing. Perhaps, once they had successfully completed their mission . . .

Beside one of the magnificent mirrors, a familiar face, the first she had seen. She smiled and nodded to Raymond Dupont. The champagne dealer was wearing a black suit and was certainly among the most elegant men in the hall. Maybe she would have the opportunity to ask his advice about a cellar master.

"Of course I can create a *champagne brut* or *extra brut*! It's just a matter of how much sugar you add, that's all," Grosse had pontificated when she raised the subject with him. "That said, the previous Monsieur Feininger preferred *champagne sec*, and I also like my champagne very sweet. But if you want a brut . . ." With a shrug of his shoulders, the cellar master had turned and walked away from Isabelle. As straightforward as the information sounded, his pompous manner had done anything but convince Isabelle.

At the moment, however, another question was much more important to her: Where were the Americans?

A loud round of applause pulled Isabelle out of her thoughts. The musicians played a fanfare and several lamps came on behind Henriette, lighting up a high pyramid of champagne glasses from all sides.

Shouts of delights rang out, and more applause.

What a lovely idea! Isabelle clapped with the rest. But when she saw who was standing beside the tower of glasses, she felt a small pang in her chest. She squeezed Leon's hand.

Daniel Lambert, Henriette's cellar master, carefully set the last glass on the uppermost triangle of the pyramid. He was focused but at the same time seemed strangely detached. With a practiced hand, he then opened the first magnum bottle and poured the champagne into the glass. The liquid overflowed, frothing and running down to the lower levels of glasses, one after another.

Leon whistled, then whispered to Isabelle, "Did you ever see anything like that? Let's hope we don't have an earthquake." He laughed a bit too loud at his own joke.

Isabelle did not reply. She was mesmerized at the sight. The glass pyramid in the golden light, the fine bubbles of champagne glittering, Daniel's gold-blond hair, gleaming in the light of all the lamps . . .

When all the glasses were full, Daniel handed Henriette the topmost glass. With a triumphant smile, she held it up before the gathered guests.

"To you, my friends! I declare the buffet open!"

Some things are the same wherever you go, Isabelle thought as she watched the guests descend on the buffet.

"Let's grab something to eat, too," said Leon. "It will help us negotiate."

Isabelle's own growling stomach agreed.

When they passed the champagne pyramid, Daniel Lambert held out one of the glasses, and she stopped. Their eyes met, and Isabelle felt a warm shiver inside. "The dress is better suited to this occasion, madame."

It took a moment for Isabelle to realize what he was talking about. The first time she had gone out into the vineyards, the first time they'd met, she had been wearing this exact same dress. Completely inappropriate, she had to admit, looking back.

"I prefer to decide for myself when a day is to be celebrated," she said, sounding rather stilted. Her hand shook a little as she brought the champagne glass to her lips.

Henriette, who was still standing beside the pyramid, followed the small scene as it played out in front of her. She looked puzzled and, pushing between Daniel and Isabelle, said, "If you will allow me, there are some important people you should get to know."

Isabelle looked hungrily toward the opulent buffet, but said, "I'd like that," and gave Leon, who was eyeing the buffet ravenously, a jab with her elbow.

"May I introduce Edgar Ruinart? This is Leon Feininger, the famous cyclist from Germany!"

Ruinart, who belonged to one of the most successful champagne houses of all time, shook hands politely with Leon, but did not seem particularly interested.

"And this is Henri Marie Lanson, the son of Victor-Marie. Since he took over at the renowned cellars in Reims, the fame of the Lanson name has grown around the world."

"You do flatter us, dear Henriette," said the handsome young man, and he kissed her hand with a smile.

"Henri, I'd like you to meet an extraordinary guest, Leon Feininger, an outstandingly successful racing cyclist. Leon's triumphs are numerous:

he has crossed the Alps on a bicycle, and last year, he took part in a twenty-four-hour track race—twenty-four hours on a bicycle."

Isabelle was decidedly annoyed. What was Madame Trubert up to, completely ignoring her like this?

"You ride a bicycle? How fascinating," Henri Marie Lanson promptly said, turning directly to Leon. "My daughter would like such a vehicle for herself. Perhaps, at your convenience, I might ask your expert advice?"

"Of course! Although I must say my experience with women's bicycles is rather limited," Leon replied. All four of them laughed; then Henriette steered them onward.

Henriette next introduced them to Louis-Victor and Léon Olry-Roederer, then the widow Clicquot's business manager, and then Charles-Eugène Heidsieck. There could hardly be any more important men in the Champagne region, Henriette told them over and over. And every time, she introduced "the famous cyclist from Germany." And while Leon innocently, cheerfully recited anecdotes from his cycling exploits, Isabelle tried in vain several times to steer the conversation around to the Feininger estate. Every time, Henriette interrupted her attempts.

After half an hour, Isabelle was on the verge of exploding. She had realized what the *vigneronne* was up to: from that evening on, no one would see the Feiningers as vintners at all. They would be no more than the "cyclist and his wife."

When Henriette wanted to introduce them to Raymond Dupont, Isabelle said, in the iciest voice she could muster, "We've already met."

Raymond smiled. "Madame Feininger managed to impress me immensely at her very first champagne tasting. She has a fine nose and a wonderful sense of the nature of a champagne. Unless my estimation is completely mistaken, we are looking at a future *grande dame de Champagne*."

"With all due respect to your estimation, my dear Raymond, it seems a little . . . bold," said the hostess, her mouth slightly pinched. "I, too, am happy to find someone who can detect a *soupçon* of lemon or a hint of pear in a glass. But to conclude a level of . . . acumen from that is bordering on the reckless." She gave Isabelle a long, almost sympathetic look.

Oh, that was . . . Isabelle opened her mouth, but then she couldn't think of anything to say in her own defense.

Smiling radiantly, Henriette turned to Leon again. "But you have proved your talent hundreds of times! It's men like you whom I really admire. But to think that your talent is being wasted now . . ." She shook her head and sighed theatrically.

"But it isn't. What makes you think that?" said Leon, happy that the conversation had come back to him.

"From my own experience, I can tell you that a champagne estate eats you up hide, hair, and all. One is a slave to the vines, year in, year out. I fear that you will find little time for riding a bicycle in the future, so"—she placed one hand on Leon's right arm and drew him away with her, without so much as another glance at Isabelle—"I have some good advice for you, young man."

Isabelle could only stand and stare as Henriette walked off with her husband. Never in her life had she been so outraged.

Raymond Dupont cleared his throat. "May I get you another glass of champagne?"

Isabelle swallowed her anger and, with feigned coyness, she said, "I would love one. I've heard there are some Americans here, too? Do you happen to be acquainted with them?"

Raymond was taken aback for a moment. Then he raised his eyebrows knowingly. "Yes, in fact. Quite a number have come over from the American Midwest. Just one moment, madame, and I'll fetch us our drinks."

And then I'll do the work myself! Isabelle thought. She saw Raymond go to Daniel Lambert, who poured two fresh glasses of champagne. A moment later, he gallantly handed her one of the glasses.

"To your health, Madame Feininger. May your every undertaking find success! Oh, I can see Greg Watson from Dayton over there, and next to him is Mr. Greenwater from Knoxville. Let's go over. Both of them were well acquainted with Jacques Feininger, by the way." Then he smiled and winked at her. "Would it be all right if I left you alone with them?"

"Feininger?" Greg Watson, his face red from the alcohol and good food, looked puzzled.

"Yes. You bought champagne from my husband's uncle, Jacques Feininger, for years. You were a very good customer of his," said Isabelle.

"Now I remember! Feininger!" the American cried, and his face lit up. "Good champagne, very sweet."

Mr. Greenwater, the hotel owner from Knoxville, nodded in agreement.

Well, that wasn't difficult at all, Isabelle thought to herself. "Very good champagne," she confirmed eagerly. "And we've got a cellar full of it. I could come up with a very good price for you! You could go home with a whole shipload."

"What a lovely idea! But . . ." Greg Watson's face clouded over again as quickly as it had brightened. "I would like very much to talk to you about that, young lady," he said. He motioned to Isabelle to come closer, and Greenwater also took a step closer. "But we have a contract with the Truberts for another three years."

If Isabelle had thought that the day could not get any worse, she was wrong. Although their hosts had ordered coaches for the guests, Leon insisted on walking home. At first, Isabelle thought he was joking. In her good shoes? But when he said, "We can talk in peace," she realized that he was serious.

It wasn't long before Isabelle realized that the fresh air and exercise were doing her good. So many impressions, so much to consider, so much that frightened her—particularly the restrictive contracts that Henriette had signed with the Americans. Another hope dashed.

They walked hand in hand, though Leon, despite his suggestion that they would have a chance to talk, was silent.

The road was lit especially for the evening by many torches. Off to their left, Hautvillers clung to the hillside, smoke rising from an occasional chimney. The night was cloudless, and cloudless nights were still cold. To their right, vineyards covered the gently rolling hills.

"It's beautiful here," she murmured, nestling closer to Leon as they walked. "I don't ever want to leave. Even the idea that we could lose all this nearly kills me." As she spoke, she felt Leon stiffen almost imperceptibly and pull away a little.

"What's the matter?" she asked, and a sudden foreboding overcame her.

"Madame Trubert made me an offer."

Isabelle swallowed. She'd suspected as much. No, she had *known* it, at precisely the moment the *vigneronne* had snatched her husband away.

"Henriette said that I could sell the place to her anytime I wanted. She'd pay a good price, and we'd be rid of this albatross forever. Let's face it—for my cycling, that's what it really comes down to."

Isabelle felt the earth disappearing beneath her feet. "What are you saying? That 'albatross' is your . . . your uncle's legacy!" She'd been on the verge of saying "your father's legacy." But she remembered how unpleasantly Leon had reacted when, shortly after they had moved in, she had pointed out the astounding similarity between him and Jacques as he appeared in the oil painting.

"Jacques chose *you* explicitly to take over the estate. He entrusted all of this to you." She pointed in the direction of their house, which they were quickly approaching. "You can't seriously be thinking about selling it!" Panic was rising inside her. This was their home, now, the home they had not found anywhere else. And they had only just arrived.

"Why not? Think about it," said Leon casually. "If we sell, we'll have enough money to last us the rest of our lives. We can do whatever we want. We could move to Reims; I know how much you loved the town. You could shop in the pretty shops there every day and get whatever you wanted. And I could finally devote myself to cycling and nothing else."

"I'm supposed to lead the life of a rich, bored housewife in Reims? Carrying on empty conversations and fighting with other women about the best hairdresser, the best hatmaker? Leon, that isn't my world!" Isabelle cried in despair. Dear God, let this be a horrible dream! Let me wake up!

"I could finally buy some new equipment and make even better times on my rides! I'd finally have some goals again that would be worth pursuing." Isabelle could hear that his daydreams were already far advanced. "I've certainly had more than enough training by riding around trying to drum up business over the last few weeks."

Isabelle felt dizzy with fear. "But we already have goals, splendid goals! We want to get the estate back on its feet, together. The two of us, doesn't that mean anything?"

"The estate, the estate." Leon waved off the word like a mosquito. "I think we simply bit off more than we could chew. Look around—nothing but problems! If you ask me, we've been deceiving ourselves. This whole adventure was doomed to fail from the start."

"Leon, that's not true," she said in disbelief. "Admittedly, our position right now isn't ideal. But a few weeks ago, we were poking around in a fog, and now we at least know how the place works. Leon, sweetheart, let's at least give this a good try! I want to lead our winery to success and make Feininger one of the biggest names in the Champagne region in a few years. Leon, please," she begged. Suddenly, every step she took was one too many. Drained, she stopped walking.

They had reached the base of the valley that separated their house from the Trubert estate and the last of the torches. From where Isabelle stood, their house was only recognizable as a black form besieged by darkness, and the way in front of them was steep and uneven, with many places one could stumble. Instead of giving her his support, as he had been, Leon was standing two paces away.

"You should listen to yourself. Champagne, day in, day out! In Berlin, you were always annoyed that all your father ever thought about was his business, but now you're no better! Don't I count anymore? I'm not interested in standing in front of everyone as the failure. I want to focus on things I understand."

Isabelle took a step back, as if someone had hit her.

Leon continued bitterly. "The last few weeks, you haven't noticed even once how much I detest all of this! Riding around only to all but beg potential customers for their business, then coming home to your disapproval when I haven't been able to sell anything again. And then you tell me that your oh-so-brilliant expert in Reims thinks our champagne is unsellable. Isn't it clear to you yet that this is all one big nightmare? It was naïve of us to think we could make a success of this place. I'm a cyclist; that's where my talent has always been, not in making wine. Henriette opened my eyes for me."

"Henriette, Henriette!" Isabelle screamed. "I hate that name, and I despise that woman! She's tipped you over like a turtle. She's spinning you around with her oily words." She began to sob. "You can't just let that witch and her garish makeup twist you like this, Leon, please." She gestured toward the rows of dark vines, where, at the end of every third row, there was a rosebush. "Do you really want to leave Hautvillers without seeing the roses in bloom?"

"The roses—as if you gave a damn about them in Berlin. Don't be pathetic," Leon snarled. "If you think you can get to me by crying, think again. If I've given in to anyone, it's to you. I've been bossed around by you far too long. I can't stand it anymore."

Isabelle collapsed. Through her tears, the vineyards that had just now been so lovely seemed to be crashing over her like a wave.

"But—"

Leon turned away. "Enough objections! *I* inherited the estate, and I'm the one who gets to say what becomes of it. I've made my decision, and nothing you say will change it."

Chapter Sixteen

Resentment and discord entered the once-peaceful house. Isabelle cried and begged, but Leon ignored her. All he could see was the million francs he would get from selling the estate. Without discussing it with Isabelle, he arranged an appointment with Henriette Trubert for the end of April. At the same time, he sent off his registration forms for the biggest races of the coming cycling season.

When Isabelle found out, she ran blindly out of the house, out into the vineyards, looking for somewhere to cry out her pain undisturbed. She had not gone a hundred yards when she ran into the arms of Micheline Guenin.

"Madame Feininger, my goodness, what's happened? Tears on such a beautiful day?"

Isabelle turned away. She wanted to be alone.

"Let's sit a moment. The ground is lovely and warm, and I think a little break to catch our breath will do both of us good, won't it?"

Isabelle had no strength left, and the constant quarrelling was taking its toll. She sank onto the grass beside Micheline. "Damn, damn!" Furious and miserable, she beat at the ground with her fists. She really did not want to talk, but before she knew it, everything came out.

Micheline listened in silence. When Isabelle was finished, she said, "But none of that is reason to despair and certainly not reason to consider selling!"

Isabelle snorted. "Tell my husband that. All he can think about is riding his bicycle. If it were up to him, he'd take off tomorrow and join the cycling circus. He's always going through the programs put out by the big organizers or reading the cycle catalogs! Now he's signed up for a twenty-four-hour track race in Paris. After that comes a one-day race from Paris to Roubaix, then the 750-mile Paris–Brest–Paris race. He's lost all interest in the estate."

"Then let him go," Micheline Guenin replied. "Pardon me for saying this, but he hasn't been a very big help so far, now has he? You can run the winery alone just as well."

"I'm supposed to run the winery? I know the top of a grapevine from the bottom, but that's about all." For a moment, Isabelle thought she must have misheard. She let out a shrill laugh.

"Now don't go looking so horrified," said Micheline, laughing. "You wouldn't be the first woman to set out on that particular adventure. The women of the Champagne region have always been an independent lot, and their men have suffered for it often enough. Just think of famous *vigneronnes* like Louise Pommery or Barbe Nicole Clicquot. Both would be among the most successful winemakers in the world. Or just look at my sister-in-law and me. We do quite well for ourselves, thank you very much. Unfortunately, you can also point a finger at Henriette Trubert, the snake! Say what you will about her—when it comes to business, she can hold her own against any man."

Isabelle sighed. "That's an impressive list, dear Micheline," she said. "Except that all your successful women—every one—were born and bred in Champagne. They were born into the world of wine, so to speak. I know practically nothing about it."

"But that isn't true, child," said Micheline gently. "Claude has been very impressed by the way that you have found your feet in the daily business of the estate so quickly. You've made a good start."

"Knowing when the chicken stall has to be mucked out or when the horses need new shoes is one thing. But it's a far cry from working the vineyards, let alone overseeing the making of the champagne. And I don't get much help from Gustave Grosse, either," said Isabelle. Micheline had sown a seed of hope in her, but she could already feel it withering again.

"A person can learn anything. If you need any advice or any help, I'll be there. Claude, too. He knows a lot more about growing grapes then he lets on."

Isabelle raised eyebrows. "Really?"

Micheline nodded. "Up to now, he's just chosen not to get mixed up in Gustave Grosse's work. Cellar masters generally are a little . . . capricious. They don't see themselves as workers but as artists. And few artists are happy to have someone else tell them how to do what they do. Blending the various types of grapes, mixing wine from different years—it's like a painter dipping into the palette and coming up with new, daring—or perhaps less daring, less successful—combinations of colors. A good champagne is like a painting that calls forth visions and makes you dream."

"Then *our* 'artist' paints with a very wide brush, and the only vision he has is a drunken stupor." Isabelle narrowed her eyes and looked at her neighbor. "But you're right. Grosse isn't the only cellar master in Champagne. I could look around for someone more capable, someone who can make modern, dry champagnes." Even as she spoke, the withered seed inside her began to swell again. "Who makes the champagne for you?"

"Me," said Micheline. One simple word, but spoken with pride.

Isabelle looked at the woman with admiration. They had become almost old friends, but she still knew very little about the Guenin estate.

"Let's get back to your problem," Micheline said firmly. "Have a little faith in yourself! You will be surprised what you can do if you only try. Or"—she frowned—"do they still tell you German women that the only way to survive as the weaker sex is at the side of a man? In case you hadn't noticed, my dear, the wind changed a long time ago!"

Isabelle's despondency abruptly transformed into a broad grin. "A fresh wind. My friends and I, in Berlin . . . we wanted that so much. Clara always said we needed a turn-of-the-century wind, one that would sweep away all the dusty ideas about us as the weaker sex!" She nodded, remembering the things that they had talked about when they were still girls. "We longed for a new age in which women were no longer second-class people but could live up to their strengths, like men. An age in which women could realize their own dreams."

"But hasn't this turn-of-the-century wind already been blowing for a long time, all over the world?" Micheline asked. Her voice was doting, as if she were speaking to a child who was slow to understand.

"If you look at me, then certainly not," Isabelle replied. Her anger at her own fearful hesitation was rising. "I came here with such great dreams, and what has become of them? I wanted to prove to the whole world what I was capable of. But secretly, I was relying on Leon taking charge as the man of the house." She looked at Micheline sadly. "But I'm afraid I've only come to understand that too late. I wanted so much to defy Henriette Trubert! It serves me right, having to pay for it now."

"Stop blathering. It's never too late to take the reins," Micheline replied gruffly. "If you really wanted them, you'd have half a dozen customers by tomorrow."

They chose a bar at the edge of the market square. The maître d' had arranged a few small round tables alfresco, and they sat down at one of them. Leon ordered them a *coupe de champagne* and water.

Isabelle smiled wistfully. "Do you remember how, after we visited the notary in Pirmasens, we drank tea because drinking champagne during the day seemed strange?"

"The rules are different here. Everywhere else, champagne is a luxury, but here it's as normal as a glass of water," Leon replied, and he smiled, too.

Isabelle's heart was beating hard. Was this the moment she'd been waiting for? Slowly, she said, "Speaking of different rules, what would you say if we held on to the estate, but you were able to concentrate one hundred percent on your cycling?"

"Having my cake and eating it too—how would that work?" Leon's voice carried mockery and doubt.

"Well, I would take care of the champagne side—all of it—and you'd be free to ride," she replied, trying to sound as confident as possible.

"*You* would take care of the winery? Don't make me laugh! What do you know about winemaking?"

"What I don't know, I can learn. Jacques's library is full of books about viticulture. Do you have so little confidence in me? You sound like my father; he always used to put me down, just like that," said Isabelle, raising her voice. The waiter, gathering cutlery at the next table, looked toward them curiously.

Leon waved it off. "You're going down the same old road. Don't! You'd have to admit that you don't have the first clue about winemaking. It's hard work, dawn to dusk, all year—how do you expect to manage that as a woman? In the end, it will be me racing during the day and breaking my back in the vineyards at night. No, thank you! Apart from that, how am I supposed to afford a new bicycle? I might as well not even sign up for the big races without a decent machine. Sorry, my dear, but your idea doesn't hold water." He picked up his glass and emptied it in a single swig.

For a moment, Isabelle sat in silence and looked at him while she sorted out her arguments anew. She had known from the start that it wouldn't be easy.

Leon went on. "Take my word for it, selling is the right decision! When I was going through Jacques's papers earlier, I discovered that the lands belonging to the Feininger estate are far more extensive than I'd thought. When we sell, we'll be stinking rich." He laughed the laugh of a satisfied man.

Isabelle took another deep breath. "If I sell the rest of my jewelry, you'll have enough to buy not only one but *two* new bicycles. We wouldn't be *stinking* rich, I admit, but we'd get by for the next few months, maybe even longer. And with a little luck, you'll be back up on the winner's podium and bringing in some decent prize money from time to time."

"That's a given! But that has nothing to do with luck; I'm in top shape," Leon said. "So we'd have the equipment question answered, that's one thing, but what would we live on, and how would we pay our bills?"

Isabelle, who had barely dared to dream that Leon would go this far with her, rejoiced inwardly.

"What would you say if, to start with, we didn't produce any champagne at all and sold the entire harvest instead? According to Micheline Guenin, the big vintners are eager to buy as many grapes as they possibly can, and at a premium price. Wouldn't that be the easiest way to pull a profit out of this year's crop?"

"Sell the grapes?" Leon looked at her aghast.

Isabelle nodded briskly. "And cover our costs and keep ourselves alive. I'm positive that we would come out of the deal well."

Leon said nothing.

Isabelle wrung her hands until they hurt. "Please give me this chance, this one year. After the harvest in the fall, we'll see where we stand. If my idea hasn't paid off, we can sell." Her pulse was racing as she held out her right hand to Leon, and after a moment of hesitation, he shook it to seal the deal.

"All right. But no complaining. The moment I get the feeling that you're in over your head, that's it. I know for sure that if Henriette Trubert can't buy the estate now, she's willing to wait."

Isabelle could hardly believe what she was hearing. She had her chance, and she would use it!

The next day, she drove into Reims again, this time with Leon at her side. Apart from a few pieces she couldn't bear to part with, Isabelle had all her jewelry with her. This time, however, when she put it on the jeweler's counter, she did so with a lighter heart. This time, she was buying herself freedom and a future.

For Isabelle, everything happened quickly. The first thing she did was summon Claude Bertrand and Gustave Grosse. She paid them the salary they were due, then said, "I have a number of changes to tell you about. The cycle racing season has begun, and my husband has decided to dedicate himself completely to his sport. You know that he is one of Europe's most successful cyclists. This means that, from now on, *I* am in charge of the estate. It is true that I don't know much about wine-growing"—she smiled, or perhaps frowned, self-mockingly—"but I am willing to learn! And it would make me very happy to know that I could count on your support. Between us, I know we can get this place under control, right?" She smiled expectantly at her two employees.

Gustave's expression was one of irascible suspicion, but Claude beamed broadly.

"I'm very happy to hear that, madame! If there's ever anything you need to know, come to me. I'll help wherever I can."

Outfitted with the most modern machine he could buy, Leon plunged heart and soul into the European racing scene. Because a cyclist had to be part of a team, he now rode for a cycling club in Charleville, a city northeast of Reims. As fruitless as his long tours had been in search of customers, they had paid off with his conditioning: physically, he had never been fitter, and it wasn't long before he was standing on the top step of the podium. After that victory, Leon popped some corks at home, and Isabelle and he celebrated his success. His self-confidence was much stronger, and now that he was doing what he really wanted to, the word "sales" never crossed his lips.

Isabelle, too, was over the moon. If she were thrifty, Leon's winnings would see them through the summer, and they could count on new earnings in autumn when the grape harvest was sold. Their fears of being able to earn a livelihood were not gone, but she could certainly sleep better than before, although, she had to admit, that was also due in part to working hard all day.

Each morning she rustled up Gustave Grosse and had him report on what he planned to accomplish that day. She read a book in Jacques's library on a vintner's typical year, and afterward she knew, more or less, what was coming in the weeks and months ahead. If whatever Grosse claimed to be doing disagreed with the program in Jacques's book, he had to come up with good reasons why before Isabelle would be appeased. She constantly asked him to explain this or show her that. Within a few weeks, she knew how best to tie young shoots to the trellises and could handle pruning shears reasonably well. She stood at Grosse's side when he sprayed the vines with a vile concoction to protect them from mildew, and though by evening the foul-smelling spray gave her an excruciating headache, she was up at dawn the next day.

Whenever the cellar master saw his new employer coming his way, he groaned loud enough for Isabelle to hear. It made no difference. If there was one thing Gustave Grosse had to accept, it was that his easy life was over.

She had daily conferences with Claude as well. Now that they had Leon's winnings and the money from selling her jewelry, all the patchwork solutions came to an end. Together, they fixed the livestock fences and nailed the loose boards on the sheep stall firmly back into place.

Claude ordered hay and straw, and when the farmer drove up with his fully laden wagon, Isabelle climbed up to help with the unloading. Two hours later, happy and satisfied, she stepped back and surveyed the full hayshed now stacked with bales for the horses, chickens, and sheep, and bravely ignored the red scratches and scrapes that the bales had left on her naked arms.

For the peacocks, Isabelle bought some mixed-grain feed, which Claude had told her would bring a new shine to their feathers. A few days later, Claude announced that the peahen was sitting on a clutch of eggs and that they could expect chicks in a few weeks.

Isabelle smiled. Peachicks, offspring of those magnificent birds . . . could there be a better sign that good times had arrived?

The first young shoots soon began to appear, and toward the end of April, the vines were covered in new foliage. If the day was particularly sunny and there had been a little rain the evening before, the canes grew inches by sundown. They climbed the trellises, clinging on strongly, twisting around every stick and every piece of wire. *Like hands the vines use to hold on*, thought Isabelle of the canes as she walked among the rows of vines early one rainy morning.

As she often did, she saw Daniel Lambert off in the distance, moving through the Trubert vineyards. Like her, he was out working every single day, whatever the weather, and there he was again on that rainy morning. In Berlin, Isabelle had hated the rain. Here in Champagne, she began to love it: rain meant growth and a rich harvest. And a rich harvest meant the certainty of money.

With this in mind, Isabelle went in search of her cellar master. He wasn't down in the cellars, so he had to be somewhere out among the vines. She searched first one vineyard, then the next, but found no sign of Grosse anywhere. Finally, she discovered him in one of the domed huts that the workers in the fields used for shelter during thunder-storms. He was wrapped up in a blanket, taking a nap!

"On your feet this instant!" she shouted, jabbing Grosse with the point of her shoe.

Grosse stood up guiltily. "Just a little break, madame."

"How can you even think of taking a break when so much around here is in such a sorry state? If I catch you napping one more time dur-ing the day, you'll be searching for a new job. Now follow me, and be quick about it!" Outside, she spread her arms wide, encompassing a large area in front of them. "Is this a vineyard or a wasteland? The weeds are growing just as fast as the vines, and they're robbing the vines of the nutrients in the soil. We have to start getting rid of them urgently. I need well-fed vines; it's the only way to produce good, juicy grapes!"

"But madame!" Grosse cried in horror. "I've got my hands full with the *effeuillage*! And I still have to finish spraying the vines for mildew. Though you have the best intentions, madame, you can't simply come along and turn everything upside down like this."

Effeuillage? She had read in Jacques's library about how unhealthy weeds were for the grapevines, but *effeuillage* was new to her. She decided to ignore his objections.

"Can't I? We start tomorrow, so start planning now. I'm going to ride down into the village to see if I can find some young men to help us. I'm sure I can come up with at least a few who'd like to earn some extra francs."

"How nice of you to drop by, my dear Madame Feininger!" said Micheline Guenin when she saw Isabelle standing at the top of the cellar steps. "Wait a moment, I'll come up. I wanted to talk to you anyway."

Micheline took off her heavy rubber apron and nimbly climbed the steps. "I was just about to come over to see you. In mid-May, after *les saints de glace*, there's going to be a festival in the village square. Claude invited me to go with him, and I wanted to ask if you'd put my hair up again, like you did before?"

Les saints de glace? Probably one of the Christian holidays here in Champagne, thought Isabelle.

"I've got a comb with a glittering butterfly on it. It will suit you perfectly," she said with a smile. Micheline's eyes lit up with anticipation. Or was it the magic of love that made them sparkle like that?

"Will you come to the festival, too?" asked Micheline. "The spring festival is always nice. Everyone's glad to have the winter behind them. We pick flowers and decorate the tables and benches. The parish priest delivers a lovely sermon, and we pray together for a good year for the grapes."

"I don't know. Leon will be racing in Milan then, so I would have to come by myself."

"But you've got Claude and me!" Micheline exclaimed. "Marie's coming, and Carla and Ignaz will be there—it's really a whole group of us."

"I'll think about it," said Isabelle vaguely. Since taking over the running of the estate, she was so tired in the evenings that she collapsed onto bed before dark and fell asleep immediately. She was too exhausted even to miss the nights of lovemaking with Leon.

"Micheline, could you tell me what *effeuillage* means?" she asked.

"It means getting rid of a few leaves around the grapes to let more light and sunshine through, so the grapes can develop better. Why are you asking about that now, though? That's something we do at the start of September."

"Hm. My favorite cellar master was trying to tell me he had his hands full right now with the *effeuillage*."

Her neighbor laughed out loud. "That old swindler from the Aube, he knows every trick in the book!"

"So do I," Isabelle replied, and she marched off to read Grosse the riot act.

Micheline Guenin watched her go, beaming broadly.

"Who would have thought?" said her sister-in-law Marie, who had just come up from the wine cellar and caught the end of their conversation. "Who would have thought our little city girl could put her foot down?"

Micheline thought that Marie almost sounded kind.

It was a few days after her meeting with Micheline that Isabelle, out on her daily rounds, discovered the first white-green flowers, low on a vine. They were only the most meager and insignificant of panicles, nothing to compare with the magnificent blooms of other plants, but Isabelle cried out so rapturously that Gustave Grosse, busy tying up vines a short distance away, looked over in astonishment. The vines bloomed every year—how anyone could be so happy about it must have been completely beyond him.

What the flowers lacked in beauty they made up for in scent, for their perfume was incredibly intense. It lay over the vineyards like a blanket of honey and passion fruit, beguiling anyone who came by. At the same time, it seemed to Isabelle, the perfume made the people strange in a whimsical kind of way. If she ran into any of her neighbors, it might happen that, instead of returning her greeting, they just stared away, pondering, into the distance. They did not see others around them but were utterly focused on the vines. They spent more time gazing up at the sky, too, and when Isabelle dared joke about it, all she got in return was a surly look.

"Actually, it has nothing to do with the smell of the flowers," Claude Bertrand laughed, when Isabelle asked him about this strange behavior. The peahen was brooding, and Claude Bertrand was in the middle of adding more straw to the wooden shed where she had built her nest.

"In the flowering stage, one bad frost can destroy the entire harvest. This is a fact, and it makes the *Champenois* nervous; they start seeing every cloud as an omen of bad weather. What we all want is a little bit of wind, because it helps pollinate the flowers."

"The wind?" Isabelle frowned. "I thought the bees took care of that."

"No, grapevines pollinate each other. A little wind carries the pollen from one plant to the next. It's ideal for the pollination to take place completely within a few days. If it's spread out over weeks, which can happen if the weather is changeable, the grapes grow at different speeds—that, in turn, leads to a poor harvest." The overseer stopped what he was doing and touched Isabelle lightly on her arm. "But don't worry. By the time we've got *les saints de glace* behind us, people go back to normal."

"*Les* . . . what? Micheline said the same thing a few days ago when she talked about the upcoming spring festival," Isabelle said. "I'm sorry, my French vocabulary has grown immeasurably in the last few weeks, but I still struggle with all the technical terms."

"Wait, I'll come up with the German word in a moment." Claude closed his eyes and started waving one hand in the air so vigorously that his dog began to yap, waiting for a stick to be thrown. "It's the . . . *Eisheiligen!* The Ice Saints. Some call it the blackthorn winter. Saint Mamertus, Saint Pancras, Saint Servatius."

Isabelle was more perplexed than ever. Ice Saints? She'd never heard of Ice Saints in Berlin.

"It's the name they use for the days in the middle of May, when the last nighttime frosts can happen. I can still remember the year 1891 very clearly. It was the eleventh of May, St. Mamertus's day, and the vines were just coming into bloom when the frost came. The next morning"—he lifted one hand and let it drop, shaking his head sadly—"the buds of the flowers were frozen, the new leaves withered and browned. Grown men howled like forgotten dogs. And they howled again in the fall, because the baskets were empty." Describing that day, Claude had grown louder than usual, and the peahen broke out in an excited hissing and beating of wings. Claude had to soothe the poor bird.

From that moment on, Isabelle also began watching the clouds and the wind. And when she opened the windows early in the morning, she held one hand outside for a long moment to see how frosty it might be. What if a night frost came this year, her very first year, and damaged the vines? It would mean the end of her plan to sell the harvest. She'd be back where she started, and Leon would push again to sell the estate.

Chapter Seventeen

To Isabelle's relief—and that of all the other growers—the night frosts of the blackthorn winter stayed away that year. The vines thrived. Now nothing stood in the way of the spring festival in the market square and the church service to give thanks.

It was a bright and sunny morning, pleasantly warm. *The best riding weather*, Leon thought as he buckled his pack expertly on to his bicycle. A change of clothes, soap, his razor, his papers, and the copy of the registration form—everything he would need. Now, where had he put the note with his itinerary?

"Do you have to go so soon?" he heard Isabelle's voice behind him. "You've only been back four days. It would be nice to go to the spring festival together."

Leon sighed. Hadn't they had this discussion the previous evening?

"You know how important Milan is for my reputation as a cyclist." While he spoke, he patted down every pocket on his jacket and trousers for his itinerary.

"In the last few weeks, you've won everything there is to win! What else is there? Wouldn't you be better off giving your body a rest?"

Found it! With the note in hand, Leon could breathe more easily. "The track race in Milan is a nice change from the long-distance races I know so well. If anyone needs a rest, it's you. Frankly, you're looking a little worn out." When he saw Isabelle's expression, he immediately regretted his words. "Why don't you come with me? You'd like Milan. We could stay for a couple of days after the race and look around the city," he said, though he knew full well that his wife would never take him up on the notion.

Isabelle promptly said, "And who'd look after the estate? Besides . . ." She bit her lip.

"What?" he asked, with a touch of impatience, and he swung his leg over the saddle of his bicycle. He had realized long ago that it was best to cut off such discussions before they got started. Isabelle saw things her way, and he saw them his way—only rarely did they find any common ground. He took a final glance at the route he had to follow, memorizing the towns along the way. He would ride from Épernay to Verdun, then on to Metz and from there along good roads to Karlsruhe. To save travel expenses and because he wanted to use the stretch for training, he was only planning to take a train to Milan once he reached Karlsruhe.

"Nothing. It's nothing," said Isabelle.

Well, then. Leon put on his most disarming smile. "Cross your fingers for me, darling. If I win this race, I'm certain to be the season champion!"

Champagne is the perfect training ground, Leon thought happily as he sped along the road to Épernay. The weather was dry, not too warm or too cold. Unless something unusual happened, he would be on the winner's podium again in Milan! His name would be known around the world, like a Moët champagne or a Veuve Clicquot Ponsardin. There was more than one way to get famous; unfortunately, Isabelle did not understand that.

One more hill, then the steep descent into Épernay. He could reach thirty-five miles an hour on that downhill, maybe faster! Looking forward to the descent, Leon pumped harder up the hill. At the top, he stopped for a moment. Without dismounting, he took a final long look over the expanse of the Champagne region. Below him lay Épernay, and behind him, farther north, was Reims—even at that distance, he could make out the towers of the cathedral.

Leon crouched low over the handlebars as he rolled away and began to pick up speed. The headwind became stronger, and he had to squint against the tiny gnats that flew into his face. One or two had found their way into his nose, which tickled uncomfortably. He blew out to clear his nostrils, then ducked even lower and gave himself over to the rush of the high-speed descent.

He had almost reached the bottom of the valley when two large gray mongrel dogs appeared on the right. They were playing and were so deep in their game that they didn't seem to see Leon. He felt hot and cold at the same time. He had a split second to assess the situation: He had to swerve, but which way? Where could he go? On the right was the stone fence the dogs had escaped through, but if he hit one of the pillars . . . And on the left was a precipitous embankment down to a meadow. A tumble there would probably be the lesser of two evils. His thought lasted a heartbeat, then he made his decision: left!

It was not the first time that he'd found himself in a tricky situation while riding. He gripped the handlebars firmly, keeping his eyes focused on the line he'd chosen. Just before he reached the dogs, he shouted, "Take off! Get away!" Maybe they would scamper and he could stay on the road? That would be the best solution of all.

Startled, the dogs stopped and turned. The larger one leaped out of the way in the direction of the fence. The smaller one was not as smart, and it jumped directly into the path of Leon's bicycle. The sound of the collision between bicycle and dog was dull and metallic; the dog squealed and howled, and Leon was thrown over the handlebars toward the embankment. He let go at the moment of impact and tried to roll over one shoulder. But at the same time, in the grass at the side of the road, he saw the pile of cobblestones, leftovers from road construction. Pale-gray granite, angular and rough, hacked from raw rock. *But this part of the road isn't even paved*, he thought, and it was the last thought he had before everything around him went black.

***

Isabelle's depressed mood did not last long. She would naturally have preferred to have her husband with her, though, especially now that she—well, she had become used to tackling things alone, but going to a festival unaccompanied was certainly something new.

She shut the door of the house and waved to Claude, who was just leading the horses in from the meadow and into the stable; he and Micheline would follow along later.

As doubtful as she had been about the village festival at the start, she was now looking forward to it. After weeks of hard work, her back was sore and her hands were callused from the hoe she had used to hack out weeds. *But she who works hard should also be allowed to enjoy herself,* she thought. When she told Micheline that she would go to the festival, she discovered that everybody in the village was helping with preparations. Some of the men carted in ice to cool the drinks, some were setting up the tables and benches, and others were practicing for the concert in the village chapel. The women were also tending to varied tasks. Some women were in the kitchen at Le Grand Cerf, preparing the food that would accompany the pig, which had already been roasting for hours on a large spit on one side of the square. Others were in charge of decorations and setting the tables.

When Isabelle had offered to help, she was immediately commandeered by Carla, who was responsible for the floral decorations.

What might Leon have volunteered to do? Isabelle wondered as she walked toward the square. Suddenly, she was overcome by regret at his absence. At the festival or perhaps afterward, a perfect opportunity would certainly have presented itself to tell him the good news, something that she didn't want to tell him just by the by. But no, he was hell-bent on his cycling!

Now don't go and spoil your good mood, Isabelle reprimanded herself.

She saw Carla Chapron sitting at a long table with several other women, so she headed toward them. Beside the table, a handcart was piled high with grapevines, and next to that a small wagon was filled with bundles of peonies and daisies. The women eagerly plucked the flowers they needed to skillfully create the garlands and wreaths.

As Isabelle got closer, she realized that one of the young women at the table was Yvette, Henriette Trubert's daughter. Blanche Thevenin, the seamstress, sat beside her. Isabelle hoped that Henriette would not suddenly appear. The woman had reacted rather coldly when Leon had given her the news that they would not be selling the estate.

"Madame Feininger, come and sit with me!" Carla Chapron cried when she saw Isabelle. "We can use all the hands we can get."

One of the older women poured her a glass of rosé. "At least let the poor girl have something to drink; it makes the work go so much easier."

"I doubt it. I've never done anything like this. I'll probably be all thumbs!" With a laugh, Isabelle threw her hands in the air.

The old woman who had poured the wine grasped Isabelle's right hand and scrutinized it. A little embarrassed, Isabelle wanted to pull back her callused hand with its broken fingernails, but the old woman held on to it tightly and said, with admiration, "It looks to me like you can do quite a lot! With hands like that, you've no need to be ashamed of the things you *can't* do. Come, I'll show you how to tie a garland."

The women's conversation was lively and funny—a bit of gossip, a bit of scandal—and all of them enjoyed the work they shared, the art of which came to Isabelle with astonishing ease. The grape-leaf garlands, into which she weaved colorful flowers, grew slowly but steadily. After an hour, Micheline opened the first bottle of champagne. The women had just toasted each other when they saw Daniel Lambert appear in the square, not far from their table.

"What's Daniel doing here, I wonder? None of the other men are around just now," said Carla.

"Good that they're not. They'd just disturb our work," one of the older women added.

Yvette and the other young girl giggled.

"He might just be going to see his sister?" said Therese Jolivet, who owned the bakery.

"Ghislaine? But she's not even there," Carla replied. "I heard she'd gone away on a trip somewhere."

Isabelle looked over toward Le Grand Cerf; from its open windows came the sound of women laughing and the clattering of pots. "Then who's in the kitchen?"

"Ghislaine's kitchen hands and a few extras," said Carla. "Someone has to prepare all the food."

"But where would Ghislaine have gone? And during the spring festival?" Therese asked. "Maybe Daniel knows more. Look, he's coming this way."

"Madame Feininger"—Daniel stopped in front of Isabelle, a grim expression on his face—"something terrible has happened. Your husband . . ."

***

All Leon could hear was the beating of his own heart. The silence made him afraid. As did the darkness. He couldn't see anything. But he smelled something pungent, sharp. Floor cleaner, like the kind his mother used. Strong enough to get off whatever muck clung to them from the farm. The Palatinate . . . but he wasn't in the Palatinate, was he? Where was he? His head ached so hellishly that he could barely string together a coherent thought.

He'd been cycling, that much he remembered. A road. Milan. He'd been on his way to Milan. But what had happened then?

He tried to open his eyes, but he couldn't. He felt as if he were inside a cocoon, unmoving, helpless. Unmoving? A new, terrifying thought sent a shiver through him. Was he paralyzed? Just the year before, that had happened to a fellow rider who took a bad fall. He tried to wriggle his toes. When he managed to do it, he felt such a sense of joy that tears came to his eyes. He sobbed aloud.

"Leon."

Isabelle! His wife was there, at his side. Relief flooded through him. He wanted to say her name, but his throat was so dry that it felt like every sound was being dragged over sandpaper. "I . . . sa . . ." Moving his lips instantly made his headache worse.

"Shh, don't speak, don't move. Everything will be all right."

He felt her hand stroking his left arm. Her touch was good—feeling it was good. He wanted to sit up, but the slightest movement sent a shrieking pain through him. He clenched his teeth to stop himself from screaming.

"What . . . happened?"

"You had an accident just before Épernay."

An accident. Two dogs. He remembered two dogs. And grass that wasn't grass, but cobblestones. He had hit one of them with his head.

"Where am I?" he croaked. He reached up with his right hand and touched his forehead cautiously, wanting to be rid of the pain. He ran his fingers over the tightly wound bandage; it covered his entire head and even came down over his eyes. That's why he couldn't see anything.

He tugged the bandage upward. The light that struck his eyes was bright and triggered another shooting pain in his head.

"You're in the hospital in Épernay. The doctors say that you were very lucky. Concussion. Some bad bruising on your chest and back and some grazing. It's a miracle you didn't break your neck. A few days of rest and you'll be your old self again, the doctor said a few minutes ago. Oh, Leon, I was scared to death!" Crying, Isabelle kissed him on his chest, arms, hands, fingers. She laughed and cried at the same time.

Leon closed his eyes again.

A miracle. He'd been given a miracle.

***

At some point, Isabelle's exhaustion caught up with her and she fell asleep. She jumped when she felt a hand shaking her shoulder.

Two young nurses were standing beside Leon's bed. While one of them changed Leon's bandages, the other said, "Madame, we're going to move your husband into the big ward. I'm sorry, but you have to leave."

Isabelle looked beseechingly at the nurse. "And if he wakes up and calls for me?"

The nurse shrugged.

Downcast, Isabelle stepped out of the room. In the corridor, she encountered the doctor with whom she had only spoken briefly.

"It is truly a miracle that it wasn't any worse," he said. "When your husband was brought in, he was covered in blood. The gash on his head and all the grazing on his body—he looked very bad. But when the nurses washed him clean, we saw that it wasn't as bad as we'd feared. Your husband had more than one guardian angel watching over him."

Still, it made Isabelle shudder to think what had happened. She didn't want to know everything in detail. She looked yearningly in the direction of the ward where the nurses were rolling Leon's bed.

The doctor spoke gently. "Go home, madame. Go home and try to get over the shock. If you don't want to drive home, there's a nice little pension just around the corner. You can't do anything for your husband here. We've given him something to help with the pain; he'll sleep soundly now for at least ten hours. Sleep is sometimes the best medicine. More than anything, he will need peace and quiet for the next few days."

Isabelle had almost reached the entrance when she heard someone weeping softly, the sound coming from a room on her left. *More like a lament,* she thought. It was a woman, and there was so much sorrow and loneliness in the sound that it almost broke Isabelle's heart. She hesitated for a moment, then walked on. She had worries of her own; someone else could console the crying woman.

But she stopped just outside at the entrance and turned back. If she didn't look in on the woman now, she would spend half the night reproaching herself.

Two gas lamps cast a dingy light over the large ward and exuded a sweet odor. Ten beds were lined up along the walls to the left and right of the door, but only three of them were occupied. The sound of weeping was coming from the last bed, beside the window. Cautiously, Isabelle approached the bed. She had no idea what she was supposed to do to console the woman. After the shock she herself had suffered, and from which she had not yet recovered, she really had no head for charitable acts. She hadn't been able to walk away, but when she reached the bed, she wished she had done just that. "*You?*"

Ghislaine's beautiful face was swollen, her eyes red with tears, her normally magnificent hair dull. When she saw Isabelle, she didn't turn away; Isabelle momentarily hoped that she would, because then she would have turned away and left. But instead, Ghislaine's tears only intensified.

"Mademoiselle Lambert, Ghislaine . . ." Isabelle said gently, fighting against the lump in her throat. *Don't you start crying too,* she commanded herself. *That won't help the woman at all.* But how could she help? If it had been Josephine, Clara, or even Micheline lying there, Isabelle would not have hesitated to throw her arms around her friend and rock her back and forth until the crying stopped. But with Ghislaine, such an embrace would have felt out of place; it would have suggested an intimacy they did not have. Instead, Isabelle pulled up a chair—the least she could do was give her a little company. Perhaps she would soon fall asleep, and then Isabelle could leave.

Ghislaine Lambert. Daniel's sister. That's why he had been in the hospital. That's why he had heard that Leon had been brought in, badly hurt.

The longer Isabelle sat there, the more she felt how tired and worn out she was. She moved her aching shoulders and concealed a yawn behind her hand. She thought of Leon, lying just a few doors away. Was he sleeping? She hoped his headaches would ease soon.

"The child . . ." Two words, whispered.

Isabelle started. For a moment, she had forgotten Ghislaine was there. Instinctively, she laid both hands on her own belly. "Which child?"

"I lost it. Early this morning. The doctor said that with work as hard as mine, it can happen." Ghislaine's eyes were bloodshot, and her arms lay on the rough, white bedcover like the limp limbs of a marionette.

Isabelle nodded, and as she did, she felt unspeakably stupid. Why did she nod? Was it because there were no words of solace that she could possibly say?

Ghislaine did not seem to notice. Instead, she whispered, "I finally had something from him that was only for me." Her voice was choked with tears.

"I'm so sorry," Isabelle said softly. So it was Alphonse Trubert's child. And Ghislaine had lost it.

Ghislaine looked at Isabelle with a strange expression, as if she only then recognized her.

Isabelle slid back and forth uncomfortably on the chair. "Can I do anything for you? Or . . . I should go."

Ghislaine closed her eyes, just as Leon had earlier. Relieved, Isabelle stood up. She turned to leave when she heard a soft voice from the bed. "Look after yourself, Isabelle. Yourself and the child, so that you don't go through what I am."

Chapter Eighteen

Isabelle heeded the doctor's advice and took a room in the pension. The next morning, Micheline and an extremely hungover-looking Claude appeared in the small breakfast room.

"How did you know I was here?" Isabelle exclaimed when she saw them.

"Where else were you supposed to be?" her neighbor said, and crushed Isabelle to her chest. She had brought along a bag of toiletries and fresh underwear.

They ate croissants and coffee together, and Isabelle reported what she knew of Leon's accident and condition. Everything was going to be all right. Micheline and Claude sighed with relief.

Together, they went to the hospital.

Leon was sleeping. Isabelle persuaded Claude and Micheline to go home again. The spring festival had carried on into the early hours of the morning, and a few hours of rest before the start of a new work week would do both of them good. It took some convincing, but they let Isabelle accompany them to the hospital entrance, where Daniel Lambert was just then approaching.

"Is your husband all right?" he asked immediately.

"He's asleep," Isabelle said. "He has a concussion, but he's doing well otherwise."

"When I saw him yesterday, covered with blood, I feared worse," said Daniel.

"Thank you for coming to tell me right away." Isabelle clasped his hands in hers. "If you hadn't, then who knows when I would have heard about the accident?" She waved in the direction of Ghislaine's room. "You've come to see your sister?"

Daniel looked at her in surprise, then nodded curtly.

"Ghislaine's in the hospital, too?" Micheline asked as soon as Daniel was gone. "Is she sick? What's wrong with her?"

Isabelle only shrugged.

Whenever Isabelle visited Leon, he was asleep. The doctors and nurses said this was normal, that a damaged body healed best when asleep. Hour after hour, she sat by his bed and held his hand. His bandages no longer covered his eyes, and she observed how his left eyelid twitched as he slept and how his cheeks flushed or paled.

Now and then, he woke up but only briefly. As soon as he realized she was there, a smile spread across his face, and he squeezed Isabelle's hand. There was so much intimacy when his eyes met hers that it sent a tremor through her. If it had been up to her, she would have sat by his bed around the clock. But the nurses kept sending her away. Couldn't she see that she was hampering their work?

A few days later, Claude and Micheline returned to the hospital to check on Leon and Isabelle. Micheline brought Isabelle a hunk of bread with cheese and a bowl of apple compote, which Isabelle ate hungrily. Apart from breakfast at the pension, she hadn't eaten anything for days. She was just finishing the last bit of food when the doctor came by.

"Madame Feininger, here again, I see. Or should I say, still here?" He shook his head. "If you don't go home voluntarily, then I'll have to ban you!"

"But I—"

"No buts, madame!" the doctor cut her off. "If you come back tomorrow or the day after, your husband may be able to leave the hospital. To do that, he will need fresh clothes. Or do you want to put him back in his torn cycling gear?"

"If I may say so, Madame Feininger," said Claude, "you do look very tired. Let us take you home. I'll be happy to drive you back again tomorrow."

It was good to be home again. She had not washed properly since Leon's accident, and now she warmed water and poured herself a hot bath. Lying in the enamel tub, she looked out the window into the green foliage of the pear tree and thought of everything that she wanted to prepare for Leon's homecoming.

She would need to have a delicious meal on the table, for one thing—something to give him back his strength. She wanted to change the bedding, too, so the bed would be fresh for him. An hour later, with wrinkled fingers and toes and feeling much more cheerful, Isabelle climbed out of the tub. She had a lot to do!

She returned to the hospital the following day. A squeal of joy escaped her when she saw that Leon was awake and dipping a croissant into a cup of milky coffee.

"If I'd known you had your appetite back, I'd have brought you some of the stew I've made for when you come home," she said gaily. Maybe she would finally be able to tell him the good news today?

They kissed long and affectionately, then Leon said, "I'm feeling much better. The headaches have finally stopped, at least, but I fear your stew will still have to wait awhile." He grimaced. "The doctors still want me to stay a day or two longer because of the concussion. They asked me to walk down the corridor this morning, and I felt dizzy; apparently I was swaying from side to side. I still need peace and quiet, they say, and medical supervision."

Peace and quiet? She couldn't help her disappointment.

"What's another day or two if it gets you back to your old self again?" she said as encouragingly as she could. "Perhaps I can speed up your recuperation with a little good news." She paused for a moment before she went on. "Claude will be shearing the sheep this morning, and he already has a buyer lined up for the wool. That will bring some money in."

Leon smiled. "Didn't I tell you it was a good idea to hang on to the sheep?" The next moment, his left eyelid began to twitch uncontrollably, and he lifted his hand to his temple.

"Leon, what is it?" Isabelle quickly took his hand and squeezed it. From the corner of her eye, she saw one of the nurses approaching.

"Nothing," he whispered hoarsely. "The pain will go away in just a moment."

"Madame! The patient needs rest! How many times do we have to tell you?"

Isabelle went to the hospital again the next morning, and when she saw who was sitting by his bed, she was speechless for a long moment. What did *she* want?

"A little sausage, some cheese, a bottle of good red wine . . ." Henriette Trubert was unpacking a basket of groceries on Leon's bed as if it were the most normal thing in the world. "And chocolate, perfect for getting one's strength back, by the way."

The eyes of the man in the next bed grew wider and wider, but Henriette just gave him an unfriendly look. Then she noticed Isabelle.

"Ah, Madame Feininger, I'm sure you have nothing against my dropping by for a quick visit with your husband," she said with a sugary smile. "When I heard about the accident, I thought to myself, how can a sportsman possibly recover on the food they serve in hospitals? I happened to be in town, so I brought a few things for him. We have to get him back on his feet, after all, don't we?"

"The doctors and I are taking care of that," said Isabelle with undisguised displeasure. She set down her own basket, also filled with fruit, sausage, and cheese, beside Leon's bed. Then she leaned over to Leon and kissed him.

"How are you feeling, darling?" she asked him gently.

"With two beautiful women here to look after me, I can only be getting better. I'm allowed to go home tomorrow morning. The doctors said so earlier."

Isabelle heaved a sigh of relief. *Thank you, God.*

"I like your fighting spirit, Monsieur Feininger. Nothing seems to keep you down for long." Henriette Trubert packed the things she'd brought back into the basket and put it on a chair beside her. "I don't want to disturb you any longer. However, I would like to repeat my offer to purchase your estate. You've just seen how quickly things can change—and painfully, too. It would be good to know that one had made some provisions for the future, wouldn't it? Two million francs would see you through to the end of your days and beyond, and you'd never have to lift a finger again."

Isabelle could not believe what she was hearing. "You've got some nerve, exploiting my husband's condition to—" she began, but Leon interrupted her.

"It's all right," he said gently. "Madame Trubert is right. The accident has truly changed my view of things. This was no simple fall. I could easily have been killed. The more I think about it, the clearer I see just how lucky I've been. God has given me a second chance." His eyes were gleaming, and for a second he looked as if he might begin to weep.

Isabelle looked at him in horror. *Don't sell! Don't make a rash decision now!* she begged him silently.

The first signs of victory flashed in Henriette's eyes. "And you would like to enjoy life to the fullest. I knew you were a smart man," she said, patting Leon's hand. "If it would be agreeable to you, I will use the time of your convalescence to have our notary draw up the necessary contracts. Agreed?"

"Leon, don't say yes!" Isabelle cried, looking at him in despair.

For a long moment, no one said a word.

"I've made my decision," Leon said, directing his words as much to Isabelle as to Henriette. "Please don't misunderstand me—cycling will continue to play an important part in my life. It isn't as if the fall has robbed me of my courage, God forbid! It's more that I've finally realized what God put me here to do. I was so blind." He took a deep breath, as if to underline the weight of his words.

Isabelle's forehead creased deeply. Leon mentioning God so frequently . . . what did it mean? He sounded practically enlightened!

"When I leave the hospital tomorrow, and in the future, I will use all my strength . . . to get the estate into shape! I have no intention of selling, Madame Trubert."

"But why . . . ?" Henriette began.

Isabelle could have jumped for joy. Instead, she stepped forward and shooed Henriette off her chair.

"Please go now," she said, as icily and arrogantly as she possibly could. "I find your chatter terribly exhausting. I can only imagine how the patient must feel!"

"What you said, do you really mean it?" said Isabelle as soon as Henriette left. She felt like kissing him from head to foot but instead just held his hand chastely.

He nodded, then pulled his hand free of hers. He fished a small worn notebook out of the drawer of the nightstand.

"One of the nurses gave me this when I told her there was so much going around in my head that it hurt." He opened the notebook, and Isabelle saw that most of the pages had been torn out. On those that remained, she saw Leon's handwriting.

"I've started a list with the most important things, the ones we have to get on with urgently in the next few months. On the estate and out in the vineyards, one step after another, you know?"

She nodded and read.

- *Replant the fallow vineyard*
- *Actively seek new customers?*
- *Sales tour together?*

Three points, two with question marks after them. Isabelle found it charming—the mere fact that Leon was thinking about these questions at all counted for something. She was suddenly filled with emotion and happiness, and she felt a swelling in her throat.

"From now on, you come first. You and Uncle Jacques's inheritance. And only then the cycling."

"Oh, Leon."

They kissed tenderly.

"We'll have none of that in here, thank you!" said one of the nurses walking past.

Isabelle pulled a face behind her. Then she turned back to Leon. Should she or shouldn't she? She took a deep breath.

"You might have to reconsider what comes first on that list. You're going to be a father, Leon. We're going to have a child."

"We . . . what? But . . . since when?"

"I've suspected it for a while, but I've only known for certain since last week." Isabelle stroked her belly automatically, as she often had in recent days. A feeling of bliss washed through her.

"An heir!" Leon beamed. "Someone to take over our work later on. If I hadn't made the right decision already, I would do it now."

Isabelle smirked. "I never thought I'd hear you talk like this. But there's one thing you do have to promise me. Later on, that we won't coddle our children or push them too hard. When I think about how I suffered because my father had everything mapped out for me!" She shuddered. "Our children should decide for themselves what kind of life they want to lead. If they want to continue with the winery, wonderful. If not, that's also fine."

"You're right, darling," said Leon tamely. "But one can hope, right?" They smiled at each other. "It took a miracle to open my eyes, but from now on, everything is going to work out. I love you," he murmured softly, then closed his eyes.

"I love you, too," Isabelle whispered back. "Tonight will be your last night in the hospital. You'll sleep in our bed again tomorrow. Sleep well, my darling."

She stayed awhile longer, sitting beside his bed, basking in their love, her trust in him, and her confidence about the future. Then she left the hospital. She would pick Leon up the next day. With fresh clothes and a fresh outlook. And then their new life could begin. Again.

***

The large round clock at the end of the corridor said it was two o'clock when Leon swayed toward the nurses' station. He had had a bad dream and probably tossed his head from side to side in his sleep. Now, his head was aching something terrible. And he was thirsty, too. A glass of water and a few drops of that horrible liquid on a spoon. Two birds with one stone.

He staggered a little. It was so far to the nurses' station. Leaning against the wall, he waited for the dizziness to pass. Damn it, if only the shooting pain in his head would pass, too!

Why didn't anyone come to ask how he was? The nurses were probably off in some corner, drinking coffee or wine. The brunette with the facial hair always smelled of alcohol. And the young, blond night nurse, she had her eye on the senior doctor, guaranteed!

Two more doors, and he would have made it. A nurse had to be there. One step after another. Hadn't he said the same thing to Isabelle that afternoon?

The next moment, he collapsed to the floor, dead.

Chapter Nineteen

Early August 1898

"I brought you soup. Eat, before the skin falls off your bones!" Ghislaine held the soup bowl so close to Isabelle's mouth that she had to obey. Isabelle was silent as she slowly spooned up the soup, and Ghislaine stood and watched her, just as silent as Isabelle. But it was not the amicable silence of good friends; it was the silence—at least from Ghislaine's side—of helplessness.

"He's been dead for nearly three months. How much longer are you going to refuse to live?" Ghislaine asked after Isabelle finished the bowl of soup. "If anyone can understand the emptiness you feel after such a loss, it's me. But sooner or later, you are going to have to start filling yourself up again. It doesn't matter with what—work, with the joy of summer, with new life . . ." As she spoke, Ghislaine rested a hand on her own belly. Unless the signs were false, she was carrying a new life inside her again. "A *bébé*—is there any greater way to honor life?"

Despite all Ghislaine's words, despite her insistence, Isabelle's gaze remained as empty as ever.

Ghislaine stood up, shaking her head. "I can see you want to be alone, but I have to tell you one thing before I go: you're not only making your own life unnecessarily hard, my dear, but our lives, too." At the door of Isabelle's bedroom, she turned back. "I can still remember very well how furious I was at you and your husband when old Jacques left you this place. Inheriting something so valuable, just like that! Something that once belonged to my family. I envied you, and I looked at you as intruders. More than anything else, I wanted to see you ruined or gone or dead. And when you arrived and Leon played the greatest sportsman and you went traipsing through the village like a princess, I saw all my prejudices confirmed. You with your pretty dresses, Leon in his cycling clothes—spoiled city folk, that's what you were!"

Suddenly, Isabelle blinked, and her eyes seemed to focus; for the first time since she had entered Isabelle's room, Ghislaine had her attention. Was it the doggedness in her voice? Or was it that she was revealing what she normally kept hidden so deeply inside, something she so rarely did?

Driven by some strange inner urge, Ghislaine went on. "But *you* changed my mind. All your husband ever had in his head was his bicycle, but you . . . you rolled up your sleeves and went to work. Whenever I left my house to go to the tavern, I saw you out working in the vineyards or talking with one of Jacques's men. The vintners told me that you were driving them around the bend with all your questions. You surprised not only me, but also Claude Bertrand, Micheline, Marie, and all the other neighbors. Your devotion to this place, your eagerness to work—even Daniel saw it. Slowly, slowly, we began to get used to the idea that the estate was in good hands, in *your* good hands. And now?" Ghislaine looked at Isabelle accusingly. "Now you're letting yourself down as well as everyone who trusted you!"

***

"Isabelle, please, you have to get up!" Micheline Guenin hurried from the bed to the window and pulled back the curtains. "The sun is shining! It's a glorious day! You could sit out on the terrace before it gets too hot and look out at the vineyards. The roses are all in bloom. You were so looking forward to them blooming, and now you're not even seeing it." When Isabelle didn't answer, Micheline continued. "We . . . could go to the cemetery together. Whenever I visit my brother Albert, I go over to your husband's grave, too, and put some flowers in his vase. But wouldn't it be nice to visit him yourself?"

Isabelle glanced at Micheline with impassive eyes.

"Well . . . maybe visiting the grave is still too painful for you," said Micheline with a sigh. "But let's take a stroll through the vineyards, at least! It would amaze you how the grapes have come on. Those pinheads have turned into little marbles, now, and they'll be ripening before you know it." When Isabelle still didn't react, Micheline babbled on. "I actually tried one of the grapes yesterday, though you'd think I'd know better by now, wouldn't you? Even when it's getting close to harvest time, they still taste terribly sour." She forced a bit of laughter.

Isabelle stared at her own hands. She noticed her fingernails were getting very long. And they were grooved and had white spots on them. Like the fingernails of a corpse.

"I've made some breakfast. Sweet nut bread. And I've brought lavender honey from Provence. Try a bite or two. You're as thin as a leaf these days. Oh, child, what am I supposed to do with you?"

The bedspread. When had it started to smell different? The perfume of the apple flowers from the old tree in the garden was gone. And the sharp smell of their nights of lovemaking. Now the linen smelled of old sweat. Of loneliness. Of nothing ever again being what it once was.

"Claude needs to speak with you urgently. The man is at the end of his tether, Isabelle! It's quite a lot for him—looking after the animals and the vineyards, too, now that Gustave Grosse has gone to his family in the south. It would be good if you could help, at least a little bit."

For the first time since Micheline had come into her room, Isabelle looked at her.

"Grosse will be coming back," Isabelle said with a flat tone. "Until he does, Claude should just do what he thinks best. He's the overseer, after all."

"But you're the boss! There are things that only you can arrange. Claude and I, we're happy to help, but . . ."

Isabelle closed her eyes and drifted off across her ocean of loneliness.

"A blood vessel ruptured in Monsieur Feininger's head. No one could have predicted it. And even if we could have, we wouldn't have been able to stop it from happening. An unforeseeable tragedy. A stroke of fate. Divine providence, madame."

The doctor's voice had revealed his shock at Leon's sudden death, but there was a trace of fatalism there as well. The man knew the limits of human existence, and experience had taught him that fighting those limits made no sense.

That's when it started. Isabelle had heard the doctor's words; she had looked into his sympathetic eyes, but she had felt nothing. From one moment to the next, her ability to feel any emotion died off like a plant fed poison instead of water. She felt no sadness, no anger, no hatred for God above. She didn't cry or scream. She didn't ask the doctor any questions, didn't want to hear any details about what happened. Why should she? The doctor was mistaken in thinking this had something to do with her.

Her husband. Dead? The man who had so many plans? The man who had been so happy to hear that he was going to be a father? Impossible. A mistake. Fate could not err so gravely. She closed her heart the way one closes one's eyes when confronted with an unbearable sight.

She had packed up Leon's things and was driven home. She sent a telegram to Leon's parents; by the time she left the post office, she had already forgotten the contents. When the pastor talked with her about the funeral, she had arranged everything as best she could. Leon was to wear his cycling clothes. And the cap he had found in Jacques's wardrobe and had loved to wear. Flowers? No, she would prefer a few tendrils of grapevine laid atop the casket. But it really made no difference. An error had been made. A nightmare, that's all it was, and she would soon awaken from it.

Almost everyone in the village had attended the burial service. The members of a cycling club came from Charleville to pay their respects. Leon's mother had come, too, and she stood silent and trembling beside Isabelle. No one could say which of them was the more pitiable, the dead man's mother or his widow.

An air of melancholy settled over all those gathered. It no longer mattered that the residents of Hautvillers had viewed the redheaded *l'Allemande* and her husband with mistrust. That many of them had ridiculed Leon's passion for cycling. That some had been angry to see Jacques Feininger's inheritance end up in the "wrong" hands. In times of need, the people of Champagne stood as one. And as a widow, Isabelle Feininger was in need.

Isabelle had stood at the grave with her face as white as the chalk of the region. She listened to words of consolation, or at least pretended to listen. Many of those at the funeral, among them Raymond Dupont, handed her an envelope. Micheline explained that they contained small donations to help offset the expense of the funeral.

The chairman of the cycling club from Charleville also pressed an envelope into Isabelle's hand and said, "Leon Feininger was greatly admired by all of us. The cycling world will be much poorer without him. If you ever need our help, just let us know."

Isabelle, who had not even known that Leon was attached to a cycling club, thanked him kindly.

Now and then, she spoke a few words with some of the visitors, sometimes even smiling, but she had let their compassion roll off her. Accepting it would have meant letting her emotions show, and that would have hurt too much. Only once did she wake briefly from her lethargy. When she saw Ghislaine standing off to the side of the crowd, she went over to her and said, "Now we have both lost what we loved the most."

Ghislaine had nodded, and Isabelle took some solace from that silent gesture.

Micheline was at the door, receiving a courier's delivery, when Henriette Trubert's coach drove up.

Henriette pointed to the bouquet of colorful gladiolas in Micheline's arms, as if to inquire about them.

"From Raymond Dupont. Flowers, pralines, cookies—he's trying everything to cheer the widow up," Micheline said.

"I had no idea they knew each other so well," Henriette said. "Well, I'd also like to cheer her up a little!" she added, and lifted the cloth that covered the basket she carried. "Almond cake, the best around."

Micheline knew that the cake was no more than a feint, and that Henriette had far more in mind than the well-being of the young widow. But she had no choice, so she showed the vintner inside.

Even as a young woman, Henriette had never been innocent. As the attractive daughter of a successful businessman, she had been idolized by every young man for miles, whereas no one had much interest in quiet, shy Micheline. They had always been worlds apart, and that had not changed as they got older. It was not that Micheline abhorred the other woman's business acumen. On the contrary, Henriette followed a long tradition of female *Champenois*. But what angered Micheline beyond all else was the brazenness with which Henriette sought to expand her holdings. An illness here, a death there, and along came

Henriette with her checkbook in her hand, ready to snap up a cellarage, a vineyard, a press. But most important of all was land, land, land . . .

Since Leon Feininger's death, the vintner had come by almost every week. Every time, she murmured a few sympathetic words in Isabelle's ear, then renewed her offer to buy the Feininger estate. The first few times, Micheline had sat beside Isabelle like a mother hen, protecting her. It was unthinkable that Isabelle, blind and confused in her grief, might simply sign Henriette's contract! But once it became clear to her that Isabelle reacted to Henriette's purrings exactly as she did to Micheline's own words, she decided it was no longer necessary to watch over her.

"So how is she? Still no sign of improvement?" Henriette asked with a nod toward the top floor.

Micheline shook her head, but said nothing.

Henriette did the same, but for other reasons. From her, the gesture signaled disgust, incomprehension, and more. "If you really cared for her, you'd get her to sell! Madame Feininger would be a wealthy woman, beholden to no one. She could go to the Côte d'Azur or wherever she wanted and wallow in her grief to the end of her days. And who knows"—Henriette let out a shrill laugh—"maybe she'll get married again, maybe to a rich widower? *L'Allemande* won't find any more happiness here in Champagne. We both know that that sorry little pile lying up there doesn't have the spine to get out of bed and lead this estate again! It looks to me as if the wood the Germans are carved from isn't as hard as they say, after all."

"Can you believe Henriette came again today?" Micheline said to Claude a short time later, while the overseer curried one of the horses out in the stable. "I told her to keep her conniving nose out of other people's business, the cow! It's outrageous how persistent she is."

Claude nodded. "She came nosing around here, too, saying I should try to talk Madame Feininger into selling. She says there'll always be a good job waiting for me with her."

Micheline looked at the overseer skeptically. "And what did you tell her?"

Claude shrugged. "Nothing. I haven't seen madame for weeks now." He lowered the currycomb and looked past Micheline, out of the stable window. "Sometimes I wonder if Madame Feininger wouldn't truly be better off if she sold. Madame is letting her grief eat her away, and the place is slowly falling apart."

Micheline could see that Claude felt at least as helpless as she did. With a sigh, she said, "You're right. Isabelle is disappearing. Whenever I take her something to eat, she turns away. Apart from the bowl of soup that Ghislaine brings her every evening, she eats almost nothing. And she should be eating for two!" Micheline sat down on one of the bales of straw stacked along the stable wall. "Does my food taste worse than Ghislaine's?" she asked, sounding rather put out.

Claude looked at Micheline over the back of the horse. "You wouldn't be jealous of their friendship, would you? Be happy that Ghislaine has stopped being so unfriendly to Madame Feininger! Isabelle can use all the sympathy she can get. And another thing: that she's expecting is only something the two of you *suspect*. I can't say that she should be eating for two."

"You haven't seen her for too long," Micheline replied. *And it's good that you haven't,* she thought. Claude would probably drop dead from shock at the sight of Madame Feininger. Her stringy, unwashed hair, the flowered dress she'd had on for so long that it was stiff with sweat and dirt . . .

For a moment, they were lost in their own thoughts.

When Micheline looked up, her eyes flashed angrily. "It really gets my goat that Henriette is trying to exploit Isabelle like that. Now, in her hour of need! And you know what else makes me see red? That lazy bastard Gustave Grosse still hasn't returned from his 'well-earned' vacation! Ha, he's probably taken a job somewhere else, and good riddance."

"Did you ever think that our good Gustave might have been paid to go away?" Claude asked grimly.

Micheline held her tongue. She wouldn't put anything past Henriette.

"The harvest is going to start in just a few weeks. So far, I've managed to keep this place going, more or less. But organizing and supervising a complete harvest? On top of everything?" Claude shook his head.

Micheline nodded. "Even Marie and I approach every new harvest with respect, and we're old hands."

"If there's any chance at all of getting this estate over the hump, then we need a new cellar master, and the sooner the better," said Claude.

Micheline shook her head. "What Isabelle needs more than anything else right now is someone who can take the reins until she can take them back herself. Whoever it is will need authority with the workers. An experienced foreman. Or an old vintner who's sold his own place but still knows the craft. That's what we need!"

"I couldn't have put it any better. With someone here who really knows how to keep things organized, a lot of things would be easier. I'd be there to help, of course. Wherever I could." Claude knocked his currycomb against the wall. "I can't understand why Leon's father didn't come to the funeral. A vintner from the Palatinate—he'd be just what we need! And what about Madame Feininger's own parents? Isn't her father supposed to be some sort of successful businessman? Berlin isn't all that far, and any man in his right mind would stand by his daughter if she needed him. If it's a factory or a wine estate he's organizing, the principle is the same. Isabelle is the sole heir of this place now. Is it all just going to fall apart?"

"She once told me that her parents didn't accept Leon as her husband and that she broke from them because of it. Terrible, what people do to each other, isn't it? Isabelle only stays in touch with one friend in Berlin. Clara's her name."

Chapter Twenty

The letter had arrived the day before. In a woman's hand, on thin, translucent paper. Clara had never seen the delicate handwriting before. Across the top of the envelope was a watermark, two letters: *C* and *G*, intertwined. Only later did Clara recognize that this was the emblem of the Champagne Guenin winery.

When she first had seen the letter, she was completely taken aback. A letter for her? She hardly ever received any mail. All the envelopes and packages the postman brought on his twice-daily deliveries were addressed to her husband, Dr. Gerhard Gropius. But this one was not. Micheline Guenin, a French woman and, it seemed, one of Isabelle's neighbors, had written directly to *her*.

It had been a long time since she had learned French in school, and it had taken Clara awhile to decipher the French. Several times, she had to resort to the dictionary, and even when she had transcribed it, word by word, into German, she could barely absorb what it said. Leon Feininger was dead? That happy-go-lucky man who'd managed to turn Isabelle's head so much that she had simply run away with him? Poor Isabelle . . . Tears came to Clara's eyes, and it took a long time for them to subside.

What Clara found at least as shocking as the terrible news was that someone was asking *her* for help. Her, of all people. Someone too stupid for even the simplest of tasks, as Gerhard never tired of reminding her. How was she supposed to help anyone? Certainly, she and Isabelle had known each other since kindergarten, and they had grown up on the same street, Isabelle in the fancy villa beside her own father's factory and Clara herself just down the street from her parents' pharmacy. Josephine, the smith's daughter, was the third member of their little band. Despite their social differences, they had been good friends. Isabelle had never flaunted her wealth but rather shared her chocolates and fashion magazines and even her coveted bicycle with her friends.

How had the French woman known about their old friendship, and how did she get Clara's address? From Isabelle herself? While Clara had thought about these things, she had carefully hidden the letter behind the mirror in the hallway, where Gerhard wouldn't discover it.

Now, the day after the letter arrived, as she checked to make sure that not the slightest corner showed beneath the broad, gilded frame, she took a long, critical look at herself in the mirror. Although she would be celebrating her twenty-fifth birthday on December 24, her doe-brown eyes gleamed, her lips were full, and her figure was still youthful. Her dark-brown hair gleamed like chestnuts fresh from their spiky shells, and her skin was flawless.

"Marriage seems to suit you. You are more beautiful every year," her mother had told her only recently. Clara hadn't replied. What could she have said? That Gerhard only pinched her in places where the bruises wouldn't show? That he didn't actually hit her anymore but made up for it by pulling her across the room by her hair?

You and your burden to bear! she taunted herself, as she stepped into the dining room, where her husband was already sitting at the table. *If Gerhard gets a little rough with you, it's because you've provoked him with some silly little mistake or other. Apart from that, he's a good man, and a good provider. Besides—your son, Matthias, is the true joy of your life. You live in a beautiful house. And as a doctor's wife, you're welcome everywhere. What else do you want?*

She sat down on her chair and gazed listlessly out the window. Rain pattered against the windowpanes, and water splashed from the gutter down onto the sidewalk below. The pale blooms of the dog-rose drooped to the ground under the weight of the rain.

"Professor Hackestorm is coming to dinner tonight. He's bringing his wife with him." Gerhard spoke so suddenly that Clara flinched.

As a rule, breakfast was a silent affair; Gerhard preferred the newspaper to a conversation with her. She had once pleaded with him to talk to her, but now she liked the silence. Silence was predictable. And it didn't hurt.

"I hope you didn't forget about it. It is immensely important for me." He was scrutinizing her over the edge of his newspaper.

When he first announced the Hackestorms' visit, she had immediately written herself a note. He could be very unpleasant if she forgot something like that.

"A three-course meal, then coffee, brandy, and sweets—isn't that what you want for this evening?" Clara recited like a schoolgirl who had dutifully learned her lesson by heart. "I'm off to Kramer's after breakfast to buy everything." And after that, she would have to go clear across the city, but Gerhard didn't need to know that. He didn't like her to be out by herself.

"I wouldn't be in your shoes if the soup is as thin tonight as it was yesterday. Or if you overcook the meat again. A good repast should put Hackestorm in the right frame of mind. But poor fare could destroy everything I have worked for in recent months. Is that clear to you, Clara?"

She nodded. Gerhard's only interest at present was for Professor Hackestorm, chief physician in the Women's Department at Berlin's Charité hospital, to send him his patients for follow-up care. Of all the areas her husband could have decided to specialize in, he had chosen gynecology, and now he wanted to make a name for himself in the field. Precisely how the cauliflower soup she was planning to serve was supposed to influence Professor Hackestorm's decision was not clear to Clara, but she would take care not to let any trenchant remarks slip. Such things did not become her.

"And put on some decent clothes. Hackestorm's wife is a demon for the latest fashions, and she'll be dressed to the nines. One can afford to be fashionable in the better circles, and *that* means that you can't be running around like a kitchen maid. Take a look at yourself, hair all stringy and plain. And your shoes look like you were wearing them while digging in the garden." His last words were spoken with even more disgust.

But I am the kitchen maid! The words were on the tip of Clara's tongue. Gerhard believed that she could manage the household without the help of a cook or maid; the only thing he had agreed to was a nanny for Matthias, and now red-cheeked Christel took care of Matthias during the day. This was a good thing. Clara worked all day to keep the house in order and cook only to play the well-groomed wife in the evenings. She looked down at her shoes. She had been out in the garden to cut a few roses, but that was before the rain. And despite Gerhard's claim, her shoes were spotless.

"I'll wear the dark-blue outfit and pearls, if that's all right with you. I could also—"

"Spare me the details! The least you might manage is to choose what to wear without my help," he growled. "I'll tell you this: if you don't pull yourself together, then my patience is going to wear very thin indeed! Just thinking about the disgrace you subjected me to when we went to the Nordstroms' is enough to drive me wild!"

Clara lowered her eyes in repentance.

The garden party at the Nordstroms' house. It had been a magnificent summer afternoon, with the air full of the scent of roses and all the guests in a splendid mood. Her pink dress and matching hat, Clara saw with relief, fitted in well with what the other women were wearing. Gerhard had immediately immersed himself in a technical discussion with a group of physicians, and she was left with no choice but to stroll through the garden alone. Everybody knew everybody else, except for her. But then, over a cup of coffee and a slice of cake, she had gotten into a conversation with a nice couple. The woman knew Clara's parents and had been a customer of their pharmacy for years. Clara was relieved to no longer feel like a fifth wheel. Suddenly, she, too, was infected by the pleasant mood of the party. She had chatted away, laughed and joked, and generally had a wonderful time. It was a nice feeling, she realized.

Afterward, she had thought she had done very well for herself. But the moment they got home, Gerhard started in on her. "What got into your head? Cavorting like that with Dr. Köhnemann, of all people?" he screamed at her. "I thought my eyes were deceiving me when I saw you prattling away with my biggest rival! Everyone is talking about his new practice on Landsberger Allee. They say it's fully equipped with all the latest technical advances—whereas I have to do the best I can with my old shack. But my darling wife doesn't think about that for a moment, oh no! Instead, she behaves like a common prostitute, without an ounce of decency or composure. Disgusting!"

He had kept it up for hours, and Clara had tried to protest a dozen times that it had all been quite harmless. But in the end, she had been forced to see that she had made a grave mistake. Yet again. At least Gerhard had not hit her.

"What's more, I expect your conversation with the Hackestorms to be cultivated. No loud laughter, none of your stupid silences. The theater, anything new in the literary world—and I don't mind if you talk about our trip to Norddeich. Then you must mention our visit to that expensive restaurant beside the Ludgeri church, where we had Paul von Hindenburg sitting at the next table. Things like that always tend to impress people."

Clara nodded, although she could barely remember their visit to the restaurant. The sea breeze blowing in her hair, the tumbling waves, and the sand between her toes—all of those had left far more lasting impressions than a meal in a gloomy restaurant.

"And don't even contemplate turning the conversation to Matthias again! To think for a second that people are interested in the development of a child—only you could be that witless." Gerhard slurped his coffee noisily.

"But other women talk about their children," Clara managed to say. "Raising children is our God-given task. You say so yourself."

Gerhard shook his head and glared at her. "Sometimes I think you deliberately try to make me angry. Yes, other women mention their brood from time to time, but none of them put on airs about it like you do. Do you think Mrs. Hackestorm sits all day in the nursery, playing silly games? A woman like her takes her *representative* obligations seriously. But you . . ." He gestured contemptuously. "Enough of this, or my mood will be spoiled before I've even finished my first cup of coffee." Without another word, he returned to his newspaper.

Clara sighed.

The minute Gerhard left, Clara ran into the bedroom and slipped out her diary from beneath the mattress. She had not managed to come up with a better hiding place, and she prayed daily that Gerhard would never discover it. She sat down at the small round side table beneath the bedroom window and looked outside for a moment, her eyes scanning the street.

A curious letter arrived for me yesterday, she began.

Not long after she and Gerhard had married, Clara found that it did her good to commit her thoughts to paper. It was a way of organizing and evaluating them. Many times, when she wrote about an incident from her everyday life, it seemed less overwhelming. Gerhard's often savage beliefs, his imperious tone when he spoke to her, his demands. Maybe she really was a little oversensitive. Was he right when he accused her of making a mountain out of every molehill? In her mind, she threw the same accusation back at him, but she would never actually say it.

She ended her entry for the day with a question: *How am I supposed to react to this cry for help from Isabelle's neighbor?* She had not gained much clarity, but she did feel a little better and calmer.

Once she had stowed the little leather book away safely, she put together her shopping list for dinner that evening. Apart from the cauliflower soup, she wanted to do chicken braised in red wine and fresh peaches with cream for dessert—she hoped that her choices would meet with the approval of Gerhard and their guests. She would easily be able to find everything she needed in the local shop, which was good, because she really didn't have much time for shopping and cooking that day. With her basket and the money allocated for the week's groceries in her hand, she looked in briefly at the nursery. The nanny was just getting Matthias dressed for a walk along the Spree; they wanted to sail boats. Clara smiled as she observed how her son pressed the carefully folded paper boat so hard to his chest that the little vessel was crumpled and skewed out of shape; it would probably tip over and sink the moment it touched the water. She gave him a kiss on his cheek, then forced herself to leave.

The letter.

There was only one person on earth with whom she could discuss it.

***

"You sit here on the saddle, both hands on the handlebars. Then you put one foot on the pedal, here, and the second—no, wait!" Josephine exclaimed as her customer was about to ride away. "I still have to teach you how to stop."

The woman, a housewife in her forties, waved dismissively. "Oh, I know all that. My neighbor bought exactly the same kind of bike from you two weeks ago and explained everything to me. She's been very satisfied with it, too. We want to go out cycling together. May I try it out?"

Josephine smiled and said, "Of course. But be careful. After the rain, the roads can be quite slippery!" The woman, wobbling a little but pedaling single-mindedly, rode off down the street. As Josephine watched, Adrian stepped out of the warehouse for their bicycle shop. Josephine's heart jumped, as it always did when she saw him. And as she had so many times, she said a silent prayer of thanks for the way her cards had fallen. Adrian. Her husband, her love. They shared their passion for not only bicycles, but also their lives.

He had a notebook in his hand and a pencil behind his ear, and when he saw her standing there, he came over. He still limped visibly with his left leg, although the robbery in America, during which he'd been shot in the knee by thieves, had happened almost two years ago. Every morning, in the hope of one day being able to walk normally again—and to ride a bicycle again—Adrian performed the exercises prescribed by his doctors. Josephine did them with him. Because of all the work in the shop, she only rarely had the chance to go riding, and she enjoyed the chance to exercise.

Adrian looked around. None of their staff was in sight, so he kissed her deeply and tenderly on the mouth. Josephine's lips parted, and she enjoyed the play of his tongue in her mouth. She felt her desire flare, and she pressed closer to Adrian. But when, from the corner of her eye, she saw her customer pedaling back toward them, she freed herself from Adrian's embrace.

They shared an intimate look, then he said, "We're going through our stock faster than expected. We've still got three hundred bicycles, eighty for women, all the rest for men." Then he winked and added, "I wonder why women's bicycles have sold so quickly?"

Josephine smiled while her customer rode a few final curves. "I wonder! All I know is that I, personally, have sold forty of them in the last few weeks." Although she knew about the sales, their inventory, and everything that had to do with the business, she still found it hard to believe how successful they had been.

When, on his trip to America nearly two years earlier, Adrian had ordered two thousand bicycles from the Western Wheel Works, a factory in Chicago, Josephine had been a little worried. What if they had miscalculated and the bicycle boom ended before it had even really begun? "Then we'll be sitting on an Everest of bicycles!" Adrian had replied, laughing. So they looked ahead instead and opened their bicycle shop and repair business. A short time later, they added a cycling school, offering their customers the opportunity to learn to ride on site. The business flourished, even more bicycles were ordered, and both Josephine and Adrian enjoyed the work immensely.

"It's amazing! I feel faster than the wind," said the woman, her cheeks red and her hair tousled as she climbed off the bicycle. "I'll take it."

Adrian and Josephine laughed as one.

"That makes seventy-nine. I think I'd better order more, and fast," Adrian said, leaving Josephine to complete the woman's purchase.

Josephine had just finished writing the amount of the sale into her books when the bell rang again, and she lifted her head, ready to greet the next customer. But when she saw who was standing there, she had to blink to make sure her eyes were not lying.

"A young, healthy man like Leon . . . dead, just like that. It hard to believe, isn't it?" Clara's eyes radiated incomprehension and despair. "I don't want to think what Isabelle must be going through. She was so madly in love with him!"

Josephine nodded. She herself had married just before Isabelle, and the thought of becoming a widow so young sent a cold chill down her spine. It took no more than a glance at her friend since childhood to know that Clara was thinking exactly the same thing.

"Isabelle needs us. That much is clear," Josephine said.

"But how can we help her? I mean, we're just her old friends. We've all been going in our own directions for quite a while. Shouldn't this be something for Isabelle's parents?"

"*Just* her old friends—the way you said that." Annoyed, Josephine shook her head. "Isn't friendship the only thing that matters? But you won't be able to count on her parents. Isabelle died for them the day she stopped doing what they wanted her to. Look at my parents. They also stopped wanting anything to do with me when I didn't do what they expected. Not everyone has a mother and father as nice as yours, Clara." But when Josephine saw Clara's guilty look, she regretted her final words. With a husband like Gerhard Gropius, Clara could use every bit of parental support she could get. "Of course it's going to take time to get over such a loss, but the letter makes it sound as if Isabelle can't even get back on her feet."

"You think so?" asked Clara, chewing her bottom lip. "Poor Isabelle."

Their silence was overshadowed by the ticking of the large clock on the wall. Clara plucked at the hem of her jacket sleeve. Josephine stared at the draft of an advertising leaflet lying on the desk in front of her. She'd been planning to give the leaflet a final once-over. The illustrations they wanted to use to explain and extol the refinements of their Crescent bicycles blurred before her eyes into a hodgepodge of strokes, curves, and dots as a thousand thoughts jostled in her mind.

Isabelle needed her help, that was certain, but how was she supposed to get away from the shop? Their summer business was booming, and even the autumn was looking good. Adrian wanted to push ahead with his new project, organizing bicycle races, in the next few weeks.

Since his injury prevented him from racing, he had turned to other ways to stay close to the sport. Now he was planning to stage exclusive track races, bringing in the best cyclists from Berlin and throughout the empire. She couldn't simply tell him that she was going off to France for some indeterminate time! Besides, why should she even feel obligated to help? In the end, she and Isabelle had no longer been close. The opposite was true, in fact: Josephine falling in love with Adrian . . . Isabelle had not taken that well at all. But at the same time, Isabelle's earlier engagement to Adrian had been a farce from the start, a business arrangement between their fathers, nothing more. Isabelle didn't want to have Adrian, but she didn't want anyone else to have him, either.

But wasn't that all water under the bridge? Wasn't the friendship that had once bound them so closely together worth more than the friction that crept into their relationship more recently? Water under the bridge! Josephine suddenly felt a deep need to stand by her old friend. Adrian would not object to her desire to go away to France, she was sure of that. If they tried, she was sure they would find a way to make everything work.

Josephine took a deep breath, then looked at Clara. "When do we leave?"

Chapter Twenty-One

"When do we leave?" Clara shook her head. As if it were that simple! She reached for a carrot and began to dice it into small cubes. When Josephine was younger, she followed whatever fancy came into her head. And it had once cost her three years in jail! Apparently, marriage hadn't changed her at all; such selfishness really did *not* become a woman.

She tossed the diced carrots into the pan with the finely chopped onion and both ingredients sizzled away gently in the goose fat.

Clara hadn't yet said a word to Gerhard about the letter from France. He would never allow her to go on this journey, not in her wildest dreams, and he'd be up in arms in seconds if she approached him with the idea. *Have you taken leave of your senses?* he would shout at her. And how could she even consider it? The cost! And who would look after the household and Matthias during her absence? *A woman's place was at her husband's side and nowhere else. Basta!* Clara could already hear his objections. Of course, she could tell him that everything could be organized. She was sure her mother would look after the house and Matthias. And their nanny would still be there. For two or three weeks, they could certainly come up with a solution. Even before she finished the thought, she felt a sharp pang in her chest. She would have to be away from Matthias for so long? She wouldn't survive it. And she probably wouldn't trust herself to go off on a trip like that without Gerhard. Who knows what might happen? On the other hand, it would be a wonderful opportunity to actually use the French she had worked so hard to learn. And Isabelle needed her.

Clara took the chicken out of the wax paper and rubbed the skin with dried herbs and pepper. Carefully, she slid the chicken into the roasting pan with the braising vegetables. It made a loud hiss in the hot oil, and Clara went over to the window to open it. Gerhard didn't like the house to smell of food.

If it were anyone else, she might perhaps be able to win Gerhard over. But certainly not when it came to Isabelle Herrenhus. And with Josephine as her traveling companion—in Gerhard's eyes, things couldn't get much worse. When he looked at her former cycling friends, all he saw were headstrong harpies. When she and Gerhard had first gotten engaged, he had tried to forbid her from seeing them, but at least on that matter she had managed to stand up for herself—they were her friends, and they would continue to be her friends even after she married! But when Isabelle abandoned Berlin for her life with Leon and Josephine went off to the other end of the city with Adrian to open their shop, Clara's contact with them had all but stopped. She had her own hands more than full with the house and her son, and her visit to Josephine today was a rare exception. Gerhard knew nothing of the occasional letters she exchanged with Isabelle or of the cookbooks she had sent.

Clara looked at the bottle of red wine from which she had just added a full glass to the chicken. It was a burgundy, from France. But where in France was Champagne, exactly?

Abruptly, she wiped her hands on her apron, then she went to the bookshelf in the parlor. The large atlas contained 170 maps, and it was one of the books that Gerhard liked to browse through in the evenings. He didn't like her doing the same, however; he was afraid that she would clumsily manage to crease a page—or even worse, tear one.

"Too much reading gives a woman headaches. You'd do better with a good handicraft," he was fond of telling her.

With fingers still smelling of onion, she leafed through the maps until she found what she was looking for. Paris, Reims, Épernay, and there—Hautvillers! Charly-sur-Marne, Condé-en-Brie, Vailly-sur-Aisne. *The* Champenois *certainly had a sense for fancy names for their towns*, she thought with a smile.

France . . . Even if the reason for the trip to Champagne was a melancholy one, the trip itself was sure to be wonderful. She had never seen a grapevine, let alone a vineyard, and apart from that trip to Norddeich, she had never even been out of Berlin. What was the French countryside like?

Clara looked over at the dining table with its white tablecloth. Goodness! Their guests would be arriving in less than three hours, and she still had to set the table, prepare the dessert, and get herself ready. And the chicken in the oven was already starting to smell a little over-cooked. She put the atlas aside. She really did not have the time for vain dreams.

"And then the girl held my skirt in her little hands and wailed, 'Why do I have to stay here? Take me with you!' Hearing things like that as often as I do, well, it nearly breaks my heart!" Natalie Hackestorm, her eyes dark with makeup, looked around the table.

Clara nodded and covertly pushed a hairpin that had worked loose from her bun back into place.

The professor's wife immediately picked up her own thread again. "Helping out in the St. Augustine Orphanage can be so painful sometimes, but when I see the loving children there, when I read them a book . . ."

While Clara passed around the platter with the chicken, she cast a triumphant glance at her husband. So much for Mrs. Hackestorm not being interested in children.

Natalie took a piece of chicken breast and sighed deeply. "If I could, I'd take all of those lovely little ones home with me and spoil them every day with food as delicious as this. You are an exceptional cook, my dear Mrs. Gropius!"

Clara smiled gratefully. Gerhard, sitting beside her, stiffened.

"Don't you dare bring those little devils into our home! I think you do quite enough donating so much of *my* money for your charity work!" said Richard Hackestorm to his wife with an indulgent smile.

"And what exactly would you have against two or three more mouths to feed at the table?" his wife shot back defiantly.

Clara held her breath. They wouldn't get into a fight here and now, would they?

"I have absolutely nothing against two or three more mouths at our table. But did it occur to you that I might want to produce them myself, my darling?" With an almost lewd gesture, he stroked his wife's cheek.

"You old reprobate," said Natalie in a smoky voice, and they broke out in a carefree laugh.

Deeply embarrassed, Clara dug into the bowl of potatoes. How could the professor and his wife break all the rules of decent conduct like that? If she tried something like that even once . . . ! With a surreptitious look at Gerhard, she saw his eyebrows were raised in disapproval, and in his expression she saw a mixture of grimness and helplessness. Clearly, he was far from pleased with the way the evening had gone so far. Usually, the men solemnly discussed medical topics while the women sat silently or, at the most, threw in an occasional admiring remark. But thanks to Natalie's chattering, the conversation had not once turned to medicine. And then came that salacious comment from the professor! Unbelievable! And who would be to blame in the end? She, of course.

After the main course, Natalie spoke at length about a charity event that she had organized to raise funds for a new roof for the orphanage. Her husband listened patiently, and he seemed utterly unconcerned that his wife was dominating the conversation.

Clara thought feverishly about how she—for Gerhard's sake—might steer the discussion to their trip to Norddeich, or even better, to Gerhard's brilliant skills as a doctor.

"I see you're planning to travel, too?" said Richard Hackestorm during a lull in his wife's monologue. "To France? Are you going over to our archenemy?" He laughed loudly.

Clara flushed and at the same time felt a chill run through her. Blast it, she'd forgotten to put the atlas away.

"What makes you say that?" Gerhard asked in surprise. "Oh, of course, travel broadens the mind, as they say, but I find it very difficult to leave my patients unattended. As a local doctor, I like to be available for emergencies day and night."

Richard pointed to the atlas, lying open on the sideboard.

"And what about that?"

Clara's jaw tightened. She felt Gerhard's interrogating eye on her, but at the same time, she saw an opportunity that would present itself only once. She began shaking inwardly with excitement. Should she or shouldn't she? Gerhard could hardly lash out at her in front of their guests, so perhaps she should risk it and raise the topic that lay so close to her heart.

"An old friend of mine, Isabelle Herrenhus—Isabelle Feininger now—lives in a town called Hautvillers, in the Champagne region," she said, unable to keep the trembling out of her voice. "I wanted to find out where that famous region actually lies."

Gerhard drew a sharp breath. He already had his mouth open to say something, but Clara didn't give him the opportunity. "Isabelle's husband died suddenly. I don't know how or why. Her neighbor wrote me a letter asking me to come. Isabelle needs someone urgently to help her get back on her feet."

Natalie laid one hand on Clara's arm sympathetically. "How terrible for the young widow! But how good it is that she has friends like you to count on."

Clara sensed how Gerhard, sitting rigidly beside her, had to make an effort to control himself. Straightening up, as if doing so might boost her own courage, she said, "Of course I feel the urge to go and help. But my son needs me here, too. And besides, it's important that Gerhard isn't burdened, which is why I hadn't yet mentioned this to him. He works so much—"

"I know Moritz Herrenhus very well," said Richard Hackestorm suddenly. Turning to Gerhard, he added, "We eat in the same club, and he is one of the patrons of the Charité. His wife was a patient of ours last year, and when he saw the physical limitations of the facilities in which we have to work, he declared his willingness to donate an annex for the gynecological wing. An extremely generous man—I had no idea that you and he were also acquainted!"

So generous that he would turn his back on his own daughter just because he didn't like her choice of husband, Clara thought. The next moment, she nearly fell off her chair with shock.

"Clara and I have known the Herrenhus family for a long time, haven't we, dear? Clara and Isabelle rode bicycles together. The businessman, Adrian Neumann, and his wife were also part of your little group, if I remember right," said Gerhard. He put his napkin aside and went on with a smile. "I thank God that I was at least able to talk my wife out of that dangerous pastime."

Speechless, Clara listened to her husband ruthlessly exploiting her friendship with Isabelle and Josephine for his own ends.

"Oh, you know the Neumanns, too, Doctor?" Natalie Hackestorm's well-formed eyebrows lifted in appreciation. "I did not know that you moved in . . . such circles."

"Adrian Neumann has already allowed his wife to make the trip to Champagne. It's so important that friends can rely on each other in an emergency, isn't it? Adrian found that out for himself the hard way." The words practically fell out of Clara's mouth before she could think about them. *Such circles*—pah!

"What kind of emergency did Adrian Neumann find himself in?" Natalie asked, curious. Clara told them the story of Adrian's trip to America and the robbery that ended with him getting shot. The Hackestorms listened breathlessly while Clara fell deeper and deeper into her entertainer role.

"Didn't you want to serve the dessert, my dear?" said Gerhard when she finished.

Red-cheeked, Clara went into the kitchen to get the peaches and cream. She couldn't do anything right with Gerhard. If she talked about children and home, that didn't suit him. But if she told an exciting story, something the guests obviously found interesting, he still wasn't happy.

She reappeared in the doorway in time to hear Gerhard say, "Well, of course my wife will be going to France! Where would we be if we couldn't help our friends in need? I'll miss my angel terribly, to be sure, but one has to make sacrifices now and then, doesn't one." He laughed jovially.

Natalie Hackestorm joined in his laughter. "A voyage to Champagne—oh, I do envy you, Clara. But is your French up to it?"

Clara waved one hand airily as she set the dessert on the table. "At school, I only had one hour of French each week, but I still read a French book now and then. Gerhard would like not only a good housewife at his side, but also a well-read spouse. Isn't that right, dear?" She looked at him as sweetly as she could and earned a cramped smile in return.

The professor and his wife exchanged a look.

"And Josephine Neumann has picked up some French by talking to her French customers. Between us, we'll get by."

Impressed, the professor's wife nodded. Then she spontaneously took Clara's hand and squeezed it firmly. "I wish you all the best for this trip. And all the best for the widow, of course. But you have to promise me one thing, my dear!"

"Yes?" Clara croaked as she served the dessert.

"That you will bring me back a crate of champagne. Moët is my favorite. It's absolutely divine."

From the corner of her eye, Clara noticed Natalie give her husband an almost imperceptible nod.

The next moment, the professor cleared his throat and said, "My dear Mr. and Mrs. Gropius, this has been a pleasant and fascinating conversation. I hope you will therefore not take it badly, my dear doctor, if we might turn to your medical work. In the next two or three weeks, I have to decide to which practices I will be sending our Charité patients for their follow-up care, and technical expertise naturally plays an important role in that. Speaking from a purely personally perspective, however, this evening has been a very positive surprise. After all, a certain reputation *does* precede you."

Gerhard's Adam's apple bobbed. "How am I to understand that?" he asked stiffly.

It was Natalie who replied, looking at him directly. "Oh, people say that your views when it comes to the fairer sex are a little . . . unprogressive. My husband, however, is a strong advocate of the emancipation of women. I would never have married him otherwise!" She let out a peal of laughter but quickly became serious again. "Again we see how much truth there is in hearsay. That you would let your wife travel alone to Champagne demonstrates not only mutual respect and trust, but also your own generosity. You are willing to make sacrifices for her sake, and I like that."

The professor nodded in agreement. "I can only work with men cut from that kind of cloth and can happily live without the old breed of diehards. Tell me, my dear doctor, how many Charité patients may I send you per month without overtaxing your capacities?"

Chapter Twenty-Two

One week later, Clara and Josephine were standing side by side on the train platform. They would go from Berlin to Leipzig and from Leipzig to Frankfurt, then on to Saarbrücken and from there to Reims via Metz.

When Josephine and Adrian embraced tenderly in parting, Clara looked away and fought back tears. Gerhard had gone off to his practice as usual, saying good-bye to her that morning in a few words and with no kiss. And she herself had forbidden Christel from coming to the station with Matthias. It was better like this. She knew that she would turn around on the spot and go home if her son started to cry. She dabbed at her eyes and nose with a handkerchief and hoped this whole trip was not one enormous mistake.

"How did you manage to talk your husband into letting you come along? You're not normally allowed to take two steps without his permission," said Josephine, once they had settled into a compartment in second class. Before that, she had made sure that her bicycle was stowed safely in the baggage section. Clara was surprised when she saw her arrive with it. What was the point of taking a bicycle?

"Gerhard is certainly concerned about my well-being, but if you think all I'm going to do is say 'yes, sir' or 'no, sir,' then you're mistaken. I can stand up for myself," Clara retorted as casually as she could, and she smoothed her hair. Even as she spoke, she thought about how much truth her words actually contained. Instead of whining and pleading as she had in the past when she wanted something from Gerhard, she had played her cards cleverly. Perhaps she should try that more often.

Josephine raised her hands defensively. "All right. I wasn't trying to attack you. The opposite, actually. I'm happy that we're traveling together. If I were doing this alone, I'd be feeling a little uneasy."

Clara accepted Josephine's words as an apology and smiled. "We're not going off to a different continent, just to France," she said appeasingly, but at the same time, her own heart was beating so hard at the thought of the nearly six-hundred-mile journey that she could feel it in her throat. She squeezed Josephine's hand in her own. "You and me, together, just like when we were children. Who would have guessed it?"

The trip was long, but not hard. Whenever they pulled into a station, the train they had to change to was ready and waiting. After the second change, they had a routine: Clara took Josephine's suitcase along with her own, and Josephine took care of her bicycle.

"Maybe I can cheer up Isabelle with a little two-wheeled tour," she had said when Clara asked her about the bicycle. It drew a lot of attention, and other passengers wanted to know about it; conversations developed and soon they were talking animatedly about their travel plans.

One older couple was on their way to Paris, where they had first met more than thirty years earlier. They held hands continuously, which Josephine found touching, but Clara wondered whether such intimacy was suitable for public display.

An actress from the Frankfurt Theater, following a long stay at Lake Constance, was on her way to take up a new job as the lead in a play by Arthur Schnitzler.

Two men introduced themselves as representatives of a glassware company in Bavaria. They traveled from one end of Europe to the other to sell their products.

A pleasant camaraderie developed among the strangers during the journey. The Bavarians offered the others bread and ham. The actress brought out some smoked fish she'd brought from Lake Constance, and Josephine ordered tea and coffee for everyone. After eating, the travelers were overcome by a satisfied weariness. Clara, too, grew tired, but instead of sleeping, she took out her diary and committed to paper all the exhilarating insights into other worlds. A trip to Paris, just for the fun of it! Three months at Lake Constance to "regain her strength" to cope with the day-to-day toil—wasn't it amazing what some people pursued? The woman had extolled the glorious landscapes around the lake in such glowing words. Clara decided that, as soon as she got home, she would look in the atlas to find out exactly where the Swabian Sea lay.

Home . . . With every mile between her and Berlin, the meaning of that word grew blurrier. In Clara's heart, a welcome indifference began to appear, sweeping aside her homesickness and worry like dust. Matthias was in capable hands—not for nothing had she interviewed thirty nannies before deciding on Christel. And her mother had promised to check in every day and cook for Gerhard. Clara thought he'd probably get by better without her, considering how he felt her as a burden so much of the time. He might only notice her absence because she wasn't there to knock around. Even if he actually missed her, well, she couldn't help that. So she relaxed and enjoyed the train journey, open to every impression that came her way.

With eager eyes, she looked out the window, where the forested hills of Taunus were rolling past. So much open country! So much air to breathe!

"How must it be, living on the land?" she murmured softly. But she received no answer, because her traveling companions had fallen asleep.

***

In four days, they reached Reims. It was just after midday when, in a restaurant beside the station, they enjoyed their first French meal: chicken in a white wine sauce and *pommes dauphines*. Josephine suggested spending a night in the town, but Clara wanted to push on and tackle the last short stretch as soon as they were done eating.

"Just imagine Isabelle's face if we come knocking on her door this evening!"

Josephine thought about it, then nodded. "Then we'll have to find some sort of vehicle to take us to Hautvillers. Shall I see if my miserable French will do to haggle a decent price out of the coach drivers in front of the station?"

A short time later, they were sitting in a coach on their way to Hautvillers. The sun was shining as they drove through the outskirts of Reims, and a soft breeze drifted across the landscape of vines beyond.

"Have you ever seen such beautiful countryside?" Clara asked euphorically. "The pretty houses, the gardens all so well tended—it's like something out of a picture book!" In every front garden they passed were bushes laden with berries, and the branches of trees drooped low and heavy beneath the weight of ripening apples and pears.

Josephine, too, was fascinated by the Garden of Eden they were riding through. "The people here seem so relaxed!" She pointed to a group of women walking along the road with hoes and baskets, unhurried, laughing and talking cheerfully. "When I think about how frantic everyone in Berlin seems to be . . . !"

Their enthusiasm only grew when they left Reims behind and were out among the seemingly infinite vineyards, where red and green grapes hung luminescent between the deep-green leaves. It was so appealing that Clara was on the verge of asking the driver to stop so that they could pick some. *I don't believe it*, she thought, when the next moment the driver, a young man of perhaps twenty, jumped down from his bench, dodged into the nearest row of vines, and skillfully snipped off two heavy, low-hanging bunches. Smiling, he handed a bunch each to Josephine and her.

"*Merci!*" they said simultaneously.

"I haven't had a man able to read what's in my mind for a very long time," Clara said with a laugh, and popped one of the sweet grapes into her mouth.

"This must be it," said Josephine, looking from the building to the address that Micheline Guenin had written in her letter. At the sight of the large house and surrounding gardens and vineyards, her eyes grew bigger and bigger. "It's like paradise! And the house . . . it's so much grander than I ever thought it would be. I can't imagine a lovelier way to live. Can you?"

Clara, still completely overwhelmed by the drive to Hautvillers, nodded in awe. Suddenly, she felt far less sure of herself than she had in the days they had spent traveling. How could anyone possibly be unhappy in such extravagantly beautiful surroundings? Isabelle had probably cut off all ties with Berlin forever. She might see their arrival as an undesired intrusion. "Should we really just barge in? Or wouldn't it be better to try and find Madame Guenin, so she can tell us how Isabelle is first?"

But even as she whispered to Josephine, the huge door of the house opened, and from inside appeared an older woman with a round face and the liveliest eyes Clara had ever seen.

"You must be Madame Gropius! And you've brought a friend along, too. *Mon Dieu*, you've taken such a load off my heart!" Before Clara knew it, the woman was embracing her warmly. "I'm Micheline, the one who wrote you the letter. Now everything will be good again."

Soon, they were sitting in the kitchen in Isabelle's house. It smelled of soup and the herbs that had been hung to dry above the window. Clara, who liked to use herbs when she cooked, sniffed: rosemary, thyme, and maybe oregano, too? The mix of odors was invigorating, practically intoxicating.

While Micheline Guenin set out water and wine on the table, Clara tried to imagine Isabelle cooking at the stove. The businessman's daughter doing housework—she really couldn't picture it. And where was Isabelle?

"She's upstairs, in her room. I was with her just now. I try to look in two or three times a day, depending on how much time I can spare. Ghislaine—she lives across the street—also comes by every day to check on her," said Micheline, before Clara had formulated her question in French. "But Ghislaine owns the tavern on the village square, and her hands are always full."

"Then I find it even nicer that the two of you have taken such good care of our friend," said Clara warmly. "How is she now?"

The neighbor shrugged. "Well, she gets out of bed occasionally, for an hour or two."

Josephine and Clara exchanged a look. That sounded good! But what Micheline said next destroyed their seed of hope before it could take root.

"But that doesn't mean she's part of this life again! Oh, no, she's lost every bit of her *joie de vivre*. She's not interested in anything. Grapevines aren't like potatoes or apples, which grow all by themselves! Vines are like small children—they need all your attention; they want to be cuddled and spoiled. Day after day, month after month, they present us with new demands. Claude Bertrand, the overseer of the estate, has been looking after the vineyards through the summer, as much as he could, at least. But a lot has fallen into a sorry state. And now we've got the harvest coming up, and there's so much that Claude really needs to discuss with Madame Feininger!" The old woman shook her head with concern. "And this year, it's all or nothing."

"Why?" Clara asked, her voice slightly hoarse. It all sounded so dramatic.

"Well, you have to keep in mind that the turn of the century is next year. More people will be drinking more champagne than usual and choosing their bottles with even more care. For the few who can afford it, for a day like that, the very best will be just good enough! So we must all be prepared with the best champagne we can make."

All this talk was exciting the elderly champagne maker, it seemed, for her cheeks were glowing red.

"But let's forget the turn of the century for now. For Isabelle, this harvest is crucial; the money she'll make from selling the grapes will have to last her for an entire year. But instead of working with Claude and preparing everything, Isabelle sits around listlessly and stares off into space. Sometimes I fear she has lost her mind. Really, I just don't know anymore." Micheline hung her head in resignation.

Clara felt her heart sinking. "It really looks so bad?"

"It's worse. Lately, word has got around the region that Isabelle can't get back on her feet. The vultures are waiting for her to finally give in. In Champagne, land is the rarest commodity of all. Only the wine grown *here* can call itself champagne! The prospect that the poor widow Feininger might sell her estate is on a lot of minds right now." A deep crease formed in the center of Micheline's forehead as she said those last words.

Clara frowned too. "But this beautiful house, the vineyards—everything looks so abundant. Isabelle isn't seriously thinking about giving it all up, is she?"

Micheline shrugged. "If something doesn't happen soon, there won't be any other choice."

Josephine gestured to the end of the long table, where a large stack of letters lay in a basket. "Is that all business mail?"

Micheline looked at her. "Not all of it. That's all the mail from the last few months. Condolences, private letters, bills, everything!" She shook her head. "Isabelle and I, we're friends now, but I would never dare to open her correspondence."

"So you're saying that since Leon died, the entire business side has been ignored?"

Micheline nodded.

Clara could hardly believe her eyes when she saw how Josephine pulled the basket over to her.

"Your businesswoman's heart might be breaking to see such neglect," Clara said sharply, speaking German to Josephine, "but we're here for Isabelle. She's our main concern, not this winery or anything else." When she saw Josephine's piteous look, Clara realized that her friend was afraid to see Isabelle; tending to the business side was only a way to postpone the inevitable.

Micheline, who had followed the exchange silently, cleared her throat. "Before you go up to see your friend, I should probably warn you."

Clara and Josephine looked at Isabelle's neighbor. More bad news . . . ?

***

She heard voices. Clara's voice. And Josephine's. That was strange. She often heard voices, but mostly it was Leon's. He spoke to her every day. She didn't understand what he said or what he wanted from her, and it made no difference anyway. He had abandoned her. She was alone. Alone on an island in a black ocean of loneliness. The voices were the waves lapping against the shore; they came and went. Sometimes she heard sounds from before she was married: the clattering of pots when her mother's new cook was in the kitchen or Josephine tossing pebbles at her window to call her down for their next bicycle ride. Life had been so uncomplicated back then.

She briefly laid one hand on her belly, which was growing larger all the time. That was the dwelling place of the pain, a pain that always reminded her of her loss. A soft knocking at the door, then. She sighed, annoyed. Why didn't Micheline simply leave?

"Isabelle?"

She felt her body stiffen. That voice . . . Her heart began to pound, and sweat broke out on the palms of her hands. She wiped them on a pillow. It wasn't possible. She was alone. Alone on an island . . .

"Isabelle." That voice again, a little louder. "It's me, Clara!"

A harsh buzzing noise filled Isabelle's head.

"Josephine is here, too. Can we come in?" The sound of robust shoes on the plank floor. Footsteps entering her room.

Slowly, Isabelle turned around. She squinted.

"You? How is . . . why . . . you've come." Words formed in her mind, and she wanted to speak all of them but could not. She wanted to let out all the suppressed screams but could not. The lump in her throat swelled and swelled.

With a cautious smile, Clara came toward her; like an angel, she opened her arms wide. "Isabelle, I'm so terribly sorry."

Those arms thrown around her, so caring, protective. The warmth, the unaccustomed closeness, so strange. Tears filled her eyes, poured hot down her cheeks, gathered at the corners of her mouth.

She had not cried for months. Instead, she had let the pain grow until it had swallowed every single feeling in her. But now, in Clara's arms, the tears so long held back came rushing out. Isabelle sobbed and sobbed. And Clara rocked her in her arms like a child.

Chapter Twenty-Three

Isabelle let herself be led downstairs without resisting. Micheline was standing in the entryway, buttoning her cardigan. With a satisfied smile, she nodded to Isabelle. "Everything will be better now, *ma chère*," she said, then she opened the door and left.

Had Micheline asked her friends to come? Feeling numb, she followed Josephine and Clara into the living room, where Josephine immediately flung open the double door to the terrace.

"What a glorious view! Can't we sit outside?" She waved out to the terrace. "This summer in Berlin has been terribly wet, and there's hardly been any chance to sit outdoors."

Isabelle shrugged. Inside, outside—what difference did it make?

Josephine grabbed a few cushions from the sofa and brought them out to the wicker furniture on the terrace. Clara had gone into the kitchen, and when she came back out, she was carrying a tray of food.

"Your neighbor made some soup. And I cut some bread and found a bottle of wine—Madame Guenin had put it in a bucket of cold water to cool. I hope that was all right? A warm meal can't hurt, especially considering your condition, can it?" Clara cast a worried glance at Isabelle's swollen belly.

That was so typical of Clara, framing every statement as a question! A trace of a smile appeared momentarily on Isabelle's face.

The three friends positioned themselves around the wicker table. While Josephine and Clara sighed with delight at the beauty of their surroundings, Isabelle blinked and looked around as if she were seeing everything for the first time. Three half-barrels full of red geraniums. Who had planted those? The sun settled gradually below the vineyards, dousing the landscape in an orange-red glow. The vines were reaching out toward the house as if they wanted to take hold of it. And the grapes! When had they grown so big? Did they still taste sour? For a moment, Isabelle was tempted to go to the nearest vine and pick a bunch. But her legs did not want to obey her mind, and she stayed motionless in her chair. She knew that she was supposed to feel something. Pleasure, perhaps, at the sight of the flowers. Shame at her unkempt appearance. Clara and Josephine had been clearly shocked at the sight of her, although they had tried hard to cover it. And she knew she should have felt hunger or at least a little bit of an appetite. Clara had gone to so much trouble to set the table nicely. But nothing came. She was still dead inside.

The wall of the house behind them radiated the stored warmth of the sun. For the second time that day, Isabelle felt herself held in a loving embrace, but this time it wasn't Clara's arms but her own house enfolding her. Her house . . . the house that she had fallen so deeply in love with before it became her prison. Tears sprang to her eyes again.

Josephine and Clara, just then dishing out the soup, exchanged a worried, helpless look.

"I'm sorry," Isabelle said once she gathered herself. "I don't know what's gotten into me." She sniffed loudly. Her crying attack had left her exhausted, and at the same time, she felt a little freer than before. "It must just be how happy I am that you've come," she said flatly.

"Don't go apologizing for crying," said Josephine. "When I think that Leon isn't here anymore"—she turned away—"I almost start crying myself," she whispered, her voice raw and breaking.

For a long moment, the only sound was the hum of the cicadas in the nearest bushes. It was Clara who broke the silence. "How did it happen?" she asked softly. "Your neighbor—who's lovely, by the way—didn't say anything about it in her letter. Can you . . . do you want to talk about it?"

Why *shouldn't* she talk about it? Isabelle closed her eyes and let out a long, deep sigh. "It happened on the same day as the festival in Hautvillers in honor of the Ice Saints, who spared us, the winemakers, this year. I asked Leon to stay. He'd been quite successful in several races in the weeks before. But he wanted to go to . . ." She trailed off, bit her lip. Where had he wanted to go? She couldn't remember, then stopped trying. "Two dogs ran under his wheels on a long, steep descent. He had a bad fall, and they took him to the hospital in Épernay, where the doctors diagnosed him with concussion." Objectively, and feeling little emotion inside, she told them the rest. "He was on the road to recovery. He was supposed to come home the next day. I'd already prepared everything for him—the house was so clean it was almost glowing, and there were flowers and his favorite meal. Then it happened: a blood vessel in his head burst in the middle of the night, and he suffered a stroke. They couldn't save him." Even as she spoke, she felt the chill coming down on her again, the icy veil that had settled on her skin like frost back then in the hospital.

Clara silently took her hand and held it tightly. The cold retreated.

"I don't know about you, but I'm thirsty," said Josephine, lifting the bottle out of the bucket. "Clara couldn't find any water in the kitchen, but she *did* manage to find this wine. Don't you think we should open it?"

"That isn't wine. It's Guenin champagne," said Isabelle when she saw the label.

Josephine immediately put the bottle back in the bucket. "I'm sorry. I didn't know."

Isabelle chuckled a little but with no real spirit. "It's all right. Here in France, they drink champagne all the time. They don't wait for special days, like we do in Germany. They even served champagne at Leon's wake. And I'm sure that Micheline would be disappointed if you didn't accept her welcome gift." She nodded encouragingly at Josephine, who immediately went back to work on the cork.

Soon came a loud pop, and Josephine poured the champagne. Each of the three women took a glass and held it aloft a little helplessly.

It was Clara who managed to break the uncomfortable silence. "To our reunion!"

"To our reunion!" said Isabelle and Josephine together.

When each of them had drunk, Josephine spoke up. "How are *you* now? Are you coping, more or less?"

Isabelle looked at her with empty eyes.

Josephine swept her arm wide. "The vineyards, the harvest coming up, and there must be a few employees here who have to be told what to do and supervised. Can you do all of that?"

"Josephine," Clara said, with a note of warning. "Isabelle, I'm sure, is in no state to talk about business matters. You haven't even eaten anything. The soup is delicious; try at least a little," she said in exaggerated encouragement.

Isabelle ignored Clara's urging. With her eyes cast down, Isabelle said, "To be honest, I'm afraid I've rather let things slide. I can't seem to rouse myself to do anything. What's the point? I can't go out into the vineyards and pretend that everything is fine! Without Leon, none of it makes any sense. I . . . oh—" She broke off and shook her head. It was the first time since Leon's death that she had tried to put how she felt into words. She had not been particularly successful, she knew. She looked at her two friends with a sudden flash of anger. Look at them, sitting there! Untouched by death—or by life, for that matter. Neither of them knew anything. Not a thing!

"How can you say that your life has no sense?" said Clara softly. "You're going to have a child, Leon's child! Are you trying to say it isn't worth living for that?"

"Leon's child," Isabelle repeated tonelessly. "He was so happy when he heard the news." She looked down at her own body as if it were something foreign. "I can't find any joy in it. I pray and I pray that everything has been a huge mix-up. A bad dream, you know? All the time, I think that Leon will be coming around the corner any minute, and I'll wake up, and everything will be good. But there's no way to wake from this nightmare." Her eyes were brimming with tears again. "I miss him so much."

This time it was Josephine who took her hand and squeezed it.

Isabelle talked, and she cried. When the sun was long gone, the air grew chilly. Clara went into the house and returned a minute later with a stack of blankets. Josephine lit two large candles. Once they had made themselves comfortable again, Isabelle went on. She talked about Leon's cycling ambitions and that he had wanted to sell the estate. She told them about her despair when he had told her that. And she spoke about her love for the house and how she had felt, for the first time in her life, that she was truly where she was meant to be.

"This is where I belong! I was so certain of that. I talked as if my life depended on it, trying to convince Leon not to sell this place. Luckily, Micheline had given me an idea of how I could earn money easily with the estate, and that was crucial. When I told Leon what I had in mind, he finally agreed, on condition that I take care of everything and that he could dedicate himself completely to his sport."

"He was confident that you could do it?" asked Clara, impressed.

Isabelle smiled and nodded. She frowned and listened to what was going on inside herself. During her narration, she had felt something, a gentle movement deep in her heart. She didn't know what to call it, only that it felt foreign and unaccustomed.

"After his accident, it was as if Leon had reached some kind of enlightenment. Suddenly, he didn't want to sell anymore and wanted to throw himself heart and soul into this place instead. We wanted to lead the Feininger estate to success, together. We were so full of hope. We wanted to show the world we could do it! And then—" She sobbed. "Nothing is how it was anymore. I'm alone, and all I see in front of me is a mountain of unsolved and unsolvable problems."

It was nearly two in the morning when Clara and Josephine went to bed in one of the guest rooms. Before that, they had cleaned everything up and taken Isabelle back to her room.

"I'm so happy that you're here," she had whispered, her last words that night.

Oh my goodness, what have we gotten ourselves into here, Clara thought, staring at the dark ceiling overhead.

"Can't you sleep, either?" whispered Josephine beside her. "I'm dead tired, really, but everything has got me too stirred up to sleep."

"I'm the same," said Clara, and turned to face Josephine. "Were you as shocked as I was at the sight of her?" Isabelle had looked like an old woman. She had tied her hair into a single braid that hung dirty and lifeless down her back. Clara was not sure they would be able to untangle it. Was it so matted that cutting it all off was the only solution? The gray smock that smelled unpleasantly of old sweat. And underneath, her distended belly . . .

"Isabelle looks far worse than the women sitting at the sewing machines in her father's factory twelve hours a day. When I first saw her, I didn't recognize Isabelle there at all. If Madame Guenin hadn't given us some warning . . . and the way her eyes are completely lifeless. Now I know what Madame Guenin meant when she said she didn't know if Isabelle was ever even listening. I feel so sorry for her! How far along is her pregnancy, do you think?"

"I guess she's in her fourth or fifth month," Clara answered, thinking about it for a moment. "But she's a bag of bones, and it makes her belly look even bigger."

Josephine rolled to her side. "A child, right now—"

"It's a blessing!" Clara interrupted her vehemently. "Children are always a blessing. It's all she has left of Leon."

"But you saw Isabelle! She isn't even able to look after herself, let alone her business. How can she possibly take care of a baby?"

"The child isn't going to come tomorrow," said Clara. "For now, I think we have to be satisfied that Isabelle actually got out of bed and came out to the terrace with us. That's more than Madame Guenin has managed in the last few months." In the darkness, she could only imagine the skeptical look on Josephine's face. "We have to be patient; Isabelle has suffered an unspeakable loss. One part of her doesn't want to believe that Leon is dead, and at the same time her grief is eating her from the inside. And because it's all so hard to bear, she's gone into a kind of shock or paralysis. You heard her say that she can't get herself to do anything."

"Ah, paralysis. As the wife of the learned doctor, I imagine you've learned something about the human soul, too?" Josephine asked, her tone ironic.

"All it takes is a little empathy, no more. Put yourself in Isabelle's shoes—after a tragedy like that, you certainly wouldn't get everything back under control from one day to the next. We have to try to lead her back to life again, a little at a time."

Josephine sighed. "But we don't have all the time in the world to do it! My own business is waiting for me back in Berlin, and Gerhard will make your life hell if you stay here longer than necessary. We should sit down and make a plan tomorrow morning." As if her words had given her new energy, Josephine stood up and went to the window to open it. The room immediately filled with the sounds of the chirruping night insects.

Clara took a deep breath of the sweet, cool air streaming in through the window. It smelled of lemons and oranges and lavender. Although everything around them was so sad, the scent made her happier than she'd felt for ages. Softly but with determination, she said, "Today, for the first time in I don't know how long, Isabelle came out of her shell. If we approach her condition like a business, we'll scare her straight back into it." Clara sat up and pointed with her chin toward the window. "Can you smell the sweetness in the air here? It's that sweetness that Isabelle has to smell again. She has to experience that life without Leon is still worth living. There's no timeline for a resurrection like that, no plan it can possibly follow."

Chapter Twenty-Four

The following morning, despite only a few hours of sleep, Clara was up early. The cry of the rooster, the chirping of the crickets, the shouts of the workers already out in the vineyards—all these morning sounds seemed so strange and refreshing. Instead of tying her hair up in her usual severe bun, she wove it quickly into a single, loose braid. Then, barefoot, she went to the kitchen and, with some effort, got a fire going in the stove. When she had two large pots of water set to heat, she went into the hallway and opened one door after another. Pantry. Utility room. Laundry. And here, the bathroom, just as she'd imagined a bathroom in such a grand house might look. A washbasin, a mirror, an ornate iron shelf painted white and topped with a stack of towels, and an enamel tub directly under the window. When Clara opened the window, the sweet perfume of roses wafted in. Following an inspiration, she went behind the house, plucked several handfuls of purple rose petals, and gathered them in her apron. A few fresh leaves from the peppermint growing between the roses, a few stalks of lavender, and last of all a handful of verbena—did Isabelle even know what treasures she had in her garden?

Back in the kitchen, she added a third pot of water to the stove and tossed in the peppermint and lavender and some of the rose petals. The water in the pot turned a pale green before taking on a pink tinge, and the delicate smell of roses spread through the kitchen. Then she went in search of soap. In the laundry, she found a ceramic jar. She expected there would be brown, sudsy lye inside, but when she lifted the lid, the soap was white and clean and fragrant. Maybe the French added perfume to their soft soap? Clara carried her discovery back to the bathroom. The soap and her herbal concoction would produce a lovely aroma in the bath.

"What are you doing up so early?" asked Josephine, who appeared in the doorway. "Isabelle is still asleep, and I'm still tired, too, frankly." She underlined her words with a very unladylike yawn.

"We didn't come here to rest," said Clara, unperturbed. "Help me carry the pots with the hot water into the bathroom, then we can put more on to heat. When the herbal mixture is done, I'm going to fix a bath worthy of a queen for Isabelle! And I've got an idea for what comes afterward."

"Aha," said Josephine.

"Do you remember that time Isabelle invited us to Konnopke's in Goethe Park and we ate potato pancakes?" said Clara, as they each took a handle of the large steaming pot.

Josephine's already doubtful expression looked even more puzzled. "*Now* you remember those greasy things?"

Clara sighed. Sometimes her clever friend could really be quite thick. "What would you say if we made potato pancakes for lunch? There are potatoes in the pantry, and I found a few apples we can use for applesauce. Maybe we can tempt Isabelle's appetite with something typically Berlin?"

Isabelle sank so deeply into the tub that only her nose and eyes remained above the surface. A few rose petals stuck to her lips, and she blew them away gently. The water was warm and smelled wonderful, thanks to Clara's herbal infusion. Isabelle felt her cramped limbs loosening up a little.

"Feels good, doesn't it?" Clara was looking triumphantly down at her. "If you'd like, I'll wash your hair for you."

Before Isabelle could reply, Clara set to work on her matted braid. Isabelle put up with the tugging and pulling, and she let Clara work the soap into her hair. Clara only meant well, after all.

"Head back!" said her friend, and the bucketful of fresh water splashed over Isabelle's head. "You'll be feeling much better after that," Clara added, when Isabelle, a moment later, wrapped a towel around her head like a turban. "Stay in the tub a little longer, and I'll bring you a cup of verbena tea. That will give you a boost."

A few minutes later, Isabelle accepted the cup from Clara and sipped obediently at the pale-green tea. Then she watched as Clara left again and felt relieved.

It wasn't that she didn't appreciate Clara's efforts. The bath was nice. The tea, too. And the smell of frying potatoes drifting from the kitchen to the bathroom was very tempting indeed. But it would have been all the same to Isabelle if she'd rubbed herself down with a cold cloth, drunk water, and eaten the potatoes raw. Nothing now was how it had been, and a handful of rose petals wasn't going to change that. Nor was the perfectly ironed black linen dress that Clara, with a motherly smile, had hung over the valet stand next to the tub.

Over lunch, Isabelle asked her friends questions so they would describe what was going on in their lives instead of prodding at her. Josephine talked about her flourishing bicycle business, and Clara talked at great length about her son, Matthias. The potato pancakes tasted good, and Isabelle even ate a second one.

After they had finished eating, Josephine asked Isabelle for a short tour of the estate. Isabelle agreed. They had come all the way from Berlin on her account; the least she could do was show them around.

They went through the courtyard and visited the horses and the peacocks. Their brace of chicks had now grown into lovely young birds—the cries of admiration and adoration from Josephine and Clara showed Isabelle that her friends were impressed. For Clara, the peafowl were the most amazing discovery; she thought they looked elegant and "aristocratic." At the sight of the blackberry bushes loaded with ripe fruit, Clara let out a little shriek. "The berries have to be picked and preserved immediately. You'll have a wonderful supply for the winter."

Isabelle only nodded slowly.

When they walked beyond the garden and into the vines, her friends' delight only grew. "All these vineyards belong to you?" Josephine said, her eyes wide.

Isabelle smiled and said, yes, they did. She crouched and picked up a handful of earth. "See the light-colored particles? That's chalk. It gives the soil good drainage. Grapevines don't like to get their feet wet. And do you see the little colored spots?" She lifted her hand and let a little earth sift through her fingers. Concentrating, Clara and Josephine followed the motion with their eyes. "The soil here is particularly rich in minerals, and you can taste that later in the champagne. The people here claim that the *terroir* here is unique . . . It's a little like magic."

Her friends listened reverently.

"This special soil, the care we take, and the good weather sent by God—that's the holy trinity here in Champagne," Isabelle went on. "A champagne dealer in Reims explained it to me like that, and I've never forgotten his words."

"Am I just imagining it, or is there a special light here?" said Clara, lifting her hands to take in the landscape all around. "It's like everything is coated with gold."

Isabelle nodded. "That comes from the chalk in the soil, too, they say. It takes the harshness from the sunlight, and the colors are less glaring, more muted, as if a painter has gone to extraordinary lengths with his work."

The wine cellar with its various levels and long corridors and the sight of the thousands and thousands of champagne bottles left the Berliners speechless. It was so cold! And it smelled so odd! Like earth and chalk and wine, all mixed together. When Isabelle told them about the useless one-eyed cellar master, her voice took on an ironic, almost joking, edge, and she noticed how Clara and Josephine exchanged an exultant look.

Isabelle smiled gently. What had *she* felt the first time she saw old Jacques's estate? The open, sweeping lands and the imposing wine cellar—hadn't she been just as fascinated as her friends were now? Hadn't her heart opened at the sight?

"As wonderful as it all looks, the Feininger estate is in serious trouble, and not only since Leon's death."

Josephine and Clara were both shocked to hear how another producer had stolen away their American customers.

"Have you found new customers?" Josephine asked.

Isabelle smiled bitterly. "Our champagne is far too sweet for European tastes. The people who drink champagne want an elegant, dry wine, not the kind of sweet champagne my old-fashioned cellar master brews."

"But . . ." Clara looked helplessly at the countless bottles. "You mean that . . ."

Suddenly, it felt good to Isabelle to destroy the romantic imaginings of her two friends. Almost with pleasure, she said, "All of this is worth as good as nothing. I'm rich in land and champagne bottles but poor as a church mouse otherwise. Apart from a mountain of problems, I've got nothing." Without another word, she left her shocked friends there and went back upstairs. It served them right!

In her bedroom, exhausted, she let herself fall onto her bed. Clara had changed the sheets and covers that morning. But instead of snuggling into the fresh bedclothes and feeling better, a sense of abandonment, of being forsaken, rose inside her. Nothing was the way it had been—and fresh sheets couldn't change that.

Chapter Twenty-Five

Over the next few days, Clara tended carefully to Isabelle, her tone invariably encouraging. She cleaned and polished the house as if she were trying to win some sort of competition. There was tea in the pot and freshly baked cake—Isabelle had to make an effort to accept so much charity graciously. But in reality, all she really wanted was to be left alone. Why couldn't Clara see that? Josephine, to Isabelle's relief, kept more to herself, but Isabelle suspected that she was active in the background. She was probably fixing up the chicken stall with Claude or busy with some other work around the estate. That had always been her friend's forte, fixing broken things. *Then she's in her element on the Feininger estate*, Isabelle thought grimly. She'd probably already been through Jacques's account books in search of orders that simply didn't exist. Isabelle could well imagine the look of horror on her friend's face! She should never have said a word about the miserable state of the business. If she'd only acted as if things were going well, then they wouldn't be so unbearably *caring* all the time!

It was good to have Clara and Josephine around. At the same time, though, everything inside her rebelled against their enforced closeness, and she withdrew to her bedroom for hours at a time. But even with eyes and shutters closed, the inner immobility that had paralyzed her for the previous weeks and months was diminished. Something had been set in motion. Sometimes she felt a flicker of dry humor, then a touch of resentment when Clara brought her yet another cup of tea. Were these stirrings the start of a return to normal life? Normal life—no one asked her if that was what she wanted or if was even *capable* of leading one again. And at the same time, she knew that her friends would not give up until everything was back on a steady course.

Late in the afternoon of the third day, Clara knocked on her bedroom door and came in. "Isabelle, your friend Ghislaine is downstairs. She's invited all three of us to her restaurant. Shall we go? You haven't been out for any fresh air yet today."

Clenching her jaw, Isabelle watched Clara set her shoes by the bed and then go to the wardrobe to find a good dress. She ordered her around, treating her like a child who had to obey! Suddenly, she felt driven into a corner by Clara's and Josephine's ministrations. She sat up abruptly and screamed, "I don't want to eat! I want to be left in peace! When will you finally get that into your damn heads?!" She snatched the shoes and hurled them across the room. One of them missed Clara by a hair.

Clara and Josephine opened the door to Le Grand Cerf and walked in to a round of laughter from a group of men standing and drinking at the bar. While Josephine looked around inside the French tavern with interest, Clara—who rarely entered such a place—was intimidated by the loud, relaxed atmosphere. She wanted to leave immediately, but after the endless discussion she had had with Josephine about coming here, she had to at least stay a little while.

"There you are!" Ghislaine called from behind the bar. "All the tables are full at the moment, but you can stand here. I'll bring you something to eat." As she spoke, she shooed aside several of the men taking up space at the bar, and they did as they were bidden without complaint.

Ghislaine set two glasses of rosé wine in front of them, then she motioned to a good-looking man with blond hair.

"Allow me to introduce my brother, Daniel. These are Isabelle's friends from Berlin."

Daniel nodded by way of hello, then returned to the conversation among the men.

"I'm so happy you're here to support Isabelle," said Ghislaine with a warm smile. "She and I . . . we both suffered at the hand of fate, and at the same time. I know what she's going through. But at some point, I got on with my life, and she is still sick with grief. What can anyone do?" She raised her eyebrows helplessly, then went back to work.

"It would certainly help if Isabelle simply pulled herself together a bit," said Josephine roughly. She was losing some of her patience with Isabelle. While she could see Isabelle was grieving, she simply could not fathom how anyone could let herself go like that while the pile of unfinished business rose higher and higher. Clara understood the depth of Isabelle's misery, but she had no desire to fight with Josephine again just then, so she sipped at her glass and pretended to study the watercolors decorating the restaurant walls. On every one was a stag. And then she realized what the name of the restaurant meant—"the great stag."

"Surplus champagne—did you ever hear of any such thing? Even the expression—surplus!—my God, these people don't have a clue!" One of the men beside Clara had abruptly raised his voice.

"Not even the merest glimmer of a clue, or they'd know that you can only snap up things that actually exist!"

The men laughed and shook their heads.

"You might find surpluses in other industries, but certainly not around here," another said in a tone both disparaging and snobbish.

The one beside him added, "All they're after is a bargain, if you ask me. Lucky for me I don't have to rely on customers like that."

Clara frowned. She could follow the broad strokes of the exchange, certainly, but she didn't understand the specifics of what they were talking about.

"Americans!" another sniffed. "What do you expect?"

"It was worth it to them to take out a full-page ad in the newspaper," said the first man, and he tapped at a rolled-up newspaper that lay among the wine glasses, ashtrays, and empty plates.

"Daniel, you've been very quiet," one of the men said to Ghislaine's brother. His tone was mocking as he continued. "Could it perhaps have something to do with an upcoming appointment in Troyes? A very important appointment that your boss arranged *just for you?*" The men laughed heartily again.

Daniel replied, "How could anyone object to visiting Troyes?" he said, and laughed with the others.

Clara smiled, too, but she wasn't sure she had figured out what the men were really talking about. If she had understood right, there were some Americans who were looking to buy champagne. But why had the men laughed so long and loud about something like that? Finally, she screwed up her courage, tapped Ghislaine's brother on the arm, and said, "Excuse me, but I couldn't really avoid overhearing a little of your conversation. May I ask what . . . I mean . . ." She trailed off, feeling embarrassed, and looked away. Barging into a conversation like that was anything but polite, she realized. What must the man think of her? On the other hand, she thought she might find out something of use to Isabelle.

Ghislaine's brother looked at her in surprise. Then his face lit up; he pushed a lock of hair out of his face and grinned broadly. He grabbed the newspaper, unrolled it, and leafed through it until he had found the page he wanted. Then, speaking so softly that no one around them could hear, he said, "Read this! And don't let what the others say put you off—this might be very interesting to one special person."

Feeling a little uneasy, Clara took the newspaper from him.

Josephine looked over her shoulder impatiently. "Could you tell *me* what's going on, too?"

"Just a moment," Clara murmured absently.

"**WANTED!**" was printed in English across the top of the full-page ad in large black letters. Beneath that, smaller and in French, she read, *"Désirez."* Then came a short text in both English and French. As Clara scanned the words, her heart began to beat so hard it almost deafened her.

Grinning broadly, she turned to Josephine. "You want to know what's going on? Then read this!" she said ominously, and tapped the newspaper ad with her finger.

Both women were so excited that it was impossible for them to enjoy the atmosphere of the tavern a moment longer than absolutely necessary. As soon as they finished the meaty ragout Ghislaine served, they left for home again.

"Americans are coming to Troyes to buy remnant stocks of champagne for their fleet of steamboats on the Mississippi!" Josephine giggled childishly. "That's too good to be true!"

Clara nodded. "It's a gift from heaven. Oh, maybe not, but it's a chance you'll only get once in a hundred years. A *once-in-a-century* chance!"

Josephine giggled again. "How fitting that the men want to buy champagne to celebrate the *turn of the century.*"

"And isn't it wonderful that they're taking care of it this year." Clara laughed, too. A great load felt lifted from her heart. What a stroke of luck that they went to Le Grand Cerf, today of all days! What if they had never even seen the advertisement? She said a quick prayer of thanks to heaven as they marched through the growing darkness to Isabelle's house. Now everything would be good again.

A cat dashed across the road in front of them, quickly followed by another, and a loud hiss sounded from the blackberry bushes on their left.

Josephine stopped walking. She looked confused. "There's one thing I still don't understand. Why were the people in the tavern laughing about it?"

Clara shrugged. "If I understood them right, there's no such thing as 'surplus' champagne. Whether you get thousands of bottles in a particular year or only a few hundred, that in itself makes no difference to the price. But if it's a champagne popular with the experts and only a small amount is available, the price can climb immensely. At least, that's how Ghislaine's brother explained it to me. Either the Americans don't know that, or they just didn't choose their words very wisely. Whatever the case may be, the winemakers see no need to sell off small 'remnants' cheaply. But it could be just what we need." They started walking again, and Josephine fell into the same rhythm as Clara.

"You're right when you say that we can be happy that the others are not interested in the Americans' offer. This could be Isabelle's saving grace. When I think about how much champagne she has in her cellars . . . it's not exactly what I'd call surplus stock. It's more like a sea of champagne." Josephine laughed gleefully. "Oh, when we tell her about this!"

"Don't get your hopes up about Isabelle's reaction." Clara sighed. "She'll probably just repeat how nothing makes sense anymore."

Josephine stopped walking again. Her brown eyes sparkled, and she said, "Don't worry. I've got a good idea about how we can drag her out of her state."

Chapter Twenty-Six

"I'm supposed to go cycling? Are you out of your mind?" Isabelle stared at Josephine in shock.

Josephine replied with a grin, "Do you think I brought my bicycle all this way for nothing? The roads here are excellent, nothing like the potholed cow paths we had to put up with back in Berlin."

Isabelle shook her head. "Out of the question. Never, not in your wildest dreams." She was angry that she'd even bothered to come down for breakfast. She should have known that her friends would have some new idea in mind to raise her spirits.

"Now don't be so stubborn," Clara said. "You can't seriously miss out on me embarrassing myself on a bicycle again for the first time in *years*!"

"*You* would come?" Isabelle could not hide her disbelief. Clara had hated cycling ever since she broke her leg the first time she tried it. On top of that, her husband was rabidly opposed to women riding bicycles, and if he were ever to catch Clara on one . . .

Clara looked at her steadily and said, "Yes, I would. And Ghislaine is borrowing a bicycle and coming along, too."

"And she's making a picnic for us, which I must say is very nice of her."

Isabelle felt her resistance crumbling. "But I'm so out of shape," she said. "And I'm pregnant, too."

"We're not out to win races. Downhill is always easy," said Josephine dismissively. "On the way here, we followed an extremely picturesque river for a while. We could ride back along that stretch. And if we get tired, we'll find a coachman to drive us all back home."

An hour later, they were ready to go. Josephine and Isabelle pushed their bicycles from the barn to the front of the house, and Clara was allowed to use one of Leon's old bicycles, which Isabelle handed over with a heavy heart. In a closet, Isabelle found a few straw hats, which she distributed to her friends as protection against the late August sun. Josephine wore bloomers and a tight-fitting jacket, while Clara and Isabelle were dressed in plaid blouses and plain cotton skirts, which they gathered at the hems with clothespins so the fabric wouldn't get caught in the spokes.

"Don't you dare go racing off downhill!" Clara said. "And not too fast around the curves, all right?"

"Clara is right. In Isabelle's condition, you shouldn't risk anything," said Micheline, who had emerged from her house with her sister-in-law, Marie.

Isabelle and Josephine exchanged a look. And suddenly it was back, the old camaraderie that had bound them in the past. They had ridden side by side for hundreds—oh no!—*thousands* of miles, each motivating the other, overcoming weariness, sore legs and backs, hunger and thirst.

Isabelle mounted her bicycle. The handlebars under her hands, her feet on the pedals—everything felt so familiar but at the same time so strange.

A moment later, Ghislaine rode toward them with a young woman in tow. "This is Sophie, the baker's daughter," Ghislaine introduced the cyclist, who stopped beside her, red-faced. "The bicycle was a birthday present from her parents. She received it in May, but Sophie hasn't trusted herself to ride it until now."

"Looks like we have the perfect group," said Josephine to Isabelle, who smiled. "Well then, shall we?" said Josephine loudly and with an encouraging nod to the others.

Their route led them down through Hautvillers and into the gently rolling hills of Champagne. When they reached the Marne, Ghislaine suggested they follow the river and ride in the direction of Tours-sur-Marne, and the others immediately agreed.

"I didn't know that you could ride a bicycle," said Isabelle, short of breath as she rode beside Ghislaine.

"You know almost nothing about me," Ghislaine replied and laughed, then she pedaled ahead to Josephine. Gritting her teeth, Isabelle realized she could not keep up. She was completely out of shape; even Clara could ride faster! Her legs were shaking as she rode alongside Sophie, behind the others.

The sun beat down from a cloudless sky, and at ten in the morning, it was already so hot that the air across the landscape shimmered. But along the Marne, a fresh breeze off the river made the cycling more comfortable, and the air smelled of watercress, weeds, and freshly cut grass. Isabelle's hands, which had been clenched around the handlebars at the start, now relaxed, and her breathing grew more regular. The road was mostly empty, and only occasionally did they pass a horse-drawn cart. Most of the farmers were busy out in the vineyards—the harvest had already begun, and apart from their small cycling group, no one seemed to be enjoying the luxury of a day off.

Leon must have ridden along this road many times, thought Isabelle. He would have pedaled through here very fast while training for his great passion, cycle racing. A smile spread across her lips, and she suddenly felt closer to her husband than she had in all those weeks of mourning.

They had been riding for a good hour when they reached a flat area by the river shaded by huge old beech and pine trees. It was the perfect spot for a picnic.

With unaccustomed hunger, Isabelle watched while Ghislaine set out the picnic on a blanket that Clara had brought. Cold fried chicken, a salad with olives and artichokes, cheese, and grapes. And champagne! The women watched admiringly as Ghislaine, with practiced ease, opened the first bottle.

"*À la vôtre!*" she said, raising her glass.

"*Santé!*" said Josephine and Clara.

"*À la vôtre,*" Isabelle and Sophie repeated, then they turned to the food.

Well fed and satisfied, they lay down in the soft grass. Before Isabelle knew it, her eyes closed. The fresh air, the physical strain, all the food . . . Of course she was tired. It felt good to get out of the house again, she realized, and it was wonderful to have her friends there with her. A lovely outing, and so much better because Josephine and Clara were finally keeping their good advice to themselves.

Isabelle was woken by the warmth of the sun on her left cheek. She sat up, dazed. A moment later, two pairs of eyes were peering at her expectantly.

"Finally! I thought you weren't ever going to wake up. We have to talk, urgently!" said Josephine. Clara nodded energetically beside her.

"Where's Ghislaine? Has something happened?" In a second, Isabelle was wide awake, her heart pounding fearfully. Cycling was dangerous. But to her relief, Josephine said, "Everything's fine. Ghislaine and Sophie have gone to the next village to find someone who can give us a lift back to Hautvillers on a cart. They've been gone a long time, and they'll probably be coming back any moment. We've got something we need to discuss before they come back!"

"What, then?" Isabelle asked reluctantly.

"The chance of a lifetime!" said Clara excitedly.

Isabelle listened in silence as her two friends told her about the advertisement in the newspaper. With the end of the century fast approaching, the Americans were predicting that their countrymen's appetite for champagne would only increase. They were coming to Troyes and holding court in the Hotel l'Esplanade. Any winemaker who was interested in doing business with them simply had to take along a few bottles of champagne for tasting and be able to provide a list of their current stock.

Isabelle, of course, could see where they were going. To stall for time, she said, "Why Troyes? It's about seventy miles south of Épernay. If these people want to buy champagne, they could make it much easier for themselves and travel to Reims."

"Micheline said that huge champagne auctions took place in Troyes a long time ago. Maybe that's why the Americans chose it. But really, it makes no difference which town they're in," Josephine said impatiently.

"Don't you understand?" said Clara, almost pleading. "This could be *your* chance to get rid of your stock of champagne, all at once. You're the one who told us that no one in Europe is interested in your wine but that the Americans prefer those kinds of sweet wines—you have exactly what the Americans are looking for!"

Isabelle looked out over the sluggish waters of the Marne and nervously tried to find something to say. "There are hundreds of vintners in the Champagne region. What makes you think I have any chance at all with the Americans?"

"Because Americans like your champagne! And besides—we'll go with you," said Josephine. "You have all those pretty dresses in your wardrobe. If we do ourselves up nicely, three *alluring* young women . . . well, if we can't bewitch the Americans with our charms, who can?"

"You make it sound so easy. Selling champagne—that takes an expert!" Isabelle said. "Leon rode from pillar to post and managed to sell next to nothing, and now you think that we three women would have any more luck? What do we know about selling champagne? I don't care how loudly the men in Ghislaine's restaurant scoffed—no one around here is going to let good business slip through their fingers. I'm telling you, there will be dozens of vintners there. The competition will be huge." She shook her head. "The trip would be doomed to failure from the start."

An uncomfortable silence followed, but it seemed as if she had succeeded in convincing her friends that their idea would not work. "In the past, perhaps, before I knew just how miserably life could treat you, I might have let you talk me into such a folly. I would have looked on the whole thing as an adventure, with nothing to lose and everything to gain. These days, I know better."

"But—" Josephine began to say, sounding desperate.

"You know *nothing* better!" Clara blurted. "You're a coward, I'd say. You have no interest at all in finding a way back into your own life, especially when it's so much easier to sit around and drown in self-pity!" As she spoke, she stood up and grabbed Isabelle roughly by the arm, pulling her to standing. "Well, if that's how you feel, you might as well go and drown yourself right now. Maybe there are some creepers down there in the water that will pull you down, and then that's it for you! You'll be with your Leon again, and someone else can look after the Feininger estate, someone with some guts. Someone like that Henriette Trubert, who can hardly wait to sink her claws into your land." Clara let out a shrill laugh. "Maybe I'll pay her a visit this afternoon and tell her that she won't have to wait much longer, hmm?"

Frozen with shock, Isabelle could only stand and gape at her friend. This couldn't be good little Clara talking like that!

"Clara? We agreed that we would try it my way," whispered Josephine, sounding almost frightened.

"My way, your way!" Clara dismissed Josephine's objection. "We traveled six hundred miles to come here and help Isabelle. Day after day, we nurse poor *madame* like a bird that's fallen too early from its nest. And for what? 'I can't do that; I don't want to.'" She mimicked Isabelle's mournful tone. "You wanted to run the winery, and Leon left it up to you to do just that. A man puts his trust in you, and what do you do with it? And what about the baby in your belly? Are you planning on telling your child that her mama is the biggest coward of them all?"

"Who do you think you are, talking to me like that? You have no right!" Isabelle pulled her arm free. Every word Clara said was like a stroke from a whip. She had never thought that her friend could be so mean to her—especially not mothering, caring Clara.

"Clara, what's gotten into you?" cried Josephine in dismay.

"What's gotten into me? Do you really want to know? I am not a grieving widow. I am a loyal and loving wife, but that doesn't make everything in my life rosy." As she spoke she seemed to crumple, like a bellows with all the air gone out of it. "Oh, it's all so unfair!" Then she burst into tears.

Isabelle and Josephine looked at each other helplessly. Josephine held out a handkerchief to Clara.

After a moment, Clara blew her nose, then took a deep breath. Red-eyed, she looked out to the river and said, "I would give anything to have the chances you have! Making decisions for yourself. Setting things in motion and making sure they go where you want them to. Instead, Gerhard patronizes me like I'm a little girl. I can't even decide what soup goes on the table. I get the housekeeping money handed to me, and I have to account for every pfennig, and I have to beg and plead for household purchases. He has to approve the weekly meal plan in advance. I have to inform him about every step I take, whether I'm off shopping or going for a walk or visiting the library, where I'm quite welcome to borrow *Gardener's Monthly* or a respectable novel, but I must never dare to open one of his precious textbooks! Women are too stupid for anything like that, in his opinion. The only thing he gives me a free hand with is raising our son, because that's woman's work. Otherwise I have as little freedom as Gerhard can possibly manage, like a dog on a short chain."

She looked up, and in her expression Isabelle saw so much despair, so much suppressed fury, that a tremor ran down her spine. She sought some kind of comforting words, some solace.

But Clara looked at her threateningly and said, "Spare me your pity. I made my own bed, and now I have to lie in it. But you, Isabelle . . . go do something with your life." Her voice was hoarse now. "Think of that wind of change. You owe it to me and all the other women who have few opportunities."

Chapter Twenty-Seven

Daniel Lambert leaned against the windowsill in Henriette Trubert's office and watched his employer say good-bye to her guest. Until a few minutes earlier, the eighty-eight-year-old Francois Leblanc had been the proud owner of a very well-situated vineyard that he had worked by himself until that day. The sale of his Pinot Noir and Pinot Meunier grapes had given the old man a good living over the years, and now the sale of the vineyard itself had made him a rich man. Even richer, however, was Henriette Trubert—in land.

When Francois was gone, Henriette turned back toward Daniel, wearing a satisfied smile.

"If only it were always so easy," she said with a sigh and sat behind her desk. "Now Francois can go and enjoy his remaining years in warmer climes, where perhaps he will be free of the pain his arthritis caused him." She gestured to Daniel to sit in the chair in front of her desk. He did so reluctantly. This close to the harvest, every moment was precious, and Henriette knew perfectly well that he had no time to chat.

"Congratulations. The Leblanc vineyard is in one of the best locations in all of Champagne," he said, because he knew he was expected to say something.

Henriette laughed. "I'm the last person you need to tell that to! Best if you could go and look it over today and let me know what condition the vines are in. The Pinot Noir, in particular, will be a wonderful complement to our champagnes." Her smile vanished and, changing the topic abruptly, she said, "By the way, I have heard that Isabelle Feininger is traveling to Troyes to meet the Americans." Although she tried to adopt an indifferent tone, Daniel could see how tense Henriette really was. Her mouth, excessively made up as usual, was slightly pinched. The dark-red satin of her dress rustled with every nervous movement.

"I don't know anything about it, madame," he said calmly, although Ghislaine had already told him. *"The two visitors are a blessing,"* she had said, full of admiration. *"They really know how to get through to Isabelle."*

"I assume her friends from Berlin have put her up to it," Henriette said promptly. "As weak as Isabelle was the last few times I visited her, she would have been in no condition for something like this. If you ask me, the widow is far too frail for the trip, and the kind of tough negotiating she'll need to do down there is certainly beyond her." Henriette's tone betrayed both annoyance and impatience.

"Why worry about where Madame Feininger goes or what she does?" Daniel asked, as innocently as possible.

Henriette looked at him suspiciously. "You know perfectly well what this is about. I need to nudge the poor widow about *this* far to get her to sell me her estate!" She held up her right hand with the thumb and index finger a fraction of an inch apart. "She would probably have signed on the spot on my next visit. And then along come these friends of hers and mess up everything. What happens if Isabelle Feininger actually manages to sell her champagne to the Americans? Most likely it will put her back on her feet again, and she'll be as arrogant as she ever was. Who knows what else those Berlin witches are whispering in her ear? She might end up wanting to *stay* here. But *I* will put a stop to that!"

Isabelle back on her feet. Daniel could imagine far worse.

It must have shown on his face, because Henriette immediately said, "Daniel, we are talking about the land of your forefathers! When it belongs to me, you can do whatever you like with it. Picture that for a minute. No more slinking like a thief through the Feininger vineyards. You could legally, legitimately, walk through Lambert land again on your morning inspections. And on New Year's Eve, for the turn of the century, there will be a champagne with your name on it: Trubert-Lambert. Isn't that what you want?" Her voice had turned velvety soft and seductive.

Daniel closed his eyes as if to protect himself from the image that Henriette was sketching out for him.

"I'd rather talk about what you want," he said brusquely. "Why is it so important to you to own the Feininger land at all? You already own practically everything around the village. Why don't you simply buy Isabelle Feininger's crop from her? The result would be the same—we would have more grapes and could produce more champagne."

"And I thought that at least you would understand me." There was disappointment in Henriette's voice, along with a little bitterness that her next words only accentuated. "It isn't enough that my esteemed husband prefers practically anything to business, but it seems I also have a cellar master without the slightest sense of ambition." She sniffed disdainfully.

"What does my ambition have to do with your land?" Daniel replied, with no less disdain. "Isn't it always *my* champagnes that bring home one prize after another from the major shows? How would you describe my efforts to create the best champagne of all time, if not ambitious?"

She had some nerve to attack him like that. He practically breathed champagne, day and night; even in his dreams, he tasted the characteristics of the individual grapes on his tongue, possessed by the idea of creating the perfect cuvée. Did she really think he only did it for the money? His love of champagne, his passion for the grapes, his ambition to show everybody what a Lambert could truly do—*that* was what drove him.

"Don't you understand?" Henriette said, her voice becoming shrill. "Trubert champagnes can only be made from Trubert grapes, and those can only grow on Trubert land! Of course I could buy grapes, but it wouldn't be the same." Now it was she who closed her eyes for a moment.

Daniel didn't know what inner demons she encountered when she did that.

When she looked at him again, she said, "Do you think I don't know how my husband's affair with your sister sullies the name of Trubert, how everyone goes on about it the moment my back is turned? He *strives* after great love—ha! How ridiculous!" she spat. "I strive after something much grander, much bigger. Love dies but land survives. *I* will be the one to ensure that the name Trubert becomes the greatest name in all of Champagne! One day it will be like this: someone who wants to drink a glass of champagne will say, 'Let's open a bottle of Trubert!' and everyone who utters that name will do so with due reverence. No one will care what my adulterous husband is up to. Trubert *equals* champagne—as it should. And this is why I've been doing some serious thinking about your meeting with the Americans tomorrow."

"Oh yes?" said Daniel sharply. "You know what I think about the whole thing. If all your salesmen weren't already away, I never would have let you talk me into making this trip, not so close to the harvest. But so be it. I'll visit the Americans, introduce them briefly to our wines, and open the doors for future business. And then I'll say a friendly *au revoir*!" He made a fluttering gesture with one hand, meant to demonstrate his departure.

"And that is exactly what you won't do. Instead, you will sell the Americans Trubert champagne with all the passion and conviction you can muster. Whenever you visit our mutual friend, Raymond Dupont, in Reims, you seem able to handle the sales side very well indeed. And you'll do something else, too, which is sell our champagnes at such an unbeatable price that not even poor desperate Madame Feininger will be able to compete. This business with the Americans is her last chance. If she misses it, then she has no choice but to sell to me."

"But—"

"No buts. Here with me, you enjoy freedoms that would be the envy of any other cellar master. Have I ever interfered with how you create your champagnes? And now, just once, I ask you for a favor." She looked at him with an expression both imploring and uncompromising. "By tomorrow evening, I want to see Isabelle Feininger broken—her and her clever friends. You know what you have to do."

***

Troyes was a medieval city on the Seine, around eighty miles south of Reims. Until well into the seventeenth century, Troyes had been a major trade center for goods of every kind: silk from the Orient, fabrics from Holland, the finest Calabrian lace, orange trees from Spain, and far more besides. All of it arrived via ship, from the sea and up the Seine to the buyers in Troyes. In return, the foreign traders loaded their ships' holds with thousands of crates of champagne. The citizens of Troyes were so proud of this that they claimed that the historical old part of the city, if seen from above, was shaped like a champagne cork, which only went to show that Troyes was at least as important as Reims for the champagne trade.

As Daniel made his way through the narrow cobblestone alleys toward the square in front of the town hall, he wondered whether the American businessmen were aware of such historical facts when they chose the city as a place to buy champagne. He had other questions on his mind as well.

Why exactly was his loyalty to Henriette dwindling? The vineyards, the wine cellar, the champagne—he and Henriette seemed to have so many things in common, but he was beginning to realize that the gap between his goals and what his employer wanted from him was growing wider and wider.

With a sigh, he straightened the backpack in which he carried two bottles of the very finest Trubert Millésime and walked on. He would certainly do the best he could with this visit; the only thing he didn't yet know was how.

The Hotel l'Esplanade was opposite the town hall on the edge of the small city square. The square was a busy place: stalls were being set up for a fabric market that would be open to the public later in the day. Bales of fabric were being unloaded from carts, and anybody—like Daniel—who wanted to cross the plaza was left with no choice but to jump over mountains of cloth.

Daniel was doing his best to placate a cloth dealer who was upset that he had accidentally touched his wares when he saw them turn a corner: three young women prettily dressed, wearing smart silk dresses, elaborate hats, and matching lace-embroidered handbags. The only thing that did not fit with the otherwise elegant image was the wooden crate that two of the women carried with some difficulty between them. The fabric merchant, who had just been vilifying Daniel, whistled admiringly. "*Mesdemoiselles*, why so fast? Perhaps you'd like to see what I have for sale? The finest silk and lace, muslin, best quality—"

"The women have better things to do," said Daniel, and took a step toward the three women. "Madame Feininger, may I help?" He pointed to the crate that Isabelle's friends were hauling between them.

"Monsieur Lambert, you're here too?" said Isabelle, and it seemed to Daniel that he saw a faint glimmer of delight appear in her eyes. As he took the crate, in which he heard champagne bottles bumping against one another, he tried to conceal his dismay at her appearance. She was so pale! And her face, so thin . . . and not only her face. Apart from her protruding belly, she was little more than skin and bones, and even the many layers of her dress could not hide that. The frailty of the woman he had once seen radiate enormous strength moved Daniel deeply. A strange fluttering made its presence felt inside him, like the beating wings of countless butterflies.

Until now, Daniel had successfully managed to shield himself from developing feelings for any other person—except for his sister, Ghislaine. He liked women, and they certainly liked him, but his relationships had little to do with true love, which came with high expectations and made one vulnerable. True love could break your heart. He knew from his early boyhood how that felt. Back then, his father had taken his own life and left Ghislaine and him alone. Being abandoned—maybe that was what he feared most. And looking at Isabelle, he saw what that could do to a person. Yet, standing in front of the pale redheaded German, everything in him wanted to take her in his arms and protect her. Nothing and nobody should ever do Isabelle Feininger harm.

"I take it we are going in the same direction," he said, his voice suddenly raw, and he nodded toward the hotel where the Americans were waiting.

"Why are you here? Do you also have leftover stocks of champagne to sell? I thought that nobody was interested in this kind of business," said the brown-haired girl who had approached him in Le Grand Cerf. She looked more elegant and confident today than she had in Ghislaine's tavern. The same was true of the other woman, who was wearing a rather dashing hat with feathers and pearls. She, too, looked at him reproachfully.

Daniel smiled. "Don't worry. I won't stand in your way."

Apart from Daniel Lambert and Isabelle, no one from the region around Reims and Épernay had made the journey south. From the southern

Champagne region, however, two hapless winemakers were already waiting in the hotel lobby. They told the others that their vineyards, like so many others, had fallen prey to the phylloxera plague, and they had no money to replant. The champagnes they had to offer the Americans were, in fact, smaller quantities of leftover stock from better days, and the money would go to feeding their families awhile longer. When the men discovered that Daniel represented the great Trubert estate, they suddenly looked especially broken.

The Americans had planned their reception for 2:00 p.m. At fifteen minutes before the hour, a pimply young man with a sparse beard appeared and asked the vintners to work out among themselves in which order they would appear before the Americans. In awe at the Trubert name, the vintners from the south let Daniel go ahead. Josephine and Clara immediately began to protest, but Daniel said, "If I am first to meet these gentlemen, then Madame Feininger will be next in line."

The other two vintners accepted that, too. As they spelled out their names for the American, Daniel leaned close to Isabelle and, with an almost imperceptible wink, he whispered, "Believe me, sometimes starting second means finishing first."

Isabelle frowned, then watched as he hurriedly crossed the hotel lobby and disappeared through a door in the back.

The three Americans had rented a salon designed for much bigger events. Transom windows that reached to the ceiling flooded the room with light, which was reflected by the stucco ceiling and red-gold walnut parquetry of the floor. In the rear third of the room, the Americans had set up a long table, behind which they sat in a row. Their young assistant sat off to one side. None of them stood when Daniel approached the table, where rows of champagne glasses stood ready for the tasting session.

After a brief, almost casual introduction of the Trubert estate, Daniel opened the first bottle of champagne while the Americans looked on with interest. One of their stomachs growled audibly.

"Damn, I'm hungry," said one of the Americans with a laugh. "Croissants and coffee isn't breakfast for a real man!"

"I could kill for a decent steak," said the man next to him. "God, I hope there's something besides organ meats on the menu tonight."

The third man gave his colleagues an admonishing glare, then he looked up to Daniel and, in surprisingly good French, said, "As you know, we're here to buy champagne for our fleet of steamboats on the Mississippi. We believe that, come the turn of the century next year, our guests will be in an especially ebullient mood, and we plan to be well prepared. What makes you believe that *your* champagne might be the right one?"

"Who says I believe any such thing?" Daniel shrugged. "You know, when it comes to champagne, it's like the clouds in the sky." He waved one hand toward the nearest transom window. "In a cloud, one sees what he wants to see or whatever his imagination can come up with. For one person, the clouds are heavenly figures; for another, they are no more than the heralds of bad weather."

The three businessmen involuntarily turned toward the window. Daniel used this brief moment to add a swig of vinegar from a small flask to the champagne bottle. As he did so, he realized that he didn't feel the slightest twinge of guilt. Hadn't Henriette herself doubted his loyalty? And wasn't she always right?

"Enough philosophy! The proof of the pudding is in the eating— I'm sure you say the same in America." With verve, Daniel swung the bottle back and forth a couple of times to mix the vinegar with the champagne, then he poured three test glasses. "A juicy steak and a glass of this champagne—is that what you had in mind?"

"My God!" cried the man who had been longing for an American breakfast, after the first mouthful. His eyes grew wide and he stared in horror at the glass in his hand. "What is that?"

"This sour swill with a steak? Not on your life!" cried the second, appalled. Daniel kept a straight face, but he was grinning on the inside.

The man who spoke good French said vaguely, "This champagne is beyond dry." He looked even more confused than when Daniel had aired his thoughts about the clouds.

Daniel sighed. "I couldn't agree more! If you ask me, a truly elegant champagne should be as sweet as the sweetest hours of love. But do you think my boss will listen to me? Every year he pushes me to make my champagnes drier and drier. 'It's the latest fashion,' he says." He leaned forward conspiratorially and said, "Just between us—I think he's just too miserly to add enough sugar to the champagne."

The three Americans exchanged meaningful looks while their assistant frantically scribbled notes on his list.

"But perhaps your customers on the Mississippi are of the more sophisticated and modern type? Then a champagne this sour would be just right."

The man still hungry for breakfast snorted. "You have no idea, my man! We Southerners are conservative to the core and proud of it. *You* might be able to hawk this to your customers as the latest fashion, but *we* certainly can't."

Daniel—who had, until today, been unaware of his acting talent—smiled innocently. "What can I say? Trubert isn't one of the great names, so what can one expect from the champagne ?" He sighed deeply. He scratched his head absentmindedly. "My dream would be to work for someone like Bollinger or Feininger . . . or for the *veuve* Clicquot! To work for the *veuve* Clicquot . . . then I would have made it as a cellar master. You know, it's the women—and especially the widows—who make the best champagne; it's been that way for centuries. If I were to work for one of the *veuves,* then I would be able to create a champagne so delicious and sweet that one would happily drink a second glass. Which is certainly not"—he waved his hand vaguely toward the bottle he had opened—"the case with this vinegar. But please don't tell my boss I said that!"

"Feininger?" One of the Americans pricked up his ears. "Don't we have that name on our list?"

Before the pimply assistant could hand over his list, Daniel said, "The *veuve* Feininger will grace you with her presence after me. Grace—a word to be taken literally with this woman. I don't know what reputation precedes *you*"—he looked the three Americans up and down—"but it must be good, or Isabelle Feininger would never do you the honor of coming here in person."

"Feininger? Odd that I've never heard the name before. I had actually counted on welcoming the representatives of such houses Moët & Chandon, Roederer, and Heidsieck," said the American on the left.

The leader of the three immediately gave his colleague a denigrating frown. "My dear Steven, you are, and you continue to be, a Philistine. Practically every child knows that the widows Clicquot and Feininger are among the greats of the champagne world." He looked solemnly at Daniel. "Thank you, monsieur, for allowing us to sample your product, but it would not meet with the tastes of our customers. If you would be so kind as to send Madame Feininger in."

***

Just as Daniel exited the salon, Isabelle was powdering her nose. Early that morning, in their hotel room, the three women had helped each other with their makeup—kohl-lined eyes, rouged cheeks, and bright-red lipstick. If they wanted to make an appearance like elegant French women, then they had to do it right, Isabelle had insisted. Clara's old-fashioned bun was transformed into an elegant French chignon, and while Josephine's short haircut had to stay as it was, she topped it with a fashionable hat. All three wore dresses from Isabelle's wardrobe, and they donned all the jewelry she hadn't sold. They surprised even themselves: they looked stylish and self-confident, and almost like real Frenchwomen.

Ever since their departure from Hautvillers, Isabelle had been vacillating between a slender hope that there might still be a chance for her and the estate and a feeling of wanting to run away.

"*Bonne chance!*" said Daniel with a wink as he held the door open for them. For the blink of an eye, his gaze met Isabelle's. Her heart thumped in her chest. *Don't get nervous now*, she silently ordered herself.

"Let's go," she said to Clara and Josephine, her voice barely a whisper.

They had barely stepped into the room when the three businessmen leaped to their feet.

"Madame Feininger!" The man who'd been sitting in the middle strode around the table and approached her. "You don't know what an honor this is for us!" He was smiling from ear to ear.

Isabelle's forehead creased. "How—" she began, but was immediately interrupted by Clara.

"As you might appreciate, Madame Feininger's time is limited—if we could get down to business immediately?" she said in French, then she smiled and fluttered her eyelids.

Isabelle and Josephine stared at their friend in surprise.

Josephine produced two bottles of champagne from the wooden crate and set them on the table. "Open these, please!" she ordered the assistant, who was on his feet as well.

Isabelle was about to say that she could take care of that herself, but then she thought better of it.

"Whatever you do, don't be seen as needy!" Josephine had advised her earlier. "Customers can sense very well if somebody has to sell something because they need the money. And they will exploit that ruthlessly; they will knock the price as low as they can and wring every possible concession from the seller! You don't want that, do you? We need to blind the Americans with self-confidence and a whiff of arrogance. You have to act like you don't need any of it."

Isabelle reminded herself of those words and, gesturing toward her friends, she said, "I'd like to introduce my two assistants, Clara and Josephine." She stressed the French pronunciation of the two names. "With an operation the size of mine, *one* assistant simply won't do." She glanced sympathetically at the pimply young man for a moment.

The Americans nodded, awestruck. "Even in America, we've heard that it's the women in Champagne who have the final word—and that it's the widows who make the best champagnes of all."

Isabelle lowered her eyes modestly. "I don't want to exaggerate, but our customers in your American Midwest have never once complained about our wines. Quite the contrary; they keep asking for more! But where is it supposed to come from?" She shrugged helplessly. "The quantity of available champagne is limited, and that's how it will always be. Unfortunately, I was unable this year to give our American customers the attention I would have liked. Otherwise, I would not be here."

"Madame Feininger has spent a long time in mourning for her husband," Josephine added. "That is the only reason she has any stock to offer at all."

Once the assistant had finally filled the tasting glasses, Isabelle nodded benevolently to the three businessmen.

"Be my guests!" She heard Clara giggle beside her and gave her a furtive jab in the ribs. Then she held her breath. Would they like her champagne? She didn't have to wait long for an answer.

"Excellent!"

"Superb!"

"As sweet and light as love itself." The man in the middle beamed. "This is exactly what I imagine a truly great champagne to be! One would gladly drink a second glass."

"Or a third or fourth," said the man on his left, raising the glass to his mouth once again.

"Certainly no shortage of sugar here. Absolutely delicious."

"With cornbread and fried chicken."

"Or a juicy steak."

The assistant, standing slack-armed by the table, licked his lips thirstily.

Isabelle let out her breath, which suddenly made her so dizzy that she had to support herself on the edge of the table. The pimply assistant was immediately at her side. "Madame, are you all right?"

It's just the relief, thought Isabelle, then she sat on a chair that Josephine had pulled up for her.

"The widow Feininger has been through a great deal in recent months," said Clara as the Americans looked at Isabelle with concern. "We already mentioned that her husband passed away . . . suddenly, in the spring—" She broke off, biting her lip.

The leader of the visiting delegation looked at Isabelle sympathetically. "Considering the circumstances, we see it as an even greater honor that you have come here today, Madame Feininger. It looks as if most of the vignerons did not consider it necessary," he added, shaking his head in annoyance. "But who wants Moët & Chandon when one can have Feininger? Your champagne will be the perfect thing for our beautiful Southern belles and their gentlemen!"

The men on either side of him murmured their agreement, and their spokesman cleared his throat.

"My dear *veuve* Feininger, I do not want to put any unnecessary demands on your time, so without further ado: How many bottles of champagne would we be able to purchase, and what price would you ask?"

Chapter Twenty-Eight

They had not touched a drop of alcohol, but the women were drunk—drunk with happiness.

"Ten thousand bottles—oh, just the number makes me dizzy!" Clara laughed hysterically.

"That's the deal of the century!" Josephine squealed.

"This could be my salvation," Isabelle sighed. Tears of relief ran down her cheeks, and she wiped them away with the sleeve of her dress. Deep inside, she felt the lid that had been screwed down tightly on her feelings over the last months begin to loosen. Was there hope?

"Could be? This *is* your salvation! With this one deal, you've become a rich woman." Josephine was radiant, as if a bucket of gold dust had been poured over her.

"From here, things can only go up," Clara agreed.

"You're really the best friends anyone could ask for. Thank you, thank you, thank you!" Isabelle embraced Clara and Josephine so wholeheartedly that all three of them nearly fell.

"The way you ordered those men around!" said Isabelle to Clara. "And you mean to tell us you play the good housewife at home? Either you're a better actress than the players we see on stage or . . ." But she had run out of words and waved it off.

"I've got some hidden talents! Maybe I should become your real-life assistant," Clara said, giggling.

Their high spirits were so infectious that more and more travelers on the platform at Troyes glanced in their direction, envious but smiling, too.

If only you knew, Isabelle thought, well aware of the people's looks.

The melancholy that thought brought with it was swept aside by the sweet taste of victory. And she could do little more for now than savor the taste, because instead of celebrating the deal in Troyes, she had to get back to Hautvillers as fast as she could. The Americans had made clear the size of their order and the terms of delivery: Isabelle had to have ten thousand bottles of champagne ready to ship that week. The question of how to pack the bottles for such a long trip put her on the verge of panic again, but only for a brief moment. *That* was something the three of them could manage; she was sure of it.

It was already late in the evening when they arrived in Hautvillers. While she did not know exactly *what* Daniel Lambert had told the Americans before she entered the room, he had clearly laid the ground for her success. It had been too easy! Should she seek him out in Hautvillers and ask him? Isabelle had kept her eyes open for him at the station in Troyes and on the train, but she hadn't seen him. She at least had to thank him.

They were all tired from the journey and the excitement of the day, but none of them even considered going to bed. After the oppressive humidity in Troyes, it was surprisingly chilly inside the house, and Josephine lit a fire in the open fireplace. Clara went to the kitchen to make some sandwiches—they had brought back two large hunks of cheese with them from Troyes—while Isabelle went down to the cellar and returned with three bottles of champagne in a basket.

Petra Durst-Benning

Josephine looked at her doubtfully. "Can you spare them?" she asked.

"A normal bottle of wine or a nip of liqueur would be more than enough," said Clara, setting the plate of sandwiches on the table.

Isabelle fetched glasses from a cupboard and said, "Don't worry. My cellars are so full that I could have sold the Americans twenty thousand bottles. Who knows, perhaps they'll order more?" As she spoke, she opened one of the bottles.

Since her arrival in Champagne, Isabelle had taken part in various tastings, not only with Raymond in Reims, but also with Micheline and other vignerons. And every time, she had been fascinated by the almost sacred ritual of opening the bottle. Now it was she who removed the cork so carefully that no more than a light hiss escaped, without the slightest trace of a pop. "Like an angel's fart," Micheline had described it once.

"Anyway, these three bottles are not from Feininger at all. They were a gift from my friend Raymond Dupont. He's a champagne dealer in Reims. The first time I tasted champagne properly was in his shop, and he actually said I have a good palate, if you can imagine that."

Both Clara and Josephine nodded, impressed.

"A man gives *you* champagne? Isn't that a bit like taking coals to Newcastle?"

Isabelle laughed. "If only it were! Raymond only ever sends me his most carefully chosen wines. Feininger champagne, I'm sorry to say, is far from that class." She held the bottle so that Josephine and Clara could see the label.

"Millésime Bollinger . . . all right," said Josephine, not sure what she was looking at.

Isabelle laughed mysteriously. "Tonight you will taste the very best that Champagne has to offer!"

"Can you smell the vanilla? And that touch of linden blooms?" Luxuriating in her senses, Isabelle kept her nose over the glass for a few more seconds, then drank a mouthful of the delicious Bollinger. "And the flavor of a freshly baked brioche . . ." She sighed almost rapturously.

"Now that you mention it, the champagne really does taste a little like pastries," said Clara in surprise. "But how is that possible?"

"It comes from the yeast during the fermentation. It leaves traces in the taste, sometimes stronger, sometimes weaker," Isabelle explained. She closed her eyes and let another mouthful of the cool golden liquid flow down her throat. It was simply delicious!

"Every champagne is made of the same ingredients. There are three kinds of grapes—Chardonnay, Pinot Meunier, and Pinot Noir—and a bit of sugar, but really not much. So you'd think that every champagne would taste the same, right?"

Josephine, who had so far said nothing, nodded.

Isabelle smiled. It felt good to share her knowledge with her friends. "The fact that they don't taste the same comes down to the art of the cellar master. He decides on the proportions of the three grapes, how long the first and second fermentations last, and how much yeast is added for the second fermentation. The cellar master also decides how many different years he'll use for a cuvée. Sometimes he'll mix together as many as fifty different wines. Can you imagine?"

Clara looked almost reverently at the glass in her hand, and she and Josephine shook their heads.

"The only condition for a cuvée is that all the wines have to come from the Champagne region," Isabelle continued. "Some people call blending the wine 'marrying,' which I think is a much better expression."

"You really know a lot about this," said Josephine and gave Isabelle a little shove.

"You've become a real expert; well done!" said Clara, with admiration in her voice. "And you haven't even been here a year."

Isabelle shrugged. "I just find champagne interesting. So I try to learn as much as I can about how it's made." Her words sounded hollow in her own ears. What she truly felt, deep down, about the making of champagne was far more passionate, more all-encompassing, but she could not find the words to capture those feelings.

A silence fell over the three friends for a long moment.

"What now?" Josephine asked after a while, looking at Isabelle. "Where do things go from here?"

Isabelle put her empty glass down noisily on the table. Then she started to open the second bottle from Raymond Dupont's gift basket. She needed to send him a thank-you card for all his attentions over the last few months. How impolite of her to have neglected that.

Thinking about the champagne dealer, she recalled the sense of being protected that she had always felt when she was around him. Raymond Dupont knew so much, and he was so experienced, moved in the best circles—perhaps he would be a good adviser for her when it came to deciding about her future?

"Well, first of all, I have to get the Americans' order done. After that, there's the harvest to take care of and buyers to find for my grapes."

Just a few weeks earlier, she had been overwhelmed by panic just thinking about the future, let alone actually speaking about it as if it were a real thing. And now here she was, making concrete plans, she realized in amazement.

"And what about that woman that Micheline told us about, Madame Trubert? She wants to buy your place come hell or high water, apparently," said Josephine, and pulled her legs in comfortably underneath her.

"She'll be waiting a long time!" Isabelle let out a harsh laugh. "I admit that when I was at my lowest point, I thought about selling and not just once. If Henriette had not been so horribly greedy, I might have actually signed in a weak moment. She certainly held her contract under my nose often enough. But she's like a shark, eating everything that crosses her path. Sometimes, when she was sitting on my bed and pretending to be sympathetic, I was waiting for a shark fin to push out through her tight-fitting dress and reveal her true character!"

All three of them giggled at the notion, then Clara said, "You're finally starting to sound like the Isabelle we used to know," and she raised her newly filled glass. "To you and your glorious future without Madame Shark!"

With a crystalline clinking of glasses, Isabelle and Josephine joined her in her toast. Isabelle took a swig of the Ruinart champagne, an outstanding drop, then she looked at Clara and Josephine seriously.

"I never would have made it without you." Tears of gratitude and hope brimmed in her eyes.

Clara just shrugged, and Josephine raised her free hand, dismissing the thought. "Oh, don't go getting all sentimental," she said, feigning imperiousness, but her own eyes were shining traitorously. "I'd much rather talk about the future of your winery. What's next on the list once the Americans' order is on its way?"

Isabelle sighed. "Then I have to see to the vineyards urgently. We should have been trimming leaves around the bunches of grapes to let more sunshine reach the fruit, but it's incredibly time-consuming work and too much for Claude to manage alone. And until now, I haven't had the money to take on any helpers." But it wasn't only the money; it was also the state she'd been in! *How many times had Micheline begged her to do more about her business in the last few months?* she berated herself.

"You don't sound particularly happy about it," Clara murmured.

"Does that surprise you?" Isabelle said. "When I first came here, I would never have dreamed that one day I'd be forced to sell the grapes. I wanted to make champagne, really *good* Feininger champagne! One with character, like this Ruinart." She held up her glass. In the flickering light of the fire, its contents shone golden. "*That's* why I read all the books in Jacques's library; *that's* why I was out in the vineyards from dawn to dusk: to see and smell and learn." With a steady hand, she refilled all three of their glasses.

"It's like liquid gold," said Clara admiringly. "I can understand very well how a drink like this could fascinate you so much."

"Champagne . . . just the word is enough to make you smile," said Josephine with a grin.

Isabelle nodded fiercely. "That's exactly it! But to manufacture a perfect champagne, it takes more—a first-class cellar master, for one thing, and that is something I lack, I'm afraid." She sniffed. "Right now, I don't even have a second-class one, because Monsieur One-Eye still hasn't reappeared. I'm slowly starting to fear that he won't be coming back at all." She shrugged. "But in any case, Gustave Grosse is not the man for what I have in mind. Nobody wants the kind of sweet champagne I have in my cellars. The Feininger champagne I want to make should ring in the new century in its own way: untroubled and as light as a feather!"

Her friends nodded, but Isabelle was not sure whether they had really understood. *Am I talking nonsense?* she wondered. "Without the right cellar master, I might as well forget about it. Do you see now why I have no other choice? Why a 'grape farmer' is all I can ever be?" She could not keep the disgust she felt out of her voice.

"I've got an idea," said Clara, breaking the uncomfortable silence that had momentarily settled.

Isabelle and Josephine turned to her immediately.

"You could open a guesthouse!"

"A guesthouse?" said Isabelle and Josephine together.

Clara seemed to relish the puzzled looks on her friends' faces. "Yes, think about it—Isabelle, this house is so beautiful, and I'm sure there are many travelers who would love to stay here. On the train here, we met an actress who spent a few months down by Lake Constance to regather her strength for her work. You could rent out rooms to people like her. You could introduce your guests to the delicious cuisine of this region, you could take them strolling through the vineyards, offer champagne tastings . . ."

"A place of calmness, a place to relax and recuperate," Josephine murmured, more to herself, then she looked up. "I'm sure you could earn good money like that. Clara and I could advertise for you in Berlin."

"Please don't!" said Isabelle, horrified at the thought. "No disrespect to your idea, Clara, but a guesthouse like that is something you would really need to have a passion for, and I just don't have that. I cherish my privacy far too much to even consider it." She sighed with regret when she saw the disappointment in her friends' eyes.

"A country hotel like that would be more something for you, Clara, but for Isabelle, it's probably not right," Josephine agreed. She turned to Isabelle. "Just now, you were talking so ardently, so urgently, about making champagne that it gave me goose bumps. If making an excellent champagne is truly your great dream, then do it!"

It isn't as simple as that, Isabelle was about to reply, but the words stuck in her throat. Suddenly, she was sick to death of her weakness, her angst, and her internal discord. She wanted to be like she once was—audacious, brash, brave. She wanted to be like Josephine, who talked about passion and about turning dreams into reality and who did just that. And she wanted to be like Clara, who could transform herself from Miss Mousy to Lady Lioness when it really mattered, when she had to tell Isabelle how she really felt. Her magnificent friends.

She felt tears coming to her eyes and fought them back.

"Me, a champagne maker—that would truly be the greatest adventure of my life," she said, her voice raw.

"I've got another idea!" Clara cried out, and both Isabelle and Josephine turned and looked at her expectantly.

Clara took a deep breath. "If Isabelle actually manages to make her once-in-a-century champagne, then we absolutely *have* to try to meet again next year on New Year's Eve."

Isabelle was taken aback for a moment, but then she laughed and said, "It's a deal! But only if I can offer you a bottle of the best Feininger champagne of all time."

They took each other's hands, as they had when they were younger. Isabelle expected them to renew their old "to the turn-of-the-century wind!" covenant.

But both Josephine and Clara seemed to hesitate.

"Before we make any promises, perhaps we should talk about something else," said Clara slowly. "Something we really haven't talked about much at all." She looked at Isabelle intently. "You're going to be a mother, Isabelle. And it's time you started to think about that. Those two things at the same time, ringing in a new century with a glorious champagne and a wonderful child—isn't that something?"

The next morning, Isabelle woke with the first light of dawn. After a quick bath, she crept quietly out of the house. The others could sleep awhile longer—what she was planning to do, she had to do alone.

The cemetery of Hautvillers was surrounded by a ramshackle knee-high wall and covered by the shade of a huge weeping willow. Leon's grave was in the last row. It was the first time since the funeral that she had visited it. Extraordinary fear had prevented her from taking this step before that day. Fear of the irrevocable certainty it would bring? Of the knowledge that it really wasn't a bad dream? Isabelle's sigh was picked up by the soft rustling of the weeping willow in the morning breeze and carried away.

There was no gravestone yet, only a wooden cross marking who lay beneath. Leon Feininger, the great love of her life. The father of her child. Instinctively, she stroked her belly with her right hand. Beyond the low cemetery wall, she realized she could see the Feininger vineyards; the sight of the vines gave her some solace, and she was glad she'd come. For a long time, she stood still and quiet, while deep inside she untied one knot after another. Leon was dead. He had taken his dreams with him to the grave. But her life went on. She would dream for two—or rather three. She smiled at the thought, her hands resting on her belly.

Earth sprinkled with white beads of chalk covered the grave. There were a few stalks of grass coming through, as well as thistles, dandelions, and other weeds. She had not thought to bring a shovel or hoe, so Isabelle began to pull the weeds out of the earth with her bare hands. In a vase in front of the cross was a single withered pink rose. Had Micheline brought it when she came to visit her brother Albert, who lay at the other side of the cemetery? She had not thanked Micheline even once for all she had done. Isabelle replaced the faded rose with three lilies she had cut in her garden. From now on, she would take care of the flowers herself. Her handled trembled a little as she stroked the chalky earth.

"Hello, Leon. It's me. I've got quite a lot to tell you."

Chapter Twenty-Nine

"Heavenly Father, Creator and Lord over the earth, we are gathered together today to praise thee and to commend thee for everything thou hast done for us. We thank thee for the blessings thou hast bestowed upon us. And we ask thee to let everything that grows ripen unto the day of harvest."

Isabelle swallowed the bitter taste that had entered her mouth as the pastor spoke. Praising God for all the good He had done? That was not something she had been capable of for a very long time. But even so, there she was, in the Hautvillers church, where every seat was taken and more people stood in the rear. She still found it difficult to be around people, but she couldn't stay away from the harvest service—for the *Champenois* it was at least as important as the Christmas or Easter service.

Strange, she thought, as the congregation began a hymn, *how every church in the world has the same smell*. In Berlin, in the Palatinate, here— they all smelled of myrrh and mothballs, of poorly aired clothes, sweat, and sins. Isabelle did not know the words, so she just moved her lips and pretended she did. She looked around the church, noticing how the altar was decorated with a cornucopia of vines and grapes.

It was the first time since Josephine and Clara's tearful departure three days earlier that Isabelle had left the house. Her fear that she would again feel as alone and abandoned as she had in the months before their arrival had quickly proved unfounded. So close to the harvest, the most important season in Champagne, the people of the region closed ranks even more than usual: Claude, Micheline, and Marie had insisted that she walk to church with them, and now they were sitting together in one of the middle rows.

And beside them sat none other than Gustave Grosse, who had returned a week earlier. "I told you I'd be back in time for the harvest," he had said with a shrug.

Isabelle hadn't known whether she should hug him or slap his face. She had immediately told him that his habits would have to change, that they had a lot to do that autumn, and that they all had to pull together to make it work. Grosse listened to every word, then asked for an advance on his salary.

Josephine and Clara had listened to their exchange in silence. "Am I mistaken, or did your cellar master reek of alcohol earlier? I must say, he doesn't seem the most trustworthy type," Josephine remarked later. "If I were in your shoes, I'd start looking around for a good cellar master as soon as I could."

Isabelle had sighed and nodded. She was happy to at least not have to deal with the approaching harvest alone. After that . . . well, she would see.

"Merciful God, protect our grapes from rain and hail, protect our vines from the phylloxera . . ."

That was the very least that God could do, in Isabelle's opinion. One row in front of her sat Therese Jolivet from the bakery and Carla Chapron and her husband Ignaz. Ghislaine and Daniel were also there, and next to Daniel sat Blanche Thevenin, the seamstress. Was she mistaken, or was Blanche unnecessarily close to Daniel?

"Merciful God, we beseech thee, hold thy sheltering hand over our vines. Give us the strength to overcome the strenuous weeks ahead . . ."

The Trubert family sat—where else?—in the front most row on the right of the aisle. The first row of pews on the left was occupied by the Moët and Chandon families, the biggest champagne producers of them all. They owned an unbelievable eight hundred and forty acres of land. True, their vineyards spread throughout all of Champagne, but the owners traditionally visited the harvest service in Hautvillers.

"Merciful God, release us from our cares, give unto us the gift of thy mercy, so that with thy blessing we may bring this year to a good and proper close. Fill our presses with grapes and fill our barrels with wine—for these things we beseech thee, O Lord. Be merciful unto us. Amen!"

"Amen!" repeated the churchgoers.

The pastor made the sign of the cross with his right hand.

"Go ye forth and praise our Father at a plentiful table!" Accompanied by the sound of bells, a buzz of voices rose as the congregation slowly filed out of the rows of pews.

"Amen," said Isabelle, too. But instead of standing up with all the others, she stayed in her seat. For the first time that day, she raised her eyes to the large crucifix.

"You sacrificed your son, and my husband. Enough sacrifices have been made. Now help me, please, to come through the harvest well, because I won't be able to do it by myself. Amen," she murmured quietly, then she crossed herself a final time.

Claude, who was still standing in the aisle, looked back at her in surprise. "Did you say something, madame?"

Isabelle smiled and shook her head, then she stood up, too. "It's strange. Church services always make me hungry, but I'm probably not the only one," she said with a nod toward the people streaming toward the exit.

Micheline, ahead of her, laughed. "That's a good thing, because the tables are going to be bending under all the good food. The harvest really takes it out of us in the next few weeks, so it doesn't hurt to build up some strength in advance, right, Marie?" she said, turning to her sister-in-law.

Marie Guenin nodded. "In Hautvillers, this meal we share before the harvest is taken very seriously. Every house contributes something. And we vignerons provide the champagne. Who knows if the harvest will be a good one, or if we'll have any reason to celebrate afterward? All the more reason to lift our glasses now!"

The evening before, the residents of the surrounding houses had carried their front doors into the village square and set them up on wooden trestles as tables. Before the church service, the women from the houses had covered the tables with white cloths and decorated them with woven garlands. In this way, they had created a single long table at which more and more people now found a place to sit. Greetings were exchanged, conversations were kindled, and the September sun, which washed everything in golden light, was praised.

Young and old, poor and rich—in the coming weeks, all of these people would work day and night, snipping off bunches of grapes hour after hour, lugging them in heavy baskets to the waiting wagons where they would be unloaded, then hauled away to the presses. They would defy the wind and weather and ignore the injured hands and aching shoulders. The grape harvest meant their income for the year ahead, and during it, everything else took second place. But they had this final day of exhilaration and freedom: the villagers were filled with the zest of life, and good cheer overflowed like the champagne that the vignerons had provided for the gathering.

Isabelle felt a lightness that had long been missing from her life. Arm in arm with Micheline, she walked toward the long table, where

Ghislaine was putting final touches on the food platters. Today, everything had to taste wonderful and look perfect!

Morels in champagne sauce, salmon poached in champagne, snails cooked in champagne and garlic, calf cheeks, various spicy tarts— Isabelle could only stand and marvel at the dishes lined up side by side along the length of the table.

"Who made all this?"

"Well, who do you think?" said Ghislaine, grinning. She patted the seat next to her, inviting Isabelle to sit. "My cooks and I, and some of the winemakers' wives helped, too. How would it be if you helped out next year? *Andouillette*, perhaps. I know how much you like it."

Isabelle groaned. "Don't remind me." She looked into one of the pots suspiciously, where several sausages were floating in some kind of stock. "This isn't them, is it?"

"Who knows? Maybe I really should try serving it to you again." Ghislaine grinned even more widely. "What a shame that your friends had to leave. I think they would have really enjoyed this meal."

They would have, thought Isabelle. *And Leon, too.* In her mind's eye, she saw him sitting beside her, chatting away. Her Leon—with his charm and humor, he had always been a welcome guest at parties.

Before she had time to get melancholic, Micheline, sitting opposite, tapped her hand. She pointed to a plate of sliced cold meats garnished with poached artichokes. "That's from me. Want to try it?"

"I'd love to," Isabelle replied. Next to her, she felt Ghislaine move over, and Daniel sat down between them. Blanche, the seamstress, was nowhere in sight, which Isabelle was grateful for. She could finally thank Daniel for whatever he had done for her in Troyes. Then she saw that he was not alone—he had Raymond Dupont with him.

Isabelle smiled shyly at the champagne dealer from Reims. She owed him her gratitude, too, for all the encouraging notes he had sent her over the last few months, all of which, until recently, she had utterly ignored. And for the champagne he had sent, of course.

"You, too, Daniel?" asked Micheline, reaching across the table with her plate of sliced meat.

With her hands trembling slightly, Isabelle took the plate from Micheline and held it in front of Daniel. "May I offer you some of this, Monsieur Lambert?"

"Are you two still so formal?" Ghislaine cried in exaggerated horror. "High time we did something about that. Daniel, I'd like to introduce my friend, Isabelle. Isabelle, may I introduce my brother, Daniel? There, done!" she said, underlining her words with lively gestures.

"Fine with me. I'm Isabelle!" She reached out one hand to Daniel.

"And with me, as long as you don't accuse me of being a saboteur again. Daniel."

Isabelle rolled her eyes. "First it was Ghislaine with her *andouillette*, and now you. Is everyone today going to remind me of the sins of my past?"

The pressure of his hand was firm and the smile he gave her warm. Would he kiss her hand? She held her breath for a heartbeat. *How can you think that?* she admonished herself.

"Daniel, what do you think? Are we going to have a marvelous year, like we did in 1889?" said Micheline, changing the subject. "Or is it going to be an ordinary harvest, like last year?" Everyone sitting within earshot turned and looked at Daniel.

"I fear the latter," he said. He raised his hand regretfully. "The grapes certainly haven't turned out bad, but June was rainy and July not as sunny as I would have liked, and the grapes are not that sweet. I'm estimating that we'll get ten percent alcohol, no more, with the sugar in them."

Why is everyone hanging on every word he says? Isabelle wondered. And what was he saying about a rainy June? Or about grapes that were not ideal? She had heard none of that before, she had to admit. None of that and none of many other things, she realized when she noticed Ghislaine's belly. Was her friend pregnant again? The morsel of meat in her mouth became drier and drier, and it was difficult for her to swallow.

"It makes me happy to see you here, Madame Feininger," said Raymond Dupont, dragging her back from her thoughts.

"The pleasure is mine, although I really have to get used to being around so many people again," she replied, looking around. "I've been something of a hermit these last few months."

"Come and visit me again in Reims! We could have dinner together or visit the opera or—"

"After today, no one in Hautvillers will have time for things like that," Daniel interrupted the champagne merchant, and his tone was unusually harsh. "We have the harvest to manage. Right, Isabelle?"

Was she mistaken, or was he deliberately emphasizing her first name? And didn't she hear some irritation, too, as he chided Dupont for making such an untimely suggestion? Isabelle looked from one to the other.

"Oh, when I think of what we managed back in 1874—remember? The first dry champagne, a fine effervescence without being fizzy, with finesse but without any of that sugary sweetness. Louise Pommery harvested later than she ever had before. The rest of us couldn't believe it! We were completely flummoxed and didn't know if we should do the same or not." Marie Guenin's gray eyes sparkled at the memory.

Micheline nodded. "Most of us harvested earlier. We were all terrified that the weather would change, but we Guenins decided to take the risk and leave the grapes on the vine for another two weeks," she said. "But should we do it this year?" she asked, deliberately slowly and looking expectantly at Daniel.

Again, all eyes were on the cellar master. But he only smiled.

How strange. Why is Micheline probing Daniel like that? And why doesn't he simply answer her questions? The *Champenois* were really a very mysterious bunch sometimes, Isabelle thought. Then she took a peach from one of the fruit platters; it smelled of sunshine, flowers, and a hint of perfume.

"Our dear Louise, God rest her soul," Marie added, and Micheline sighed. "Without her and her courage to try something new, we'd probably all still be making sugar-sweet champagnes instead of our wonderful bruts."

"What's wrong with a sweet champagne, madame?" asked Gustave Grosse, who was sitting beside Claude.

Isabelle noted with disgust that she had lost count of how many times her own cellar master had refilled his glass with champagne. Nothing had changed there, certainly.

"Wrong, for example, is the way it sat like lead in my cellar—and still would be sitting if a sign from heaven hadn't led me to the Americans in Troyes," Isabelle said.

Everyone at the table laughed—all except Gustave Grosse.

Turning to Daniel, she said quietly, "Of course, I don't know *what* you said to the Americans that had them eating out of my hand like that, but it helped. Thank you for that."

Daniel gestured dismissively.

"I think we could use a sign from heaven, too," said Micheline, looking intently at Daniel again.

"Have I missed something?" asked Isabelle, smiling. "Have you turned into some sort of oracle for a good or bad harvest?"

Daniel grinned and was about to answer when he suddenly stopped.

Isabelle followed his gaze and saw Henriette Trubert, dressed in a thundercloud of purple lace, approaching where they sat. There was no sign of her husband, Alphonse.

"Raymond . . . didn't you want to join us at our table?" she said, fixing the merchant with a frown.

Raymond Dupont smiled. "Henriette, *ma chérie*! You know what they say: settle where the people sing! I am so extraordinarily happy that our beautiful widow Feininger is in fine form again. And a little bird has whispered in my ear that she is ready to do great things—my congratulations, madame!" He raised his glass in a toast to Isabelle.

Isabelle smiled, but she wondered how he had heard about her plans. She hadn't said anything, and she was sure that neither Josephine nor Clara had. Had he simply given voice to a hunch to annoy Henriette?

Henriette looked at him disparagingly, then she turned to Isabelle. "So Madame Feininger is in the mood to celebrate? But that should be no surprise. That was quite a trick, selling your sweet concoction to the Americans. Much better than pouring it all down the drain, wasn't it? Oh, *here* is where I find my dear cellar master. Daniel, don't you think you should be gracing our table with your presence?" The expression through her heavy makeup was *not* happy. Daniel merely raised his glass as if proposing a toast to his employer.

With a little sniff, Henriette swung around to where Gustave Grosse was sitting; he nodded almost imperceptibly to her.

"The Americans were very happy about my champagne," Isabelle replied, wondering at the same time whether she had just imagined the look that had passed between Henriette and Grosse. "But you are right, Madame Trubert, sweet champagne is truly a relic of the past. As Monsieur Dupont has already said, I have very different plans for the future." She looked to Raymond, and they shared a conspiratorial smile.

Henriette raised her eyebrows in mock surprise. "As I hear it, you don't even have a buyer for your grapes yet, and you're talking about *plans*? Or"—a flash of hope kindled in Henriette's eyes—"do you mean you want to accept my offer to buy your place after all?"

"I think you must have misunderstood me," said Isabelle. With satisfaction, she watched Henriette's expression darken again immediately, and she realized that everyone at their part of the table was listening to the exchange.

Henriette narrowed her eyes at Isabelle. "You'll regret it," she said so quietly that only those sitting very close could hear.

"If there's anything I regret, it's the fact that I let life frighten me after Leon died," Isabelle retorted. "But that is behind me now. I will not let myself be intimidated again, not by God, not by the devil— and certainly not by you." She held Henriette's glare steadily. "And I'm not selling my grapes, either. Instead, I'm going to roll up my sleeves and make the best Feininger champagne there has ever been. *Vive la Champagne!*" she said, raising her voice and her glass for her last words.

"*Vive la Champagne!*" cried everyone at the table.

Henriette snorted and swept away in a rustle of purple lace.

Chapter Thirty

The next day, a wave of unrest rolled through the village. Wine lovers had traveled from around the world to savor the very special atmosphere that only the grape harvest in Champagne had to offer. Suddenly, there were unfamiliar faces everywhere: casually dressed journalists there to report about the annual hustle and bustle, elegant wine experts, enraptured actors, and wealthy businesspeople. Everyone wanted to watch as the grapes were harvested, so later, with a glass of champagne in their hand, they would be able to say, "I was there when this was born!" In Le Grand Cerf and other restaurants and hotels, the finest dishes of the region were served, and wine knowledge was passed around at the tables. Every bed in every guesthouse was booked solid, and the hoteliers rubbed their hands together at the idea of the profits.

The majority of newcomers, though, did not need hotel rooms and could not afford fine meals in the restaurants. They traveled on foot or in rickety horse-drawn caravans and built their camps on every available patch of meadow and every open backyard. These were the people who'd come to help with the harvest; they had traveled from various

European lands, and some from poorer areas of France, to earn a few francs picking the Champagne grapes.

When Isabelle looked out her window one morning, she saw three of these caravans on the meadow at the back of her garden. An hour later, there were ten of them. The weathered, windowless carts and the horses that pulled them all looked as if they had seen better days. Isabelle was astonished to see a small group of women lighting a fire in the center of their camp, as if it were the most natural thing in the world. The wood for the fire came from a stack that Claude, whenever he had a little time, added to, with an eye on the approaching winter. Children and a pack of dogs ran around, shrieking and barking. And if Isabelle's eyes weren't deceiving her, a few of the children were helping themselves to her blackberries. What did they think they were doing?

She was on her way outside to stop them when she ran into Claude Bertrand.

"Don't go trying to read them the riot act," he warned. "Every year, more than ten thousand itinerant pickers come to the region, and they have to set up their camps somewhere. Without them, we would not manage to get the harvest in at all, so be glad that they have showed up! And one more piece of advice: if a few tomatoes or eggs disappear in the next few days, or perhaps even a chicken, turn a blind eye. If they go too far, then of course you have to step in, but as a rule they know they have to behave."

"Then it would be for the best if I went and said hello?" said Isabelle meekly as she watched the women setting up clotheslines across the meadow.

Claude shook his head. "It isn't necessary. All of these extended families have a leader, and usually one leader speaks for several clans. *He* will come to *you* and agree to the conditions for this year's harvest with you or with Gustave. That's the tradition, and it's best to hold to it."

"Conditions?" Isabelle asked with a frown. "He should know how many pickers I need and what they get paid for their work, shouldn't he?"

"It's not as simple as that, I'm afraid," Claude replied with a laugh. "These people work hard, and in the evening they want a little more in their hands than a crust of dry bread. But you will find all of that out in the next few days." He patted Isabelle on her arm and strolled away, whistling, his dog at his side as always.

Quite apart from the unrest that the influx of travelers brought with it, something else was in the air. Something invisible but so intense that Isabelle felt she could grasp it. Every morning, when she went out to inspect her vines—something she had started doing again after Clara and Josephine left—she saw the older and more experienced men out prowling through the vineyards, each with a retinue of younger followers. The plump bunches hanging from the shoots were so densely packed that it was impossible to push a finger between the grapes. The older men plucked off the outer grapes and crushed and rubbed them between their fingers, feeling the grapes and their juices. Some of them relied on their tongues, too, to judge the sugar content of the grapes. One might taste the grapes with eyes closed, while another might look up to the heavens as if God owed him an answer. Now? Tomorrow? The men were watched breathlessly by their entourages. And whenever Daniel appeared somewhere, the tension went up another notch. How would *he* assess the grapes? When would *he* begin to pick? Isabelle had come to understand that Henriette's *chef de cave* was considered *the* master of his trade.

Like the other vintners, Isabelle found herself furtively observing the Trubert vines, waiting to see if Daniel was going to finally signal the long-awaited start of the harvest. Independently, though, she tried to feel her way into the nature of her vines for herself. The sunshine of the last few weeks had dried the soil and the vines now had to push their roots deeper and deeper to get even a little bit of water. With every passing day, she noticed, it became easier to pick the bunches from the shoots, and the deep color of the grapes grew darker, too, with the violet taking on a touch of black. And the balance between sweet and sour changed constantly, she realized, as she crushed the grapes on her tongue. Even the shoots looked different than they had just a few weeks earlier: now, they had developed an almost cork-like structure. But the question was, what did all these observations add up to?

"Not a thing, madame," Gustave Grosse replied harshly when she encountered him out in the vineyards one morning. "All the hard work and headaches that go into figuring out the best time to start the harvest; it's out of all proportion! Forget the weather—exactly one hundred days after the vines are in full bloom, the grapes are bright. It's as simple as that. Just as a woman's pregnancy is also fixed: it's always nine months, come rain, hail, or sleet." As he spoke, he stared in a less-than-seemly way at Isabelle's body.

"If you're so clever, then I really wonder what you were doing over in the Trubert vineyards. I just saw you coming from there," said Isabelle with a nod toward Henriette's hillside. She narrowed her eyes and looked again. Was she mistaken? Were Daniel and Henriette standing together, over there among the vines?

For a moment, Grosse's self-confidence seemed to waver. "Well, I . . . I thought . . ."

Isabelle's face contorted in mockery. "Oh, admit it. You listen to every word Daniel Lambert says, just like everyone else."

Grosse snorted. "Daniel Lambert can go hang! Who knows how long this good weather will hold? I recommend we start harvesting the red grapes tomorrow."

There were, in fact, two harvest periods; Isabelle knew that much from reading Jacques's books. There was one for the red Pinot Noir and Pinot Meunier grapes, and a somewhat later harvest for the white Chardonnay grapes.

"But isn't it true that the grapes become even juicier and put on a lot of weight in the final stage of growth?" she said, stalling for time. Something inside her was balking at making a final decision.

"That's true enough," her cellar master replied. "For a few days at the end, their weight stays the same; after that they begin to shrivel and dry out. Do you want to risk that?"

"Of course not. But my feeling is that we should still wait a day or two. Has the leader of the pickers gotten in touch with you? According to Jacques's paperwork, he always had about fifty pickers a year, so I think that ought to be sufficient again this year. Did you tell the man that?"

"All long finished," Grosse said dismissively. "Those people know they could do far worse than work here. Jacques Feininger looked after the pickers well. He gave them decent food and wine, and at the end of the season, there was always a big feast with two pigs on a spit. If you do the same, you'll have no problems with these people. Don't worry; you've got me here!" he added, lifting his chin.

Isabelle, who could not decide if that was more a curse or a blessing, sighed. Then she took a deep breath and said resolutely, "Let's give the grapes just a bit more time. Meanwhile, you can wash out the barrels again. In the two big barrels for the Chardonnay, I found some sticky residues around the top edge from old foam. You know as well as I do that cleanliness is paramount for making champagne."

Gustave Grosse shrugged, unmoved, and said, "As you wish, madame."

***

"In the final stage of maturity, the sugar content of the grapes increases one last time, and this has exceptionally positive effects on the flavor, as you know. My advice would be to leave the grapes on the vines for another two, maybe three, days," Daniel said insistently. He was very close to wringing his hands and openly pleading. In the last few days, he had said the same thing to Henriette so many times that he could recite his litany in his sleep. "The weather will hold. You would not be taking a risk, I promise you."

"You promise!" Henriette repeated disparagingly. "It isn't enough that the others look up to you like the God of grapes; now you think you're the Almighty yourself, don't you? It's high time somebody brought you back down to earth." She took a step toward him, so that her face was only inches from his. He could smell her foul breath and see the furrows around her mouth. Her eyes flashed as she said, "Every day we wait costs us money I don't want to spare. I have called for the workers to be here at ten on the dot, and they will start picking *at ten!*" Stiff-backed and with her head held high, she turned and walked away.

Daniel watched her for a moment. He should have been furious. He should have ranted and raved, because she had flicked away him and all his expertise as she would an annoying mosquito. But all he really felt was resignation—resignation paired with something else for which he could find no words. Had he become jaded from being through far too many scenes like this in recent years? Had Henriette lost the power to move him, deep down, because of that? If that was the case, it was time he looked around for a new job.

"My God, Monsieur Lambert, something's got your hackles up! You look like you've been watching it rain for a week." The voice, coming so unexpectedly from right beside him, made him jump.

Isabelle Feininger. He had seen her in the distance but had not heard her approach. She was wearing a green plaid dress, the color just a shade lighter than the green of her eyes. She had tied her red hair into a loose braid that hung down her back. She looked beautiful.

"I thought we were using first names?" he said with mock severity. It pleased him to see a touch of color come to Isabelle's face.

"I'm sorry. I'm just not used to it."

"Maybe that's because we see each other so rarely? But to come back to what you said, what's got my hackles up has a name: Henriette." He smiled wryly. "Every year, it's the same—Madame Trubert and I have different views when it comes to deciding the right time to start picking. But I can't do anything. She's the boss."

"I've just been having the same discussion with my cellar master! Monsieur Grosse was far from amused when I told him we're still going to wait another day or two," said Isabelle, slapping one hand over her mouth in phony horror. "Don't tell me I'm turning into Henriette Trubert, or I'll throw myself off the nearest mountain!"

There was something conspiratorial about the way they laughed together, and Daniel felt his bad mood evaporating.

"I admit I feel far from certain about what I'm doing," said Isabelle, becoming serious again. "But my instinct tells me I should give the grapes more time." She shrugged.

"Then trust it!" said Daniel bitterly. "If I had my way, I'd wait, like you. Unfortunately, that's not how things work here. Which is why I am about to go back to the Trubert estate, round up the workers, and pick grapes that are two days from reaching perfection."

"Ah," said Isabelle. That one small word contained more understanding and sympathy than if they had spent hours talking about their mutual antagonist.

Their eyes met, and they shared a momentary smile, then Isabelle turned and pointed to the nearest vines. "When I first came here, the vines were weeping. And now they are proudly bearing fruit." Her voice had turned a little raw, almost reverent. "This might sound strange to you, but for me, this ripening process is little short of a miracle. If there's a God anywhere, then He shows himself in this."

Daniel nodded. Isabelle Feininger had changed so much! In spring, at their first encounter, she had been little more than pretty: arrogant, supercilious, and at the same time an empty shell. She had gone parading among the trellises as if she were at a fashion show. Today, though, in her simple linen dress, her hair braided, wearing no makeup, she looked like a beautiful, down-to-earth woman. Was it the loss that she had suffered that had sharpened the contours of her face? The passionate timbre of her voice when she talked about the vines, the strength and power that she radiated with her every movement— everything about her presence seemed to make the air vibrate. But at the same time, he sensed a vulnerability in her, a depth of feeling that moved him like nothing else had in his life. And as before, in Troyes, he felt that urgent need to take her in his arms and protect her. *Watch out, or you'll fall head over heels in love with l'Allemande!* a quiet voice in his head warned. Or had he already?

Instinctively, Daniel looked along the way that Henriette had gone. Even though she acted with utter indifference whenever Isabelle's name came up, Daniel did not believe for a second that his employer had so easily resigned herself to Isabelle's decision to continue running the Feininger estate and actually make champagne. Now that Henriette knew that his loyalty had its limits, she would look for other ways and means to get what she was after. Who would her new allies be? Or had she long ago found a willing adjutant for her intrigues? He knew that Gustave Grosse had been slinking around the Trubert estate recently. Was Grosse the person Daniel had to warn Isabelle about? He had no proof that Grosse intended any harm to Isabelle, just an uneasy feeling about the man. And what if he scared Isabelle unnecessarily? That was the last thing he wanted.

As they went their separate ways, Daniel decided to keep a closer eye on Grosse in the next few days. And he would ask around—for now, he could do no more.

Chapter Thirty-One

"What do you mean, the pickers haven't come?" Isabelle glared at her cellar master in disbelief.

It was early in the morning, and the sun was just beginning to rise beyond the valley, its crimson rays dousing the landscape in an almost surreal light. The previous evening, she had informed Claude and Grosse that the harvest was to begin today. Claude had already hitched the horses to the wagon, loaded up dozens of baskets of different sizes and all the shears he could find, and rolled away toward the vineyards, where he and Gustave Grosse were going to distribute the baskets and shears to the pickers. Isabelle had followed them on foot, her heart beating hard and a smile on her lips. Her first harvest! Finally, it was starting. She would not miss the opportunity to say a word or two of greeting to the pickers. At least, that had been the plan . . .

"I can't explain it," said Gustave Grosse, his eyes scanning the vineyards. "The lazy oafs simply didn't show up even though we'd agreed on everything."

As he spoke, Claude came running up with a grim expression on his face. "They're working for the Truberts! Henriette promised them a higher wage and a bottle of wine a day for every picker. They ran like rabbits." Claude was puffing angrily, but Isabelle could see that the old man had turned almost white with fear.

"But . . . that's not right! They're camping on my land, so they should come and do their work for *us*! Tell them I'll pay just as much as Henriette."

Claude's expression turned even darker. "I told them that. They wouldn't listen!"

Dazed, Isabelle sat down on one of the border markers that separated her land from her neighbor's.

"What now?"

"I could go and ask Micheline if they can spare a few men," Claude suggested halfheartedly—he seemed far from comfortable with the thought. The Guenins would certainly not be happy about giving up any of their pickers.

"Forget it! We won't get far with a handful of men," Gustave Grosse immediately countered.

"Maybe we can still find some workers among the itinerants?" Claude was beginning to sound desperate.

"As if you'll find anyone sitting around a campfire unemployed today." Grosse spat on the ground beside him in disgust.

"I thought you had everything under control, and now this," Isabelle growled at Grosse. She had questions she wanted to ask: Had he actually spoken with the pickers at all? Was he more interested in working against her than for her? But the idea of this level of deception was simply too monstrous to consider, let alone voice.

Her first harvest. And now it was all threatening to come crashing down. She was close to tears. What was she supposed to do now? Go to Henriette and confront her? The old fox would just shrug it off, as she had when her salesman had stolen away Jacques's American customers. Isabelle let out a strangled scream. The notion that her workers were now harvesting Trubert grapes while her own fruit rotted on the vines was almost more than she could stand.

She looked over toward the Trubert estate, then at the other villages dotting the wide landscape. At harvest time, as Claude had explained to her weeks earlier, they were practically deserted. Every man, woman, and child was either busy in their own vineyards or in those of an uncle or a neighbor. She looked to the heavens for help. *Oh, Leon, what would you do now?*

Something sparked in her mind. It was not exactly a thought, but something far more vague. Then a voice. A sentence.

"If you ever need our help, just let us know." She had never in her life needed help more than she needed it now! But who had made her that offer? Who, when, and where? She frowned, trying to remember, but it was difficult. Leon's funeral . . . strangers in cycling outfits. A cycling club, from . . . Charleville? The members had come to pay their last respects to Leon. A smile played around her lips as the memory came to her.

The two men looked at her in disbelief. What was there to smile about now?

Isabelle took a deep breath, and then she said, "I have an idea. I admit it's rather crazy, but I want to leave no stone unturned." She pointed to the wagon loaded with baskets and shears. "Monsieur Grosse, you can pack those away for today, but with a little luck we will be able to start with the harvest tomorrow. Claude, I want you to help me with the wagon; we have a long road ahead of us."

The road to Charleville was mainly through flat land, but the pregnancy had made Isabelle's back hurt, and with every pothole they hit, she winced. Claude kept giving her concerned looks, but Isabelle simply gave him a brave smile in return. Now was not the time to start whining. She had one chance and no time to lose. The grapes were waiting.

In Charleville, a sleepy town about as big as Épernay, it was easy to find what she was looking for. The local cycling club's oval racetrack was displayed prominently on a large sign at the start of the town and showed them which way they had to go. *Please, God, let me find a few men riding laps . . . men with the time and willingness to help me out of this!* She prayed as Claude brought the wagon to a stop at the entrance.

Luck was on her side. The chairman of the club, who had expressed his condolences to Isabelle at Leon's funeral, was there. He remembered Isabelle immediately. He showed her into the small clubhouse and offered her some water, then asked an elderly woman working at the bar to make her something to eat. Isabelle accepted gratefully and asked that someone take something out to Claude, who was waiting outside with the horses.

"What's on your mind? How can we help you?" the chairman asked her then. He was a tall, gaunt man around fifty years of age.

While Isabelle, who actually hated the idea of having to ask anyone for help, haltingly explained the situation she was in, more and more cyclists joined them at their table. Perhaps the Charleville men felt flattered that she had come so far just to find them. Perhaps it was her plaintive appearance—or her pregnancy—that made them so attentive and sympathetic.

"I'd pay for your work, of course. And every picker will get a bottle of champagne a day. If you drink it or sell it or take it home would be up to you." She smiled, looking from one man to the next.

She had hardly finished when the chairman looked around and said, "Leon Feininger had a great sporting spirit. How could we not lend a helping hand to his widow, right, men?"

A murmur of agreement rose from those gathered.

"I'm a teacher, but if someone shows me how to pick a bunch of grapes, I think I can pick it up fast enough. Good thing we've got the autumn vacation right now," said the man sitting directly across from Isabelle.

"I've got more vacation than I want," sniffed the man beside him. "Since my boss let me go, all I have is vacation, but no money. I'd be glad to earn a few francs."

"Me, too!" threw in another. "Then I can get that new bicycle sooner and finally whip you on the track." The men laughed.

"Picking grapes isn't hard," said one of the older riders—Isabelle had heard the others call him Yves. "My brother and I used to help out every year with the harvest in Bordeaux; we've got family there. If I ask Luc, I'm sure he'll come, too."

The men were already talking about the trip to Hautvillers—by bicycle, of course. They had no problem with camping in Isabelle's barn. "After a day's work in a vineyard, you'll be tired enough to sleep standing up," said Yves.

The chairman grinned with satisfaction and said, "Well, madame, I think you can count on twenty to twenty-five of us. When and where do you want us?"

As soon as the horses had had enough time to recover, Isabelle and Claude made the return journey to Hautvillers. There was still a lot to do before their helpers arrived.

The following morning was dry, and it promised to be another beautiful day, not too hot and with no threat of a thunderstorm; one could not ask for better harvest weather.

"Pick a vine and start at the bottom; work your way up with a great deal of sensitivity." Gustave Grosse was talking to almost thirty cyclists from Charleville; the men were standing in a circle around him at the start of the first vineyard. Each carried a steaming cup of coffee in his hand, and a few of them were eating bread with cheese that Isabelle had prepared. Claude had told her it was crucial for the men to get a good breakfast before they started work.

Despite everything, Isabelle had worried the entire night about whether the men from Charleville would keep their word. Starting at sunrise, she had kept a lookout over the valley, and when she finally saw the armada of bicycles working their way up the hill to Hautvillers, she was so relieved that she almost burst out crying.

Choking back tears, she had told the cycling club chairman, "I'll never forget this."

But he had just waved it off. "Don't mention it, madame. In an emergency, we cyclists help each other; we're willing to set off in the middle of the night, if the occasion demands."

Grosse continued his tutorial: "Never, never squeeze the bunches too much or damage them. If you do, they'll start to ferment right away, and that would be a tragedy. If the skin gets damaged, it darkens the juice, and that's something that has to be avoided at all costs. If you get rotten grapes or ones that aren't yet ripe, throw them right to the ground, not in the basket, understood?"

The men nodded.

Claude had given half of the men a pair of shears and a small wooden basket each. The other half of the group was empty-handed; these men would act as *porteurs* and take the full baskets from the pickers, then tip them carefully into the large baskets, which they called *mannequins*. After a few hours, the men would swap roles. Grosse and Claude would supervise to make sure the system worked.

Isabelle spoke next. "We're starting with this vineyard. These grapes are Pinot Meunier; their skin isn't quite as delicate as that of the Chardonnay grapes, but they still have to be treated with the greatest care. Just imagine that you're holding grapes made of glass in your hands," she said. She had picked up that pearl of wisdom from one of Jacques's clever books. Gustave Grosse tossed her a surprised and not particularly pleasant glance, which she happily ignored. She clapped her hands and said, "All right, let's get to it—here's to a good harvest!"

Isabelle could not remember anything ever being as much fun as picking the grapes. Wearing an old dress, her wild locks bound with a scarf, her sleeves rolled up to the elbows, she worked alongside the men as well as her belly allowed. Cutting off bunches of grapes with the shears was not difficult, but it was more strenuous than it looked. The grapes were heavy in her hands, and the juice ran over her fingers so that, after a short time, both the shears and her hands were uncomfortably sticky. Even so, her small wooden basket filled so quickly that her *porteur* had trouble keeping up with her.

After two hours, she saw Claude approaching.

"I hate to disturb you when you're working, madame," he said with a smirk. "But the men will be expecting a solid lunch. Perhaps you should see to that instead."

Feeling a little embarrassed, Isabelle straightened up. *My God*, she thought, *I'd forgotten about that completely.*

Back in her kitchen, she quickly unfolded Clara's last letter. She had asked her friend for recipes that would feed large numbers of people, and Clara had written back to her shortly after her return to Berlin.

> *Dearest Isabelle,*
> *The time I spent on your winery will be etched in my memory forever, and I think each day about the next time we meet. Now I am back in my everyday Berlin life. And you must surely be in the middle of harvesting your grapes. It is nice to be home again, but I would so love to be with you, as well! I'd cook for all of you and draw a footbath for you in the evenings to soothe your aching feet . . .*

Isabelle quickly scanned the well-intentioned but—just then—not particularly useful lines. On the back of the page, she found what she was looking for.

> *If you have to cook for many people, then the word you have to remember is potatoes!*

Clara had written in her fine, flowing script, underlining the word *potatoes* heavily.

> *They are the most filling of all foods. Cook as many potatoes as you possibly can in your biggest pots early in the morning, and you can conjure up all sorts of different dishes from them.*

Too late for "early in the morning"! Isabelle chewed at her lip as she filled several pots with a few inches of water. Luckily, she had a good fire going in the stove, and the water quickly came to a boil.

> *Render a little bacon, then bake the potatoes in the bacon fat until they're golden brown.*

Still reading Clara's instructions, Isabelle reached into the potato sack next to the oven. Now she had to be just as quick with the potato knife as she had been earlier with the pruning shears!

Potatoes with chopped bacon, a huge plate with sliced green cucumbers, and a bowl of peaches, halved and drenched in champagne—if anyone found Isabelle's lunch unusual, no one let on. Instead, the men dug in heartily and drank carafe after carafe of water and at least as many bottles of red wine. Isabelle worried that all the wine might go to the men's heads, but at the same time, she was glad that her food had met with such a favorable reception.

It warmed Isabelle's heart to watch the men sitting around the large wooden table that Claude had dragged out of the barn and set up at the foot of the vineyard. All of them laughing and joking, all in high spirits and enjoying the camaraderie that came so naturally to them. This was just as she'd imagined the harvest to be! She absolutely *had* to write about it to Clara and Josephine.

The work was hard and the hours long. Apart from the break for lunch, they did not stop again all day.

"You can rest tonight, but now the job is to get the grapes into the presses. We don't want to let madame down, do we?" Claude implored the men again and again. "The widow Feininger isn't sitting around. This evening, there'll be a big pot of pork sausages, mustard from Dijon, fresh bread, and wine, as much as you like. Now isn't that something to look forward to?"

And so the men kept working, despite aching backs, tired arms, and sore legs, until the sun dropped below the horizon.

Instead of hauling everything back down to the vineyard, Isabelle served dinner for the pickers by candlelight out on her terrace, although neither Claude nor Grosse could join them for that. They were in the press-house, supervising the processing of the grapes picked that day. Before the harvest began, Claude had managed to hire a few of the older men from the village to operate the press—it was tricky work, and too much depended on it to put it in less experienced hands.

"For the next few days, we won't be eating or sleeping much. That's just the way it is at this time of year, madame," Claude had said, almost apologetically, when she asked him where he was going when it was late and everyone else was just sitting down to eat. Isabelle promised she would check in on him later.

When the pot of sausages and the breadbasket were empty, one of the men unpacked a violin and started to play. Unlike Isabelle, all the men seemed to know the song, and they clapped and sang along with the violinist.

Isabelle couldn't stop smiling, and she opened a few more bottles of wine.

The first day was over. They had done it!

Chapter Thirty-Two

The pickers were back among the vines by four in the morning. Isabelle had read that the best way to retain the fine, fruity aroma of the grapes was to harvest them early in the morning.

"In return, you can finish earlier!" she had told the men from Charleville, convincing them to get back on their feet again after so few hours of sleep. With Gustave Grosse watching over the work in the press-house, Claude was left to supervise the vineyards alone, so Isabelle was doubly surprised to see him appear in the kitchen at midday. Instead of spending the first few hours helping with the picking, she was preparing breakfast, lunch, and dinner for thirty hungry men.

"Has something happened?" Isabelle asked.

He shook his head. "The men are doing the best they can, but thirty pairs of hands simply aren't enough to do the work that used to be done by fifty. We need more pickers, or we're not going to get the harvest in on time."

Isabelle furrowed her brow. "What difference does one day more or less make? As long as the weather holds . . ."

"We're talking at least a week. That's how much longer we'll need," said Claude. "And I doubt this spell of good weather is going to hold.

If you look to the west, that narrow, dark band on the horizon does not augur well. I can already feel it in my bones: there's a front coming. It's still a long way off, but that can change fast. We need more people, and we need them urgently, madame."

His dog barked as if to endorse its master's words. Isabelle tossed the dog a sausage that had been meant for the bean stew. She looked in desperation at her overseer. "For heaven's sake, where am I supposed to find more pickers?"

Daniel's eyes burned as if he had washed them with salt water. His arms were so tired that the slightest movement was a chore. His legs were as heavy as lead, his feet swollen, his shoulders . . . he couldn't feel his shoulders anymore. And he no longer heard the din and frantic activity in the press-house at all, though it surrounded him day and night. Being able to sleep eight consecutive hours again—eight? Two or three would do!—seemed impossible. And yet he felt optimistic, standing, as he had for days, beside the Trubert press while he oversaw the men filling and working it. So far, not one of their own people or any of the foreign pickers had gotten sick or injured, and there had been no fights or other trouble. With a little luck, they would get through the last three or four days of the harvest without incident. Daniel yawned and rubbed his tired eyes, then Henriette's voice pulled him out of his thoughts.

"Well, are you pleased with the quantity and quality?"

In the low light of the press-house, he turned to Henriette. "It could be worse," he said. In truth, he was extremely satisfied with the harvest. The grapes were almost flawless and had a fuller aroma than they did the year before. But sharing that satisfaction with Henriette would have spoiled it for him. *She's your boss. She has a right to know things like that,* he berated himself in the same instant, but he still did not say any more.

They stepped out into the open air together. After the darkness of the press-house, the bright sunshine hurt Daniel's weary eyes. A deep gong rang loudly. The gong had become a tradition at the Trubert estate, and it was rung to signal the start of every meal.

"You look as if you could use some food yourself," Henriette said, and stroked Daniel's arm.

"A good idea," he replied, pulling his arm free of her touch. At the thought of eating, his stomach growled. He could not remember the last time he had eaten.

"Strange," he murmured as his eyes swept across the vineyards. "Most of the Feininger vines still haven't been harvested. But Isabelle Feininger wanted to start picking one day after us." He saw pickers at work in only one vineyard close to her house, where Pinot Meunier grapes grew, but the vines were otherwise deserted. Isabelle . . . even in the bustle of the harvest, the German constantly found her way into his thoughts—which surprised him.

"Considering your newfound interest in the widow, I thought you would already know, my dear," said Henriette. "But I'll tell you what poor Isabelle's problem is: her pickers have all abandoned her. With the handful of people she has, she'll never manage to get her grapes in!" There was satisfaction—or triumph—in Henriette's words.

Daniel turned quickly to Henriette. "What? But why . . ." Was *l'Allemande* such a terrible boss? Isabelle certainly did not seem to be a slave driver. Had she been unable to pay the pickers? But he could not imagine that; she had the money from the Americans, after all.

The corners of Henriette's mouth rose in a spiteful smile. "And this is the best part: I managed to get the regular Feininger pickers to work for us. They're picking in the Leblanc vineyard and all the others I've bought in the last year. Everybody has a price—I've been convinced of that for a long time, and it's proved true. For a few more francs and a bottle of wine a day, getting them was easy. Oh, Daniel, don't tell me you didn't notice that we've got fifty more pickers than usual!" She shook her head and clucked her tongue.

Daniel had, indeed, hired the pickers, but his best foreman managed them in the vineyards. He glared at Henriette in disbelief. "You stole Isabelle Feininger's pickers?"

"If looks could kill . . . ," Henriette cooed, taking a step back in exaggerated fear. "Don't be like that, my dear. If you'd done what you were supposed to do in Troyes, I wouldn't have been forced to take such steps, and the Feininger land would be mine by now."

"What a greedy old viper you are." He couldn't believe he worked his fingers to the bone day and night for her.

"A viper who gets what she wants," said Henriette maliciously, then she turned away. "The food's getting cold. You'd better hurry."

Though he felt like nothing more than walking away, he followed Henriette into the empty warehouse that they had converted into a cafeteria for the harvest workers. He had no appetite anymore, but there was something else—or rather, someone else—he wanted to deal with.

It didn't take Daniel long to find out who headed the clan that should have been working for Isabelle: Pedro Garcia Àlvarez. It didn't surprise Daniel in the least since it was well known that Àlvarez always asked for more from his employers than he passed on to his people. Because few vintners cared where their money went as long as the work was done well, Àlvarez lined his own pockets without his people finding out about it. What was equally well known was that the Spaniard was a Casanova from whom no woman was safe. Àlvarez cheated his people out of their hard-earned money and cheated on his wife as well.

Until that day, Daniel had had almost nothing to do with the man, but that was about to end.

The Spaniard sat at one of the best tables, directly beside where they served the food. While the plates of most of the pickers were empty, and the men and women were getting up to go back to their strenuous work, Àlvarez was treating himself to seconds. When he saw Daniel approaching, he paused momentarily, then calmly continued eating.

Daniel stood in front of the man. "I need to talk to you, right now." He nodded toward the warehouse door.

"And if I don't need to talk with you, monsieur?" Àlvarez replied languidly.

"Fine with me," said Daniel with a shrug. "I can just as easily talk to your people. I'm sure they'd be interested to hear how *skillfully* you negotiate their wages." He gestured to those leaving to wait a moment longer.

Maria Àlvarez looked curiously at her husband.

"Something the matter?" asked one of the workers. A restlessness stirred among them.

"If you know what's good for you, you'll come with me now," Daniel whispered to Àlvarez. The Spaniard followed him without another word.

***

While Isabelle served potato soup to the pickers, she kept glancing at the sky with concern. The sun was still beating down mercilessly, but along the horizon, there were high white streaks of clouds.

"Your soup's delicious, madame," said one of the cyclists, holding his bowl out to Isabelle. Forcing a smile, she filled the bowl again. She wanted the men working, but she knew how hard the picking was. To be able to get through the afternoon shift at all, the midday break and a fortifying lunch were vital. Soup packed with meat, plus bread, cheese, and vegetable fritters—every day, she put out more on the table.

Oh, let them eat in peace and enjoy the break, she thought with resignation as she scraped the last bit of soup out of the pot for herself and sat down at the table to eat. *An hour more or less isn't going to make a difference; either way, we'll only get half of it in.*

A sparrow hopped from the sunlight into the shadow cast by the long dining table. Ignoring the crowd of men, the bird hunted for fallen crumbs, and Isabelle tossed it a crust of bread.

"Madame—look!" Claude Bertrand, sitting beside her, jabbed her in the ribs. He was pointing to the road, where thirty or more men and women were walking toward them.

"What's this now?" Wide-eyed, Isabelle stared at the group, which was led by a wiry man with receding black hair. His expression was anything but friendly.

Isabelle frowned. Was she mistaken, or were these the same people who camped down at the bottom of her garden? Were they breaking camp? Why else would they be walking around like this in the middle of the day?

"Christ!" said Claude Bertrand. "If that isn't Àlvarez and his clan! That's the lout who should have been working for us. Leaving us hanging like he did—I'll tell him a thing or two!" He stood up angrily and rubbed his hands together as if he were about to attack the man.

"Claude," Isabelle said, with a note of warning. "No arguments now, please. Let's hear what they have to say first."

Her overseer gritted his teeth, but he nodded as the Spaniard walked up to them, hooked his thumbs into his waistband, and rocked provocatively from his toes to his heels and back again. Then he said, "We've been sent. They say you need help."

Isabelle looked at the man in confusion. "But . . . who sent you?"

The man dismissed her question. "That doesn't matter. For good pay and food, we're willing to work in your vineyards. That's what matters." He peered critically at the plates of the cyclists, as if to check that what Isabelle served was good enough.

Isabelle could have jumped for joy. This man was her savior! But she put on her sternest voice and said, "I'll pay you the wage we'd already agreed. You can't expect any more, not after you abandoned us. But I'll gladly add a bottle of wine per day for every worker. Does that sound good?" She looked from one to the other and heard a general murmur of agreement. Their leader nodded.

She clapped her hands. "Then what are we waiting for? To work!"

"You'll get pruning shears and baskets from me," Claude added grimly. "Let's get one thing straight: I want to hear you singing while you work. Have I made myself clear?"

The workers nodded while their leader spat disdainfully onto the ground.

"What did you mean by that?" Isabelle asked a little later, as the new pickers headed back into the vineyards with the cyclists.

Claude grinned. "Around here, we say that if you're singing, you're not stuffing your mouth with grapes. Not that we'd have to worry about that. These people must be sick of the sight of grapes by now. I just wanted to rile Àlvarez a little."

Chapter Thirty-Three

The two horses worked more the days of the harvest than they did through all the rest of the year. With their heads bent low, they leaned into their harnesses, hauling one brimming cartload of grapes after another to the press-house. Where the leather straps lay against their hides, the horses' hair was dark with sweat, which in turn drew the flies. Although Àlvarez's men and women already had the Trubert harvest behind them, they also pulled their weight at the Feininger estate. The cyclists, spurred by the hard work of the itinerant harvesters, picked up their paces. And row by row, the grapes disappeared.

The baskets were unloaded in front of the press-house, their contents inspected briefly by the cellar master. The grapes were then poured into the press, which could hold almost ten thousand pounds of grapes. When this quantity—called the *marc*—was reached, seven men positioned themselves around the wheel; when they turned it, the heavy plate known as the *mouton* sank onto the grapes, squeezing out their juice. The work had to be done with care so the red color from the skins didn't mix with the juice, which had to stay as light and clear as possible. Two pounds of grapes would later be transformed into a little more than one bottle of champagne. It made Isabelle dizzy to think what a treasure, what wealth, was flowing through her press.

Thanks to Jacques's books, Isabelle had a good idea of what happened when the grapes were pressed. Most valuable of all were the first five hundred gallons of juice. The first half of that was called the *première cuvée*. The next hundred and fifty gallons made up the *deuxième cuvée*, and the final hundred were the *troisième cuvée*. These five hundred gallons formed the basis for the most valuable champagnes. With every subsequent pressing, the flesh of the red grapes came into more contact with the skin, and the juice consequently took on a reddish coloration and lost some of its aroma. This juice could be made into very drinkable champagnes, but they were generally less elegant or full-bodied than those of the first pressing. Of course, every pressing was stored in a separate barrel.

But for all she had learned, nothing from any of the books had prepared her for the feverish atmosphere in the press-house, which held an almost magical attraction for Isabelle. Every night, when she had her duties as cook and hostess behind her, she visited the press-house and stood by the entrance, always taking care not to get in anyone's way or disturb the complicated handling processes. Every night, as she stood at the entrance, she was struck by the unique smell of grape juice, fermented fruit, and sweat, and she breathed it in greedily; it represented the basis for her own future security and her great goal of creating her own champagne. And every night, not without anxiety, she marveled at what she knew was only a seeming chaos but in reality was the perfect coordination of many experienced hands.

Supervised by Gustave Grosse, the press-house men worked day and night in two shifts. Filling the basket, pressing, scooping the grapes that clung to the sides back into the middle with a wooden scraper, pressing again—juice flowed from the grapes, and sweat streamed from the men.

The vineyards and the press were like two worlds, completely separate from one another but existing side by side. The longer the harvest went on, the slower the vineyard workers moved. No one spoke much; they were in tune with one another and certainly too tired to fight.

In the press-house, though, the atmosphere grew more tense with every passing day. A false word, a tiny shove, and a fight would ensue, only to be nipped in the bud by the cellar master. Time was much too precious to be wasted with fighting. But speed alone was not enough to do the work; the press demanded the greatest concentration: each type of grape and each pressing had to be pumped into separate tanks—*cuves de débourbage*—that were stored in a cellar one level deeper. There, the juice could rest, and contaminants like stems, skins, sediment, and insects were removed. Later, the juice was pumped through the complicated system of pipes into another cellar, where it would be stored again, this time in barrels, and undergo the first fermentation. For Isabelle, this was one of the trickiest stages of all. God forbid someone forgot to note the necessary information for a barrel or accidentally mixed two kinds of juice. That nearly happened once, and Isabelle was amazed to see the otherwise so apathetic Gustave Grosse start to rage at such sloppiness. She would gladly have been there herself to supervise, but she had to trust her cellar master and his workers.

***

Two weeks into the harvest, the vines looked as tattered as molted birds, and the pickers in their filthy aprons looked nearly as bad. At some point, the last vine was picked clean, and the barrels that had spent the year empty in the extensive cellars beneath the estate were all filled again with fresh grape juice.

As the harvest had drawn to a close, Claude had told her that throwing a party to celebrate was mandatory. Isabelle had merely smiled at her overseer. She had long ago made all the arrangements for just such a party, and she had done so in style.

Now, her terrace was lit up like a theater stage. White candles flickered on the long wooden table, and the full moon cast a generous silver glow over everything. Small bouquets of lavender and roses released their sweet scent into the warm September night and blended with the spicy aroma of the suckling pig that had been sizzling on a spit since early that morning.

Isabelle, her eyes shining, sat beside Claude at one of the tables, soaking up the atmosphere, which was so unlike anything she'd experienced before. The other seat beside her was reserved for Gustave Grosse. He and the men from the press-house were still finishing up but would join the celebrations soon.

A few of Àlvarez's men played guitar and violin, and everyone sang, danced, laughed, ate, and drank. The night was long, and sleep was the last thing on anyone's mind.

"Leon would have enjoyed a party like this," Isabelle murmured.

Claude, who had been talking to the man sitting opposite, abruptly turned to Isabelle and said, "As successful as this harvest has been, you've done your husband the greatest honor. His legacy could not have been better managed."

Isabelle smiled sadly. "Do you really think so?"

Claude nodded, then went back to his conversation.

He's probably right. I can be proud that everything has gone so well, she thought. Really, she felt pride along with many other emotions. The harvest was over. But she had no real time to rest, for new tasks already awaited her. Would she be able to cope with them, too?

She was so lost in her thoughts that she did not notice Gustave Grosse until he was standing beside her. He smelled of sweat and grime. His eyes were bloodshot, his gaze almost mad as he held out a small glass of ruby-tinted juice.

"Here, madame! The last *vin de cuvée* we pressed. Would you like to try it?"

Isabelle held the glass up to the candlelight. "Isn't it a little too red?"

"Don't worry. The color will be eaten by the yeast."

Only half-appeased, Isabelle lifted the glass to her lips. Instantly, everyone around her fell silent, and all eyes turned to her expectantly.

The juice tasted sweet and sticky, but that was all she could say about it. She looked at the people all around and smiled, then called out, "It's going to be a wonderful vintage!"

Enthusiastic cheers rose on every side. Everyone had been part of the harvest's success, and they all enjoyed this moment of triumph.

Tears came to Isabelle's eyes. "Thank you all!" she called, her voice breaking. "You were wonderful."

More cheering. Goaded into it by his friends, a good-looking Spaniard with blazing eyes—one of Àlvarez's men—jumped to his feet, went to Isabelle, and bowed before her with a flourish.

"Boss—would you honor me with the first dance of the evening?"

Later, all the gaiety and noise grew too much for her. The child in her belly was restless and tired, too. She slipped away from the festivities and walked toward her vineyards.

Moonlight glimmered over the landscape, and the outlines of the bare vines looked as if someone had traced them with a fine quill in an ink drawing. It was so quiet, so peaceful. Even the wild creatures out hunting in the night made no sound.

Halfway to the vineyards, Isabelle sat on a weathered bench. She breathed in deeply; the air was still permeated with the sweet smell of the grapes and the smoke from the many campfires that dotted across the landscape. The bonfire sparks lit the night like fireflies. Someone up in heaven also seemed to have lit a bonfire—a flood of stars sparkled like priceless diamonds across the firmament. Directly in front of her, the evening star glowed. Isabelle smiled. A deep feeling of peace filled her, and she willingly gave herself over to it.

"Leon," she whispered, looking up to the sky, "believe it or not, we did it!"

What no one believed possible had come to pass. She had done it. Her first harvest was in.

No time to rest . . . but she had at least a little more time for other things, and she was looking forward to things slowing down. She had not seen either Micheline or Ghislaine for days, and she wanted to write letters to Josephine and Clara, telling them all about her harvest adventure. And then . . . Pondering, she stroked her belly. From now on, she would take better care of the child. Leon's child. Instead of ignoring its presence, she would nurture and care for it as she did the vines.

She sighed deeply. In that moment, she did not want to think about all the other duties and tasks ahead. It did her good to simply sit and enjoy the silence, and she did not want to spoil that.

But a moment later, she saw a dark figure coming down the path. She frowned, suddenly put out: Who could want anything from her just then? Had two drunks started a fight that she—the boss, as the people had begun to call her—would have to settle? Or was someone coming to fetch her back to the fire? Wasn't she to be granted just a few silent minutes to herself?

She only relaxed when she saw who it was.

"Isabelle?" Daniel Lambert looked surprised to find her there. "Don't you have your big harvest party tonight?"

"Sometimes finding a quiet corner is the best thing that can happen to a person," she replied.

"And sometimes not," Daniel replied with a wry smile. "One can also enjoy such tranquility in company. May I?"

He gestured toward the seat beside her, and she nodded hastily.

For a little while, they sat side by side, neither saying a word. Daniel's body radiated a pleasant warmth, and Isabelle unconsciously leaned toward him. "I guess the Champagne region is the only place in the world you can see stars like this." She swept one hand across the spangled sky.

"And yet, some people see only the darkness but not the stars," Daniel replied.

"I was like that myself, for a long time. I had to learn to see the stars again," said Isabelle thoughtfully.

The silence that settled again was more charged than it had been. A light tremor ran through Isabelle; it was not uncomfortable but made her a little bit afraid. She moved away from Daniel a little, then stretched her arms over her head to ease her aching muscles, sore from hauling pots, pans, and mountains of tableware. As she did so, it occurred to her how good it would probably feel to lay her head on his shoulder. *Any other mad ideas while you're at it?* she immediately scolded herself. "I'm slowly starting to feel like I've got more wine than blood in my veins," she said. "A strange feeling . . ."

Daniel laughed. "Anyone born here has wine in their veins from birth. It looks to me as if you're heading toward becoming a real *vigneronne*."

She looked at him sidelong. "If I think of Henriette, I have to wonder if that was meant as a compliment or an affront."

"That's up to you," he replied just as lightheartedly. Then he became more serious. "Well? Did Àlvarez and his people do a decent job?"

"*You* sent them?"

He shrugged. "Unfortunately, I only found out too late what was going on, or I would have done something much earlier."

"Thank you," Isabelle murmured after a few moments. "I don't know why you're doing all this for me, but without you I would have been lost . . . more than once."

Then she felt his lips on her mouth. The contact was simultaneously as light as a feather and intense. As startled as she was by the sudden kiss, she certainly felt a flame spark to life inside her. Carefully, she opened her lips a little and felt his tongue, probing. He did not taste of wine, she was surprised to discover, but of clear spring water.

Just for a moment, she imagined what it would be like to make love to Daniel, to take her pleasure in his gentle touch, to respond in kind, experiencing that ecstasy and release together. But that could not be; she would never allow it! She was Leon's widow, and she would be true to him beyond his death. Shocked, she pushed herself away from Daniel.

Daniel smiled. "I wish you all the best, my *vigneronne allemande*. May your champagne be as tantalizing as you are."

"You frighten me," she said, unsettled.

"Do you think I feel any different?" he replied. "You scare the *hell* out of me. That kiss—it came as unexpectedly for me as for you. I had no plans to fall in love with you. Being in love makes you vulnerable. But it looks like I've lost the battle. So I'm asking you, be forgiving with me." Even in the dark, she saw that the fine lines around the eyes in his weathered face grew deeper as he smiled.

Isabelle could only return his smile with difficulty. Too much was going on in her head. Daniel's confession had shocked her. What feelings did she hold for him? All she knew was that, whenever she was near him, she felt that subtle trembling, like the beat of a butterfly's wings against the inside of her stomach, pleading for release. It was something she could only remember from when she had first fallen for Leon. And now she felt the same way around Daniel.

"I don't know if I'm ready for a new love, or if I ever will be," she said, more to herself than to him. "Though I'm getting through the days better than I was, I'm still so sad that I've lost Leon. The sadness comes and goes like waves, and I never know when the next one is going to crash over me. What if I'm lying in another man's arms then?" She waited for an answer. When Daniel said nothing, she continued. "I have so many things still ahead, and I don't know if I'll be able to deal with them. I'm going to be the mother of Leon's child! And there's the champagne—it's supposed to be something exquisite, the kind of champagne you find once in a hundred years, and it's my *first* champagne. I won't be able to do it with Gustave Grosse. Sooner or later, I'll have to look around for a new cellar master, someone more talented. Someone who shares my vision. And then I have to look for new customers. And then, and then . . . !" She shook her head. "So many new things . . . and a new love on top of everything? I'm too big a coward for that."

"You are the bravest woman I have ever met." There was so much longing in his voice, so much tenderness and depth that Isabelle was afraid she would drown in it. Abruptly, she jumped to her feet, her skirt catching on a splinter on the rough wooden bench. She heard a soft tearing sound. Ignoring it, she looked at Daniel.

"Me? Brave?" Her laugh was shrill. "Try telling that to Clara and Josephine. They know what a coward I am. I'm sorry, but I'm not the right one for you. The best thing you could do would be to leave me in peace. There's no room in my life for this kind of thing."

Without another word, she walked away.

***

It was the first performance of the new season, and every seat at the opera in Reims was sold out. Now that the harvests were over and the cellars of champagne were full again, the *Champenois* wanted a change, and they wanted to be entertained. The director of the opera was an experienced elderly man from Paris, and he knew what his audiences were after, so he had decided on a performance of Jules Massenet's *Manon* to kick off the season—a love story as dramatic as it was ill fated, set in the times of Louis XV. Beautiful women, rich noblemen, magnificent costumes and even more magnificent backdrops, and bold, risqué dialogue—that was something the champagne makers could identify with! But there was one visitor that evening who could not identify with that.

Raymond Dupont shifted restlessly in his seat in one of the red-velvet-clad boxes. Manon Lescaut's arias were scraping his nerves raw, as if someone were dragging a knife across a china plate, and he did not find her constant vacillating between her lover, Le Chevalier des Grieux, and her lover's rival, the wealthy Monsieur de Brétigny, to be even the slightest bit prurient, but rather simply repugnant. Why were the two men blind to the underhanded game the profligate beauty was playing? How was it possible for grown men to let her run roughshod over them like that? Where was true love, great love?

Raymond had no idea why he was so worked up. It was an opera, no more.

Was it to do with all the busy weeks he'd been through lately? Endless days in his shop, followed every evening by the mandatory excursions with his wealthy customers out into the countryside to enjoy the atmosphere of the harvest. Only when he had gone to such pains to ensure the well-being of his spoiled clientele did he realize the truth: there was no one—truly no one!—who cared about *his* well-being. There he was, the *grandseigneur* of Champagne, a pillar of Reims society, all alone in the world. When, late in the evenings, he returned to his apartment, his two thousand square feet of luxury, it welcomed him as cold and as deserted as a grave. Now that the harvest was over, the Champagne party season would begin, and he would have to work even more. His customers relied on his advice, so this meant numerous tasting sessions and as many painstaking conversations. Sometimes his clients even expected him to pay a visit to their venue before he selected a champagne for the event.

Work, work, work, never time for anything else.

And my love life is in the doldrums. Not the slightest sign of a liaison, he thought grumpily as beautiful Manon sank into the arms of de Brétigny.

As the curtain fell and a melodic gong rang for the thirty-minute intermission, Raymond sighed. With a friendly smile at the other guests in his box, he fled to the champagne bar, awaiting the onslaught of the guests in the gaily lit foyer.

He ordered a *coupe de champagne* and gazed at the other opening-night visitors. Everyone was there: the Ruinarts and the Moëts, Maurice and George Roger from Épernay, Louise Pommery's son Louis, Joseph and Georges Bollinger. Each of those esteemed men was escorting an elegantly dressed woman . . . couples, wherever Raymond looked. He frowned; so this was where all his hard work had taken him—instead of a beautiful woman at his side, he was standing at the bar like something ordered but never picked up. It would actually have been up to him, then, to approach one or another of the winemakers he could see around him. A compliment here, a quick chat about the next tasting session there. But instead of turning on his usual charm and working on his contacts, he stood there with his smile frozen in place and hoped that everyone would leave him in peace. *What is wrong with you?* he asked himself. He needed a rest, some time to turn his thoughts to other things.

He probably would have sunk even deeper into his gloomy musings if he had not seen Alphonse and Henriette Trubert walking in his direction just then. Raymond was taken aback; he had not expected to see them together in public like this. Every sparrow in every bush was whistling about how Alphonse's lover, Ghislaine Lambert, was expecting his child. But it looked as if Henriette didn't care at all; with her back straight and her head held high, she strutted through the foyer, greeting friends and acquaintances on every side.

"Raymond, my dear!" She stopped in front of him, a predatory smile on her face. Returning her smile, he kissed her on both cheeks and did his best to ignore the red lipstick smeared on her teeth. He could no longer remember what it was that had once attracted him to this woman. Her husband seemed to be thinking along the same lines, because as soon as Henriette spoke to Raymond, Alphonse took the opportunity to escape.

"A ravishing production, don't you think? I find the composition both ingenious and refined, and with a distinctive atmosphere to boot." Henriette rolled her eyes in feigned rapture.

Since when did you become an opera expert? Raymond wanted to ask his erstwhile lover, but he suppressed the urge. Like Raymond, Henriette only went to the opera to see and to be seen; the play beyond the stage was far more interesting to both of them than the efforts of the *professional* actors. In the past, on several occasions, they had laughed about this common ground.

"Cat got your tongue, or is it something more dire?" Henriette gave him an unladylike jab in his ribs. "Talk to me. Your silence is gradually getting embarrassing. People are starting to stare."

Pull yourself together, Raymond warned himself, and not for the first time that evening. He was depressed, and it was not a mood he was familiar with. It scared him, and it made him angry. But instead of uttering either a moody quip or the kind of compliment women like Henriette liked to hear, he sighed deeply.

"I think I'm getting old," he heard himself say, to his own horror.

Henriette, who assumed he was making a joke, laughed brightly. "Won't we all be sooner or later? I know exactly what you need, my dear," she whispered in his ear.

"How can you know that when you yourself are still in the bloom of youth?" he said, finally managing to conjure up his usual charm.

Henriette raised her thin, plucked eyebrows coquettishly, then she hooked her arm into his.

"Let's take a little walk," she said, and strolled off with him toward one of the two terraces that framed the opera house. Every gas lamp along the marble balustrades was lit—the operagoers wanted to show off their splendor wherever they went, after all.

Outside, they set their glasses down, and Henriette immediately said, "I've heard that Isabelle Feininger has also managed to get her harvest in, albeit only at the last moment and by getting over some serious obstacles."

Raymond laughed. "And who was behind those obstacles, I wonder? None other than you!"

Henriette did not dispute his claim but merely waved her hand in casual dismissal, as if Raymond had mentioned a trifle. "One way or another, she will lose her estate. Am I supposed to wait for the next charlatan to come along?" she said, then went on without waiting for Raymond to reply. "Jacques Feininger was not cut from the right cloth to run a winery, nor was Leon Feininger, and Isabelle Feininger most certainly is not. It is high time that the estate found its way into the right hands."

"And the right hands would be yours?" Raymond asked drily. Why was she telling him this?

Henriette looked at him confidently. "I'm not trying to disguise the fact that I would like to have the Feininger lands. I look out my window every morning, and when I see the Feininger vineyards, I am overcome by a desire to own them. They would, so to speak, set the crown on my holdings."

Although it was nothing new, Raymond suddenly found Henriette's habit of talking about "her" property, as if she alone owned the Trubert estate, extremely disagreeable. In fact, he was finding this entire discussion disagreeable!

"At the same time, I am not ignoring Isabelle's well-being for one moment," Henriette continued. "She's still young. She should marry again. A well-to-do man would lay the world at her feet, a world where she could be a princess instead of a drudge who slogs away from morning to night. The kind of life due to a fine young lady from imperial Berlin—that's what I would wish for Isabelle Feininger. Wouldn't you?"

"What do you want, Henriette?" Raymond asked impatiently. He picked up his glass and drained it in one draught, then turned as if about to go back inside.

"Only what's best for you, darling," she replied with a saccharine smile. "It's clear to me that being alone all the time isn't doing you any good. You look tired and somehow . . . joyless. A new love would buck you up! A young woman who would appreciate a man as mature, clever, and attractive as you are. A woman like Isabelle Feininger would breathe new life into your dusty bachelor existence. There's more to life than work, my dear!"

"I won't argue with that," he noted, his voice sarcastic, but at the same time he was trying to hide his surprise. Could Henriette read thoughts? A beautiful woman, desire, excitement—there was nothing like that in his life; he'd become as flat as champagne left to stand. But it was almost humiliating that one of his former lovers should rub salt into the wound. "But you really don't need to worry about my love life. I'm discreet, that's all," he added.

"Discreet or not, my eyes and ears miss very little, as you are well aware. I've observed on several occasions that the widow Feininger appeals to you—at our own annual soiree, for one, and at the festival in the village. The way you look at her, the way you hang on every word she so much as mutters."

He laughed then. "Don't you have anything better to do than spy on me?"

She went on, unperturbed. "The German is a highly desirable woman. My own dear cellar master also seems rather taken with her, though with Daniel I'm not sure what's got him more fired up: Isabelle Feininger the woman or the thought that he might finally be able to take back control of his forebears' estate. He wouldn't be the first man to marry for money!" She sniffed in disgust.

A tangle of thoughts filled Raymond's head, and he had trouble sorting them all out. "Daniel Lambert has his eye on Isabelle Feininger?" he pressed, realizing how stupid the question made him sound.

Henriette nodded. "And because of that, he's undermined me several times. I'd toss him out on his ear for his disloyalty, believe me, but I'm afraid I'd never find such a talent again for my cellars."

Now it was Raymond who nodded. Daniel had always been the best cellar master in the region—and to keep him, one might have to swallow a little pride, and gladly so.

"Daniel and Isabelle Feininger . . . ," Raymond said, pondering. The idea did not please him.

Henriette looked at Raymond through narrowed eyes. "Do you really want to give Daniel free rein? In the past, you got any woman you wanted—could it be that you've lost your touch?"

"Could it be that you're sticking your nose in where it really doesn't belong?" Raymond shot back. "At the moment, I simply have no time to play the gentleman, not for Isabelle Feininger or any other woman. Business comes first—you'd understand that better than anyone, wouldn't you?"

Again, she ignored his remark. "Just imagine . . . you and Isabelle, traveling together. You could show her the world and discover it again for yourself. You could feast on her youth like a bee on nectar. You'd have to sell the estate, of course. It would only be a burden. And you know I'm willing to pay the best price for the Feininger land. After that, you'd be free, and you'd have the sweetest life ahead of you. Oh, to fall in love all over again . . ." Her voice was as smooth as honey, her sigh covetous.

Raymond felt desire stir inside him. A smile crossed his face, alluring images playing out in mind's eye. He would never lower himself to admit that Henriette was right, but it was not to be denied: the old coquette had shown him exactly how to add some fresh spice to his life.

Chapter Thirty-Four

Two different ways of life permeated the region, it seemed to Isabelle. Before the harvest, fear that poor weather or even one big storm could destroy a year's work at the last moment dominated the mood. But now the harvest was over and the fear had dissipated. People were happy and liberated again. Ignaz and Carla Chapron invited Isabelle to a small party to celebrate the sale of the cooper's new barrels. And at Ghislaine's Le Grand Cerf, the vignerons sat, hour after hour, with onion tarts and new wine for lunch, leisurely reviewing the year behind them. A round of champagne, then a round of spirits—with the millions of gallons of grape juice stored in their cellars, the *Champenois* were willing to open their wallets wider than usual. The diners and drinkers gossiped to their heart's content, spreading and then dissecting the latest rumors. A great deal of attention was given to the question of how high the price of champagne might go for the turn of the century.

At least as much attention, however, was paid to Daniel Lambert's departure from the Trubert estate. It was said he left right after the harvest, more or less on the spur of the moment. And now he was working for Perrier-Jouët, a well-known champagne house in Épernay. But the hows and whys of it all were open to wild speculation. A scandal involving Daniel and Henriette Trubert? Or simply a good offer from Perrier-Jouët, one that Daniel could not refuse? That charge was disputed instantly. For Daniel, making champagne was an art, not a business. Others asked whether the vineyards of Hautvillers were perhaps no longer good enough for him.

Isabelle and her neighbors Micheline and Marie Guenin were also to be found in Le Grand Cerf on more than one afternoon. They ate grape cake and washed it down with champagne, and Isabelle listened closely to the talk about Daniel. Confessing his love for her in the vineyard had certainly been shocking, but had she been right to run away as she had, as if he were snapping at her heels? What if he left because he was upset by the way she reacted?

She turned her attention to Micheline and Marie. The sisters-in-law were busy knitting children's clothes. "That will be lovely," she said, pointing at the sweater Micheline was working on. "Claude is going to help me paint an old cupboard tomorrow. I want to use it to keep the baby's things in later. Clothes and toys and such." With every passing day, her anticipation grew, and with it, the preparations for the arrival of the new child.

"Why don't you knit some clothes for my child while you're at it?" said Ghislaine. She smiled as she came to the table with a pot of coffee in her hand. Her belly had grown considerably, and she carried her new curves with pride.

"Of course, my dear!" Micheline beamed. But Marie scowled—she would not knit a single row for a child conceived in sin.

"If you would like, Madame Feininger, I'll put together a little cradle for your baby," Ignaz Chapron called from the next table.

"Only if you promise that the cradle will look like a champagne barrel. They say the children here are born with wine in their blood, so a bed like that would be just the thing," Isabelle replied with a laugh.

"Then why don't I take a barrel and cut it down the middle? Then I'll have two cradles, one for Ghislaine's child, too."

Everyone laughed, and the mood grew even brighter.

Wherever she went, whomever she met—Isabelle's constant companion was the warm feeling that this was where she belonged. The people of Hautvillers were no angels. They had their rough edges, their weaknesses. But when it really mattered, they helped each other out of a tight spot, just as Daniel had done with her, several times now.

His disappearance hit her harder than she liked to admit. On her walks, she often looked over to the more distant vineyards, hoping to catch sight of him. He wouldn't spend all his time in Épernay, would he? He would have to visit his sister and his old home occasionally. But with every week that passed without that happening, her disappointment grew. She missed Daniel Lambert.

After weeks spent out among the grapevines, the wine cellars became her second home in autumn. Holding tightly to the handrail, she descended the steep wooden stairs every day and listened to the brisk bubbling in the giant vats. The fermentation of the juice was in full swing, and the gurgling sound made Isabelle think of a witch's brew.

So it was all the more surprising when she went into the cellar one December day and was met by an uncanny silence.

"It's finished fermenting," Grosse explained as he threw open the enormous rear-opening gate of the cellar. "Now we've got to leave all the doors and windows down here open; the cold from outside will stop the process completely, so no bacteria can spoil the wine."

Isabelle carefully climbed one of the small ladders and looked down into the large vats. Just a day or two before, all she'd been able to see was a cloudy liquid, and the fermented juice now had a silvery glow from the light pouring in and was as clear as glass. She let out a small enraptured cry.

"The yeast and all the sediments have settled. The champagne looks clarified! This is when you have to pump it into another barrel, isn't it?"

"The *première soutirage*. Exactly." Gustave Grosse nodded. "But a day here or there makes no difference. Let me do my job! Weren't you going out in the vineyards with Claude today?" Without another word, her cellar master disappeared into one of the side passages.

Instead of following Grosse and accosting him about his attitude, she simply watched him walk away. She had to start looking for a new cellar master, and the sooner the better.

To calm herself, she walked along the main passage of the cellar, where dozens of large wooden barrels lined the walls. It was so quiet, like being in a cathedral. And she felt so safe, so sheltered down there in the darkness! Was it the same for the child inside her body? Tenderly, she caressed her belly.

She had read in Jacques's books that the *assemblage*—the first blending of the wines—took place immediately after the *première soutirage*, and that it was one of the most important moments of the entire year for a champagne maker. This year, the blend was even more important than ever. Her turn-of-the-century champagne had to be something different—elegant, not too sweet, but also not so dry that it scratched your palate. With floral nuances and a spicy undertone. It had to contain the multitude of aromas that Isabelle herself wanted to take with her into the new century. But her dream of a champagne was something she could only realize with a cellar master who understood her ideas and was able to put them into practice. A true master, someone like Daniel Lambert.

When she stepped out into the open air, she was so deep in her thoughts that it took her a moment to realize what had changed. Outside, it was at least as quiet as it had been inside the cellar.

The first snow of the year! Delicate flakes fluttered down from the sky, covering the land as if with a veil of the finest lace. Isabelle let out a small enraptured sound. The fields of vines looked enchanted, like a fairytale landscape. Her anger at Grosse was forgotten, and the unsolved problems were as well—for a few long seconds, Isabelle gave herself over completely to the memories rising inside her.

The first snow in Berlin. In her parents' house, making preparations for Christmas. The huge tree they had, and all the countless presents. With the valuable jewels, the expensive porcelain figures and silver boxes, Isabelle often had the feeling that her father, far more than trying to make her or her mother happy, was trying to show off just how much he could afford.

And then there was the meager Christmas the year before, at Leon's parents' house, when she and Leon had crept away before the midnight mass to celebrate the "festival of love" in their own way. Leon . . .

Snowflakes settled on her eyelashes, where they melted and then the cold water trickled down her cheeks. Isabelle blinked. Christmas this year would be different. There would be no wonderful gifts, no magnificent tree. She would not be able to sink into Leon's arms. Still, there was no reason to cry. She was not alone. Ghislaine had invited her over, and Micheline wanted to join them, too. Or she might just make herself comfortable at home, wrap up by herself, or rather with the child she carried. Leon's child . . . wasn't that as rich a gift as she could want?

A smile flitted across her face, but it was replaced a heartbeat later by a frown. Only two weeks to Christmas, and she hadn't bought a single gift! She had new boots in mind for Claude; his old ones were falling off his feet. And she'd get some kind of sausage for his dog, of course. Micheline would love some red lipstick, she knew, and she could find some nice soap for Marie. She should give Ghislaine something for her child, and she wanted to buy something for her own child, too! If only she knew whether it would be a boy or girl . . . perhaps a rattle, then, to be on the safe side?

So many plans, so many ideas. Feeling on top of things, Isabelle turned and walked around to the house entrance. She had to go to

Reims urgently, not only because of the Christmas gifts but, more important, to ask around about a new cellar master. But first, she had to attend to the vineyards.

An hour later, she was wearing her warmest jacket and three pairs of woolen socks inside her boots when she headed out. When she reached the manure pile, Claude was already waiting for her—along with the horses and a wagon filled with manure.

"Madame, what we have ahead of us today is really too strenuous for you."

"Don't worry. I won't do too much." She would really have preferred to spend the day indoors, baking cookies or knitting the baby blanket she'd been working on.

"Of course, madame. Also, the vines need to be untied, and we have to dig drains, too; we don't want the winter rain to wash away all the good soil. But I have to ask, why don't you let Grosse do these things? For a woman—and especially for one in your condition—it's too hard, far too hard."

"Oh, Claude," Isabelle said. "You know better than me how our wonderful cellar master is with hard work. I could chase after him from dawn to dusk, but that would take just as much out of me as if I did the work myself." She sighed. "I'm just so sick of the man."

"What are you doing about it?" Claude asked.

"What am I supposed to do? I can't just conjure a new cellar master. You know as well as I that experts like that don't grow on trees. But don't worry. I'm keeping my eyes and ears open! I know things can't go on as they have, and as soon as I've found the right man, you'll be the first to know. Now let's get started, before I freeze to death."

Claude's expression grew grimmer. "Three hours," he said. "After that, you go home and rest; I don't care how far along we are. And all you do is shovel. I don't want you carrying any buckets. If you feel ill, even a little, we stop."

"Aye, aye!" said Isabelle, then she climbed up onto the wagon.

"When are your friends from Berlin coming back?" With a cluck of his tongue, he set the horses in motion.

"Josephine isn't coming anytime soon. Her husband is in America on a business trip, and she can't leave. But Clara would like to come again at the start of the year." The midwife that Carla Chapron had recommended and with whom Isabelle had first met a few weeks earlier had estimated that the child was due around January 5. It eased Isabelle's mind immensely to think that she would not be alone then.

"High time for someone to watch out for you," said Claude Bertrand, and he muttered something else that Isabelle didn't catch.

She glanced fondly at him. "Thank you," she said, and squeezed his arm. "You're an old grouch, but I'd be lost without you."

The work was both hard and boring. A shovelful at a time, Isabelle filled the buckets with manure, which Claude then spread at the base of the vines. After three hours, they had completed no more than three rows. The snow had stopped, and an icy wind now whipped across the land; still, the sweat trickled down Isabelle's weary back. She hoped that she would not catch a cold.

Finally, she said to Claude, whose face was as gray with exhaustion as her own, "We're getting nowhere. I never imagined it would be this much work. We need help from the village; we'll never manage it alone."

The overseer nodded, relieved, and promised to ask around for a few helpers. They drove the horses back to the estate in silence and parted company at the stable.

What I wouldn't give for a hot bath, she thought, though it meant having to heat many buckets of water and haul them down to the bathroom.

Her visions of a relaxing bath burst like soap bubbles, however, at the sight of two men with the olive skin of more southern regions, unloading sacks of—what?—from a cart in front of her house.

"What are you doing? What is that? I didn't order anything," she said, perplexed.

"Bonjour, madame," said the two men simultaneously. "Cork delivery, just like every December. The finest Catalonian cork. Monsieur Jacques knows about it. Perhaps you could call him?"

"Monsieur Jacques is dead," she said. "Corks for the champagne bottles?"

The two men nodded. "Monsieur Jacques always paid cash. Who's going to pay us?"

The cork dealers' cart had just disappeared around the first curve when another cart came into view.

Isabelle frowned. What now? She crossed her arms and waited for the driver to turn his wagon around in front of her house and park it.

"Bonjour, madame!" the man cried with a tip of his hat and a smile that revealed several missing teeth. "Another year gone, can you believe it? I've brought the bottles, just like every December. Three thousand of the finest glass bottles the Argonne has to offer!"

With a sinking heart, Isabelle watched as the man and his helper unloaded crate after crate, directed by Gustave Grosse, who apparently had been woken from his afternoon nap by the clattering of the bottles. She knew she should have been happy that Jacques had organized the regular delivery of the bottles and corks. But she could see the money she'd made from the Americans melting away like the first snow, and it made her nervous.

"Our bill, madame! And could you spare us a bite to eat and a bit of water and hay for the horses?"

Once the bottle merchant and his helper had eaten a chunk of bread with butter and the horses had been tended, they set off toward the next of their Hautvillers customers.

"Until next year, madame!" the driver called cheerfully from his seat atop the wagon.

She nodded vaguely. Who knew what next year had in store? Drained, she wrapped herself up in a blanket on the chaise longue in the living room, where a warm fire crackled in the tiled stove. A hot bath? She was too tired to even think about it!

When she awoke the next morning, it took her a moment to realize where she was. The fire had long since burned out, and the room was chilly. Had she really spent the entire evening there, with nothing to eat and wearing dirty clothes? Shaking her head, she set off for the kitchen. Claude was right. She really had to start taking better care of herself. To make up for it, she prepared a hearty breakfast.

Afterward, she left the house and took her kitchen scraps out to the chickens. It had begun snowing lightly again, but this time Isabelle had no eye for the beauties of nature. After she had collected the eggs, she headed straight for the wine cellar, where she needed to give Grosse a talking-to. He could at least have told her about the delivery of corks and bottles so she hadn't looked like an idiot!

She already had one hand on the solid handle of the main door when a sharp but muted roar from inside the cellar made her jump. Cannon shot? In her cellars?

Isabelle put down the basket of eggs and pushed the door open, at first just a little, then wider. Good God, what had that been? An explosion? Isabelle looked around helplessly. No sign of Claude anywhere near. What if her cellar master had been hurt and needed help? She didn't want to put herself or her unborn child in danger.

"Monsieur Grosse?" she shouted through the open door. "Gustave? Is everything all right?" When she heard no answer, she gingerly stepped inside and took a few steps toward the stairs. A new detonation sounded, and she stopped in her tracks.

"Monsieur Grosse! What's going on down there? Say something!" Her heart was beating hard and her knees were shaking as she leaned over the railing.

"Everything's fine," she heard from one of the lower levels.

Isabelle's relief almost made her dizzy. As quickly as she could, she descended the stairs to the floor below. On the second to last step, she trod on something soft and round, and her foot slipped out from under her. She automatically clenched both hands around the railing—a fall would be all she needed!

Angry, she looked down to see what she had slipped on. A cork! What the devil was a cork doing on the steps? With her lips pressed together and her eyes on the floor ahead of her, she went on in the dark.

The next moment, she almost fell over in shock. Big, pointy shards of glass; smashed necks and bases of bottles; dangerous little glass slivers; and more corks covered the floor and some of the steps. Champagne was spreading over the ground and collecting in puddles; white foam was sticking to everything.

"Dear God—what is going on here?"

Grosse, in the low light of a gas lamp, was halfheartedly at work with a dustpan and broom. He glanced up at her only momentarily.

"A minor mishap, madame. A few bottles exploded. It happens sometimes. I'll clean it all up immediately, and then it's done."

"Minor mishap? Have you gone completely insane? This is hundreds of bottles! A small fortune just went to waste here!" Isabelle was screaming so loud that her voice broke.

"Now don't go getting so upset," said Grosse, and it seemed to Isabelle that he was trying to hold in a smile. "It's only last year's champagne, and you don't like it anyway."

"Oh, so that means it's all right for the bottles to explode? You . . . you are the clumsiest oaf I have ever laid eyes on!" Shaking with fury, Isabelle snatched an unbroken bottle from a rack on her left and threw it at Grosse's feet in disgust. "If that's the case, then here's another one! And another! And another!" She pulled out one bottle after another and smashed them before the astonished eyes of her cellar master, who was now standing up to his ankles in champagne froth.

"Is it a *major* mishap yet?" she asked, her voice icy. "Now get to work and clean it up!"

Chapter Thirty-Five

With tears of anger—at herself, especially—streaming down her cheeks, Isabelle threw some clothes into her suitcase. Why hadn't she sent Gustave away on the spot? Taken away his key to the cellars and said, "Go! And don't come back!" She slammed the lid of the case closed, picked it up and, groaning, carried it down the stairs. Then she took a deep breath and asked Claude to harness the horses and take her to Reims. He did as bidden, and when he helped her into the coach he asked, "Is everything all right, madame?"

"Nothing is all right, but that will change soon enough," she muttered.

"How long do you expect to be away?" he asked.

"Perhaps one night; perhaps longer. I'll be doing some Christmas shopping and otherwise just looking at different things . . . because I'm so sick of some of the things I have to look at around here!"

Reims was at least as lovely in the winter as it was in the springtime. The crystalline chill that blanketed the open countryside lost some of its bitterness among the buildings and city streets. And the people of Reims knew how to look after themselves in winter, as attested to by the luxurious coats of the women and fur-lined hats worn by the men.

Isabelle watched a woman in a particularly fetching sable coat stroll past, but her reverie soon evaporated. God knew there were more important things in the world than beautiful clothes! She took in the magnificent white sandstone buildings, gleaming in the wintry sunshine. Instead of decorative flowers, garlands of ivy and fir now graced the entrances of the elegant shops. The air was filled with the smell of chestnuts and roasted almonds and the pungent odor of hot spiced wine sold by street vendors. Isabelle bought herself a small bag of almonds but decided to pass on the mulled wine—the midwife had advised her not to drink any more alcohol so close to the birth. So she ate the almonds and admired the window displays, which could hold their own with those in Berlin, Paris, or any other big city. The *Champenois* certainly appreciated the finer things in life.

After purchasing some of the Christmas gifts, Isabelle decided to treat herself to a cup of hot chocolate at one of the many cafés. While she was waiting for it to arrive, she felt the tension ease in the back of her neck. Hautvillers and all the worries of the estate were suddenly far away. It was so good to simply sit there and do nothing! On her previous visits to Reims, she'd always been in a hurry: visiting government offices, shopping for food or for supplies needed around the estate, the visit to the notary after Leon's death. But today, all she had to do was take care of herself. She decided that in the future, she would come into the city more often and not wait until she was ready to explode. A bit more shopping after the café, a visit to the hairdresser, and she would be ready for the most important point on her agenda for the day.

"For a few bottles of champagne to burst like that, well, it's nothing unusual, my dear Isabelle. The whole business of making champagne is unpredictable, and no winemaker really knows today what he will have to deal with tomorrow. If you ask me, the carbon dioxide content of the bottles that exploded in your cellar was probably too high; they were under too much pressure. Or you might even say the champagne was *en furie*," Raymond Dupont explained with a smile. The moment Isabelle had entered his shop, he had put everything aside and locked the front door to give her his undivided attention. It flattered Isabelle a little that such a busy man would give her so much of his valuable time.

"When I saw all the mess, I turned into a fury myself," she said, gritting her teeth at the recollection, but deep inside, her anger had evaporated long before. She casually looked around his shop; the atmosphere of wealth and excess enveloped her like a warm blanket.

"In the past, fifty or a hundred years ago, the bottles were not as good as they are today. The cellar masters and growers were so afraid of exploding bottles that they wouldn't venture into their cellars without an iron mask to protect themselves. Haven't you ever wondered why so many of them have scarred hands? Or why your own cellar master only has one eye? Accidents with flying glass were part and parcel of the business back then."

"There's really nothing you don't know about champagne, is there?" said Isabelle thoughtfully. "But you're talking about the old days. My supplier from the Argonne, at least, assures me that his bottles are of the highest quality. If something bursts in my cellar, then it's because my cellar master is incompetent."

Raymond laughed brightly. "I wouldn't dare contradict you!"

"If the incident this morning had been the only one . . . but there have been so many." She lifted both hands helplessly. "I feel like I'm marking time, going nowhere. The mountain of questions and problems is simply not getting any smaller." *And the cork and bottle deliveries put a considerable dent in my finances, too*, she thought.

Raymond took her hand. "Keeping in mind that you are—and please pardon the expression—a foreigner, you're holding up very well indeed. That said, looking at the situation objectively, the task you've set yourself is simply too much for a woman to take on alone. If you at least had someone to help . . ."

"How very true," Isabelle sighed. "Dear Raymond, I need a new cellar master urgently. Would you happen to know someone?" She squeezed his hand, which was still holding hers, excitedly.

But Raymond could only shrug regretfully. "I wish I did. I began asking around on your behalf some time ago. It was clear to me from tasting that too-sweet champagne you brought that your cellar master isn't any good. But so far, despite all my contacts, I've come up empty-handed." After a momentary pause, he went on. "It seems there isn't a decent cellar master for miles around in need of work."

Isabelle slumped in her chair. "A skilled cellar master is the only thing that can save me."

"I wish I could help you, Isabelle. But manufacturing champagne is a ruthless business. Nowhere else in the world can one earn so much money with wine. In 1868, around fifteen million bottles were sold. Today, thirty years later, you can double that number. Every vigneron knows that, and every one of them will do what they can to be top of that heap! Now, so close to the turn of the century, the whole game has taken on a new dimension. Anyone with a decent cellar master would be stupid to lose him now."

"Then you mean I might as well pack my bags?" said Isabelle, discouraged.

"Not at all! I'll keep asking around for you," said Raymond. "You should not give up hope; greater miracles have happened."

Miracles! Isabelle had given up on miracles long ago. The very thought of going back to her daily battles with Grosse was almost unbearable.

"Now try to think of something more pleasant. A woman in your condition shouldn't be getting so worked up," he said, then he nodded toward the light-yellow box embossed with the emblem of the children's shop down the street. "I see you've bought some things for your baby. Wouldn't you like to show them to me?"

Isabelle allowed herself to be distracted by the tactic, and after she had presented the woolen baby clothes and Raymond had admired them, she did, in fact, feel a little better. But then Raymond said, "Have you already found a wet nurse and a nanny for the baby? Through my customers, I know of a number of women here in Reims who come highly recommended. Young women from the Alsace region are said to be especially doting."

"A wet nurse? What makes you think I would need someone for that?" Without thinking, she placed one hand protectively over her belly.

Raymond seemed taken aback. "If I may be permitted to ask, are you planning to take care of both your child *and* the estate?"

Isabelle's answer was tentative "We will have to wait and see."

"Of course," said Raymond. Then he stood up brightly. "And now, I think, we've spent enough time on problems! It would be my great pleasure and honor to invite you to dinner. A woman I know has just opened a new restaurant on Rue Buirette; the food is excellent."

Candlelight, damask and hothouse roses on the tables, soft violin music in the background—Isabelle leaned back, relaxed, in her chair.

Raymond, studying the wine list, looked up and smiled at her. "Did I promise too much?"

Before Isabelle could reply, the restaurant owner appeared at their table. She and Raymond exchanged a few words, then he ordered for Isabelle and himself. Isabelle, who had struggled with the copious menu, was relieved.

In his shop, their talk had been mostly business, but now their conversation was much lighter. Raymond told anecdotes about his capricious customers—no names, of course!—and Isabelle told him about her cycling adventures. Raymond was deeply impressed to discover that she had taken part in a long-distance race in Denmark.

When the main course was served—capon stuffed with chestnuts—Isabelle felt better than she had for a long time.

"How is it that a man like you isn't married?" Even as she asked it, she wondered if the question was appropriate.

But Raymond did not seem put off by her curiosity. "Maybe it's just that no woman ever wanted to put up with an old codger like me for life."

"I can't believe that," Isabelle spontaneously replied. "Old codger? But you're so . . . so"—she flicked her left hand in the air as if trying to find the right adjective—"so wonderful."

Wonderful? he thought.

"I'll have to take your word for that." Raymond grinned. "Then perhaps it's that a wonderful man would also like to have a wonderful woman at his side?"

"So you're selective," said Isabelle triumphantly. Just as she'd thought.

"Selective, demanding, critical—too critical? Who can say for certain?" The champagne dealer gave a little shrug. "In any case, if I met the woman of my dreams, I would marry her in an instant." He raised his wine glass, looking deeply into her eyes as he did so.

Isabelle, suddenly a little uneasy, looked away.

When Isabelle arrived back in Hautvillers late the following day, she felt refreshed and happy. The evening with Raymond, his undivided attention, the marvelous candlelight dinner—it had all been good. She had listened almost spellbound to the stories he told of his travels and his life. Afterward, he had accompanied her back to her hotel and kissed her hand charmingly in farewell.

"It would be my greatest pleasure to invite you to celebrate Christmas with me in Reims. I'll be putting on a small dinner for some close friends," he had said before departing. "We could take the opportunity to get to know each other a little better."

As much as Isabelle enjoyed his company, she had turned down the invitation as nicely as she could. In her condition, she had no desire to spend an entire evening sitting at a table with people she didn't know, even though they were Raymond's friends. Apart from that, his remark about the woman of his dreams had unnerved her a little. The way he had looked at her as he said it . . . but she was a widow, and an extremely pregnant widow at that, who would be bringing a child into the world in the new year. It was hard to imagine that a man might see her as anything else, and she certainly didn't have any interest in an affair. And yet it pleased her that Raymond wanted to get to know her better. As she opened the door of her house she concluded that going to Reims had been a fine idea and that Raymond Dupont's company had done her good.

The next morning, there was a rapping on her door. When Isabelle saw Claude Bertrand's face, she knew instantly that something bad had happened. Her feeling of well-being from the previous day evaporated, and the iron ring of worry and fear clamped itself around her chest again.

"Wolves have killed two of the sheep," he said with a grim expression. "We have to come up with some way to protect the animals."

Isabelle pulled her shawl closer around her shoulders. "But . . . didn't you say they could stay out in winter and all we'd need to do was feed them hay?"

"Normally, that would be true. But if the wolves are going through the vineyards looking for food, it points to a hard winter ahead. And if they are successful once, as they were last night, then they'll come again, maybe even in the daytime. Which means we have to shelter the animals in the stall."

"The whole winter?" So many animals closed up in such a small space? She was no expert in raising sheep, but even she could see that what Claude was proposing was far from ideal.

Claude shrugged.

"Then what are we waiting for?" she said, buttoning her jacket.

"You don't really want to *see* what's happened, do you?" The horror in the overseer's voice hung in the chill air as little white clouds.

"Who cares if I want to or not? I have to get a clear picture of the situation before I can make a decision," Isabelle said. For a brief moment, she thought longingly of the warm semolina pudding she'd been planning to make. Again, a day not going as she'd planned. Again, new concerns.

The white snow was colored dark red where the two cadavers lay. The wolves—the paw prints suggested there had been a small pack of them—had fed well on the two dead sheep, going first for the innards. Stomach, liver, heart—none of those organs remained. One of the sheep was missing its head; a wolf had probably carried it off to a patch of bushes to eat undisturbed. Meat, intestines, and scraps of hide were strewn across a wide area, and the rest of the herd surrounded the dead animals.

Isabelle shuddered. The lump in her throat felt like lead, and tears came to her eyes. Compared to this, a few exploding champagne bottles were a trifle.

"I'm truly sorry, madame, but I didn't expect something like this," said Claude quietly as he stood beside her. "The wolves would normally be eating berries and fruits now. It's unusual for them to take sheep this early in winter, and not a good sign at all. We'll have to take better care of the peacocks and chickens in the future, too, or they'll be at least as easy prey as the sheep."

Isabelle wiped one sleeve over her eyes. "Are you saying the wolves would dare to approach so close to the house?" She couldn't seem to do anything about the slightly hysterical tone in her voice.

"I hope not, madame." His face was a mask of concern. "If I see one of them, I'll shoot it myself. I keep my shotgun ready at my front door."

Isabelle, however, was not reassured by that. "Do you remember how happy Leon was to see that we still kept sheep? Maybe that's why I've held on to the animals."

Claude nodded.

"Leon would certainly not like it if I got rid of them." But Leon was dead, and she was responsible for the living. She pulled herself together. "We'll go over to the peacock pen and the chicken stall in a minute and check that everything is in order. If necessary, we'll double the wire netting to keep the wolves out. As for the sheep . . . it's my fault that this happened. I should have looked for a buyer for them long ago. Could you take care of that?"

Two days later, a man came for the sheep. Isabelle watched silently as the new owner, a shepherd from the nearby village of Romery, drove the animals down the narrow street with the aid of his two dogs. She should have taken this step much earlier. The few francs that the sale of the wool brought in would not have made her much wealthier, not when she factored in the cost of feed and shelter for the sheep. With the shepherd, her sheep were in competent, knowledgeable hands—he had enough hay for the winter and a large, safe stall where they could get through the cold months safely. So she had done the right thing.

But it still hurt to see the small flock trotting away. Was it just the start of the sell-off? What part of the Feininger estate would she have to part with next? One of the vineyards? The horses?

Abruptly, she turned away from the street. What nonsense! The cold and her fat belly must have been putting such stupid thoughts in her head. *Enough of this for today*, she commanded herself. There was still so much to be done before the child came.

Chapter Thirty-Six

On December 23, the postman knocked at Isabelle's door and unloaded a crate of champagne from his handcart. Isabelle smiled when she recognized Raymond's elegant handwriting on the card that came with the champagne, on which he had renewed his invitation for the following day. If her situation had been any different, she might well have accepted.

"And two parcels from Berlin, too," said the postman.

Isabelle was thrilled to receive them.

Inside again, she made herself comfortable in the warm living room. With great care, as if she were handling the finest lace instead of coarse packing paper, she unwrapped Josephine's parcel. Inside, she found an elegant Christmas card decorated with glitter and two smaller packages on which was written *Open Only on Christmas Eve*. No doubt there was something inside for her baby to wear, Isabelle suspected, or perhaps even a shawl for her?

In Clara's parcel, too, she discovered a brightly wrapped bundle and a tin box of homemade cookies; Isabelle could already smell the cinnamon through the packaging. Ignoring the sweet allure of the cookies for the moment, Isabelle reached for the far more tempting letter that Clara had sent.

Berlin, December 13, 1898

My dearest Isabelle,
I hope this letter finds you well and happy. So close to giving birth, life for a mother-to-be becomes difficult. I well remember waddling through our apartment like a duck. Everything hurt: my swollen ankles, my back, my breasts . . . Gerhard always says that rest is a cure-all for every womanly ailment, but you and I both know that the daily housework won't do itself. This means you have to stay strong until the day of birth.

With a smile, Isabelle scratched her stomach, the skin of which was stretched uncomfortably—much longer, and she'd explode! Apart from Ghislaine, she had no other female friends her own age in Hautvillers, so it felt even better to read Clara's understanding words. She riffled quickly through the thin letter paper, which smelled lightly of lavender, to read of Clara's plans for her New Year's visit, about which Isabelle was over the moon.

Unfortunately, I also have to give you some bad news. Gerhard received an invitation for the New Year's Eve ball of a countess, to take place on their country estate out near Potsdam. She is one of his patients, and he apparently helped her out of an awkward situation. She has promised to introduce him to other women at the ball—all potential patients for him. Becoming the high-society doctor, that's what my husband is striving for. It is inconceivable to him that I wouldn't accompany him on such an important occasion, which I'm sure you can understand, can't you?

Dear Isabelle, it gets worse. The way things look, I will have to postpone my visit to you until the start of February. There are several appointments here in Berlin, in January, that simply can't be put off, unless I want to get into serious trouble with my husband. It breaks my heart, believe me, to have to write these words.

Your true friend, Clara

Isabelle let the letter drop. No shared laughter. No heart-to-heart talks. No "Frau Doctor" to hold her hand when the time came. Through the last few weeks, she had held firmly to the thought that she would not be alone when she went into labor. Now she wouldn't see her dear friend, and she would have to come up with something else. Perhaps she could start to stay with Micheline and Marie shortly before the baby was due? Or maybe even move into the hospital in Épernay. The falling snow, heavier now, outside her window caught her eye. But she did not like the thought of holing up in the very same women's ward where Ghislaine had lost her child. And then there were her own memories of Leon in the hospital. No, she did not want to bring her child into the world in that atmosphere. She would ask the local midwife to spend the night at her house, though doing so was certainly unconventional.

After a long moment pondering the issue, she shook her head and stood up. She had things to do for the next day, baking and cooking for Christmas. Ghislaine had invited her, Micheline, and Marie for dinner, as well as Claude Bertrand and his dog. Each of the women had promised to contribute something to the meal to take some of the load off Ghislaine, who was keeping her restaurant open until late in the afternoon. Isabelle was planning a spicy pie with steamed herbs and ham, one of Clara's recipes; it had already gone down very well indeed with her pickers. Micheline and Marie were going to roast a duck—no doubt the Christmas table would be groaning under the weight of all the delicious food.

For the first time since reading Clara's letter, a trace of a smile reappeared on Isabelle's face. She was not going to be alone on Christmas Eve, and that counted for a lot. And maybe she'd see Daniel again. Ghislaine had not expressly mentioned that her brother would be there, but it was Christmas, after all.

Another thought entered her mind, and it made her frown. Where would Gustave Grosse spend the big day?

Since the incident with the exploding bottles, he had done everything he could not to cross her path. But now she felt obligated to find out what his plans for the holiday were. She pulled on her heavy coat and set off for the wine cellar.

She found Gustave on the uppermost level of the cellar. On a square wooden table in front of him stood a number of large glass bottles filled with liquids in a range of colors, from clear to pale yellow. They looked like champagnes at different stages of maturity. On the floor beside the table were many more of the bulbous bottles, some of which were filled with even more luridly colored liquids.

"What are you doing?" asked Isabelle, without a word of greeting.

Grosse was pouring champagne out of one of the bottles into a bowl; he glanced up momentarily. "I'm just starting with the first *assemblage.*"

Isabelle thought she had not heard him right. "Didn't I tell you we were only going to start with that in mid-January?" she said. "And what is all that?" She fluttered her hand toward the ominous bottles. Without waiting for him to reply, she moved closer and read the label on one of them: *jus de poire.* On the next one: *jus de pommes.*

"Pear juice, apple juice, beetroot juice, and cognac?" She let out a shrill laugh. "What business do any of these have in blending *champagne*? And what were you planning to do with all that sugar?" She pointed to a large linen sack with *sucre* printed on it.

"A little sweetness, a little extra flavor and color, have never hurt anyone, madame. You want your turn-of-the-century champagne to be something special, don't you?" said Grosse, with an aggressive undertone. "Now don't go looking all horrified! This is common practice. Take my word for it. Unfortunately, I wasn't able to get my hands on any port wine at short notice. Port gives champagne a very full-bodied bouquet."

A loud ringing started in Isabelle's ears, so loud that she thought she might faint on the spot with the dizziness it caused. Adulterated champagne! In her cellars! That was the final straw.

Her right arm shot out like an arrow toward the exit.

"Get out!"

"Oh, don't go getting upset. I've just begun; I can't just put it all down and—"

"Get out!" she screamed, and took a threatening step in his direction. She was on the verge of picking up an empty bottle and bashing it over the man's head. "You're fired. Pack your things and go. I never want to see you again!"

The moment Gustave Grosse was out of sight, Isabelle felt a sharp stabbing pain inside her, and she doubled over, folding like a penknife. Dazed, she lowered herself onto one of the stools beside the square table. *Damn it all, I shouldn't get so worked up!* she thought. She forced herself to breathe more slowly and evenly. The wooden barrels lining the walls left and right caught her eye. Inside them were stored the individual champagnes waiting to be blended into her turn-of-the-century champagne. *Maybe for the* next *turn of the century*, Isabelle thought bitterly.

On Christmas Eve, Isabelle set off with Micheline, Marie, and Claude for Christmas Mass. Ghislaine, who was still busy in her restaurant, was going to meet them at the church. Light flakes of snow sprinkled down and settled in Isabelle's hair.

"A white Christmas . . . in Germany, that was always something special, like a gift," she said. She looked down at the thin sheet of snow underfoot; every step they took left fresh prints. There was something so full of promise about the fresh snow that it brought a small smile to Isabelle's face.

"A white Christmas is something special for us, too," said Micheline.

Marie and Claude murmured in assent. Isabelle's elderly neighbor pointed to the houses they were walking past. "On Christmas Eve, we like to put candles in the windows. How beautifully they shine through the drizzling snow."

Isabelle nodded, moved.

The evening was a merry affair. Maybe it was the sociable atmosphere, or maybe the gallows humor of it. Whatever it was, Isabelle's description of giving Grosse his marching orders was so dramatic that all the guests were practically in hysterics.

"Well done, dear," said Micheline through tears of laughter, and patted Isabelle's arm.

"But what now? I wanted to make a champagne suitable for the end of the century, and now I don't even have a cellar master." She looked around at her friends helplessly.

"Better none at all than one like that," was the unanimous opinion, as was the consensus that Christmas Eve was not a night for dwelling on one's problems.

"There's a solution for everything," said Micheline laconically.

Isabelle would have loved to believe that were true.

After dinner, Claude and Micheline began to sing Christmas songs, and Marie and Ghislaine joined them. When Claude's dog began to howl along, the singing dissolved into laughter.

Isabelle knew neither the lyrics nor the melodies they were singing, but she hummed along, struggling all the while against a deep disappointment. She had been looking forward so much to seeing Daniel.

When he did not appear for dinner, Ghislaine remarked, "No doubt he's found some new lover in Épernay and is celebrating the evening with her."

That only made Isabelle gloomier.

The walk to the church and back had exhausted her, and although she had only eaten a little, the hearty food was sitting heavily in her stomach. She longed for her bed, to be able to stretch out, lay her hands on her taut belly, sleep, and get the last days of her pregnancy behind her as well as she could. The midwife had come down with whooping cough, which ruled her out for the birth, so Isabelle had decided after all to go into the hospital in Épernay and wait for the birth there. *If only it were already behind me*, Isabelle thought—not for the first time—as she kneaded her fingers into her aching back.

By eleven, she'd had enough. Yawning, she stood up and said good night. The others were in such a happy mood that they only nodded briefly in response.

The hot water bottle was waiting for her beneath Jacques's old eiderdown. A candle was burning on the night table, and beside it lay a French copy of *Madame Bovary*, which Isabelle had read years earlier in German. *A few more pages before I fall asleep*, she thought, as she looked out the window: outside, the gentle sprinkle of Christmas snow had transformed into a considerable winter storm, and the snow was falling so heavily that she could no longer see the houses across the street. That was probably the reason Daniel had stayed in Épernay.

Isabelle had just pulled on her nightgown when she felt something warm and wet between her legs. She looked down in shock at the huge pool spreading around her feet. *No! Please, not yet,* she thought. The child wasn't due for another twelve days!

She had not even finished the thought when a cramping pain shot through her. Whimpering, she gripped the foot of the bed to hold herself upright. After a few deep breaths, the pain receded, but it came back again the next moment, red as fire and with razor teeth, tearing at her insides and robbing her of air. Helplessly, Isabelle looked around the room. If she managed to make it to the window, she could open it and scream for help. She knew for certain that she wouldn't make it back to Ghislaine's.

***

Never would Daniel have thought that it would take him so long to get from Épernay to Hautvillers. Everything had started out so well: a vintner visiting relatives in Épernay had offered him a ride back to Hautvillers, and Daniel had been happy to accept. But not long after setting off, the one-horse chaise bumped heavily over a stone in the road. The next moment, it began to wobble alarmingly. A broken wheel! On Christmas Eve. And no one close by who could help them out. The vintner had elected to stay with his young and inexperienced horse, so it fell to Daniel to walk back into Épernay in the increasing snowfall to try to chase up a replacement wheel. It annoyed him to know that, in the time it took him to find a new wheel, he would have made it back to Hautvillers easily on foot. Two hours later, they were finally able to drive on.

By the time they arrived in Hautvillers, it was snowing so heavily that he could hardly see the horse in front of him. He hoped that Ghislaine had saved something for him to eat; his stomach was growling audibly. But it was not only his hunger that was causing such a strange sensation in his stomach; it was also the thought that he would once again see Isabelle Feininger.

The vintner dropped him at the bottom of the street. There was still a light on inside Ghislaine's house, Daniel realized as he drew closer, but most of the neighbors' houses were already dark. When Daniel looked across to Isabelle's place and saw a light there, too, his heart sank. She had already gone home.

Without warning, a piercing scream cut through the night, so raw and penetrating that not even the heavy snowfall could muffle it. The scream had come from Isabelle's house. Daniel felt hot and cold at the same time. He threw his bundle on the ground and ran to her door. He banged and shook at it, but nothing stirred on the other side.

"Isabelle!" he called out, and threw himself so hard against the solid oak that the iron fittings groaned loudly. But the door didn't budge.

Another scream. Shrill. Fearful. Kicking in the door was an impossibility. Did Claude Bertrand have a key to the house? Or the Guenins? A long, lamenting wail, like that of an animal caught in a trap, jerked him back to the moment. Damn it, he had no time to lose. He tore off his jacket, wrapped it around his right fist, and smashed in one of the windows beside the door. Glass shattered, falling into the snow and inside the house. Daniel knocked away the shards of glass still caught in the frame. Then he climbed through.

Breathing heavily, he stood in the entry hall in which he and Ghislaine had spent their childhood.

"Isabelle?" he called out.

It was pitch-black on the ground floor, but he knew the house inside out. Without hesitation, he charged up the stairs to the second floor, where he could see some weak light.

He found Isabelle curled up on the floor of her bedroom.

"Daniel . . ." Her eyes were glassy, and she whispered, "The baby . . ."

Then Daniel was next to her on the floor. He slipped his hands under her arms and pulled her up. "Come on, let's get you onto the bed." Isabelle screamed again, so full of pain that Daniel paused for a second, then heaved her onto the mattress. His heart was beating hard as he stroked her pale face. Her eyelids were fluttering so fast that he was afraid she'd fall unconscious at any moment. *How many hours has she been in such agony?* he wondered, deeply worried. *And why wasn't anyone with her?*

His eyes quickly scanned the room where, many years ago, his parents had slept. No bowls of hot water, no clean sheets or towels, no scissors or knife to cut the umbilical cord—there was nothing to show any sign of preparations for a birth. The contractions must have taken Isabelle by surprise.

Daniel could not remember ever having felt so helpless in his life. In a wine cellar, he could handle any crisis that emerged, but when it came to giving birth, he didn't have the first clue what to do.

"Isabelle, I'm here. You have to tell me what to do!"

He tried to get her to look at him, but Isabelle's body arched in pain again.

"Get Ghislaine. She can—"

Her cry rang loudly in his ears. The thought of leaving her alone, even briefly, was horrifying to him. But he turned away and, taking the stairs two at a time, sprinted from the house and along the street, running as if his own life depended on it.

Ghislaine knelt between Isabelle's legs. Sweeping her hair out of her face, she said, "Daniel, sit behind her and prop her up. I can already see the head. One or two contractions, and the baby will be here!"

Isabelle, overcome by a new surge, screamed. Then she felt Daniel's arms around her. He held her head in both hands and stroked her sweat-soaked hair tenderly out of her face.

"You can do it, Isabelle. You're the bravest woman of them all. You'll be through it soon, soon!"

His words, spoken so close to her ear, soothed her. But the next moment came the irresistible urge to push. She felt the baby's head slide out of her along with a rush of liquid, then the rest of the body followed. But the baby didn't cry immediately.

"You have a girl," said Ghislaine, and sniffled a little.

"But she's not crying. Why isn't she crying?"

"Not to worry. She's breathing. She's just a quiet one." Ghislaine's hands shook as she wiped down the small smeary body with a corner of the soiled sheet and handed the child to her mother. Daniel pulled open a cupboard and rummaged inside for a clean blanket. When he found what he was looking for, he tenderly wrapped Isabelle and the child in it.

Isabelle smiled gratefully. "A Christmas child."

Ghislaine was standing beside the head of the bed, her hands folded as if in prayer. But then she suddenly called out, "Scissors! I need scissors to cut the umbilical cord. And hot water. I hope Micheline has all that ready." She ran down the steps toward the kitchen.

Exhausted but happy, Isabelle looked down at the tiny creature in her arms. The girl had eyes set far apart, tiny ears, and a small bud of a mouth. She looked at least as exhausted as Isabelle herself felt. Apart from the red shimmer of fuzz on the child's head, Isabelle could see no resemblance to either Leon or herself.

"But you're still too small for that. Isn't that true, my Marguerite?"

Marguerite. For weeks, she had been wondering what to call her child. A boy would have been Leonard, of course. But for a girl, making a decision had been difficult. Now the name had come to her out of nowhere. Marguerite. What beautiful eyes she had, with their long lashes, and those perfect rosy lips . . .

"Marguerite? It's a good name. She is an exceptional beauty," said Daniel, as if he could read Isabelle's mind. "Like her mother."

Isabelle held Marguerite's tiny wrinkled left hand in her own and said with a smile, "You've hardly been in the world a minute, and you've already learned your first lesson about men: don't believe a word of their smooth compliments. The way we both look right now is very far from attractive."

Before she knew what happened, Daniel's lips touched hers. Isabelle had never felt so much empathy in a kiss, so much warmth and tenderness. With her eyes closed and the infant's warm body pressed close, she gave herself over to Daniel's lips. They only separated when they heard the clatter of feet on the stairs and Ghislaine's and Micheline's excited voices.

"You've saved my life yet again," said Isabelle, with tears in her eyes. "I'd been looking forward to seeing you again so much. But when you didn't come to Ghislaine's, I—" She swallowed, then said, "I thought you were spending Christmas Eve with a new love in Épernay." She rocked Marguerite lovingly in her arms as she spoke.

"A new love?" said Daniel gruffly, and shook his head. "You're the one my heart longs for, and you know that well enough. Whether you like it or not, I'm staying here to look after you. I don't want to be saving your life every minute, but I'm sure I can get your cellars and vineyards in order. I know my way around here a little, after all." He grinned mischievously.

"But what about Épernay?" asked Isabelle in disbelief.

He waved it off as if it were nothing.

Then my greatest wish would come true, Isabelle thought. But just as a huge weight lifted from her heart, a sense of trepidation came over her. Daniel Lambert as her *chef de cave,* could that work out at all? What if he wanted more than she was prepared to offer? She liked him very much. She could trust Daniel, and she knew that. He was a man of character and principles. It often felt as if they thought and felt the same way. If she were to be honest with herself, she had missed him a great deal during his time in Épernay. Even so, the birth of her child only added to her worries and obligations, and she could hardly add a new love on top of everything. Besides, she would feel like she was cheating on Leon.

"I don't know if I can afford a cellar master as famous as you. Besides—" She broke off when Marguerite made a small whimpering sound. Isabelle looked first at her child, then at Daniel, and a frown crossed her face.

"Is she hungry?" For a moment, she felt panic. She had been hoping that the nurses in Épernay would show her how to breast-feed. Now she would have to find out for herself.

As she unbuttoned her sweaty dress, Daniel turned away and went to the window. Isabelle sank back into the pillows, then she lifted Marguerite to her right breast. The baby's small mouth closed hungrily around her nipple, and her daughter began to suck. The moment was so deeply affecting for Isabelle that a tremor shook her body and tears came to her eyes.

Hesitantly, Daniel turned back to her. Looking at the mother and child, his Adam's apple bobbed. He smiled gently and said, "It looks like little Marguerite will be putting some demands on her *maman* for quite a while. That makes it so much more important for you to have help in the vineyards and in the cellar. Together, we can turn the Feininger estate back into one of the great estates, I promise you!"

She narrowed her eyes a little. "You would really give up your job in Épernay to help me?"

He nodded. "What I do there is so dull I might as well get a job in a factory."

"And . . . if it doesn't work out, after all? Daniel, please don't get your hopes up too high," she said softly, talking about far more than just the business.

"And don't you think too much about it." He moved back to the bed, placed one arm around her shoulders, and pointed toward the window and the dark, snow-covered vineyards beyond. "Look at the vines in winter, the way they hibernate. Their branches are so thin, it's hard to imagine that in just a few short months, they will come back to life. But they will, and that's why we nurture them and protect them. There's no security in it, certainly no guarantee of success, only the hope that something good will come from the work we do." He looked at Isabelle. His eyes were full of love and confidence as he said, "I ask for nothing else from you, Isabelle. Give us the time to ripen together, and to grow."

Chapter Thirty-Seven

Isabelle was the happiest woman in the world. The birth had exhausted her, but she could not stop gazing at her daughter in admiration. Only occasionally did she put Marguerite in the cradle that Ignaz Chapron had, in fact, built for her from half a wine barrel, which was now beside her bed. Whenever she could, she carried Marguerite in the crook of her arm or lay down with the baby on her stomach. The tiny fingers and fingernails, the little feet, her heart-shaped mouth, rosy skin, and red fuzz—Marguerite was simply perfect! And she was an exceptionally quiet child; she slept a lot and rarely cried. At the same time, feeding her required all of Isabelle's strength and patience. Sometimes, Marguerite acted like she was hungry but then turned her little head away the next moment. At other times, she suckled for a few moments, then fell asleep at Isabelle's breast. Making sure she was well fed sometimes took hours.

"Is it normal for an infant to drink so poorly?" she asked Ghislaine, worried.

Ghislaine shrugged. "Some children are big eaters; others are not. You have to be patient. She will probably start to eat better soon."

"Marguerite is just a very special child," said Micheline, though she looked a little sad as she said it.

Isabelle squeezed her friend's hand compassionately; Micheline had remained childless.

Ghislaine and Micheline kept Isabelle well provided with good food, and the other neighbors also came by to see mother and child. They all poured out their admiration for Marguerite, except Marie, who remained somewhat reserved. At the start, Isabelle was a little taken aback by the behavior of her neighbor, but then she recalled a conversation with Micheline in which it had come out that Marie's own child died shortly after birth. It probably still hurt the woman to be around a newborn baby, Isabelle sadly realized.

Claude and Daniel came by every day, and they kept her updated on the vineyard and cellars. Since it had become clear that Daniel would be the cellar master for the Feininger estate, the old overseer hadn't been able to stop smiling.

"Finally, things are turning for the good!" he said, at every chance he got. And Isabelle nodded vehemently every time. Raymond had predicted that she would not be able to find a cellar master anywhere in Champagne. Now, she not only had her Christmas-born child, but also the best cellar master anyone could name! So much good fortune all at once struck her as a little uncanny. But more good news was to come.

"Things are, let's say, rather chaotic down in the cellars," said Daniel when he visited her two days after Christmas. "I'm spending most of my time looking for things. Grosse neglected to mark most of the barrels, but I've managed to figure out what's what by tasting. You've got good fundamentals, something we can really build from."

Isabelle's relief was palpable; in fact, she could have shouted for joy. And it got even better when Daniel said, "As far as I've been able to judge, the wines you've got after the first fermentation are clean, and the quality is good. Thank God you were able to stop Grosse from spoiling them. I've also turned up a few old treasures down there, things I'm guessing you don't even know about. Mature champagnes and reserve wines, all about six years old. They come from the days when I was still working for old Jacques. If we mix everything together, we'll end up with a very decent wine for the end of next year." He grinned.

"Mix everything together? Don't play modest for me!" Isabelle teased. She sat up expectantly in the bed. "When do we start with the *assemblage?*" Weak from the birth or not, she didn't want to miss that important moment.

Daniel laughed. "Easy, easy! The still wines are in a resting phase, and that will last another five or six weeks, until mid-February. We'll only start with the *assemblage* then. So you've got plenty of time to get back on your feet."

"A resting phase?" Isabelle said with surprise. "Then why did Grosse want to start blending the champagne before Christmas, even though I'd told him mid-January?"

"No idea," said Daniel grimly. "Though we're better off waiting a few more weeks." He seemed to be struggling with something. Then, slowly, he said, "I can't prove it, but for a long time I've suspected that Grosse has actually been serving a different mistress altogether, one who certainly doesn't have your best interests at heart. In any case, I've seen him talking with Henriette Trubert more often than I'd expect."

"Henriette and Grosse?" Isabelle's brain began to churn as if a dozen steam engines were turning at once. Grosse—a saboteur. A bungler, employed and paid by Henriette Trubert?

Suddenly, the many pieces of the mosaic, the small stones she'd been stumbling over in recent months, came together to form a single picture. The missing pickers. The exploding bottles. His disgusting adulteration of the wine. Why hadn't she put two and two together? How could she have been so stupid? Stupid and blind!

"He'd better brace himself! I'll pull the truth out of him like a carrot out of the ground," she said dourly. "And then I'll go to the police and—"

Daniel interrupted her with a gesture. "Don't think I wouldn't do the same. But it wouldn't work. Grosse is stupid, but not so stupid that he'd admit anything to you. There's no proof, which means we can't make a move against either him or Henriette." His eyes flashed with suppressed anger. "But if the man ever crosses my path in the night, I won't be responsible for what happens."

"You wouldn't get your hands dirty on someone like him, would you?" said Isabelle, shocked. The fierce look in Daniel's eye worried her. "In Germany, we say that revenge is a dish best served cold."

Daniel opened his mouth to say something, but thought better of it. After a moment of silence, he said, "You're right. Let's focus on what really matters. Let's make a champagne unlike any other! A success like that will hit Henriette harder than anything else will. We have a saying here in France, too: success is the best revenge!"

***

Two days before the new year, Raymond Dupont drove out to Hautvillers with flowers in one hand and a bottle of champagne in the other to invite Isabelle to a New Year's Eve party. She invited him in, and they spent a pleasant hour chatting together by the fire. But she turned down his invitation. Traveling to Reims in the middle of winter with an infant, even one as quiet as little Marguerite, seemed an impossibility.

Ghislaine and Daniel also invited her to spend New Year's Eve with them—and Isabelle was tempted to accept. In the end, though, she decided to spend the last night of 1898 alone with Marguerite. She wanted to reflect on what a year it had been, the most turbulent she had ever experienced. So much had happened, both good and bad. People had let her down, and people had pleasantly surprised her, too.

As the hands of the clock ticked toward midnight, Isabelle shed a few tears. There was still a chasm inside her that had once been filled by Leon. She thought of her parents, too. They were grandparents now and didn't even know it. *It probably makes no difference to them*, Isabelle thought bitterly. She wondered whether the day would come when she and her parents would make contact again . . . perhaps a letter, one day . . .

And how were Josephine and Clara? The three friends wanted to celebrate their turn-of-the-century wind together the following year, but would they manage it? The transformation of the nineteenth century into the twentieth—what a great moment that would be. The notion frightened Isabelle. After everything she had been through, she hardly dared to even speculate about what the next few weeks would bring.

At the stroke of twelve, she opened a bottle of Feininger champagne. She looked over at Marguerite, who was sound asleep in her cradle. Her daughter was quite a beautiful Christmas gift. Daniel was right: she thought too much about things. Wasn't it better to enjoy the moment?

***

The weeks passed, Isabelle regained her strength, and the day of Clara's arrival drew closer. Isabelle cleaned the house until it sparkled. She wanted everything around her clean and beautiful. A new life. A fresh start. She wanted to see it in every vase filled with evergreen, in every polished silver platter, and in every dust-free volume on her bookshelves.

"Now the jacket and the cap, and you're nearly done!" Isabelle pressed a kiss to Marguerite's head. How fine and fuzzy her hair was! First, she put the baby's arms into the sleeves, then she carefully buttoned up the heavy woolen jacket. The entire champagne region had been covered in frost since the New Year. Now, added to her concerns for what the unusual chill would do to the vines, she had her concerns about Marguerite. For a child so small, catching a cold could end badly, and it was better to avoid the risk altogether. She added a warm cap and a scarf made of angora wool. As always, Marguerite let Isabelle dress her without crying or swinging her arms, which Carla Chapron had told her was common among other children.

"So little and you're already a fashion plate, aren't you?" Isabelle smiled, picked her daughter up, and laid her down in the pram that she had ordered through a department store in Reims. In the entry hall, she pulled on her own warm jacket and scarf, which she'd especially need later on, down in the cellars.

Today was the day of days. Today, she and Daniel would begin blending the champagne. In recent weeks, Daniel had tasted the contents of every barrel in her cellars and had selected the wines that he wanted to use for this year's cuvée. Now she would get to see the cellar master's art. Daniel's concentration had to be complete and all his senses alert to be able to imagine what the final result would taste like when he blended the wines. Even though Marguerite hardly ever cried, what if she did today and disturbed Daniel at such a crucial point in the process? Besides, it was far too cold in the cellars for an infant.

Although Isabelle had thought Clara would watch Marguerite, her friend's arrival had been delayed until the end of the month. Luckily, Ghislaine always offered to look after Marguerite when Isabelle had something to do. "It's good practice for me," she said. And Marguerite was already accustomed to Ghislaine. So they set off for Ghislaine's, but when Isabelle knocked, she found Ghislaine dressed in her best clothes. "Alphonse has invited me to Paris for a few days!"

Isabelle nodded. She understood. Time to spend with her lover was a rare commodity for Ghislaine.

She knew, too, that Micheline, whose duties included being the cellar mistress at Champagne Guenin, would be busy blending her own champagne. Isabelle pushed the pram over to Carla Chapron's house, but the cooper's wife was in bed with a cold.

What now? Would Claude be prepared to look after Marguerite? She had not even finished the thought when she remembered that her overseer was away in Épernay to buy new fencing materials for the peacock pen.

Coming up to the Guenin house, she paused. Maybe she could ask Marie Guenin? She hadn't seen her elderly neighbor for weeks. While Micheline was her friend, the only connection Isabelle had with Marie was that of good neighbors, but neighbors could help each other out, couldn't they?

Isabelle knocked on Marie's door. But instead of the door, one of the ground-floor windows opened. Marie looked out. Isabelle had the sudden impression that the old woman's face might break into a thousand pieces.

"Yes?" said Marie, her mouth tight.

"Good morning, Marie! I wanted to ask if you might be able to look after Marguerite, just this once." Small white clouds appeared in front of her mouth in the winter air as she uncertainly put forward her request. "It would only be for two or three hours," she added. "I have to go down to the cellars."

As usual, Marie had her hair tied back in a tight braid, which made the skin on her face look unnaturally tight. A slight nervous twitch beneath her right eye quivered as she looked first at Isabelle and then at Marguerite in the pram. Her lips were pinched, and when she finally opened her mouth to reply, all the color had drained from her face.

"Isabelle, please don't think ill of me, but . . . I can't take your child. I would do any other favor for you, but bringing that child to *me*, of all people . . . no, I'm sorry."

Thunderstruck, Isabelle could only watch as the window closed again. What in the world was that all about?

***

Daniel looked around the small room at the back of the house with satisfaction. It was just what he needed for the *assemblage*. In contrast to the dark, cold, stuffy wine cellar, the room was dry and bright, and it didn't smell. There was no mold on the walls and no moisture that could have a negative impact on his work. Inside, he was not only protected from all kinds of weather, but he could also lock the room thanks to the large padlock that Claude had bought for him in Épernay. He didn't believe that Henriette would go so far as to send her saboteur Grosse back to the Feininger estate, but better to be on the safe side!

In the center of the room, he and Claude had set up an enormous table on which almost three dozen bottles now stood—fresh wine from the recent harvest and samples of the various reserve wines that he had found in Isabelle's cellars. There were also several bottles of finished champagne in a bucket of ice water, a small surprise that Daniel had prepared for Isabelle. He was excited to hear her reaction.

Claude had brought in a few chairs as well. On a sideboard, there were more glass containers; Daniel would use these for blending his new compositions. A large spittoon was at the ready—like any good cellar master, Daniel would not swallow the wines as he tasted them but rather spit out the mouthfuls.

He walked over to the window. The air glittered like crystal, and everything was silent and peaceful. Even the birds that hadn't flown south were keeping their chittering to themselves, as if they knew the significance of the day. Now all that was missing was Isabelle.

Daniel already had a very good idea of the champagne he wanted to create for her. But he wanted to find out first if his own concept matched with what she had in mind. This would be their first mutual champagne, after all!

A wry, self-mocking grin appeared on Daniel's face. What strange impulses were these?! All these years, he had prohibited Henriette Trubert and Jacques Feininger from sticking their noses into his work. Whenever they had tried, he'd turned downright cantankerous. And now here he was, anxiously waiting for Isabelle to appear, when he should have been well underway with the work by now.

His grimace turned into a broad smile when he heard steps outside. "I'm in here! You weren't looking for me down in the cellars, were you?" he called out, straightening the chairs. He wanted Isabelle to feel comfortable in the room. He opened the door. "An *assemblage* would have been impossible in there, so I set up everything here—" He broke off with a frown when he saw her distraught face. "Has something happened?" He looked into the pram and was relieved to see Marguerite lying inside, wide awake. He quickly pushed the pram close to the rear wall, where the temperature was warmest.

Isabelle sat down. Haltingly, she told him what had happened when she tried to find someone to look after Marguerite. "You should have seen the look on Marie's face. For her, it was simply inconceivable that I would bring Marguerite to *her*—what did she mean by that?" Perplexed, she looked up at Daniel.

Daniel let out a heavy sigh. He crouched beside Isabelle and stroked a few strands of hair out of her face. How beautiful she was!

"Marie can be a little . . . strange, sometimes. Don't take her words too much to heart. You know her sad story, don't you?"

Isabelle nodded. "Yes, but that's no reason for her to be so mean," she said, crying.

Daniel looked at her earnestly. "When God created the grapevines, he didn't make them all the same. Each one, in its own way, is unique and beautiful. Anyone who doesn't understand that can't hope to understand life." He looked at Marguerite, who had fallen asleep again, then handed Isabelle a handkerchief.

"But what is so different about my child?" she whispered.

"Don't waste too much energy thinking about it," Daniel said. "Let's get to work; we have a lot to do today." He sat down opposite her. "Before I start with the *assemblage*, I'd like to hear what you imagine your champagne should be. A good champagne should make a statement that the person drinking it understands after a few mouthfuls. It has to have character, its own persona." He leaned across the table as he continued. "I can create a light, bubbly champagne or one as elegant and rich as an expensive perfume. I can make a champagne that would appeal mostly to younger drinkers or one that older connoisseurs would enjoy, people who appreciate a woodier undertone and more mature nuances. Everything depends on the proportions of the different wines."

Twisting the handkerchief in both hands, Isabelle listened attentively. Then she blew her nose so loudly and so indelicately that they both had to laugh. Then, it was as if the air had cleared. She was completely focused on the task ahead.

"I am honored that you are asking me for my opinion, but I honestly have no idea about the making of champagne. For me, it's not just a science but also an art form."

"Art or science or whatever, I'd still like to know what comes into your head when you think about the coming century, what you see in your mind's eye."

Isabelle sighed. "If you'd asked me that before Leon's death, I would probably have answered you wholeheartedly, talking about freedom and a new feeling for life and about great opportunities ahead." Her voice was full of irony. "That the new century would bring with it a fresh wind, something new especially for women—it's something that Clara, Josephine, and I have always longed for and talked about. Our turn-of-the-century wind was supposed to sweep aside all the prejudices about women as the weaker sex." Her gaze had drifted, and Daniel sensed that her thoughts were far away. After a long moment, she looked at him again.

"When I was a child, the adults often said 'Men plan, fate laughs,' and I never understood what they meant. Now I know that it isn't necessary to always be making plans down to the last detail." She sniffed softly. "Of course, it's always been important to have a goal, and that won't change. A person with no goal is like a piece of flotsam, pushed back and forth by the tides of life. My goal is to preserve Jacques's and Leon's legacy for my daughter. But recent months have also taught me not always to be thinking about tomorrow but to enjoy the moment. To take pleasure in life, to laugh, and to be lighthearted, because everything can change tomorrow." A little embarrassed, she waved off her own words. "I can talk some rubbish, can't I? But that's what you get for asking."

"It's not rubbish, none of it! With champagne, all that matters is the moment; what you just said was exactly on the mark." He jumped up, went to the bucket of ice water, and came back with one of the champagne bottles. Its temperature was perfect. With practiced ease, he opened the bottle and poured two glasses, then handed one to Isabelle. The champagne had a delicate rosé tint, as if a rose petal had been floating in it. It was topped with a thin white foam that was visibly disappearing—a sign of the highest quality.

"Everything in life is as ephemeral as bubbles of champagne. What counts is to make the most of every moment, to take life as it comes, as it is. When you open a bottle of champagne, you're not waiting for the magnificent moment. You making sure that *this* moment is magnificent. That might well explain the great allure of champagne." He swung his glass expertly to awaken the liquid inside it, then he raised it to Isabelle. As she took a mouthful, he did not take his eyes off her. The green of her irises was even more vivid than usual as her expression turned to one of rapture.

"This is simply delicious! Countless tiny bubbles exploding in my mouth . . . it's as if it's trying to make me laugh!" She smiled, then took another big mouthful and rolled it around in her mouth before she swallowed it. "Incredibly fresh and invigorating. I can taste a little strawberry, vanilla, and there's a very slight sweetness to it, like fine sponge cake." She shook her head in confusion, then put the glass down. "What in the world are we drinking?"

Daniel smiled. Raymond had told him that Isabelle had an exceptional palate when it came to picking out the nuances of a champagne.

The man hadn't been exaggerating—Daniel couldn't have described his champagne better himself.

"Feininger champagne from 1892," he said, as casually he could. "The third level down in your cellar is full of this *assemblage*; I'd say several thousand bottles. They're from the time when I worked for Jacques. I created it back then so that several years to mature would do it good; now's the perfect time to drink it.

"You're kidding! I've had this in my cellar all along?" Isabelle blinked in disbelief. "This wonderful rosé color! I've never seen a color like it."

"It reminds me of your hair with the morning sun shining on it." Daniel quickly looked away, wanting to hide the deep feeling Isabelle aroused in him. Then he refilled the glasses. "Jacques wanted to conquer the European market with this champagne, but it never got that far. It seems he preferred to sell Grosse's sweet brew over this exquisite champagne." Daniel shook his head in bewilderment. "But so be it. For us, it's pure serendipity that I rediscovered these bottles."

Isabelle reached across the table, took Daniel's right hand in hers, and squeezed it. "Can't you make an identical rosé champagne for the new century? Then we'd have something really very special to offer, wouldn't we? I've never tried anything like this, not even with Raymond."

Daniel laughed, then. "And there's a good reason for that. Hardly anyone would even attempt to make a rosé champagne, because they're extremely difficult to produce. Even with the most careful *assemblage*, there's no telling how the color of the blend will develop in the months ahead. In the worst case, you don't get a rosé tone at all, but a dirty blue or green. And then the entire cuvée would be lost. Most cellar masters who try for a rosé champagne add cochineal to a white wine. Cochineal is a red coloring derived from beetles. But I personally would never use something like that; for me, it's tantamount to fraud. The color has to come from the skins of the grapes."

Isabelle nodded rapidly. "Adding color to champagne—that's just another kind of adulteration!"

"That's exactly it," said Daniel. "But to come back to your question, yes, I am certain I could produce another champagne of this quality. But to do that, the champagne would have to mature until at least the summer of *next* year, and ideally longer."

"But we don't have that much time. The turn of the century would be over!" Isabelle cried in horror.

"But you can sell the 1892 cuvée as your turn-of-the-century special. It certainly has the class. And it would make you quite rich in the process. I'm sure of that," Daniel replied calmly. "And then you can sell the wines I'm making today in the future."

"I thought the juice we got from last year's grapes would go into the champagne for the end of the year. Now I'm not sure." Isabelle was completely confused.

"I know that with the twentieth century approaching, some wine-makers are selling everything they've got. But a champagne so young is still too rough, not rounded enough, and for the great celebrations ahead, it would simply not be good enough. I'd feel like a swindler if I sent you out with that in your hand. But if that's what you insist on . . ." Daniel shrugged.

Isabelle looked at him in consternation. "And I thought I understood at least a little about this business." The next moment, she jumped to her feet, embraced Daniel, and planted a kiss on his cheek. "What would I do without you? Thank you for your good counsel. I will sell your mature rosé champagne, and I will do so with pleasure and pride. Against our turn-of-the-century Feininger, every other champagne will look anemic!"

Chapter Thirty-Eight

When Clara awoke, she did not immediately know where she was. The chirping of birds outside her window, the lavender scent of the bedclothes, the weight of the blanket . . . everything sounded and felt unfamiliar, but not uncomfortable. Almost unwillingly, she opened her eyes and found herself back in Isabelle's guest room, where she had slept for the previous five nights.

She turned and looked out the window. It was only the end of February—another of Gerhard's engagements had kept her in Berlin longer than planned—but there was already a hint of spring in the air. Around Isabelle's house, winter jasmine and witch hazel were in bloom, exuding a warm, matchless perfume.

Clara's brows furrowed as she thought of the horrible stench that plagued Berlin's streets. The stink of the ever-increasing number of factories, the gray smoke rising from the chimney of the smithy, the sharp odors from the shoemaker workshops—and on top of it all, the waste produced by humans and animals alike in the confined spaces of the city. When the fog from the hinterland around Berlin closed in, it was so hard to breathe that Clara worried about the health of her son. At three, Matthias was still a delicate child; a puff of wind was enough to give him a cough or cold.

"That comes from you coddling him all the time," her husband always said disdainfully. "A cold rubdown morning and evening, that would toughen him up!"

Clara sighed. Gerhard didn't have to put up with Matthias's shrill screaming if the washcloth was just a shade too cool.

She wondered how Matthias and her parents were getting along. Sophie and Anton Berg pampered their grandson exactly as they had pampered Clara as a child. They were probably spending wonderful days together without giving a thought to what she, Clara, was up to.

She rolled to her side and sighed. How lucky she was to have such a cheerful, healthy son, notwithstanding his tendency to catch colds! The thought that not every mother was blessed with such happiness saddened her. *Don't dwell on it*, Clara chided herself. *Don't think. Just be.*

Lying in bed longer than necessary—what a luxury! It was impossible at home. Gerhard wanted to see a perfectly set breakfast table every morning and a no less perfectly prepared wife. To manage everything to his satisfaction, Clara had to rise an hour earlier than he did, for she still had no one to help her in the household.

Thoughts of home were so exhausting that Clara closed her eyes again.

When she woke a second time, Isabelle was standing beside her bed. She was carrying Marguerite on her right arm and a cup of tea in her left hand; she set the cup down on Clara's nightstand. It smelled of hay and wildflowers.

"Well, sleepyhead! Did you forget that we've been invited to visit Raymond Dupont today? If we want to make it to Reims by lunchtime, you should drag yourself out of bed."

Isabelle was so cheerful these days! It was such a contrast to Clara's previous visit, in the aftermath of Leon's death.

"Good morning, you two." Clara stretched languidly, then smiled and tickled little Marguerite's feet. Instead of kicking her legs as Matthias would have, Marguerite just rested her head against Isabelle while she looked at Clara with her large eyes.

Outside, a cloud crossed the bright winter sun, and inside, Clara's mood darkened a little. When she thought of the terrible task ahead of her, she came close to tears. How would Isabelle react when she told her that? She pushed herself to a sitting position and forced herself to think of other things.

"Are you really sure that I'm supposed to come with you to this birthday party? I don't know anyone, and I don't even have a gift for Mr. Dupont. Maybe it would be better if I stayed home and looked after Marguerite."

Isabelle dismissed her doubts with a wave of her hand. "I probably don't know anyone there, either. And when Raymond heard you were visiting, he expressly invited you along, too. It's important for me to see him; I need to get his advice on marketing our new champagne. Besides, Ghislaine is already looking forward to watching Marguerite. Now climb out of bed and make yourself beautiful. If you like, we can do each other's hair, and you're more than welcome to borrow one of my dresses. No doubt Raymond has invited only the *crème de la crème* of Reims society."

Clara felt a nervous twinge in her stomach. She hoped she'd be able to behave herself appropriately in such a smart crowd.

Sensing Clara's insecurity, Isabelle said, "Don't worry. We won't stay out too late. I still have to pick up Marguerite from Ghislaine later tonight." She gave her daughter a kiss on her forehead.

Marguerite . . . The sight of the child awakened a deep sadness in Clara. Maybe it would be good to spend the evening in Reims. Elegance and luxury all around instead of a conversation that she would rather put off until the end of time.

***

Raymond Dupont looked around with satisfaction at the guests seated at his birthday table. The mayor of Reims was there with his wife and daughter, and they were accompanied by other honored guests from the city. Louis Pommery had come from the eponymous wine estate, and his sister and brother-in-law, Guy de Polignac, sat beside him. Then Joseph Krug II, Maurice and George Roger with their wives from Épernay, and Henriette and Alphonse Trubert—the champagne-making elite of the region were gathered at his table. The only one missing was Edgar Ruinart; the old man had an audience with the czar of Russia—something Raymond had accepted as an excuse for missing out on *his* party.

Apart from the champagne barons, Raymond had invited a prima ballerina from the Paris Ballet, with whom he had spent an exhilarating night on one of his journeys, as well as a breathtakingly beautiful actress from the theater in Reims. Both women seemed spellbound whenever he opened his mouth to speak. The title "Madame Raymond Dupont" for both of them seemed to promise as much prominence, wealth, and fame as any *comtesse* or baroness. In the light of the chandeliers, their fake diamonds glittered across their revealing décolletages and in their elaborate hairdos. The scent of their excessive perfume drifted across the table until, in Raymond's exceptionally sensitive nose, it congealed with the delicious odors of the fine food into a florid mess.

But even if they had smelled as delightful as a May morning, for Raymond the two women were only there to decorate his table, like the long-stemmed roses and the napkins fringed with Brussels lace. A hunter like himself did not appreciate the rabbit throwing itself in front of his rifle—if the women did not know that, then they had a great deal to learn about life and men.

The woman sitting to his right, however, was of a completely different kind! Isabelle Feininger. She, too, wore jewelry. She, too, had her hair elaborately braided and pinned. But with Isabelle, it all seemed more natural, a more casual elegance. She wasn't trying to impress anyone. The same was true of the way she handled herself in such illustrious company. With her wit and her stimulating observations, one was happy to overlook her occasionally stumbling French. It was quite usual for the nobles of Europe to speak fluent French; it was *the* language of court, after all. But for an ordinary citizen of another country to speak French so well was remarkable; that, at least, was the unanimous opinion of the men seated around the table. The women, however, regarded Isabelle more dourly. The ballerina, especially, cast baneful glances in Isabelle's direction whenever she could, but Isabelle ignored them.

Likewise, Isabelle paid her old nemesis, Henriette Trubert, no attention. When, earlier, she had become aware of Henriette's scrutiny, Isabelle had nodded to Henriette with a gesture at once chilly and regal. *Bravo!* Raymond had silently saluted her. In the Champagne region, it was impossible to avoid one's enemies, so it was all the more important to encounter them with your head held high.

"Well, how's the suitor business going?" Henriette had asked him earlier that evening. He had been on his way to the kitchen to give his cook final instructions for the meal when she intercepted him. "I really hope that wedding bells will soon be ringing for you and your young bride. You've been lonely far too long."

Raymond had asked himself countless times what he had ever seen in this woman. The nosy way she pried into his life, and—even worse—the way she was now making him a pawn in her own game repulsed him. The only thing that mattered to Henriette was adding another precious stone to her crown with the Feininger estate. *And why not?* he had still thought the previous autumn, when she had spoken to him the first time about Isabelle. *Let her get her claws on the Feininger lands, if they mean so much to her.* But he had changed his mind. He could find a buyer for the Feininger estate anytime he liked. It would serve Henriette right if *he* took *her* aside at his wedding to tell her they wanted to sell the estate to someone else. Or that they already had.

"Don't worry on my account, my dear. With all my work, I have no time left to be lonely." He had said nothing of the progress he had been making with Isabelle. And even if he had wanted to, it would have been hard for him to put it into words. He was reasonably sure that Isabelle liked him, or she would not always ask him for his advice. Or did she see him only as an adviser, the avuncular friend? Were there deeper feelings there? It was time for him to find out, before someone else got in ahead of him. He did not like that Daniel Lambert was now Isabelle Feininger's cellar master. He would much rather have been her only white knight in her time of need. But why think about it? Daniel might be the best cellar master in the entire region, but he didn't have Raymond's ways and means for courting a woman. If everything went as he imagined it would, Isabelle Feininger would soon be melting like ice in his hands.

Watching over his champagne glass, Raymond frowned. Joseph Krug was openly ogling Isabelle Feininger. And George Roger could hardly take his eyes off her. But hardly anyone so much as glanced at Isabelle's friend. Poor nondescript thing.

For a moment, Raymond didn't know if he should be happy or upset at the attention Isabelle was attracting. But it consoled him to think that a single word from him would be enough to have her all to himself again.

The five courses of his dinner were absolutely sumptuous, the champagne sparkled in fine crystal glasses, and the conversation around the table was just as light and sparkling without turning superficial. Everyone knew everyone else, and they certainly had enough to discuss for the next few hours. His physical presence as their host was no longer an absolute necessity. It was entirely up to him when he left the room with Isabelle.

It seemed to him to be a good sign that the widow had come to him to ask him for his professional advice, despite the fact that she had Daniel Lambert working for her. Daniel might well be a genius in the wine cellar, but he had no idea at all about selling champagne. Which fitted in nicely with Raymond's plans . . .

How delicious she smelled! Of soap and mother's milk. How good it would feel to lower his lips to her breasts and—aroused, Raymond shuffled a little in his chair, then turned to the woman he was imagining.

"My dear Isabelle, you still had a question or two for me, didn't you? If you like, I'm sure we can excuse ourselves for a little while and dedicate ourselves to your concerns."

***

"Daniel created this champagne when he was still Jacques's cellar master. I had no idea I had such a treasure in my cellar." Isabelle laughed excitedly while Raymond Dupont opened the bottle that she had given him.

Clara could see from the fine film of condensation that had formed on the bottle that the champagne had now cooled sufficiently. She smiled and thanked Raymond for the glass he had poured for her. But she had no idea how to taste champagne properly. This was Isabelle and Raymond's field; she was happy enough just to escape the exhausting company at the table, especially because she hardly understood a word any of them said. And she had put so much store in her good school French, she thought rather downheartedly, while the champagne dealer took a large mouthful from his glass.

"Daniel thinks I should offer this champagne for the end of the year's festivities. A rosé with a shade of vanilla and a hint of strawberry, plus . . ."

"Accents of sponge soufflé . . . and lemon zest," Raymond added. He and Isabelle laughed conspiratorially.

Clara shook her head. How could anyone taste all that from one mouthful of the stuff? And both of them had exactly the same experience? It was very mysterious to Clara. While they went on talking about aroma, color, and taste, Clara covertly looked around the inside of Raymond Dupont's living room. Dark-green silk wallpaper covered the walls, and gold-framed paintings of hunting scenes kept the room from appearing too gloomy. A chandelier was suspended from the ceiling. It was at least six feet across and hung with many different forms: droplets, crystals, spheres, prisms. The furniture was all made of pearwood and richly inlaid.

Immeasurable wealth, and yet it all seemed so undemonstrative. Raymond was not a man who acted self-important or came across as a braggart. It wouldn't matter if Gerhard treated patients until midnight every night or if she combed through every shop in Berlin for beautiful things; they would never have enough money or good taste to achieve anything like what Raymond had in that room. *Gerhard would turn green with envy if he could see all this*, Clara thought, and almost regretted not having her husband at her side.

"I think you could well and truly conquer the European market with this champagne," said Raymond after a second mouthful. "People would gladly accept another glass of this champagne—the perfect drink for the parties that will mark the turn of the century. Providing, of course, one can find the right customers for it."

"The turn-of-the-century champagne . . . The winds of change are blowing," Clara murmured in German, before she could stop the words coming out.

Raymond Dupont raised his eyebrows inquiringly.

"*Champagne de vent de siècle*, roughly," Isabelle repeated in French. "It's a little wordplay my friends and I once came up with." She tilted her head to one side. "I wonder if that would be a good name for my champagne? They say one should always take an original tack with the marketing."

Raymond nodded. "True enough, but the name should not be as complicated as that. Besides, what does wind have to do with a rosé as captivating as this?" He raised the glass to look at it in the light of the chandelier. "If you would allow me a personal observation, my dear Madame Feininger, the color reminds me of the red tone of your hair. There is something feminine and delicate about it, but at the same time, it does not lack any strength."

"Daniel said the exact same thing!" cried Isabelle in astonishment.

Clara noticed how Raymond's brow momentarily furrowed at Isabelle's remark. Aha, he was jealous of the cellar master!

It had already occurred to her on her last visit, following Leon's death, that their host had his eye on Isabelle. No man sent so many get-well wishes, pralines, and champagne baskets without an ulterior motive. But Isabelle seemed oblivious to the man's courting. And she always wanted to be so worldly! Clara smiled to herself.

"What would you say if this unusual color were to make an appearance in the name of your new champagne? *Rougette Feininger*—that has a wonderful ring to it."

"*Rougette Feininger*." Isabelle looked intensely from the man opposite her to the glass in her hand and back again. Her eyes shone brightly, and she said, "That's a perfect name! Raymond, you are truly a treasure!"

For a moment, Clara thought her friend might stand up and kiss him. He, at least, seemed to be expecting as much, the way his eyes gleamed. But instead, Isabelle reached across the table and took Clara's hand. "Dear Clara, what do you think?"

"It's a wonderful name," said Clara with a smile. "It's just . . ."

"Yes?" said Raymond and Isabelle at the same time.

Clara bit her lip. Wouldn't she ever learn to keep her mouth shut? Gerhard was right when he accused her of putting her nose in wherever she felt like it and making a fool of herself.

"Oh, come on. What is it?" asked Isabelle impatiently.

Clara pointed to the champagne bottle. "The label! Excuse me for putting it so bluntly, but it looks so . . . plain. Besides, it says 1892, and I have to ask myself what that number has to do with the turn of the century. I don't know what it would cost or if it's even possible, but couldn't you get a new label designed? Something that looks more feminine and more . . . modern? Then one would see at a glance that a fresh kind of wind is blowing in your cellars."

Before Isabelle could say a word, Raymond Dupont cleared his throat. "My compliments, Madame Gropius, I could not have put it better myself." He bowed to Clara, and she immediately blushed.

Then Raymond took Isabelle's hand. "In the Champagne region, there is a great tradition of women making outstanding champagnes, or at least putting their names on them. The most famous champagne queen of all time was the widow Clicquot, the *veuve* Clicquot." He stood up, crossed to a sideboard, took out a bottle of champagne, and held it for Clara and Isabelle to see.

Clara read the large letters on the cognac-colored label. "Veuve Clicquot Ponsardin."

"I know that your husband's death is still painful for you, but perhaps you should also throw your widow status into the ring? What do you think of Veuve Rougette champagne? We add a visually arresting label—with your portrait on it; why not? I already have an idea for that. Isabelle, the buyers will be lining up for your champagne!"

***

What a day it had been! Although the trip to Reims and the party had taken their toll, Isabelle was too exhilarated to sleep. She flopped into a deep armchair in front of the fireplace in the living room, listening with one ear for any sound from Marguerite, who was in her cradle in the next room. The child had already been asleep when Isabelle collected her from Ghislaine, and it had been difficult to get her to wake up for a feed. Her sweet daughter! A surge of motherly love washed over Isabelle with such force that it almost made her cry.

With a shawl around her shoulders and her feet pulled under her, Clara sat opposite Isabelle in another armchair. She did not try to stifle a generous yawn. The clock on the wall struck ten.

"Tired?" Isabelle asked. She hoped her friend didn't want to go off to bed too soon. There was so much to talk about!

Clara shook her head. "I wouldn't say no if you offered me another glass of your outstanding champagne. I never get to drink anything so good in Berlin."

"Nothing simpler," said Isabelle, and jumped to her feet. A minute later, they were raising their glasses to each other, enveloped in the warmth of their friendship. Over the rim of her glass, Isabelle peered intently at her friend. "Honestly, now—have you ever heard of that painter whom Raymond thinks would be the right one to paint my portrait for the champagne label?"

"Pierre-Auguste Renoir?" Clara nodded. "But only because there was a long story about him and his work in the last issue of *Gardener's Monthly*. They even reproduced a couple of his paintings. I liked them so much I thought about cutting them out and framing them to decorate our living room."

Isabelle frowned. "I see. And how does Renoir paint?"

"You ask some questions! As if I'm any kind of expert," said Clara with a laugh, but then continued: "They call his style impressionist. Broad brush strokes, daring combinations of color. But the article also said that in recent years his work has developed, and he's tending more toward classicism. Painting beautiful women is one of his specialties, and his portraits certainly have a special radiance and are brimming with *joie de vivre*. If you look at it that way, he'd be ideal for what you want to do."

"But would such a famous artist paint a label for a bottle of champagne?" Isabelle's brow furrowed again. "Raymond mentioned that he lives in the southern Champagne region, so paying him a visit would certainly be conceivable. Still, I don't know . . ."

"If you ask him nicely enough, I'm sure he'll say yes," Clara said. "Besides, you'd be paying him for his work. Even artists need more than love and air to live."

Isabelle nodded thoughtfully. "You're probably right. Oh, I'm so glad I get so much support, from all of you!" She stretched her arms high in the air, and now it was her turn to yawn. "Daniel in the wine cellar, Raymond with his ideas about how to sell it and what to call it. And the label, of course. I know, I know, that was actually your idea," she said, laughing, when she saw Clara's offended look. "And now Raymond has asked me to join him on his next sales trip through Europe. He wants me to meet his most important customers and to make sure they buy my champagne—what did I do to deserve all this?"

"Oh, I'm sure I can answer that," said Clara, her tone ironic. "The man has his eye on you. It's as simple as that. I'm sure he's looking forward to a 'business trip' with you very much indeed."

"Nonsense! You certainly have an imagination. Raymond is a good friend. He knows I'm still in mourning for Leon and that I have a young baby—he would never try to court me in this situation."

Clara's silence said a great deal more than any answer would have. Isabelle had already decided to move on, but then Clara raised the topic again. "If I were you, I wouldn't be so quick to push the idea aside. Considering the admiration in his eyes whenever he looks at you, he'd lay the world at your feet. You could still do what you want with your life, but without a care in the world, and in luxury to boot. A man who does all the work—sometimes that can be a great advantage."

"And I'm supposed to marry him for that? Please, Clara, we're not living in the Middle Ages," said Isabelle defensively. She felt walls going up, deep inside. She and Clara had always had different opinions about most things in life. *Anyway, there's Daniel to think about*, she thought.

"Time will tell," said Clara.

Isabelle nodded vaguely. She had no desire to fight and decided to change the subject.

"Vienna, Munich, Berlin—I get so excited when I think about such a big trip. But I wonder if these are really the right cities for selling my champagne?" As she had done several times already that day, she vacillated between euphoria and gnawing doubt.

"I wouldn't be at all surprised if your Raymond organizes an audience for you at the emperor's court. But what's far more important"—Clara paused dramatically—"is that we could have another reunion, all three of us! After this trip, Gerhard won't let me go again so soon. And now that Josephine is expecting, too, I know she won't be taking a long journey. It would be perfect if you could come to Berlin."

Berlin . . . The idea of it made Isabelle uneasy. She could see her friends again in Berlin, certainly, but also her parents. Did she really want that?

Sometimes it seemed to Isabelle that the day she left Berlin, she had been caught in a whirlwind that had not yet let go of her. New, exciting events were happening all the time, in her own life and in the lives of those close to her. Now Josephine was pregnant, too. All three of them, mothers—a few years earlier, none of them would have given the idea a second thought. Perhaps they had more in common than they realized?

"What do you think—could I take Marguerite with me on this trip? Or is she too young?" Isabelle's biggest concern was where she could leave her daughter when she went off with Raymond. By the time they were on the tour, Ghislaine would be busy with her own child. Isabelle couldn't expect her to look after Marguerite as well.

Clara sat up straight in her armchair. When she looked up, she had a strange expression on her face. "I think we need to talk about Marguerite," she said.

"What about her?" Isabelle asked. Clara's voice had taken on an odd, unfamiliar tone. A bead of sweat had formed on her upper lip, as if she were struggling hard with something.

Clara leaned forward. "There is something . . . not right about your daughter. You should take her to a doctor as soon as you can. A specialist."

Her words came out of the blue and were as sharp as the lash of a whip. Isabelle let out a shrill, disbelieving laugh.

"*What* did you say?"

Clara looked at her and nervously wrung her hands. "Haven't you ever noticed how sluggish Marguerite's reactions are? When you tickle her, for instance? Or how slowly her eyes follow your hand if you hold a toy in front of her and move it back and forth? Infants usually bend their arms when they lie down, but Marguerite's arms hang loosely. And isn't she quick to tire when she suckles? I mean unusually quick to tire?"

"Have you gone mad?" Isabelle cried out. "You're acting as if Marguerite is infirm, as if she's some sort of halfwit! That's the biggest load of . . . nonsense I've ever heard." But as she spoke, a cold chill ran down her spine. She had the sensation of losing her mind then and there.

"Isabelle, please . . . I . . . I'm not saying this for my own amusement or on a whim! Marguerite is a beautiful girl. And I love her as if she were my own daughter," Clara said. "But the way her eyes are farther apart than usual, her flat nose, her little mouth—those are all signs of . . . a very particular condition. I know I'm just a doctor's wife, but—"

"Yes, that's right!" Isabelle cut her off. "You are *just* a doctor's wife, so what do you know? Coming in here and scaring me; that's so terribly *mean*!" Suddenly filled with loathing, she glared at her friend. "What can I do if your Matthias screamed the roof off day and night when he was a baby? I remember perfectly well how desperate you were back then. You couldn't calm him down with anything. Some days, his screaming was so bad that you had to take him to your mother because you couldn't put up with it anymore. Is that what's causing your envy? My Marguerite is just a good child, especially good. And she's beautiful, besides. Don't talk to me about wide-set eyes and small nose—do you think she'd look better with a hooked nose and beady little witch eyes?" Trembling from head to foot, Isabelle rose to her feet. "You come here, a guest in my house, and you push a dagger into my heart? If that's what you call friendship, then no thank you!" Sobbing, she turned away and went into the next room. She picked up Marguerite from her cradle and, without another word, ran upstairs to her bedroom.

Chapter Thirty-Nine

The days until Clara's departure were intolerable. The two friends said barely a word to one another and avoided each other as much as they possibly could. Isabelle made sure that Clara did not set eyes on her daughter again. She could have forgiven Clara almost anything, but not the words she had spoken that evening.

When the fifth of March arrived, the day that Clara was to leave, both were more than relieved. Choking on her tears, Clara whispered an apology, but Isabelle didn't want to hear it.

Clara's coach had just turned onto the main road when Isabelle called Claude to her.

"Hitch up the horses, please. I need to visit the hospital in Épernay," she said.

"Madame, I hope you have not come down with something? Or little Marguerite?"

Faced with Claude's concern, Isabelle's stony expression softened momentarily.

"I'm sure everything is all right," she answered quietly. It irritated her to realize that she did not sound as convincing as she would have wanted.

"I'm not a specialist in children of this kind," said the doctor, when he and Isabelle were sitting opposite each other in his office. "But with your daughter, a developmental delay might very well exist."

"And what does that mean?" Isabelle said, a crease appearing between her eyes. Children of this kind?

The doctor had spent more than an hour examining her daughter. He had checked her reflexes and her eyes. He had measured the circumference of her head, and he had pinched her arm until she cried.

"Strange. She barely whimpers," he had said.

"She's a good baby! She's just tolerating this," Isabelle had replied, upset, and she had hurriedly taken the child back from the nurse who held her while she was being examined.

Now she asked, "What, in your opinion, is wrong with my daughter?"

The doctor raised his shoulders. "At this stage, all I can give you is a provisional diagnosis, madame. I advise you to seek out a specialist I know, a man more thoroughly versed in Down syndrome."

"Down syndrome?" The crease between Isabelle's eyes deepened. "You don't know what Marguerite has, but you have a name for this mystery illness? How am I supposed to understand that?"

"It is not unequivocally clear that your daughter suffers from this syndrome," the doctor said, trying to sound appeasing. "There are certain signs, no more." He took a sheet of letter paper and dipped his quill in an open inkpot. "I'll write down the address of the specialist. With a referral from me, I'm sure you'll be able to get an appointment soon. I'll just slip my bill for today's visit into the same envelope."

The specialist was in Reims. Isabelle and Marguerite went there the next day. Appointment or not, she would not leave the old-fashioned practice before the doctor had seen her child. They had to wait three hours, and people came and went the whole time. Isabelle sat as if in a trance, rocking Marguerite in her arms, and was only vaguely aware of mothers with their children entering the waiting room and leaving again. A boy of about three had a large misshapen head and sobbed the whole time. A girl about the same age rocked back and forth constantly and made terrible noises. Another woman carried an infant in her arms. She looked over again and again at Isabelle, and it was clear she wanted to talk. But Isabelle purposefully looked out the window. None of this had anything to do with her.

"Marguerite's heart seems to be fine," said Dr. Rainier Martin after listening through a stethoscope.

Isabelle pressed her lips together tightly. She had not come to have Marguerite's heart checked. She watched every part of the doctor's examination with an eagle eye. Some of what he did merely repeated what the doctor in Épernay had done, but Dr. Martin also listened to her heart, poked at her head for what seemed like an eternity, and measured her limbs. To Isabelle's horror, he then placed the little finger of his right hand in Marguerite's mouth to test her sucking reflex. The child immediately began to cough and wheeze and then to cry. How could she do anything else?

When he was finished with his examination, Dr. Martin asked Isabelle to sit with him at his desk.

"About thirty years ago, an English doctor by the name of John Langdon Down first recorded the symptoms of Down syndrome. It's a hereditary disease. Now that I've examined her, I can make a tentative diagnosis, at least, that Marguerite suffers from the syndrome. Scientific research in this area is still in its proverbial infancy, but we do have a number of very reliable indicators," the doctor said.

Isabelle flushed hot and cold. She hugged her daughter even more tightly. This was the second time that she had heard the name. Down syndrome.

"Inherited? But I'm perfectly healthy! So was my husband."

The doctor ignored her objection. "Little Marguerite shows some of the typical signs, with the emphasis on *some*. The flat, broad face and the somewhat smaller eyes—"

"So my child could also be healthy?" said Isabelle urgently. Marguerite was so pretty. How could the doctor see anything wrong with her?

"Well, I wouldn't call her healthy. There is, for example, the unusually large gap between her big toe and second toe." He looked toward Marguerite's feet, which were once again wrapped up warmly. "A typical characteristic of children suffering from Down syndrome. There is also clear hypotonia of the palatal region, from which her sucking difficulties stem."

"But isn't it the case that some children are simply better at suckling than others?"

Tentative diagnosis? Separated toes? Isabelle's mind was reeling.

"Of course," the doctor replied patiently. "But you would not be here if that were her only problem." He scribbled something on a piece of paper. "If you doubt my diagnosis, you are naturally welcome to seek out another specialist. I recommend Charles Fraudand in Paris, a student of John Langdon Down's." On a second piece of paper, he added together a few numbers. "That comes to eighty-seven francs, madame."

Feeling numb, Isabelle drove back to Hautvillers with her sleeping child. She had insisted on a more thorough explanation, and the doctor had responded with more technical terminology about the condition, but Isabelle still didn't feel well informed. How Marguerite would develop, what effects the syndrome would have on her life—to these questions she had received only vague answers.

"Generally speaking, in their first five years, children with Down syndrome show only half the development of a normal child. But many of them catch up with a large part of their development later on," the doctor had said, and Isabelle's relief had been great. But her happiness at that news was short-lived.

"Others, however, remain underdeveloped throughout their lives. On top of the mental difficulties they face, there are also health problems . . . respiratory infections, for example, and leukemia."

Leukemia. Isabelle suddenly had the feeling that she was about to step through a door and fall and fall and . . . But her daughter was healthy!

"Madame, there is no need to be excessively alarmed. There are now exceptionally good curative establishments for serious cases," the doctor said.

That had been enough for Isabelle. Without another word, she paid the man, and just as silently she climbed into the waiting coach, ignoring Claude Bertrand's inquiring look. She didn't want to talk about any of it, because if she did, she would transform it into a fact.

In Hautvillers, she had Claude drive her straight to Le Grand Cerf. Ghislaine was sitting behind the counter, reading a book; there were no customers at all, and Isabelle breathed a little easier. With the last of her self-control, she forced herself to make a little innocuous conversation, talking about the unusually mild start to March, about the work to be done soon in the vineyards, and about how glad she was to have Daniel working for her that year. She drank a Marc de Champagne brandy. The strong spirits, however, could not rinse the bitter taste from her mouth. Somehow, Ghislaine had heard that Isabelle had been to see a doctor with Marguerite. Of course, she wanted to know how it had gone and what the result was. But Isabelle waved it off.

"Nothing certain, not yet," she said, her voice unsteady.

Ghislaine embraced her warmly. "Forget the doctors and enjoy your child. Marguerite is the sweetest, loveliest child in all Hautvillers!"

Isabelle gave her a pained smile. "I know that you're about to have a child of your own, but I must ask if you would be able to take Marguerite overnight, just this once. I need a little time for myself."

"Say no more," said Ghislaine, and laid one hand reassuringly on Isabelle's arm. "It's so quiet here in the restaurant that I'm going to close early tonight. Marguerite will be fine with me. And if I really do go into labor tonight, Daniel can still look after your daughter."

Lethargic as an old woman, Isabelle unlocked her front door. Micheline, just then stepping out of her house next door, waved, but Isabelle pretended she did not see her elderly friend. Don't speak. Not with anyone. Be alone. Die, or act as if you had.

Inside, it smelled as it always did. Of the work boots in the closet, to which a little soil always seemed to cling. Of the preserved sauerkraut, apples, and old potatoes in the pantry. From the kitchen came the smell of coffee and baked white bread. The plate and cup from her breakfast still stood on the table, unwashed. Everything was as it always was. And nothing would ever be the same again.

Isabelle put her bag down in the hall and hung her coat on one of the coat hooks. It was Daniel's day off, which was good, because it meant she could open the door to the cellar unnoticed and descend the narrow stairs. She didn't want champagne, not then and perhaps never again. As if in a trance, she went to a wooden cupboard where Jacques kept his wine collection. Without looking at the label, she grabbed the closest bottle. Red wine. Then she took a second. Back in the kitchen, she found a corkscrew and a glass. She had not eaten anything the entire day. Her stomach was filled with sorrow and fear.

With the bottles jammed under her arm, she climbed the stairs to the second floor. In her bedroom, she unlaced her boots and tossed them across the room. Then she lay back against the pillows.

Petra Durst-Benning

The wine tasted sour and bitter. She emptied the first glass in a single draught, then poured herself a second and stared off into space.

"A typical characteristic of children suffering from Down syndrome."

"If you doubt my diagnosis, you are naturally welcome to seek out another specialist. I recommend Charles Fraudand in Paris."

"There is something not right about your daughter. You should take her to a doctor as soon as you can."

"When God created the grapevines, he didn't make them all the same. Each one, in its own way, is unique and beautiful."

Everybody had known it. Micheline, with her tormented eyes every time she looked at Marguerite. Daniel, with his comparison to the vines. And probably Ghislaine and Claude, too. Clara had simply been the first to call it by name.

Only she, the mother, had been blind.

Down syndrome. A name for something she did not understand, could not understand, did not want to understand.

"Isabelle, please don't think ill of me, but I can't take your child. I would do any other favor for you, but bringing that child to me, of all people . . . no, I'm sorry." In one of their first conversations, Micheline had told her about the misfortune that her brother and his wife had suffered.

Isabelle simply had not been listening closely enough. Too many new impressions had been raining down on her. A disabled child; she did not doubt that it was a sad affair. But that had all happened so many years earlier, long before she had met Marie. *What did it matter to her?* she thought, but realized she was being unfair.

Without warning, she felt nauseous, so nauseous that she thought she would throw up. She put the wine glass down and forced herself to swallow; too much spittle was in her mouth. She felt dizzy. She leaned back on the pillows, then raised the glass to her lips and drank again. The nausea gave way to a burning sensation in her gullet.

400

"On top of the mental difficulties they face, there are also health problems . . . respiratory infections, for example, and leukemia."

A choking sob escaped Isabelle's throat. Would her child ever even be able to speak? Tears flowed down her face but she made no effort to wipe them away. Nothing mattered anymore.

"There are now exceptionally good curative establishments for serious cases . . ."

Isabelle's heart felt clenched. Never, *never*, would she give Marguerite up. It would be like cutting off her right arm. Or her leg. Or as if someone tried to cut Leon out of her heart. Marguerite was his bequest to her, just as the estate itself was.

The estate. Everything had been going so well. She had found new hope. Things were looking up! And now . . .

Another struggle.

And, once again, she was alone. Would she have the strength to get through everything still ahead?

Dear God above, please make it all just a bad dream. Why are you doing this to me? Why me? What law did I break to make you punish me so severely? What law did Marguerite break? She's still so small, an angel.

All the hard work last fall! Isabelle put down her glass on the marble top of the nightstand so hard that a small piece of glass splintered off the base.

Her big belly had gotten in her way the entire time, and she still remembered the sharp, stabbing pains in her back. But she had gritted her teeth and gone on with the work. Everyone had told her to take better care of herself. But she didn't want to hear a word of it. Let them give their good advice to someone else—the business came first!

And now? What would become of the business now? Would she have any time left at all for anything that didn't have to do with looking after Marguerite?

Maybe if someone had done something earlier? Shortly after the birth? What was the name of that specialist in Paris? Fraudand. She had to visit him. The doctors in Reims and Épernay were useless.

Isabelle's nose was running, and she could hardly breathe. She wiped her nose with her sleeve. Drank another mouthful as the last of the daylight vanished.

Maybe everything wasn't as bad as they said. And the doctors, those know-it-alls, had just put a fright into her.

Please, dear God . . .

The birth. Here, in this very room. Isabelle could still smell the blood and other fluids. And all the hours she had tried in vain to press the child out. Was that when Marguerite had been damaged? The doctor in Reims had said that wasn't possible and had talked about it being hereditary.

Isabelle pressed her eyes closed so hard that it hurt. And what if it was really her fault? Why hadn't she gone into the hospital in Épernay much earlier? Why had she taken such a risk? The midwife had calculated that Marguerite was only due on the fifth of January, and no one expected it all to happen on Christmas Eve.

So many mistakes. How could one woman make so many mistakes? *Please, dear God, if you exist, then punish me. But leave the child alone.*

At some point, Isabelle fell asleep. It was a restless sleep, and after twelve hours she woke up feeling as if she'd been through a wringer. Her head hurt, her shoulders were tense, and her chest was tight. She still had not opened her eyes completely when the ghosts of the night before returned. She looked at the two empty bottles and the red rings they had left on the white marble of the nightstand.

She had wanted to get drunk, had hoped that by doing so she could flee the truth. Don't think. Don't feel. Act like everything is as it was before. Another one of her stupid ideas. If anything mattered now, it was to keep a clear head and not waste her strength. With little more than a trace of her former energy, she got out of bed.

Marguerite needed her.

***

Daniel looked with pride at the enormous tanks on the second level of the cellars. The tanks were all filled with a rosé-colored liquid. The air was filled with its delicate aroma.

He had done it. He'd created the perfect cuvée, a rosé champagne that was light and sparkly. Now he had to hope that the color did not change during the next steps in the manufacturing process. By his reckoning, they would be able to fill around twenty thousand bottles, which would bring in a healthy sum for Isabelle in the next two years, money that the estate urgently needed for investments in the years ahead.

This champagne would catapult the Feininger estate back into the first ranks, Daniel exulted. Back where it belonged. Back where it had once been in the days when his father had run the place and the Lambert name still graced the labels. Names—for Daniel, they meant little. What mattered much more was what was inside the bottles—and what the people who bought it experienced when they drank it.

His life had changed so much since coming to work at the Feininger estate. It was the place he had spent his childhood, the same farm that his father had lost in a game of cards to Jacques Feininger, and he knew every stone in the cellar walls. He knew every vineyard, every vine. The feeling that he had come home only grew stronger with all the hours he worked in the cellars.

And then there was Isabelle. Whenever he went out walking among the vineyards, whenever he crossed the yard, he kept an eye out in the hope of seeing her. When he saw her, his heart jumped. *You're as besotted as a kid*, he mocked himself silently. But at the same time, he knew that his feelings for Isabelle Feininger went far deeper, that it was love.

He was about to climb the steps out of the cellar when he saw a light appear above. A moment later, Isabelle was standing in front of him, pale and bleary-eyed and with a hard look to her that he had not seen before.

His heart was spilling over with love, but he forced himself to give her no more than a noncommittal smile as he said, "I was about to come and get you. The *assemblage* is finished; tomorrow, I'll start with the filling. Would you like to try a glass?" He swept one hand out grandly, taking in all the tanks.

"Maybe later. I have to talk to you. Can you come up?"

"I don't know how to tell you this," Isabelle began slowly, when they were sitting together in the kitchen a little later. A strand of hair came loose from her carelessly woven braid and fell across her face. The redness of her hair against her almost translucent skin only served to highlight her pallor. Daniel could not remember seeing a more beautiful woman, despite Isabelle's obvious distress.

"Why don't you simply say what it is? You know you can always rely on me."

"But you can't rely on me!" she blurted. "Nothing in my life is simple. Every time I think things are starting to get better, fate comes along and slaps me in the face, and I'm back on the ground again." Tears came to her eyes, and she wiped them away furiously. In a voice heavy with emotion, she said, "Marguerite is sick. Very sick. She . . ."

Daniel listened in silence as she described her visits to the doctors. Down syndrome—he had never heard of it before.

"From now on, I have to be there for Marguerite, and that's all. Do you understand?" She looked pleadingly at him, her eyes wide. "I know it's the last thing you want to hear from me, and I feel terrible about doing this to you. You gave up your job in Épernay to help me, and we wanted to whip this place into shape together, but the way things look now, it's impossible. How can I think about going on a business trip through Europe with a sick child? How am I supposed to find the peace of mind I need to sit for hours—or days!—for a painter to paint my portrait for a new label for the bottles? It's madness!" She threw her hands in the air in despair. "How am I supposed to think competently about anything that isn't connected to Marguerite? From now on, my daughter needs all my attention. I have to look for a specialist who can help her, for a school where she can get the support she'll need later, for . . . oh, I don't know what else . . ." She slumped in her chair. "All I know is that, yet again, all my plans have come to nothing. The most important thing is that I have to be there for my child. I'll do anything for her, anything!"

There was an unshakeable conviction in her eyes. Isabelle the brave.

The old kitchen clock above the sink caught her eye. "I have to go soon. Marguerite is at Ghislaine's house. I won't entrust her to a stranger ever again. I was just so terribly . . . exhausted, yesterday."

"Ghislaine's a stranger?" Daniel raised his eyebrows.

"That's not what I meant," Isabelle said hurriedly. "But I can't ask someone else to look after Marguerite! What if something happened, some kind of emergency? No, I have to take care of her myself. Besides, Ghislaine will soon have more than enough to do with her own child."

Isabelle looked like a desperate lioness—one that someone was trying to separate from her young.

"What is it? Why don't you say anything?" she asked after a long moment of silence. "Don't you think my plans make sense?"

Daniel looked across the table at her. A brave woman. A fighter. One who did not accept help easily. Her world had collapsed around her, and she created another one. And now she needed to do that again. He could understand her so well, and yet . . .

He leaned back in his chair and closed his eyes for a moment, then began to talk. "I was eight years old when my father died. Ghislaine was ten. Our father killed himself, but you knew that. And we had lost our mother a few years earlier. Becoming orphans in such a tragic way, well, the people in the village were overflowing with pity for us. Nobody dared to speak loudly or laugh when we were around, and no one even thought about making a silly joke! Everyone looked at us with such somber expressions, all the time. The poor little orphans—that's who we were. Nobody invited us to other children's birthday parties or asked us to go on any adventures. When the other kids went out stealing apples, they didn't want us there, even though I had always been the one who climbed the tallest trees. But everybody seemed to think that everyday life wasn't appropriate to our mourning. And so they tiptoed around us, all the time."

Isabelle was listening intently to his words, but he could not read from her face what she thought about his story. When she said nothing, he continued. "You don't know how many times I wished that someone would simply act normal around us! That someone would give me a clip on the ear if I answered back or that the aunt that we grew up with would send me to my room for all my impudence. But it didn't matter how unruly I was; I got away with it. I was the poor orphan, after all. Then I began to play tricks on the people around me, and the tricks got worse and worse. It got so bad that I burned down one of the protective huts in a vineyard—burned it to the ground. Everybody knew who was behind it, but nobody took me to task." He shook his head. "When I think about it today, the never-ending pity was, for me, almost worse than anything else."

Isabelle's expression was solemn. She sat there, listening, her head lowered.

Daniel reached across the table and lifted her chin a little so that their eyes met. With great tenderness in his voice, he went on. "Do you want to turn your daughter into a cripple with excessive care? Do you want her to feel every day that she isn't normal?" He shook his head adamantly. "If you really want to help Marguerite, then treat her as normally as possible. Let her be herself. If she needs help, you will be there, and the rest of us, too. Isabelle, you are not alone!" he said forcefully. "Ghislaine, Claude, and Micheline—we will be there for Marguerite and you, always."

"But—" Isabelle began.

"No buts," Daniel interrupted. "Here on the estate, Marguerite has the best possible surroundings to grow into a happy person. If you let her."

"But she is so helpless, I have to . . ."

He stood up, moved around the table, and crouched beside Isabelle. With infinite gentleness, he wrapped his arms around her, and she did not resist.

"Everything will work out. We simply take each day as it comes, all right? We make good champagnes, we laugh, and we cry. We live. We love."

Chapter Forty

One suitcase and one travel bag—Isabelle wanted no more with her for her journey to Essoyes so she could manage her bags herself instead of hunting for a porter at every train station. She had stood in front of her wardrobe for a long time deciding on the perfect dress to wear for her portrait sitting with Pierre-Auguste Renoir. Something elegant, something extravagant? Or maybe something simple that would show her more as a person? Perhaps something light, more fitting for the warm sunshine of March? But something in a heavy velvet might be better—the champagne with the new label would be finding its way to customers' tables in the coming fall and winter, after all. In the end, she settled on a sleeveless silk dress in an elegant aqua shade that was decorated with two silk roses on the generous neckline. Isabelle thought that the green shade showed her red hair to advantage; she hoped the painter would agree with her.

When she set off for Essoyes, it would not have been true to say that she was at peace with the world or herself, but she was able to keep from sobbing as she said good-bye to Marguerite, who slept peacefully in the arms of her new nanny, Lucille. The friendly young woman was the daughter of Daniel's previous employer in Épernay and a trained nurse who couldn't pursue her profession in the hospital, because she was fiercely allergic to the disinfectants. Daniel had described Lucille as absolutely trustworthy and had recommended wholeheartedly that Isabelle take her on. After a few trial days to start, Isabelle realized how fortunate they were to have Lucille. The young woman fell in love with Marguerite at first sight, treated her with the greatest tenderness, and called her *ma chouchoute*—my beloved. She had also found a wet nurse for her daughter for the time she would be away. Lucille had to visit the woman twice a day with Marguerite, and the infant would also have reconstituted powdered milk. Isabelle had not known that powdered milk existed, but according to Lucille it had been available for years and was a blessing to mothers who, for whatever reason, were not able to breast-feed their children. Lucille knew everything there was to know about caring for infants, and Isabelle felt sure there couldn't be a better nanny for Marguerite.

Daniel and Micheline had come to the house to wish Isabelle bon voyage. Ghislaine had sent her best wishes for the journey as well; a few days earlier, she had given birth to a healthy baby boy, and she was still rather unsteady on her legs and preferred to stay home.

Her friends now stood beside Lucille and Marguerite like the pillars of a fortress. Isabelle started to tear up, so she was glad to hear Claude Bertrand noisily clear his throat.

"Madame . . ." He was going to drive her the short distance to Épernay, where she would take the mail coach south; a seat had already been reserved for her.

The journey took her via Mailly-le-Camp and Arcis-sur-Aube to Troyes, and from there to Essoyes. Isabelle had written the painter a letter explaining what she wanted. Renoir had immediately sent her a cordial invitation to visit him at his house in the country and had added that it would be an honor for him to paint a champagne widow.

I hope he finds me pretty enough for his canvas, Isabelle thought as the coach rolled through the blooming countryside. In the meadows between the cultivated fields, wild daffodils competed with primroses, and crocuses and blue hyacinths were in full bloom. Sweet aromas drifted in through the half-open window of the coach, heralding the promise of the warm months ahead, and the annually recurring miracle of nature's reawakening was the main topic among the other travelers in the mail coach.

Essoyes was a picture-book village. Whitewashed houses had small front gardens, lethargic cats lolled on sun-drenched windowsills, and washing lines had gleaming white sheets fluttering in the wind. *A place where the world is in order,* thought Isabelle, as she walked through the village with her bags, but then she immediately corrected herself. She had thought exactly the same on her arrival in Hautvillers. *What dramas are unfolding behind these flower boxes and windows?* she wondered, passing by one particularly pretty house. Or was it just normal life, with all its highs and lows? The thought consoled her.

To her surprise, the great artist did not live in a grand mansion, but in a completely normal house with a huge garden. Wherever Isabelle looked, she saw rose bushes and the canes and shoots of climbing roses, but they were only just beginning to bud.

"I regret not coming in June, now. The sight of all the roses in bloom must be extraordinary," she said as she followed Renoir through the garden and into his studio.

The painter nodded. "It's one reason I prefer to live in the country. I see the shifting seasons far more directly out here. They are as perishable as our own lives."

Isabelle smiled thoughtfully. "On days like this, I feel like I'm in the summer of my life. So many aspirations, so much drive to *do* something, but I know the feeling can vanish again tomorrow. Then I'm left more with the sense that the autumn of my life is already here."

"Autumn has its good sides, too, but you, my dear Madame Feininger, seem to me to be spring itself!" the painter said, and his smile deepened the lines of his face. He opened the door to his studio and ushered her inside.

It was almost as bright inside as out, a result of the high, uncurtained windows. Countless canvases were stacked against the walls, and Isabelle wondered what was on them all as she breathed in the smells of paint and turpentine.

Pierre-Auguste Renoir pointed to a wooden stool in the center of the room, a few feet from his easel.

"Please be seated, Madame Feininger, and we can start right away. We have a lot of work ahead of us."

Before she sat down, Isabelle reached into her travel bag for the champagne bottle she had brought with her and set it on a small table covered with tubes of paint. "My customers are supposed to celebrate the turn of the century with this champagne. If you like, I'd be glad to open this bottle for you so that you can get to know the taste of it."

Renoir, however, turned down the offer with a shake of his head and instructed her again to sit on the stool. "A new label with your portrait, am I right?"

Isabelle nodded as she sat on the stool. "It should look more feminine than the old label, more elegant and modern. The aim is to make the bottles stand out from the masses." The sunlight fell through the window directly onto her face and she squinted, but a moment later her eyes had adjusted to the brightness. Her face relaxed, and her shoulders sank. She breathed in deeply, enjoying the sun's warmth.

"Tell me something about your estate and your plans," Renoir said, and Isabelle told him about the new start she and Daniel were making with the place together. When she spoke about her turn-of-the-century wind, the painter applied the first brushstrokes on his canvas. When she had finished telling him about what she and Daniel were doing, he looked up and said, "You speak with so much fire and commitment! I can almost picture your estate in my mind. And your youthful esprit, your passion—if your champagne is only half as captivating as you are, Madame Feininger, then it will be a tremendous success. I can promise you one thing today: you will have the most beautiful label of all time—with you as my model in front of me, it will be child's play."

Renoir completed Isabelle's portrait in just five days. It showed a young woman with a mature expression: her vibrant eyes shone with a mix of confidence and mischievousness, as if she were about to say, "Hello, life, what challenges do you have in store for me now?" After all that life had thrown in her way in the past year, it astonished Isabelle to see that she still possessed such radiance. The colors were both expressive and soft, caressing more than vexing the eye. Isabelle was so enchanted by her likeness that almost the moment she arrived home again, she invited her neighbors and friends to her place to present "her Renoir" to them.

Now, early on a Saturday afternoon, standing in the kitchen with Lucille and arranging cheese snacks and fruit on a silver platter, she could hardly wait to see how the others reacted to it.

"It's just gorgeous!" Micheline cried, clapping her hands enthusiastically.

"A portrait by one of the most famous painters in the world." Carla Chapron sighed longingly. "What wouldn't I give for something like that." She looked at her husband, standing beside her, as if challenging him, but the cooper pretended not to notice.

"Now, don't go getting ideas; you're not nearly as pretty as that," said Ghislaine, good-naturedly mocking her friend. She was standing with the others in front of the small semicircular table on which Isabelle had set up the painting.

"Ghislaine!" hissed Carla immediately.

But Isabelle only laughed. "She's not exactly wrong. Monsieur Renoir really painted me in the best possible light. But I don't mind at all. For the champagne label, the portrait has to be as beautiful as possible. Isn't that true, Monsieur Dupont?"

The champagne dealer nodded. "You look like a true champagne queen! If you will allow it, I'll take it to my label maker first thing on Monday, then I can show you the first drafts of the design at the end of next week. Once you've decided on a label, we should get it to the printer immediately. We have no time to lose if we want to present Feininger champagne in its new brand-new guise on our sales tour."

Isabelle nodded. "What do you think of it?" she asked, turning to Daniel, who had so far been silent. His champagne glass was still full, she noticed. Suddenly, it seemed incredibly important to her to get his approval, too.

Daniel shrugged and said, "If you think it's worth going to all this trouble. I believe the quality of our new champagne speaks for itself." His smile seemed forced. He put down his glass. "I have to get back to the vineyards. Work is waiting."

"But it's Saturday afternoon!" Ghislaine said, perplexed.

It took an effort for Isabelle to hide her disappointment. "I'll come along in a few minutes," she said quietly.

Raymond Dupont, who had stayed in the background during this exchange, stepped forward and said, "I thought we might go over the final details of our tour?"

"If you look at it realistically, the entire world champagne market is dominated by about ten or twelve companies. We're talking about the big names—Pommery, Moët & Chandon, and Veuve Clicquot Ponsardin. These companies invest enormous amounts of money in advertising and other publicity, and their agents are at work practically around the clock. The opera, the racecourses, casinos—you'll find the champagne sellers wherever the rich play," Raymond explained, once the others had left and they were sitting opposite one another in the living room.

"Considering that competition, how am I supposed to get my foot in the door?" Isabelle asked with concern. She dared not even think what would happen if the sales tour was not a success. It would be the end; she would be penniless. A large part of what she had earned from the Americans had already been spent. And almost every day, Daniel came along with new ideas about how the winery could be modernized and the vineyards replanted. And all of it cost a mountain of money.

She shifted Marguerite from her right arm to her left. She looked so cute when she slept!

Raymond opened to another page of his dark-brown leather-bound notebook.

"The year before last, more than twenty-four million bottles of champagne were sold—I think we'll manage to sell yours as well." He smiled encouragingly at Isabelle. "With the quality and the attractive exterior, and by that I don't just mean the bottle . . ."

Isabelle felt her worries draining away again. "Oh, Raymond, what would I do without you?" Spontaneously, she leaned over and grasped his right hand.

"In this huge and extremely difficult market, the art is finding the right niche," Raymond went on. "We can forget the Russian market. The agents from Moët, Roederer, and Ruinart are tripping over each other there. The English are great lovers of champagne, too, but a few of the big names have sewn up that market." He waved his arm as if to say, *But who cares?*

"The Americans, as they always have, prefer sweet champagnes, which puts it out of my reach, too," Isabelle added. "That really only leaves Europe."

Raymond laughed out loud. "The way you said that makes it sound like Europe is just a backwater. Wait until you meet my clientele—with a little luck, they will soon be customers of yours, too."

It was late in the afternoon when Raymond left, and the sun was still high enough to bathe the countryside in its warmth. When Isabelle was finished feeding Marguerite, she laid her in her pram and pushed her outside. A little fresh air would do both of them good. In front of the house, Isabelle hesitated. Should she stroll into the village and pay Ghislaine and her new boy a visit? But following an instinct, she walked instead in the direction of the vineyards. As she pushed the pram over the bumpy grass path, she reviewed her conversation with Raymond. He had so many facts and figures at his fingertips—he really knew his field well. Unless things went completely wrong, their journey would indeed be a success. The thought should have made her happy, but deep inside, Isabelle felt a touch of unease that she couldn't explain.

Her expression only brightened when she discovered who she had unconsciously been seeking. Daniel.

"So your admirers have already left?" he said, without looking up from his work.

"And you? Still not finished?" she replied, referring to the binding wire with which he was affixing an over-long vine shoot to a wooden frame.

Their eyes met, and they smiled.

While Daniel calmly went on tying other shoots in place, Isabelle lifted Marguerite out of the pram. Then she sat down on the soft, mossy earth and arranged her daughter on her lap, where she went on sleeping. Wistfully, Isabelle gazed out at the last thin rays of sunshine descending over the vineyards.

After a few minutes, without a word, Daniel sat beside her. Only then did she notice that he had a small backpack with him. Was he going into the village that evening, or maybe even to Épernay? Isabelle felt a pang in her heart.

"Being able to sleep in any place at any time . . . it's a talent only babies and young children have." He stroked the sleeping child's cheek tenderly. Then he looked up at Isabelle. "Satisfied with Lucille?"

Isabelle nodded. "More than you know. She's a gift from heaven. When I put Marguerite in the pram just now, Lucille gave me a rather doubtful look, as if she would have preferred to keep Marguerite with her." She smiled. She had never thought that a stranger might love her child as much as she herself did. "Why did you leave so soon earlier? I wanted to share a toast with you, to a good year for winegrowers."

"A good year for . . . !" Daniel snorted softly. "We don't need snacks or parties for that, but hard work, sweat, and God's blessing."

"Oh, Daniel," said Isabelle, her expression a little pained. "Yes, I'm proud of the painting, and I was happy to show it to everyone. But all the rest . . . I'm not doing it for the fun of it! You know how important this trip is for us. We can't survive without new customers. I'm happy that Raymond is offering me his help so generously."

"Generous?!" The mockery practically dripped from the word. "Haven't you ever asked yourself *why* he's doing it? He could sell Feininger champagne directly from his shop, but no, he has to go away with you on a long trip to promote it!" He tore a handful of grass out of the ground and threw it away angrily. "I can picture it exactly, you know. How he'll present you as *his* 'champagne queen.' The two of you, staying in elegant hotels, you on his arm . . ."

"Champagne queen—that's nonsense! I'm just a housemaid in disguise." Isabelle laughed, but it sounded false. It wasn't as if the same thought hadn't occurred to her. Sometimes Raymond looked at her strangely, as if he, like Daniel, had fallen a little bit in love with her. And then there was the way he'd remarked, just before Christmas, that he would marry the woman of his dreams in an instant. Had Clara perhaps been right? And now Daniel, too?

"In case you hadn't noticed, Raymond is just as charming with every woman," she said delicately. "Why should he behave any differently around me? And he didn't organize this trip especially for me, as it happens. He planned it to deepen his *own* clientele. You really are seeing things that aren't there." As she spoke, a small smile played around her lips. Daniel sounded like a jealous husband!

Instead of answering, Daniel pulled over his backpack, untied the top, and took out a loaf of bread, a hunk of cheese, sausage, a bottle of champagne, and two glasses.

Isabelle's brow furrowed when she saw the second glass. Had he been counting on her coming out here? Or had he been planning to share his repast with someone else? *Now who's the jealous one?* she asked herself scornfully.

He handed her a piece of the bread and sausage and opened the bottle. He poured a little into his own glass, sniffed it for a second, then held the straw-yellow liquid against the light of the setting sun. Satisfied with what he saw, he took a mouthful; when that seemed to measure up, he poured both their glasses full.

With anyone else, Isabelle would have seen this routine as pedantic. Or even worse, as pompous. But with Daniel, every gesture showed no more than his love for champagne.

"People are rarely what they appear to be at first glance. Few act with noble motives; most have only their own interests at heart," he said, handing her a glass. "I just don't want anyone to hurt you."

"I know," Isabelle replied gently. They clinked glasses, and when she drank, the liquid was soft and spicy on her tongue.

She thought about how comfortable it was to sit there with Daniel and say nothing as they looked out over the valley. His body radiated more warmth than a heavy wool blanket. *Wouldn't it be lovely if he were to take me in his arms, right now?* The thought flitted through Isabelle's mind before she could stop it. *And what if he really did?* she immediately wondered, her inner voice harsh. *You'd turn away like some straitlaced virgin, reprimand him, and blather something about "unnecessary complications."*

Would she really?

If she were to be honest with herself, she had to admit that the more she was around Daniel, the more attractive she found him. His very nature, which she had come to know more in recent months, was of honesty and kindness and perseverance when it really mattered. She could rely on him and trust him. But she liked his wavy hair and his copper-brown eyes, too. On his forearms, wispy red-gold hair covered his lightly tanned skin.

Isabelle looked at him out of lowered eyes and saw the pulse beating at his throat. And suddenly, she felt lonely and vulnerable.

He turned to her then, and kissed her. His lips on hers. Soft, and yet so firm. As his lips parted, Isabelle had the sensation that a door to a secret garden had been thrown open. His breath was warm and carried promise. Instinctively, she followed his movements. He tasted of wine but also of something more austere—it was the aroma of the vines, transformed into his very own scent. His lips wandered from her mouth to her cheek, her forehead, her eyes. He asked for nothing, gave all he had, and still Isabelle had the feeling of being unable to get enough of him. But then Marguerite squirmed on her lap, and he gently released her.

His eyes were filled with tenderness as he said, "While you're away . . . promise me you'll take care of yourself."

On May 2, Raymond and Isabelle planned to travel to Munich, the first destination of their tour. Vienna and her hometown of Berlin would follow; all in all, the journey would last several weeks.

To be separated so long from Marguerite and everything she loved and held dear . . . and not being in Hautvillers on the anniversary of Leon's death—more than once, Isabelle came close to sending Raymond a note to cancel everything. But every time, she pulled herself together again. She had to look ahead. Marguerite's future depended entirely on Isabelle's own destiny. And that of the Feininger estate.

The closer the day of their departure loomed, the more nervous Isabelle grew. She had no time to help Daniel in the vineyards, and there were no more intimate moments between them. Isabelle didn't know if she was supposed to be happy about that or not, but there was simply too much she had to organize for the time she'd be away. Raymond was taking care of all the details of the trip itself, but Isabelle had to make sure that many crates of Feininger champagne were dispatched to the addresses Raymond had given her in Munich, Vienna, and Berlin. Isabelle was surprised by the quantities Raymond had requested from her. She'd assumed that a single trial bottle per customer would be enough. It also struck her as unusual that some of the addresses to which the champagne was to be shipped were those of private homes. But Raymond no doubt knew what he was doing.

Another concern that occupied a lot of her time was her wardrobe. On this trip, she would not be traveling lightly. Raymond had asked her to be prepared for any circumstance—major receptions, private dinner parties with future customers, perhaps a visit to the horse races, or attendance at garden parties and the opera. Isabelle carefully selected everything from simple cotton dresses to elegant ball gowns, and packed it all between sheets of tissue paper in her luggage. *It looks like I'm going away forever*, she thought with a frown as she finally closed the belt around the last case.

May 2 was grim and gray, and it might have been a November day but for the spring growth on the grapevines and trees. Fog hung over the vines and made no sign of lifting, and the mercury barely rose above fifty degrees. Dressed in her traveling clothes, she gave her serious-looking reflection a final once-over before leaving the bedroom. In the mirror, she saw a woman who looked as if she were about to go to the gallows rather than on a fabulous journey, but she was simply unable to plaster on a smile. Her feet felt heavy as she descended the stairs.

"Is everything all right?" she asked Lucille, who was standing in the kitchen humming a tune to herself and peeling kohlrabi for lunch. The question was unnecessary, for Marguerite was sleeping peacefully in her crib by the window.

Lucille smiled. "As soon as Marguerite wakes up, I'll warm some water and give her a bath. Our little darling always loves that. Don't worry, madame. I'll watch out for her as if she were my own."

"Don't worry." Easier said than done. Isabelle sighed, gave her sleeping daughter a kiss, and went out to the vineyards. It was time to say good-bye to Daniel.

She had not reached the first row of vines when she saw Micheline coming toward her, or rather, running toward her.

"Micheline . . ." Isabelle began, but the older woman waved off the pleasantries and did not slow down as she passed Isabelle.

"No time, Isabelle, no time, I have to get more . . . !"

"More?" More what? Frowning, Isabelle watched her friend scurry past. As much as Isabelle hated good-byes, a quick adieu couldn't hurt, could it?

When Isabelle finally spotted her cellar master among the vines, she frowned more deeply. Dressed in gray protective overalls, Daniel was standing among the vines with their delicate spring leaves and spraying them with a strange-looking liquid. Beside him stood several metal drums that presumably contained whatever it was he was spraying. He was so focused on his work that he did not hear her approach.

"Daniel! What in the world are you doing?"

He jumped at her voice. Then he put the spraying equipment down on the ground and went to her.

"Isabelle . . ." He did not seem especially pleased to see her.

"What are you doing?" Isabelle asked again. "And what's gotten into Micheline? She just ran past me like the devil was after her."

Daniel sighed deeply, his eyes wandering from the metal canisters to her. "Oh, Isabelle, I wanted to spare you the bad news on the morning of your departure."

"What bad news?" Isabelle almost shrieked.

"Yesterday evening, Micheline discovered some galling on the underside of the young leaves on some vines in her northern parcel. The galls are little brown growths that don't belong there."

"So what?" asked Isabelle, her impatience growing. A bit of discoloration on the leaves wasn't the end of the world, was it?

"It means that phylloxera aphids have returned to Hautvillers. A few years ago, we had an infestation of the things; that time, we got off lightly. This year, God only knows."

Isabelle took a deep breath. "But . . . who . . . how . . ." This couldn't be happening. Isabelle's knees grew weak just thinking about it. She sat down helplessly on one of the drums.

Of all the bad news that might affect her vines, this was the worst she could think of.

In recent years, phylloxera had decimated large areas in the southern part of Champagne. Hundreds of livelihoods were lost, and it would probably be generations before the vineyards were fully restocked. The vintners she had met in Troyes, who were trying to sell their champagne to the Americans, had had tears in their eyes when they told her about the blight that had befallen them.

"How could this happen?" she cried in despair, and with a hint of accusation in her voice. "What makes you think that they're here in our vines, too?" She stood up, almost in a panic, and plucked off a few young leaves. "Look! They're perfect. The prettiest May green you'll see. If we have to worry about anything, then it's the Ice Saints just around the corner."

"Misery loves company—you're right about that," said Daniel through gritted teeth. "The fact that our vineyards aren't yet showing any signs means nothing. Phylloxera live underground. They latch onto the roots and spread a deadly fungal infection in the process. The fungus kills off the roots. By the time we would see the first signs on the plant itself, it's too late. But if they've reached Micheline's vines, the danger is on the way!" He kicked so furiously at the ground that he broke out little chunks. Then he pointed to the spray bottle. "That's a mix of water, sulfur, and copper."

"Insecticide? That should take care of them, shouldn't it?" Isabelle looked trustingly at Daniel.

He shrugged. "It might stop them from spreading this far. But if they're already here, then nothing will help."

In her mind's eye, Isabelle saw an image of grapevines picked clean. Vines with neither leaves nor grapes. Dry, lifeless wood . . . is that what would greet her on her return?

"Oh, Daniel." Her voice was no more than a whisper. She had a sudden, almost overwhelming impulse to jump up and run away, to flee the constant stream of problems.

"Don't hang your head just yet. If we're lucky, this particular storm will pass us by," said Daniel softly, and he sat on one of the canisters beside her. He took her hand and squeezed it. For a long moment they sat there, staring at nothing.

It was Daniel who broke the silence. "I have an idea that I'd like to discuss with you. It would protect us from the phylloxera once and for all."

Isabelle turned to listen.

"I'd like to replace all our vines, bit by bit, with phylloxera-resistant rootstock."

"Phylloxera what?"

"Grapevines that are resistant to the aphids. You need to have what they call *vignes-mères*—mother vines or rootstock—that are absolutely resistant to phylloxera. This rootstock would then have our grape varieties grafted onto it. They specialize in producing these *vignes-mères* in the south, and I'd like to order plants for our vineyards from there. Not for all of them at once, of course, but we should start with at least a few acres. What do you think?"

More costs, thought Isabelle anxiously.

"But aren't we already too late in the year?" she asked. "I remember reading in one of Jacques's books that new vines are always planted in March."

"Better late than never." Daniel shrugged. "Besides, the two women we'd need to have for the grafting—the two real experts—wouldn't have had any time in March. Every year, they spend March and April working for Henriette Trubert." His expression darkened at the thought of his old employer.

It was no different for Isabelle. The old witch was one step ahead of her, yet again.

"I have no doubt that it's all very expensive," she said despondently.

"I know a few of the *vignes-mères* suppliers very well. I could try to arrange a deferred payment with them. I'm sure they would agree to being paid in three months' time. And as far as the two women are concerned, they're incredibly fast. They can do up to fifteen hundred plants a day and do outstanding work. If you agree, I'll book them for two days at the end of May."

"Do I have a choice?" Isabelle sighed.

"If we want to survive in the long-term, then no." Daniel embraced her and kissed her tentatively on the forehead. "We'll make it! Don't worry. I'll take care of everything while you're gone."

Pressed to Daniel's chest, Isabelle noticed from the corner of her eye Claude leading the two horses out of the stall. He would hitch them to the wagon and drive it around to the front of the house. And suddenly, the torment of parting was too much for her. What would she have given to be able to stay there in Daniel's arms? But at the same time, any doubt she had had about her pending journey dissolved instantly in the face of this new threat. The pain she felt at leaving, her fears—she had to forget all of it. She took a deep breath and said, "You're right. We can't capitulate to a tiny aphid. I'll go sell your champagne. For what we have ahead of us, we'll need every franc I can bring back home."

Chapter Forty-One

"Faster! Faster! Gallop, you miserable nag!"

"Come on, White Princess!"

Wringing her hands, Isabelle stood in the grandstand at Vienna's Freudenau Racecourse and, like the other spectators at the racetrack, cheered on her favorite. She had no eye for the virtues of the facility itself, the beautiful country meadows on which it was situated, or even for the radiant May day that flooded the track and the visitors with sunshine from a clear blue sky. The place smelled of sawdust and horse sweat, expensive perfume and excitement. But all that held Isabelle's attention were the goings-on down on the track, even though, when they had first arrived, Raymond practically had to force her to bet a few coins on one of the horses. Isabelle had no desire to stand there like a spoilsport, so she chose a mare simply because she liked her name. And now it looked as if White Princess might actually gallop home first.

"Run, White Princess, run!" Isabelle cried. In her excitement, she dug her fingers into Raymond's right arm. The women around them had long before given up their aplomb and were jumping around and cheering or cursing, depending on which horse they had bet on. The men acted more casual about the whole affair, but if one looked more closely, one could see that they gripped their walking sticks so tightly their knuckles turned white. One man sucked so forcefully on his cigar that the ash tumbled onto his jacket.

The last race of the day finished with White Princess placing second. Isabelle still beamed; she would never have believed that a visit to the racecourse could be so exciting.

"What amazing fun that was!" said the owner of the Hotel Imperial, patting at her red cheeks with gloved hands. "Maybe I should get out of my office more often!" She giggled girlishly.

Her friend, Countess Esterhazy, nodded. "We needed a Frenchman to come along and drag us out of our ivory tower." She spontaneously squeezed Raymond's arm. "No wonder we look forward so much to your visits. You've always got something new on the boil."

"If you say so," replied Raymond, with both charm and modesty. Then he looked around at the group that had gathered around him. "May I invite you all, ladies and gentlemen, to a little refreshment? Fresh strawberry cake at the Spritzer Café and perhaps a glass of champagne?"

Isabelle smiled when Raymond offered his arms to the two women and led them in the direction of the elegant café on the fringe of the racecourse. Chatting happily, the rest of the group followed them.

"Well, my dear widow Feininger, what do you think of our Vienna?" asked Gottlieb Bauer, another of their little group and the owner of one of the most splendid restaurants in the city, at Stephansplatz.

"It's beautiful!" Isabelle reeled off the list of the sights she had already visited. She was also astonished by the outstanding celebrity of Raymond's business contacts. Most were purveyors to the Imperial and Royal Monarchy, but his clientele also included Countess Esterhazy. If the countess decided that she preferred a particular drink or dish, then its respective vendor would do well to have plentiful stock of it, because half of Vienna would soon be following suit.

"I am so glad to be able to experience so many wonderful days here in the city," Isabelle said.

"And Vienna is proud and happy to be able to welcome the renowned and beautiful widow Feininger as its guest," Gottlieb Bauer replied.

The group sat down at a sunlit table by the window. Small bouquets of roses decorated the table, which had been set with white damask, Nymphenburg porcelain, and silver cutlery. Two champagne coolers stood by the table—it came as no surprise to see the Veuve Rougette in them: Raymond had already informed the owner of the café in advance about exactly what he wanted. Her escort was a perfectionist, no more and no less.

Raymond, of course, could have sought out each of his customers individually in their respective places of business. He could have sat himself down at a table, pulled out a list of what he had to offer, and introduced one champagne after another. But traveling like this, he sold champagne in a far more elegant and less obtrusive way, with a style that Isabelle had first had the opportunity to observe in Munich.

Raymond took his customers out of their usual surroundings, offering them something out of the ordinary, and relying on what he called the "champagne state of mind"—a great help when it came to placing large orders—to develop all by itself. For many Viennese, a visit to the racecourse might be nothing special, but for these men and women, corseted tightly within the inflexibilities of social convention and business appointments, Raymond's invitation was an adventure. At first, it had confused Isabelle that one hardly so much as mentioned champagne during such outings. Now, she smiled as she remembered their first meeting in Munich.

They had spent hours sitting in the English Garden with the owner of Munich's largest gourmet food shop. Like Isabelle, the woman was a widow, and together they had talked about the breeding of standard poodles, the businesswoman's personal hobby. With every stud that the woman spoke rapturously about, Isabelle grew more and more unsettled. At breakfast, Raymond had boasted that he was counting on an order of twelve hundred bottles of Feininger champagne, so when—blast it all!—would the talk finally swing around to business? Isabelle had put together a carefully worded speech about the ambitious goals that she and her cellar master were pursuing, and it seemed that no one wanted to hear a word of it.

"Word of your success as a breeder has naturally spread far beyond Munich," said Raymond when the woman was done telling them in detail about her most recent litter. "Though I don't own one myself, I love dogs above all other animals. As a token of my recognition for your breeding work, I had a crate of Feininger champagne sent to you last week," he went on. "A first-class Feininger rosé—nothing else would do. I trust it was the right choice for you and the buyers of your puppies?"

Horrified, Isabelle inhaled sharply. Her champagne was supposed to be sold in the woman's famous gourmet shop, not set before any old dog owners!

"Ah, the widow's pink champagne. Just delicious." The woman nodded with satisfaction. "You know," she said in her strong Bavarian dialect, "the people only ever expect the best from us, not only with the dogs, but with everything." She turned away from Raymond and looked at Isabelle. "It's a good champagne you've got there, Frau Feininger. And such a pretty picture on the bottle. I wonder if the artist might paint my dogs? How many bottles of Veuve Rougette could we have?" The last question was again directed at Raymond.

Raymond's face transformed to a look of concern. "Not as many as I'm sure you would like," he said with regret.

"But—" Isabelle began, only to be immediately interrupted by Raymond's warning glance.

"Oh, come now," the businesswoman had said, poking Raymond playfully in the ribs. "Getting me all excited and then ducking? That's not fair! Two thousand bottles is what I want. We've got a big year this year!"

"So what do you say, shall we take a ride on the Ferris wheel in Prater after this?" said Raymond now, when they all had their strawberry cake in front of them and had clinked their glasses of Feininger champagne.

Instead of answering, the owner of the Hotel Imperial peered as if in a trance at the countless tiny pearls in her glass. Countess Esterhazy, too, seemed to have no great interest in a ride on a big wheel. "Ravishing," she sighed, over the top of her glass. "My dear widow Feininger, you have created a wonderful drop here! From now on, this is the only champagne I drink," she announced, and took another big mouthful.

Isabelle smiled delightedly.

"A wise decision," said Raymond, and lifted his glass in a toast to the countess. "There is only one drink on earth that can make a beautiful woman more beautiful—champagne! I would add that rosé certainly does justice to its name; it adds a special rosy hue to a lady's complexion."

"Then I shall make sure I keep a little private stock of Feininger Rougette," said the manageress of the Hotel Imperial, patting her cheeks, again pale, affectedly.

"And what about a little for me, my ladies?" said Gottlieb Bauer then. "If I may be permitted, I would very much like to stock Veuve Rougette myself. In the coming months, Stephansplatz will host celebrations practically back-to-back—not including New Year's Eve. I can tell you now that the guests at my restaurant will have a great thirst for champagne."

Raymond smiled mildly. "It will take me a small miracle to satisfy all your wishes, you know!" He winked gleefully at Isabelle.

"Today, we're going to treat ourselves to a day off, just for us," said Raymond during breakfast the next morning in the elegant dining room of the Hotel Imperial. Isabelle, who was reading a note she had just received from Lucille, nodded absently. Marguerite was developing wonderfully well, Lucille wrote, then she listed all the things that she and little Marguerite had been doing together. It seemed the young woman had gotten into the habit of going out into the vineyards with the pram and lending a hand among the vines. She enjoyed the work very much, Lucille wrote, and the fresh air did Marguerite good. How reassuring. And yet the thought of red-cheeked, full-breasted young Lucille working side by side with Daniel did not please Isabelle at all. More important, though, she appreciated the brief updates, which reassured Isabelle that Marguerite was not wanting in any way while she was gone.

"Did I hear you correctly? We have no business scheduled for today?" she asked when she had folded Lucille's letter again and tucked it into her handbag.

"You have just over a third of your champagne stock left. I'm sure you'd like to create as much of a furor with that in your hometown as you have in Munich and Vienna, wouldn't you?"

"If anyone has caused a furor, then I would look no further than yourself," Isabelle replied rather ruefully. "I'm coming to think that my being here isn't really necessary at all. *You* are the one persuading these people. You and Daniel's artistry."

So they had already sold most of it! Raymond had the exact numbers in his order book—he received a commission for every bottle sold, after all—but Isabelle had kept a rough count in her head as well, and she was happy to have that confirmed. She tore excitedly at the crumbly croissant on her plate.

Raymond refilled her coffee. "Practicing your false modesty, my dear? Every one of my customers has assured me of how happy they were to meet the beautiful, clever widow Feininger in person."

Isabelle smiled. "Let's not argue about who is more responsible for our success. The main point is that our trip *is* a success!"

"That, my dear, is beyond doubt." Raymond took another sip of coffee. "I do, in fact, have one appointment late this afternoon, but I won't be introducing your champagne there. My other brands have to have some exposure, too. But until five this afternoon, we're as free as two birds." He made a playful fluttering movement with his hands. "We could take a walk through the city, go to one of the many museums, visit the Spanish Riding School, or stroll through the garden at Schönbrunn Palace—whatever you feel like."

Isabelle leaned back in the soft upholstery of her chair. "A day for nothing but pleasure," she said pensively. "I can't remember the last time I had a day like that. At home, it's always work, work, work. You finish one task, and the next one is already waiting for you."

"A woman like you ought to be enjoying her life, not spending her days slaving like a farmer's wife," he said reproachfully. "May I make a suggestion? Let's just go for a walk. I am certain we will see Vienna at its best."

And they did. They ambled along Mariahilfer Strasse, where elegant shops were lined up side by side. So many beautiful things! Again and again, small cries of delight escaped Isabelle. When her feet began to ache, they stopped a carriage, which took them to the Hotel Sacher. There, they drank hot cocoa, and Raymond nagged Isabelle into trying a slice of the hotel's famous Sacher torte.

"If you keep forcing food into me like this, I won't fit into any of my dresses anymore," she protested, laughing, then immediately stabbed the chocolate cake with her fork.

In Alfred Gerngross's department store, Isabelle spent a good hour going through their enormous selection of fabrics. Her dresses still fit her, to be sure, but her wardrobe, most of which had come with her from Berlin, was hopelessly old-fashioned. Alongside the stylishly dressed women she was meeting, she felt like an ugly duckling, and she did *not* want that to happen the next time she went abroad. She had just decided on a length of taffeta and another of silk. She wondered aloud about which seamstress in Hautvillers she could entrust with the valuable cloth, and Raymond asked whether they might not do better to look for a ready-made dress.

They moved on to Herzmansky's store on Stiftgasse, where Isabelle stared in disbelief at the racks of hundreds and hundreds of dresses. Day dresses and opulent ball gowns made of fine silk and warm woolen fabric. Matching gloves, hats, and scarves were displayed in glass cabinets, and the store even sold shoes. Isabelle would have loved to try on every dress, but when she saw the prices, discreetly attached at the hem of each dress, she blanched. A single dress cost more than she paid Claude and Daniel together in a month!

Raymond, noticing her reticence and interpreting it correctly, said, "You have brought me a great deal of luck on this trip, Isabelle. Not only has your champagne sold well, but the other brands I represent have also. Allow me to make a gift to you of two or three dresses, please! And look at these wonderful shoes; you should try them on, too." He repeated his offer so insistently that Isabelle finally gave in.

While Raymond sat in a leather armchair and accepted the offer of a glass of cognac, Isabelle followed one of the saleswomen into a spacious changing room. She tried on first one dress and then another, proudly presenting them to Raymond, who turned out to be not very helpful, because he found *all* of them beautiful. Isabelle giggled. It was like being a child again, when Papa accompanied her and *Maman* when they went shopping.

"Send them to the Hotel Imperial," Raymond instructed the saleswoman when he had paid for the three dresses that Isabelle liked the most. Then she took his arm, and they stepped back out on the street. Isabelle, dizzy from trying on so many dresses, followed him blindly, and it was only when they had gone several blocks that she realized they were not walking in the direction of the hotel, but back toward the store where she had first looked at all the fabric.

Raymond, who saw the puzzled look on her face, stifled his smile. "Thought we were finished, did you? No, it can't be that only Mama Isabelle gets to pretty herself up; we're going to buy some of that lovely material, and you can have something beautiful tailored for your little daughter as well. I'm sure I saw you admiring some delicate pink lace earlier."

Isabelle was in seventh heaven.

***

The blissful feeling did not subside later that evening. "What a good idea to come here," said Isabelle, taking a bite of her grilled mackerel.

When Raymond returned from his business meeting, he did not take her to an elegant restaurant as he normally did, but out to Vienna's expansive Prater park. Now, they were sitting in one of the rustic restaurants that offered simple fare in the shadow of the huge Ferris wheel. It was a warm evening, and the Prater was full of young couples in love, holding hands and laughing as they strolled among the trees and across the meadows. The smoky smell of the mackerel that Raymond and Isabelle had decided on for dinner mixed with the scent of the roses, in full bloom, that climbed the wooden wall of the restaurant.

Were the roses in her vineyards blooming, too? she wondered. As quickly as the question appeared in Isabelle's mind, so did it disappear again. Hautvillers, the vineyards, the phylloxera—it was all so far away.

"The simplest things in life can be wonderful when one enjoys them together," said Raymond and he smiled fondly at her. "What is it they say? Joy shared is joy doubled."

Isabelle nodded. "And nothing is worse than loneliness." *Like the time after Leon died,* she thought to herself. For a moment, neither said a word, but then Isabelle dragged herself out of her gloomy thoughts. She took a sip of her wine and said, "This trip . . . to be honest, I was a little afraid of it. I had no idea what was waiting for me out here. And now, every day is more beautiful than the one before it. If I just think of all the wonderful people I've had the honor to meet . . . and the elegant hotels, the many unforgettable moments. Like this one." She swung one hand wide, a gesture encompassing the whirl of activity in the Prater. "I truly believe that today was one of the loveliest days of my life."

"And yet, the best is still to come: your triumphal march to Berlin!" said Raymond.

"Triumphal march—that remains to be seen," Isabelle replied, frowning.

She was, of course, looking forward to seeing Josephine and Clara again. Clara especially, from whom she had not heard since her last visit and to whom she wanted to take a huge bouquet of flowers to apologize for her own unforgivable behavior.

"Visiting my old hometown again—frankly, the thought makes me feel a little panicky. Back then, you know, I left Berlin literally overnight and followed Leon blindly. My father had completely different marriage plans for me, and after I left, he cut me off; I was supposed to marry into Berlin society, and those people, I'm quite sure, did not think very much of my actions. And now I'm supposed to sell my champagne to the *same* high society?"

Raymond, who had been listening closely, laughed out loud. "Don't lose any sleep about Berlin society. Between us, we'll have them wrapped around our little fingers. But your parents . . . have you really lost contact with them completely?"

Isabelle nodded unhappily.

"That can be changed," said Raymond slowly. "An arranged meeting . . ."

Isabelle shook her head. "I don't know." One hand went to her throat as if to loosen a too-tight collar. "Meeting them again, after all that's happened?"

Raymond smiled gently at her. "It's just a thought, no more. I want you to be happy and to feel comfortable. Nothing else matters."

"I *am* happy. This whole trip is like a long, lovely dream. After all the troubles in the last few months, I never would have thought it possible to feel so . . . so at ease again." She shook her head. "And I owe all of it to you." She took his hand and squeezed it.

***

A carafe of fine mineral water stood on the nightstand, and beside it, a bowl of sliced fruit. The chambermaid had turned back the eiderdown for the night—in the Hotel Imperial, no luxury was spared when it came to the comfort of tired travelers. But Raymond felt anything but tired just then; in fact, he felt more fresh and alive than he had felt in a very long time. For a moment, he considered going back down to the bar for a cognac, but then he thought better of it. Early the next morning, they would be leaving for Berlin. The trip would be long and arduous, and it would be better to have a good night's sleep behind him before embarking on such a journey.

Raymond was about to climb into bed when he noticed the cream-colored envelope lying beside the fruit bowl. His curiosity turned to a deep frown when he recognized the handwriting. What in the world did Henriette Trubert want from him?

Hautvillers, May 15

Dear Raymond,
I hope my letter finds you in good health. Everything is running as usual here in Champagne. Last week I was in Reims and decided to visit your shop. Your assistant there, Madame Colette, was as stiff as if she had swallowed a stick, and I am far from confident that your customers are happy with her, or if you will be happy with her revenues.

Raymond grimaced. It was May 22, so the letter had been posted a week earlier. Madame Colette was the spinsterish daughter of a vigneron. She certainly understood something of the industry, but had such an aloof manner that she could almost be described as unsociable, not an ideal trait when one worked in the sales field. His customers would have to accept it until Raymond found someone to replace her because if everything went according to plan, he would be traveling more often in the future.

Do you remember the trips we took together? We never made it beyond Paris, but we had some wonderful times, didn't we?

Why was Henriette going back over that old history *now*? Was she getting sentimental in her later years? And, more important, why had she written him the letter at all? He could not remember telling her about the route he would be following, which meant that she must have gotten his address in Vienna from Madame Colette. He read on, and Henriette's intentions quickly became clear: her insatiable nosiness. And greed.

> *I hope your courting of your wife-to-be has been a success? The mental picture I have of the young widow Feininger lying in your arms makes me very happy. You have been alone far too long, my darling. And loneliness makes old men strange. Besides, I'm sure you will do your best to talk your future bride into getting rid of that millstone, namely her estate, as quickly as possible. You should be free to share a wonderful, unfettered life, after all. And to travel to whatever far-off countries you like. You know I'm ready, and that I pay well. My offer will convince even you, my shrewd businessman.*

Raymond did not know if he ought to laugh or be outraged at such brazenness. Typical Henriette!

But if anyone had a couple of aces up his sleeve, he did. Dear Henriette did not know it yet, but she was the last person in the world he would sell the Feininger estate to. But all of that was a long way off, and he still had a good deal of work ahead of him.

Work—the word sounded so dry. *Winning Isabelle was not* work, he rebuked himself. She was the most captivating being he knew. He could have sat for hours, just looking at her. It was no different for other men, he knew, and he practically nourished himself on the envious looks cast in his direction whenever he appeared with Isabelle on his arm. She was clever, articulate without being talkative, and she had a wonderful sense of humor. She could even laugh at herself—a talent very few people had. She was the woman he had spent his life waiting for. After all his professional success, winning Isabelle would be the crowning achievement of his life. Through her, he would dupe old age: when he was around her, he felt younger and more agile than he had in twenty years. "Madame Isabelle Dupont"—the name rang softly and harmoniously in his ears.

But did she feel the same way? Could she imagine a life at his side? After all the long coach rides and train trips, after all the excursions, dinners, visits to the opera, and everything else they had done together in the last few weeks, he still could not say with any certainty where he stood with her. It was clear to him that she felt some affection for him. She showed him as much, again and again, like that same evening in the Prater. And she admired him greatly as a businessman.

He frowned. Or did she still only see him as a fatherly friend?

Raymond suddenly had the feeling that he could not spend a minute more than necessary with this question. He dressed quickly, snatched up the key to his room, and went out.

Down in the bar, he was met by the sound of a piano being played softly. A few night owls, returning from the opera or the theater, were seated at small tables and drinking champagne or wine. Raymond took a seat at the bar and ordered a cognac. Then he leaned back to listen to the piano. It wasn't long before his earlier train of thought returned.

In the first two weeks of their journey, Isabelle had been as skittish as a young horse under a saddle for the first time. Her thoughts were constantly turning to her daughter and the estate. Did they really have phylloxera to deal with now, too? What would the rootstock cost that Daniel wanted to order? Things had been particularly bad in Munich on the anniversary of Leon's death, where she had come to breakfast distraught, her eyes red from crying. That same day, Raymond had scheduled an appointment with an important customer, but it would have been impossible to take Isabelle with him in that state. To sell champagne, or anything else, one needed to be in a good mood. So he had ordered a carriage and instructed the driver to take Isabelle for a long drive along the meadows beside the Isar river. The green of the meadowlands and the sound of wavelets along the shore had apparently done her good, for when they met again in the hotel late that afternoon, she was in much better spirits.

The pianist reached the end of his melody, and the guests responded with light applause. Raymond waved the young man over and pressed a coin into his hand. Then he asked him to play something jauntier. Maybe that would turn his head to happier thoughts. When he thought about it, however, he realized that he was not actually unhappy, but simply impatient. And Isabelle was not the kind of woman whose heart could be won in a hurry.

In any case, he sensed that her anxiety and thoughts about her home had diminished over the course of their journey, and that she was more . . . with him.

Raymond emptied his glass. The big question was, would she say yes if he asked her to marry him?

Deep inside, he believed that she would, but a grain of uncertainty remained. He hoped that, in Berlin at the latest, he would feel wholly confident. If everything went as planned there, Isabelle could hardly do anything else but accept him.

Chapter Forty-Two

It was an odd feeling to walk again through the streets where she had grown up, and Isabelle hoped she would not see her mother or father by accident. The farther she walked along Görlitzer Strasse, the stronger the feeling of strangeness became. Had it really been only two years since her sudden departure? It felt like decades.

The old shoemaker's shop was still there, and the pharmacy run by Anton Berg, Clara's father. Reutter's Emporium, the department store on the corner, had actually gotten bigger, and a milliner's had opened up next door. Despite its inviting display, Isabelle had too much on her mind to spend very long looking at the pretty head coverings. From the Görlitzer train station came the brake squealing and hissing of arriving trains, while from the smithy operated by Josephine's father came the penetrating stink of singed hooves. Luisenstadt still seemed to be a lively part of the city. Only at Josephine's former workshop were the shutters closed, and the house that Isabelle's friend had inherited from old Frieda gave an impression of being looked after but not lived in. Isabelle frowned. Hadn't Josephine and Adrian moved in there after they were married? She hadn't heard anything about them moving. Confused, she walked in the direction of Clara's house on the next corner. Clara would know.

"Isabelle! What a surprise."

"Bonjour, Clara!" Isabelle did an exaggerated curtsy. "I'm sorry I couldn't say exactly when Raymond and I would get here, or I would have gotten in touch," she said and handed Clara the bouquet. "That's for you. I know I can't possibly make up for my intolerable behavior when you visited, but I would at least like to apologize." Less flippantly, she added, "I simply did not want to believe that something was wrong with Marguerite, you know?"

Hesitantly, Clara accepted the bouquet through the half-open door. "That really wasn't necessary," she murmured. "Is Raymond . . . also here?" She looked almost fearfully over Isabelle's shoulder.

Isabelle laughed. "Oh, God no! I left him in the Grand Hotel. I prefer to meet my girlfriends unaccompanied. But don't you want to offer me a cup of coffee? Or have I come at a bad time? I can go to Josephine first, and we could meet later on. Where is she, by the way? Did she and Adrian move?"

Clara, still standing in the dim light of the hallway, nodded. "Adrian's father gave them a villa on the edge of the city. He wanted his grandson to live in a house that befits his station." There was more than a trace of mockery in her voice, but the next moment her shoulders slumped. She sounded as if she were in an abyss of despair as she continued: "Isabelle, I'm so sorry, but today is really not a good day for a visit. Gerhard is—" She broke off as if she had changed her mind about saying the words. "Isabelle, I beg of you, watch out for yourself and make the right decision! Once you've made your bed, you have to lie in it, no matter how hard it is. Raymond adores you; I saw that in Reims. You would be well off with him at your side!"

Isabelle wanted to laugh to lift the weight off the moment, but the laugh stuck in her throat. "What's going on, Clara? You're being so strange!" She narrowed her eyes to get a better look at Clara's face in the low light. Was she mistaken, or was there a blue shadow beneath Clara's left eye? A terrible thought came to Isabelle.

Clara immediately took a step back. "Everything is all right," she said with a forced smile. "It's just that I don't have any time today for a gossip over coffee. Gerhard needs me at the practice."

"But I was so looking forward to talking to you. And I would love to see little Matthias again." Isabelle was both disappointed and confused.

Clara sighed. "Matthias is with my mother, and it is better if he stays there today. Now go, please!"

Josephine skillfully screwed a small gas lamp onto an old bicycle. "There. Now Mr. Draber can ride safely through the city in the dark, too. Can you hand me that rag?"

Isabelle, sitting on a stool in Josephine's bicycle workshop, did as she was asked. "Almost like old times," she said and smiled. "Do you remember? Just after you opened your old repair shop, I stopped in to visit you. Then someone knocked at the door and this self-important civil servant came in. He wanted to give you a friendly reminder that you had to pay your taxes."

Josephine, dusting the lamp, groaned. "I was so stupid and naïve! I'd thought of everything except actually registering my business. Thank God you were there; I wouldn't have been able to deal with the man alone."

For a moment, they reveled in the old familiarity. Then, with a little difficulty, Josephine stood up and ran her hands over the swell of her belly.

"I need a break. There's a little restaurant just opened up down the street. They serve the best pea soup in Berlin. Shall we go?"

"I'm worried about Clara," said Isabelle, sitting with Josephine. Bowls of soup and large mugs of coffee were between them.

Josephine chewed at her bottom lip, but said nothing.

"Clara? What's the matter?" asked Adrian, who had spontaneously decided to join them.

Isabelle looked at her former fiancé. Marriage suited him: he gave an impression of satisfaction and happiness.

Isabelle put her spoon aside and told them about her strange meeting with Clara at her front door. "Do you think that terrible Gerhard beats her?" Simply asking the question was bad enough for Isabelle; the thought was truly horrible.

"If I ever see him try it . . . ," said Adrian grimly.

Josephine's expression was less dire. "Frankly, I wouldn't put anything past that man," she said with disgust. "A while ago, I saw Clara and she looked out of sorts. Her right arm was red and swollen. She said she'd fallen awkwardly in the garden, but somehow I didn't believe her at all. I wanted to get her to talk about it, but she closed up like a clam."

"That's terrible," Isabelle breathed.

"It was embarrassing for her that you saw her in that condition. Nothing is supposed to muddy the image of the fine doctor and his dutiful wife," said Adrian, topping up Josephine's cup with fresh coffee. She thanked him with a smile, then remarked, "Clara is ashamed, and I understand that. But if she doesn't confide in us, we can't help her."

"Clara knows that the two of you will always be there for her. When she's ready, she'll turn to you for help," said Adrian, and he stroked his wife's cheek lovingly.

They're so close, and they understand each other so well, thought Isabelle. She felt a prick of envy in her chest.

"Raymond adores you . . . You would be well off with him at your side."
She suddenly heard Clara's voice. It was true: with Raymond, she really did feel safe and appreciated. On the other hand, it wasn't as if she pined for him whenever he left the room. Her thoughts were interrupted by Adrian saying good-bye. He had to go—work was waiting.

He'd barely left when Josephine said, "Clara is pregnant again, you should know."

"She's pregnant? But . . ." Isabelle tried in vain to come up with a connection between that piece of information and Clara's state just now.

"It looks to me like the good doctor did not particularly welcome the news of this second pregnancy," said Josephine. "He'd like to invest every extra penny in his practice, but now that Clara is pregnant, he'll have to fork out a few marks for a nanny."

"And so he hits her?"

Josephine shrugged. "I don't know. But I can promise you that I'll keep an eye on Clara. Enough about that sad subject. I'd rather hear how love is treating you. You traveled here with that charming champagne dealer. Is there anything in that? The two of you . . . ?"

Isabelle laughed. "What do you want to hear? That I've fallen head over heels in love with Raymond?"

"Why not?" Josephine replied briskly. "Or do you have your heart set on your new cellar master, the good-looking—what was his name again?"

At the thought of Daniel, Isabelle's stomach immediately did a little somersault.

"Oh, Jo," she said, with torment in her voice. "I just don't know anymore! Back then, when I ran off into the unknown with Leon, I let my emotions drive me. Not that I regret what I did," she hurriedly added. "But a little more consideration wouldn't have hurt. Times have changed; I just don't want to make another mistake. Now and in the future I must let good sense be my guide."

"Getting fainthearted?" Josephine looked at her friend teasingly. "I would have believed anything but that."

"What does that have to do with a faint heart?" Isabelle replied, annoyed. Then her watch caught her eye. "So late already, my goodness! The hairdresser that Raymond ordered for me is coming to the hotel at three." She quickly began to rummage in her handbag for money. "I have to go. Raymond and I have been invited to the Berlin Palace. Can you imagine? The invitation was signed by some high-ranking general, apparently an old customer of Raymond's. When I think I might actually see the emperor, it makes me feel almost ill, I'm so excited! Raymond says that Kaiser Wilhelm only ever drinks German sparkling wine but that his generals are far more open to a glass of champagne. It would be a sensation if they actually bought *my* champagne, so cross your fingers for me, all right?" She kissed Josephine on both cheeks in farewell. "Good business and financial security—that's what matters to me. And Marguerite, of course; in the end, she's the reason I'm doing all this. Maybe I'm not cut out for love at all."

Instead of answering, Josephine only smiled.

Half an hour before the start of the formal dinner at the palace, the guests streamed into the foyer of the Berlin City Palace, each couple competing in elegance with the others. *How fortunate that I let Raymond talk me into a new evening dress in Vienna*, Isabelle thought. In her emerald-green silk dress and matching accessories, she felt slim and beautiful and could hold her own with any of the women there. But not even her elegant dress could help her overcome her nerves, and with every step she felt less and less sure of herself. As she cautiously checked her pinned-up hair, she glanced covertly at her escort. In contrast to her, Raymond seemed entirely in his element in the German emperor's home. And he was certainly among the best-looking men that evening—with his black tailcoat, white starched shirt, top hat, fine kid gloves, a gold pocket watch, and then his handsome face, which was accentuated by the silver streaks in his hair. Among the men present, Raymond looked the most aristocratic of all.

"I'm so nervous," she whispered to him.

"What about?" he whispered back. He smiled and nodded a greeting to someone, exchanged a few words, paid a compliment here and there. As he had in Munich and Vienna, he seemed to know everyone there with any rank or reputation.

"I have the feeling that everyone is looking at us," said Isabelle with a pained smile. There—wasn't that an old admirer of hers? Baron Gottlieb von . . . she could no longer remember his name, but she did have a clear memory of how he and his mother had always smelled terribly of mothballs. He was high on her father's list of prospective marriage candidates. And over there, wasn't that Irene Neumann, Adrian's sister? Isabelle's stomach roiled even more. Oh God, who else would she bump into tonight?

"They're only looking because we make such a splendid couple. Try to relax a little," said Raymond. He patted her hand where it rested on his sleeve.

Isabelle breathed in and out deeply. Raymond was right. Her nervousness was silly. She forced herself to let her eyes roam around the room. The hundreds of candles burned beautifully! And all the lovely flowers, deep-red roses, and the scent of the most expensive perfumes—everything was so opulent, so magnificent! And no doubt that they would have interesting guests at their table, and the imperial kitchen would serve all kinds of wonderful dishes. An evening like this was a rare experience, and she was determined to try as hard as she could to enjoy every minute of it. And if, finally, a small order for her estate came out of it, then all the better.

Fortified by her new resolution, Isabelle took Raymond's arm, and they walked in the direction of the various dining rooms. They were halfway down the long hallway when she abruptly stopped walking.

"What is it?" whispered Raymond.

"Up ahead, at the doorway to the semicircular balcony." Isabelle licked her lips, which had suddenly become so dry that she could hardly speak a word. "My parents."

Raymond followed her gaze. "How lovely," he said with a smile. "Then let us wish them a good evening." Gently but firmly, he began to walk fast.

"Isabelle!" Jeanette Herrenhus stared at her daughter in disbelief. "What are you doing here?"

Any other mother would have embraced her daughter without an instant's hesitation, perhaps even planted a kiss on her cheek. But Jeanette Herrenhus did no more than stiffly hold out one gloved hand. *Still the chilly beauty, I see*, thought Isabelle, and she felt a spasm of deep sadness.

"I heard that you had been widowed. My condolences," said Moritz Herrenhus in place of a greeting; he sounded far from sympathetic. "But I see you have found a replacement," he added, looking Raymond Dupont up and down. "Aren't you going to introduce us?"

How could her father be so brutish and mean? Isabelle wanted to simply walk away without another word, but Raymond stood his ground as if rooted to the spot. He seemed determined to put this encounter behind him in a cultivated manner, and Isabelle was left with no choice but to follow his example.

"May I introduce Monsieur Raymond Dupont. Jeanette and Moritz Herrenhus, my parents," she said tightly. For a moment, she toyed with the notion of telling her parents about Marguerite, but then decided against it. A disabled child—she could imagine Moritz Herrenhus's disparaging remarks about that.

Raymond turned to Isabelle's mother. He gave her a consummate kiss on her hand and said, "Until today, I thought that Isabelle's beauty was a gift from God. Now I know better—it comes from an angel."

Were her eyes deceiving her, or did her mother actually blush? And the way she laughed . . . Isabelle found it embarrassing.

The two men shook hands, and her father cleared his throat. "Who would have guessed that we would meet in the Berlin Palace? But now that we have, we should make the best of it and spend the evening together." His expression was as single-minded as ever, and it was clear that he expected Isabelle to agree. Turning to Raymond, he said, "We'll be dining in the yellow salon. I know the maître d' well, and if you agree, I could ask him to modify the place settings so that we can sit together."

Isabelle's heart skipped a beat. Anything but that! But the next moment, she felt Raymond's soothing hand on hers.

Raymond smiled. "A wonderful idea, but I hope you will understand that we have to decline your offer. We're sitting in the main gold hall. At the emperor's table."

"A wonderful idea, but . . . we're sitting at the emperor's table!" Isabelle mimicked Raymond's grave tone of voice. Her eyes sparkled with mischievous glee. "I will never forget the look on my father's face! As we walked away, I wanted to look back just to see it again. But leaving them standing there was certainly the most elegant move." Isabelle giggled playfully. What an evening!

"Let's celebrate," Raymond had suggested when the imperial dinner was over.

"But what exactly would we be celebrating? There's so much," Isabelle had replied boldly. She followed Raymond into the elegant bar that, located so close to the Museum Island and the palace, had become a popular meeting place of the rich and beautiful of the city.

Raymond, of course, had ordered champagne for both of them. It must have been something special, Isabelle realized, because two waiters came to their table to serve it. One of them brought a wine bucket and glasses, while the headwaiter of the establishment, with a solemn expression, began to untwist the *muselet* surrounding the cork. He was about to remove the foil when Raymond took the bottle from him.

"But, sir—" the headwaiter said, perplexed.

"Thank you. I'll do that," said Raymond, waving the waiters away.

Isabelle grinned. "You don't like to give up the reins, do you?"

Raymond smiled. "It is my great pleasure on our final evening in Berlin to open this bottle for you. This is an 1874 Pommery—in my opinion, it is the best champagne made in the last fifty years."

"The first time I entered your shop, you were talking about just this champagne. And you're right: today is one of those days when only the very best will do," said Isabelle, raising her glass exuberantly to Raymond. The two glasses clinked loudly, which drew looks of disapproval from several guests. Isabelle didn't care. She felt better than she had in a long time! The elation she experienced when they simply walked away from her father . . . She beamed radiantly and said, "All my life, my father wanted only one thing: to be accepted by high society. Then along comes his good-for-nothing daughter and upstages him." She shook her head. "And I still have no idea how you managed to engineer two places at the emperor's table."

"Wouldn't it be a terrible thing if I were unable to surprise you still, after the short time we've known each other?" With a secretive smile, he refilled her glass. "A toast to the new champagne supplier to the Imperial Court!"

"An order from the court of the German emperor, oh my . . ." Isabelle let out a joyous squeal, which brought more condemning looks. She raised her glass to her lips and drank quickly. "I'm sorry. I'm just so terribly excited. If my father only knew. In all his years as a factory owner, he hasn't delivered so much as a sheet to the palace. It would have been his greatest dream." She set her glass down, her hand shaking slightly. She almost pinched herself to make sure all of it was true.

"You know what they say: you reap what you sow," said Raymond, then he lit a cigar.

The first bottle of Pommery went down so quickly that Raymond hurriedly ordered a second. The ice-cold, foamy champagne tasted so delicious that Isabelle felt as if she could not get enough of it. The second bottle was soon empty, too.

When they left the bar two hours later, everything was more than a little blurry. It was a warm night, and although it was well past midnight, many people were still out and about. Couples strolled across bridges, holding each other close. Men lurched drunkenly through the streets, and a few streetwalkers were on the lookout for customers. Isabelle glanced around, trying to think, but for the life of her she could not say in which direction their hotel lay. She held on to Raymond's arm and let herself be led.

"What would I do without you?" she whispered, and nestled closer to Raymond. He put one arm around her protectively, and they made their way slowly toward their hotel, surrounded by swarms of nocturnal insects and the quiet splashing of the Spree onto its banks.

Arriving in the lobby, Isabelle stopped in her tracks, looking wide-eyed and disappointed at Raymond, and said, "If it were up to me, this night would last forever!" She lifted the hem of her dress a little and began to dance around the room, but on the second turn, she became dizzy and staggered.

Raymond, who had just taken both of their room keys from the night porter, caught her before she could fall.

"I think that's enough for today. Come on, I'll take you to your room."

With a blissful smile on her lips, Isabelle stumbled up the stairs to the first floor. Her head was still filled with the many conversations of the evening, and with the music, the tinkling of glasses, the carefree laughter. She hummed softly to herself while Raymond unlocked her door for her. "Madame," he said, and held the door open theatrically. "If I may be of any further service?" he said, mimicking the deferential tone of the bellboys.

"You should stop putting all these silly ideas in my head. Tonight I'm the champagne queen, and when I wake up tomorrow morning, I'll be the housemaid again. That's just how it is, isn't it?" said Isabelle, and her laugh came out sounding a little too shrill. She quickly pressed a kiss to Raymond's lips. "Thank you so much, so much. For everything!" she whispered drunkenly. "You put the world at my feet today."

His lips tasted of champagne and of the cigar he had smoked in the bar. Before she could separate from him again, his arms closed around her.

"Not only the world, but my heart with it."

The first thing that crossed Isabelle's mind in the morning was not how nice it was to once again wake up next to a man. The feel of soft breathing beside her, a warm body. Nor was it anything about how good it felt to be desired and caressed as a woman. The first thing she thought when she opened her eyes was: What have I done?

A soft groan rose from her throat, and she hurriedly pressed her lips together. But Raymond, lying on his back, relaxed, went on sleeping soundly. No snoring escaped his lips; no frown marred his face. Even in his sleep, he looked self-possessed, almost superior. Isabelle edged away from him with care, not wanting to wake him with some careless movement. She wanted to get out of the bed, to run away, far away! She wanted to be alone, to think about what had happened. To breathe in some fresh air, clear her head so she could think coherently. But she stayed where she was. In the bed that she had made.

She and Raymond. He was a handsome man and always so attentive to her. The ball, the wine served in the palace, and then all the champagne at the bar . . . She was not surprised that she had lost her head. She hoped that she had not made too embarrassing a spectacle of herself. If only she could better recall all that had happened! But the previous night was like a patchwork quilt in her memory, with pieces missing everywhere.

But was she taking it too easy on herself by blaming all her levity and recklessness on the alcohol? Hadn't last night been the natural consequence not only of that night but of all the weeks that preceded it? Had she simply refused to acknowledge the direction their relationship was going? And there was Daniel back home . . .

Her head swimming with thoughts, Isabelle stared toward the window. The heavy velvet curtains were still drawn. It would have been easy to extend the night, to pick up where they had left off hours earlier. To press her body to his, her body as a gift of love. Instead, Isabelle covered her nakedness with the silken bedcovers.

Lying in Raymond's arms had not been uncomfortable. The opposite was true, in fact—he knew how to give a woman pleasure. A flame had been kindled, and yet their lovemaking had not turned the flame into an all-consuming fire, as it always had with Leon. All Leon had to do was touch her to make every fiber of her body tremble; with Leon, her heart overflowed with happiness, and her soul rejoiced with love. But where had her heart and soul been the night before with Raymond?

Raymond awoke a little later. He blinked twice as if to reassure himself of reality, then a smile spread across his face. He propped himself on one elbow, kissed Isabelle softly on the forehead and said, "Thank you for last night. It was wonderful."

Isabelle smiled back tensely. Before she could ask him to leave her alone, he had already stood up and was gathering his clothes from where they lay strewn around the bed.

"Breakfast in two hours?" Without waiting for her answer, he left the room.

A gentleman to the core. And understanding, too. Filled with relief, Isabelle looked at the door he had just walked through.

Now they were sitting on opposite sides of a table in the hotel's breakfast room.

"May I order you an egg? Or some smoked fish?" asked Raymond, handing the basket of bread across to Isabelle.

"Thank you, yes. Something savory would do me good." She nodded in the direction of the high windows. "Another sunny day. Good traveling weather, isn't it?"

"The heavens smile when angels travel—isn't that what they say in Germany?"

They laughed together. Two travelers, two people who liked each other, who passed the marmalade and honey and made conversation. And who talked to each other like strangers.

In the train to Frankfurt—the first leg of their homeward journey— Raymond began the conversation that Isabelle had been fearing since she awoke.

"Isabelle . . . ," he began, and Isabelle knew exactly what was coming from the way he intoned her name. She looked around, as if for an escape route or someone to distract them, but just at that moment the first-class compartment was empty. "Until now, I have chosen my words with care, but now that I would like to confess my love to you, I no longer know how to begin." He lifted one hand in a gesture of helplessness.

Silence, sometimes, is golden, Isabelle wanted to say, but she held her tongue. She had never experienced Raymond at a loss for words.

"I have met many women in my life, but none was ever good enough for me. All my life, I've dreamed of a woman like you, and I was on the verge of losing hope. Then I met you, and my dream came true after all. Do you still remember the first time you came to my shop? To me, then, it felt like a fateful encounter."

Isabelle's smile was constrained. "Fate, coincidence—who can say for certain?" Life had taught her not to read too much into such events.

He waved one hand dismissively, as if to keep away anything that might divert him from expressing his thoughts.

"Since I've known you, my days have been brighter, as if the sun has been shining down forever." To underline his words, he gestured toward the radiant blue sky curving over the landscape around them. "Dear Isabelle, could you imagine a life at my side? We could travel, spend our nights in magnificent hotels, see the world. My place in Reims is luxurious and big enough for both of us. We could run my business together. You with your charm, and me with my expertise." He took both her hands in his; Isabelle felt the pressure and warmth of his fingers. "Isabelle, marry me, and I'll give you a heaven here on earth. I think I've shown on this journey, at least a little, that I am capable of that, haven't I? The honor alone of being allowed to sit at the German emperor's own table . . ."

Had he been trying to bait her with that? She frowned, and then she said, "And I am thankful for all of that. But your proposal still comes . . . very suddenly."

"Suddenly? After last night . . ." Raymond smiled. "When a woman gives herself to a man, he can surely take that as a sign of her favor, can't he?"

Embarrassed, Isabelle turned her eyes away. So this is what she got . . .

For a long moment, neither said a word. Then Raymond spoke again. "Think about how good it would be. After all your hard work, it's time—high time—that you enjoyed your life. You're young; you're beautiful. Why would you want to waste your beauty and energy growing grapes? Look no further than Henriette Trubert to see what that kind of life can do to a woman."

Isabelle laughed for a moment. "That's all well and good, but then who's supposed to look after the estate? I have no interest whatsoever in selling; that place is my husband's legacy, and I will do everything I can to keep it safe for my daughter."

"So far, you haven't exactly had an easy time of it. Without Daniel's help and my own, you would hardly have managed it at all," Raymond replied, rather directly. "Daniel Lambert grew up on your estate, and he knows it ten times better than you. With him to lease the place, the vineyards and the entire operation would be in the very best hands. Let him look after all of it—you'd be doing the right thing!"

Isabelle nodded, considering the idea. Daniel Lambert and the Feininger lands were as interwoven as the tendrils of two grapevines growing side by side. In her mind's eye, she saw him standing among the vines, trimming a too-long shoot, tying another in place. All these things were second nature to him. Daniel . . . A wrench of longing tugged at her heart.

Raymond, encouraged by her nodding, went on. "And your daughter, of course she would have the best of care. There are outstanding homes in Reims; the Sisters of Notre Dame have an excellent name when it comes to . . . special children. Many of my well-to-do customers have left their children in the care of the sisters. They—"

"Marguerite in a home? Never!" Isabelle interrupted him sharply. Her heart began to beat faster, as if she were confronted with a terrible danger. "Marguerite is the best thing that ever happened to me. She belongs to me, and whatever may come, I will never separate from her. No one, no man in this world, would be worth separating from her." Her eyes sparkled fiercely, if she were ready to physically defend her daughter there and then.

"I know how much your daughter means to you," Raymond said appeasingly. "It was a suggestion on my part, no more. There are so many possibilities, and possibilities can always be discussed, can't they?" Suddenly, his voice sounded like an out-of-tune instrument.

"Please give me some time." With those words, Isabelle had broken off their discussion.

Frankfurt. Saarbrücken. Metz.

A silence had settled over them, a silence that grew more agonizing with every passing minute. With every small movement she made—shifting in her seat, fetching something from her handbag, opening the window a fraction—she sensed Raymond's gaze on her. He was waiting for her answer. And he expected a yes.

But with every rattling mile in the train, Isabelle put more and more distance between her and her traveling companion. And with every mile that drew them closer to Champagne, her conviction grew that the night she had spent with Raymond had been a mistake. A serious mistake. The whole trip, the new customers, the prestigious orders that had secured her financial future—she would be grateful to him for all of that, forever. And though gratitude and affection might be siblings, they were not lovers.

In Reims, they went their separate ways. Isabelle promised that she would be in touch. Raymond replied with a small nod. He had enough experience in life to know that no answer was also an answer. Whether he could accept that was another matter entirely.

Isabelle had sent a message to Lucille from Berlin to advise her she would soon be home; she had not, however, been able to tell her the exact day on which Claude should drive into Reims to collect her. But in front of the Notre Dame cathedral, as usual, there were horse-drawn coaches willing to take paying passengers to Épernay, Hautvillers, or wherever else they were headed. Isabelle quickly negotiated a price with one of the drivers. Instead of sitting inside the coach, she asked the man if she might sit next to him on the driver's seat. She needed desperately to breathe some fresh air.

With a cluck of the driver's tongue, the horses got moving. The last stretch. Isabelle breathed in deeply, trying to calm her inner trembling. She would soon be home! Finally, after all these weeks, she would be able to take Marguerite in her arms and kiss her again. She would see Daniel, too. And her vineyards. And then there was Micheline, Ghislaine, Claude, and Lucille. Her friends . . . she had brought something with her for each of them, and for Marguerite, of course, she had several presents. She wanted to ask the driver to go faster, but she knew she would be asking in vain; the coachmen did everything they could to protect their horses and keep them fit for pulling heavy loads of champagne.

While Isabelle struggled with her impatience, the horses trotted sedately through the forests that lay between Reims and the vineyards of Hautvillers.

And then it came—the moment she had unconsciously been waiting for throughout the entire journey. The forests cleared, and in front of them lay the Montagne de Reims, the endless sea of grapevines. Gently rolling hills that fell away and rose again, lush green over the silvery, chalky earth, and in between the deep-red blooms of the roses.

A blissful smile spread across Isabelle's face. The gentle breeze carried the scent of the roses to her, and once again, the magic of the Champagne region took her as a willing captive, just as it had the first time she had arrived there.

How little I knew back then, thought Isabelle. *How self-important and presumptuous.* No wonder Daniel had looked down on her, the city girl, and mocked her. Many things had changed since then. *She* had changed, and the trip with Raymond had contributed to that. Now, at least, she knew what she did not want: a life in a gilded cage. She had escaped from that once before, and she would never again allow such shackles to be put on her. She did not need that kind of security; her vineyards, her vines, and her friends gave her all the protection she needed.

All around, winegrowers and their helpers were at work with hoes, shears, and other tools. They stamped on spades to loosen the earth, carefully tied young shoots in place, snipped off superfluous leaves.

What tasks would be keeping Daniel and Claude busy right then? And what about the phylloxera? Isabelle moved back and forth restlessly on the driver's seat; she could hardly wait to finally be home again and to hear all the news. Home . . .

The idea was simultaneously so comforting and so affecting that Isabelle could not contain a small sob.

"Everything all right, madame?" the coachman asked.

To his astonishment, she laughed out loud. Yes, now everything was all right.

The four wheels of the coach had not stopped turning when Isabelle jumped down from the driver's seat. She opened the door to her house while the driver unloaded her copious luggage. No one responded to her calls, but instead of being disappointed at the lack of fanfare on her return, Isabelle smiled. She knew exactly where everyone would be.

She was still wearing her good city shoes, and the ground underfoot felt as soft as a velvet carpet. The blue sky with its wispy, feathery clouds was as beautiful as a painting. She made her way calmly in the direction of the vineyards. Now that she was finally home, there was no longer any need to hurry.

Soon, she was approaching the first vines. The leaves were a lush green, the grapes the size of cherry pits, and she saw no signs of phylloxera.

"Thank God," she murmured to herself. At least that particular disaster seemed to have passed them by, and the Ice Saints, too. If it looked this good everywhere . . .

When she heard the sound of hoofbeats behind her, she turned around. It was Claude with the horses and cart.

"Madame Isabelle, you're back! How wonderful to see you again!" He brought the horses to an abrupt halt. "Lucille and little Marguerite are with Daniel and the others in the southwest vineyards, all the way back. Come, I'll drive you!"

Isabelle jumped deftly up onto the seat. In the back of the cart, on the open tray, she saw a large basket with bread, carafes of water, sausages, and other food. She smiled. "Have *you* been feeding the workers while I was away?"

"Someone had to," Claude grumbled. "Dear Lucille eats no sausage or ham herself, so she doesn't serve it to anyone else, either. Daniel and the day laborers kicked up a fuss when all they saw on the table was cheese and bread."

Isabelle laughed. "Looks to me like you've been keeping everything well under control in my absence." *What day laborers?* she wondered at the same time. Well, she would find out everything that mattered soon enough. From Daniel.

"Oh, we've been working shoulder to shoulder. But we missed having you here terribly," Claude replied. Somewhat abashed, he looked straight ahead and added gruffly, "I, for one, am very glad to see you back."

"And I'm so happy to finally be home again," said Isabelle. "And starting tomorrow, I'll be preparing the meals again!"

"That I'm happy to hear, madame. But tell me, how was your trip? Did the people like our champagne?"

"They liked it very much indeed," she replied proudly. "Thanks to Monsieur Dupont, we've sold all our 1899 stock. Now we just have to keep our fingers crossed that the new customers are satisfied and stay with us in the years ahead," she said, though the last words were spoken more to herself than to Claude. Raymond Dupont wouldn't work against her, would he? Out of spite at her rejection? No, she could not believe he'd be like that. The man was loyal through and through.

"Now you. What's new in the village?" she asked, and not just to distract herself from her thoughts, but because she really wanted to know.

"Oh, this and that," Claude said mysteriously. "I've just come from the church down below . . . We should have met on the way up here." He looked at her with a mischievous grin. "Micheline and I want to get married, before the harvest. I went to talk to the minister about it."

"You're getting married? Congratulations!" Isabelle cried. "That's fantastic. But . . . why now?"

Her elderly overseer shrugged. "Well, we wanted to tie the knot earlier, to be honest. But last year was all so topsy-turvy. But now that Daniel is here, and everything is looking so good . . ."

Isabelle nodded, deeply moved. She laid one hand on his arm. "Last year took it out of all of us. But with every catastrophe, you were there for me, and I'll never forget that. Thank you," she said. From the corner of her eye, she saw Claude redden.

"See the men over there?" he said, and pointed to a group of young men, many of whom were familiar to Isabelle. "Those are the day laborers I was telling you about. Hardworking lads, they've already helped us replant part of the vineyards. With the new vines Daniel brought in, we won't have to worry about the phylloxera in the future. And you won't see a weed in sight; the men are more than worth their wages. Everything is in very good shape."

Isabelle could clearly hear the pride in his voice.

But at the same time, she was only half listening to him. Her gaze was fixed on the child's crib with the white canopy that was set up in the shade, among the picturesque vines. A few steps away, Lucille was clearing weeds from between the rows of grapes.

"Marguerite . . ." Isabelle felt the tears come to her eyes. She jumped down from the coach.

"Madame! Welcome back!" Lucille's face lit up when she saw Isabelle coming through the vines. Right away, she picked up Marguerite carefully from her crib and handed the child to her mother, then retreated a few steps.

"Marguerite, your mama is home," Isabelle pulled her daughter close and closed her eyes as she held her tight. She had been waiting so long for this moment.

"Isabelle," she heard the next moment. No more than a whisper. And the greatest declaration of love she could imagine.

Isabelle opened her eyes. "Daniel!"

He looked at her inquiringly, but Isabelle said nothing more. Instead, she smiled, and in her smile was all the love, sincerity, and devotion she was capable of.

Their lips found their way together, hungrily, while Marguerite reached out for the sun with her little hands.

Lucille, standing beside Claude and watching the small scene with him, asked in surprise, "Daniel and Madame Feininger? Did you know about that?"

"*Know* would be claiming too much, but I did suspect it," said Claude happily. "And hoped for it!"

"Will I ever know what it means to be in love?" With a sigh, Lucille looked over toward the day laborers, who were taking the food Claude had brought out of the cart. One black-haired youth looked bashfully back.

Claude put his hand on the young woman's shoulder. "Everything in life has its day. Love comes to those who believe in it."

Notes

The research behind this book was unique, from my own trip to the Champagne region to my talks with the vintners and other experts to a number of exceptionally inspiring champagne tasting sessions—only rarely have I ever been able to experience so many sensory impressions. I also delved into a great deal of specialist literature. The book that helped me the most in all this was *Champagne: The Wine, the Land and the People* by Patrick Forbes. The first edition appeared in 1967, published by Victor Gollancz Ltd., although I worked with the sixth edition from 1983. It is a true classic, and I don't believe there is anything comparable on the German market. I was so fascinated by Forbes's masterful explanations of champagne production, its history, and the history of the vignerons of the region that I practically devoured his book, page after page, and not just once. It was so thrilling that as soon as I put his book down, all I wanted to do was take all my newfound knowledge and put it into this novel.

Making champagne is an astoundingly laborious business. Enumerating every individual step in the process would have been outside the scope of my story; instead, from all the individual processes, I selected those that fit well into the framework of the novel. This meant leaving out several steps and changing the chronology of some others in regard to the champagne and other aspects.

I'm happy to give a couple of examples of where I took such creative liberties—not only with the champagne-making process:

- In earlier days, bottles of champagne tended to explode primarily in July and August. In Isabelle's cellars, this happens in December.
- The sausage delicacy known as *andouillette* is mainly served in the city of Troyes, in the southern part of the Champagne region. In my novel, this sausage is also eaten in Hautvillers. Poor Isabelle!
- Once or twice, I have played with the geography. Charleville, for example, is a long way from Hautvillers, but Isabelle has to get *someone* to harvest her grapes, after all!
- The first champagne to use the Dom Pérignon name was the 1921 vintage, which was first sold in 1936, but I could hardly leave such a famous name out of my champagne novel.

A word about the famous widows of Champagne.

The region has always been characterized by the vigor, courage, and ingenuity of the Champagne widows—the *veuves*. In an era in which only men normally had any say, the *veuves* were responsible not only for an army of employees and their families, but also contributed decisively to the international renown of the famous drink.

Who hasn't heard of Madame Clicquot, the *veuve* Lily Bollinger, or the widow Louise Pommery? Other famous widows were Camille Olry-Roederer and Mathilde Laurent-Perrier. Behind many of the best known champagne names stands not only an exciting woman, but also an equally dramatic history.

After the death of Francois Clicquot in 1805, Barbe Nicole Clicquot took over the leadership of the family champagne business. The young woman, with a daughter of her own, had no idea at all about the business side of the operation, but she quickly acquainted herself with all the relevant issues and became a spirited businesswoman. In economically difficult times, she succeeded in making the Clicquot champagne house flourish. Thanks to her hard work and skill, Veuve Clicquot Ponsardin was soon served at every aristocratic table in Europe.

Louise Pommery was the mother of two children, Louis and Louise, when she became a widow in 1858 and assumed control of the Pommery cellars. She was one of the first who dared produce a dry champagne, and she did so at a time when sweet champagnes had been the fashion for decades. Under her leadership, Pommery became one of the leading champagne brands and remains so to this day.

Lily Bollinger also became world famous. In 1941, in the middle of the Second World War, she took over the operations of the Bollinger champagne house—at a time when people had far more on their minds than drinking champagne. And yet, over the years, she managed to double Bollinger's champagne production. The house of Bollinger continues to be one of the great names in the industry today.

I have written Isabelle's story as a homage to the great women of Champagne. Like them, Isabelle is unique, even if not as real.

For anyone who now has a taste for more champagne stories, I recommend taking a look at my website at www.durst-benning.de. You will find more gossip about champagne, some wonderful recipes, and my travel diary, which includes all the settings in which the novel takes place.

Acknowledgments

I owe a debt of gratitude to the outstanding German sommelier Natalie Lumpp, who put me in touch with a great many experts and who also took the trouble to proofread my novel. Any errors that still exist in these pages are mine alone.

My thanks also go to Alexandra Durin-Hepke from the Berlin champagne dealership Champagne&Compagnie. Without her advice, our trip to Champagne would certainly have been less fruitful. Alexandra was born in Reims, the capital of the region, and in the champagne field, she is an expert par excellence.

Perhaps you're curious to know what becomes of Clara? Book 3 of my Century Trilogy will be appearing soon.

I wish you hours of reading pleasure.

About the Author

Photo © Privat

Petra Durst-Benning is one of Germany's most successful and prominent authors. For more than fifteen years, her historical novels have been inviting readers to go adventuring with courageous female characters and experience their emotions for themselves. Her books and their television adaptations have enjoyed great international success. Petra Durst-Benning lives with her husband in Stuttgart.

About the Translator

Australian-born and widely traveled, Edwin Miles has been working as a translator for fifteen years.

After studying in his hometown of Perth, Western Australia, Edwin completed an MFA in fiction writing at the University of Oregon in 1995. While there, he spent a year working as a fiction editor on the literary magazine *Northwest Review*. In 1996, he was shortlisted for the prestigious Australian/Vogel Award for young writers for a collection of short stories.

After many years living and working in Australia, Japan, and the United States, he currently resides in Cologne, Germany, with his wife, Dagmar, and two very clever children.